Reviews for "

"In the spirit of Sholem Alei............ These stories of identical twins, confused from birth, will charm with their simplicity and sincerity." — *AudioFile*

"...a good story very well told" — *The Jewish Independent*

"Wired Words/Electric Prose... Weekly installments... are short enough to read easily on the screen and they carry readers into an ongoing story." — *The Providence Phoenix*

"...it's clear from the start that there is nothing factual about this book, which traces the lives of the Schlemiel family and the community that surrounds them. [Readers] will really get the humor written between the lines.... the mix-ups are many and the potential for laughter abundant" — *Jewish Book World*

For "A Village Feasts"

"Abrahmson's prose savvily mixes the homey and the surreal, and he's a master..." — *Publishers Weekly*

"...wryly funny with dollops of heartwarming schmaltz." — *Kirkus Reviews*

For "Winter Blessings"

"...utterly charming...a large side order of whimsey... so right and so touching... This Chanukah, who could ask for anything more?" — *The Times of Israel*

For "A Village Romance"

"Abrahmson outdoes himself..." — *AudioFile*

"Engaging tales... Village stories that deftly lift a curtain on a world of friendly humor and touching details of Jewish life." — *Kirkus Reviews*

Also by Izzy Abrahmson

The Village Life Series
The Village Twins
Winter Blessings
The Village Feasts
A Village Romance
The Cracked Potter
The Council of Wise Women

As Mark Binder
Fictions
What Cheer!
The Groston Rules
A Dead Politician, an Undead Clam,
and an Ancient Horror
Loki Ragnarok
It Ate My Sister
The Zombie Cat
The Rationalization Diet

Stories for young people
Cinderella Spinderella
The Bed Time Story Book
Kings, Wolves, Princesses and Lions
Genies, Giants and a Walrus
Classic Stories for Boys and Girls
Tall Tales, Whoppers and Lies
It was a dark and stormy night…
Stories for Peace
Transmit Joy!

THE
COUNCIL
OF WISE
WOMEN

Izzy Abrahmson

Light Publications
Providence

The Council of Wise Women
by Izzy Abrahmson
Copyright 2024 by Mark Binder

Cover design by Lou Pop
Book design by Beth Hellman
Copy editing by Jessica Everett

Bulk discounts and licenses to reproduce excerpts from this book are available
for schools, churches, synagogues, mosques, book clubs, and other civic groups.
Please email: licensing@lightpublications.com

For information about author visits and story concerts
by Izzy Abrahmson and Mark Binder,
please visit
izzyabe.com
markbinderbooks.com

Softcover Print ISBN: 978-1-940060-63-7
eBook ISBN: 978-1-940060-65-1
audiobook ISBN: 978-1-940060-64-4
Library of Congress Control Number: TO COME

Printed in the United States of America
Electronic edition originated in the USA
10 9 8 7 6 5 4 3 2 1

Light Publications
https://lightpublications.com
PO Box 2462 • Providence, RI 02906 • U. S. A.

Dedication

For my parents

"A man is only a man. But a woman? Is a woman!"
— *Rabbi Shmuel Kibbitz, the first rabbi of Chelm*
(and the current Rabbi Kibbitz's great-great grandfather.)

"I'm a mother, a wife, a daughter, a sister, a cook, a cleaner, a healer, a shopper, a bookkeeper, a reader, a lover, a yenta, a grandmother, a thinker, a planner, a comforter, an organizer, an adversary, and a friend. Which one do you want today?"

— *Mrs. Chaipul*

Part One

The Mother

Chapter One

First Born

The child's eyes were beautiful. They were brown, inquisitive, open already, and looking at her new world.

Her mother, Sarah Cohen, was exhausted. Childbirth hadn't been as difficult as her own mother had warned, but it had been labor. Long and painful, but with this delightful girl at the end nestled warm in her arms.

"Not again!" Mrs. Chaipul, the midwife, muttered.

Her words sounded worried. Sarah looked up from the babe. "Is everything all right?"

"Perfectly," answered Mrs. Chaipul. She patted Sarah's hand. "I didn't mean to startle you. Where is your husband?"

"He said he was going to Smyrna to buy some cloth. He should be back any time."

Mrs. Chaipul shook her head and clucked her tongue. What was it about the men of Chelm that they were never around for this moment? Perhaps it was true everywhere. Men always seemed to have appointments in other parts of the world when their wives were giving birth.

"Do you mind holding her?" Mrs. Chaipul said.

Sarah smiled, "Not at all."

"Because we're not done."

Again Sarah felt nervous. "What do you mean?"

"Twins," Mrs. Chaipul said, "A double blessing. I'm sorry. I should have caught it earlier. It's all right. I had plenty of experience with the Schlemiel twins. Born twelve hours apart. That was a challenge! This will be easy. Well, not easy, but... Just follow my directions and begin pushing again."

Twins? Sarah's mind began to spin. She was ready for one

child. She was ready for a daughter. But another? Two mouths to feed? She remembered what happened to Rebecca Schlemiel after her boys were born. The fighting, the arguing, the confusion, the exhaustion. It was crazy. It was impossible. No. It was a dream. Perhaps she was asleep even now.

Then she looked at the girl in her arms. The baby's brown eyes were staring at her with hope and love and curiosity.

It would be a shame to wake up from the dream and leave behind a beautiful soul like this.

She felt something moving.

"When would you like me to push?" Sarah asked.

"Now would be nice!"

* * *

The door to the Cohen house slammed open as Benjamin Cohen ran inside.

"Shut the door!" Mrs. Chaipul shouted. "It's still winter time and the cold won't do anyone any good."

The panting tailor shut the door behind him. "Are they all right?"

Mrs. Chaipul nodded, "Everyone is fine.

Benjamin gave her a grin and a hug. He reached for the knob to the bedroom door, and then he stopped. "How many fingers and toes?"

Mrs. Chaipul calculated for a moment and then answered, "A hundred."

"A hundred!" Benjamin smiled. Then he paused, "What?"

Mrs. Chaipul nodded. "I assume you have all of yours, and Sarah has all of hers."

"Yes," Benjamin said, "Yes."

The old woman shrugged and sipped her tea. "I have all of mine."

Benjamin's face knitted into a frown as he calculated. "That's twenty extra."

"It is."

"I don't understand." Benjamin was imagining a hand with five extra fingers. A foot with five extra toes would need a specially made shoe. Were the fingers and toes on the same arms and legs or were there extra arms and legs? "I thought you said that everyone was all right!"

The exhausted midwife spooned more sugar into her tea. "They are. And if you made it your business to be here on time, instead of gallivanting around the countryside without a care in the world, you would understand and I wouldn't have to explain everything to you."

Benjamin put his hands on his hips. Mrs. Chaipul was a rather important woman in Chelm, but she was still just a woman. Yes, she ran the only kosher restaurant. Yes, she was the closest thing the village had to a doctor, veterinarian, and midwife. Yes, she and the rabbi seemed to be engaged in perpetual negotiations for marriage. But still. This was no way to treat him in his own house on the afternoon of the birth of his first child.

"Tell me woman," he demanded, "what is going on?"

Mrs. Chaipul peered at Benjamin. She shook her spoon at him. "You need to learn more manners. And you owe me an extra chicken."

Such insults and insolence! Benjamin could barely restrain himself. Enough talking with this foolish woman.

He yanked the door open and marched into his bedroom.

The sudden noise, draft, and light from the kitchen startled Sarah, who was dozing. She looked up. "Benjamin?"

"It's me," he whispered. The curtains were drawn, and for him, the room was quite dark. "Ow!" He banged his knee against a chair that shouldn't be there. "Ow, ow, ow!"

"Are you all right?" Sarah asked.

"I'm fine." He rubbed his leg. "How are you?"

"I'm tired. I'm exhausted. But I'm fine."

"And the child?" he asked. He hated asking. He was afraid to ask. What was the point of hiring a midwife if she wouldn't give you a simple answer to a simple question?

"They're fine," Sarah said.

He was closer now, and as his eyes adjusted, he could see the smile on his wife's face. She looked pale, but so wonderful.

"'They?" he said. "Twins?"

A nod. "A boy and a girl."

"Really?" he said in amazement.

Sarah stared at her husband. "You think I'd make something like this up? You think I'd lie at a time like this? You think you wouldn't figure it out in a moment whether we have one baby or two?"

"No," he said. Why was everyone picking on him? "I'm just surprised."

"Me too," Sarah said. "I was. So are they."

"Who was born first?"

Sarah glanced to her left and smiled. "She was."

Benjamin frowned. "Really? Let's tell everyone that he was."

"What? Why?"

"Because being first born is important to a boy."

"I don't understand."

Benjamin nodded. "You're not a boy." As the third son in a family of seven children, Benjamin knew how much his older brothers had lorded over him. "We'll just tell everyone that he was born first. It's important. It's crucial."

"Crucial?" Sarah said. "I don't know that we should lie about such a thing."

Benjamin frowned. "Have you ever been held upside down by your ankles over a cesspool?"

"No!" Sarah said. "Are you threatening me?"

"No, no. Not at all!" Benjamin answered quickly. "But I have been. By my older brothers. I still remember the smell." He shuddered in revulsion.

"They were so cruel to you."

"My brothers were bigger and older," Benjamin explained. "It's the way of the world."

"But she's only older by a few minutes," Sarah said. "And she's no bigger than he."

"Minutes matter." Benjamin was firm about it. "So, we'll tell them that he was born first. We'll tell Mrs. Chaipul. She'll have to agree."

"All right," Sarah answered weakly.

"May I pick him up?"

"Yes, of course." She felt the weight lift from her right side.

"He's handsome."

The exhausted mother smiled. "Yes, he is."

"I have a son!" Benjamin Cohen said proudly.

"And a daughter," Sarah added.

"Yes, yes, of course." Benjamin reached out a finger and touched his daughter's cheek. "A daughter as well. But a son! Think of that. A son!"

Until that moment, Sarah had loved her husband, but just then she felt her heart breaking, and for an instant she hated him.

"Give him back to me," she demanded. "Now."

"Why?"

"He's hungry. We're tired. We need some rest. You got the fabric you wanted. Go to work."

Benjamin surrendered the boy. He noticed, but dismissed, the curt tone of his wife's voice. She was tired. And a son was something to be proud of.

He turned and banged his shin. "Ow! Who put that chair there!"

When she heard the door close, Sarah Cohen hugged her children tightly, but gently.

"You are both mine," she whispered. "You are both important."

Chapter Two

Cry Me a River

Almost a week after the birth of her twins, Sarah Cohen was not doing well. She couldn't stop crying. She'd cried for three days and had soaked through every single handkerchief and towel in the house. The tears kept running down her cheeks like the twin branches of the Uherka River during flood season.

Chelm is nestled in a valley. To the north are two small round hills that are known on maps as West Hill and East Hill, which the townsfolk sometimes call Sunset and Sunrise. A small stream meanders west of Sunset, down the valley, and through the farmland, skirting the edge of the village. An offshoot of the great Bug River, this shallow brook makes a somewhat revolting, gurgling, and coughing sound that gives it the name, Uherka.

The image would have seemed funny to Sarah, if she weren't so upset.

For the first time at a Sabbath dinner, Benjamin hadn't complained that the chicken soup wasn't salty enough. Sarah had wanted to laugh, but was afraid to smile because she thought she might scream. During the meal, she'd managed to keep her composure, but as soon as one of the babies began to cry, she used it as an opportunity to flee from the table and bawl with the chorus.

For his part, Benjamin Cohen was getting seriously worried. He'd gone so far as to speak with several of his friends over lunch at Mrs. Chaipul's restaurant. They had all assured him that it was normal for a wife to feel a bit down after giving birth.

"My mother used to help my father with the challah," said Reb Stein, the baker. "After I was born, she beat the dough so much that Papa had to have a mid-winter special on braided matzah."

"Every time my wife has a child, I give her a new ring to cheer her up," Reb Cantor the merchant said with a cluck. "Each time it has to be a bigger one. More expensive. When my last son, Joel, was born I had to give her a diamond. If we have another child, I may go bankrupt."

Jacob Schlemiel, who had twin boys of his own, patted Benjamin's shoulder and sighed. "Just wait," Jacob said. "You think that's bad? It gets worse. But you'll survive"

Their kind words had not been very reassuring.

After Sarah fled from the table, Benjamin cleared and washed the dishes. Ordinarily he would never have washed the dishes, because that was a wife's job. It didn't do to meddle with other people's business. But however much it might set a bad precedent, he felt that just this once it wouldn't hurt. It might even help.

He was wrong.

The next morning Benjamin was awakened to shrieks.

"What did you do?" his wife was shouting. "What did you do?"

Running from the bedroom still in his nightshirt, Benjamin first took a moment to check and make sure that neither the babies nor his wife were bleeding. Then he asked, "What's wrong?"

"What did you do?" Sarah screamed. She stared at the empty dining room table, and began flailing her arms toward the dish cabinet where he had carefully placed each hand-dried plate.

"I cleaned up."

"You cleaned up?" Sarah snapped. It wasn't a question so much as an accusation. "Did you clean up?"

"Yes," Benjamin said, nodding. "That's what I said. That's what I did."

"You call this cleaning up?" Sarah's voice was shrill.

"No. I call that an empty table." Benjamin was doing his best to keep his calm. "Cleaning up is what I did last night after you went to bed."

Sarah snatched a plate from the shelf. "Look at this. Look at this. What do you see?"

Benjamin looked. "A plate. A clean plate."

"There is no design on it!" Sarah screamed. "You washed the designs off the fine china plates!"

Benjamin frowned. "There were designs on the plates?"

"Flowers. It was a flower pattern. It was our wedding present from my mother, may she rest in peace. You washed them off."

"The plates were dirty," Benjamin said. "I scrubbed them clean."

"You don't scrub those plates clean," Sarah barked. "You wash them gently."

"The food was stuck on!" Benjamin said, defending himself.

"Then you soak them overnight. And in the morning, you wash them gently."

"Look," Benjamin took a deep breath. "We only used two plates last night. We still have another six left."

"The whole set is ruined!" Sarah wailed.

"I'll buy you new plates," Benjamin said.

"You can't!" Sarah sobbed. "My mother hand-painted those plates herself, and she's dead!"

There wasn't anything Benjamin could say to that. He looked around the room and saw that his tiny son and daughter seemed to be watching the whole exchange with small smiles on their faces. Were they mocking him? Did they think this was amusing? No, they were just little babies. They didn't know what was going on.

Sarah had collapsed into a chair. Her face was buried in her hands.

Benjamin put his hands on her shoulders and tried to comfort her. "At least," he said, "Mrs. Chaipul will be providing the plates at the bris."[1]

Again, it was the wrong thing.

Sarah's shoulders tensed. "The bris?" she spat. "Again with the bris? Is that all you can think of is the bris? Is the bris?"

"Sweetness, you're repeating yourself."

"I know. I know," Sarah said. "That's because you don't seem to understand. You don't understand."

"What?" Benjamin said, again trying to break through. "What don't I understand?"

---

[1] bris: a ritual circumcision ceremony. Usually catered. You should know that, although we've footnoted some of the Yiddish and Hebrew words, there's also a glossary at the back of the book.

"The bris this. The bris that! This, that. The bris!"

"I don't quite follow you," said the poor husband.

In Chelm, a bris is more than just a ritual circumcision. It's an excuse for a party. Everyone in the whole village gathers in the synagogue's social hall and claps with joy as the small surgical operation is performed. Of course, before young Rabbi Yohon Abrahms arrived, old Rabbi Kibbitz loved to terrorize fathers by saying, "Don't worry about paying me; I only take tips!"

Benjamin shuddered at the thought of the mohel's knife

"Of course you don't understand," his wife continued. She shrugged his hands off her shoulders. "You don't understand symbology. You don't understand duplexity. You don't understand!"

Benjamin Cohen got down on his knees in front of his wife. He looked up at her face and said, "I don't understand your words. I don't understand your tears. Tell me."

Sarah blinked. Benjamin had beautiful blue eyes. She loved looking into them. Sometimes she felt she could get lost in those eyes. She looked away.

"We have two children."

"Yes," he agreed. "I know. No sooner than one stops crying the other starts."

"But we will only have one bris."

"We only have one boy." Benjamin shrugged. "If we had two boys, like the Schlemiels, we'd still only have one bris, but with two snips."

"But what about her?" Sarah gestured at one of the babies.

Benjamin didn't know how his wife could tell which one was which. Then it occurred to him that she must have set them down in their crib in order. He'd have to watch and pay attention.

He smiled. "We'll give her some wine."

"That's not what I mean," Sarah wailed.

"Trust me," he said, "you don't want to ask Rabbi Kibbitz to circumcise her."

"That's not what I mean!" Sarah wailed.

Benjamin smiled again. He waved a teasing finger at his wife and chided, "You're repeating yourself again."

Sarah's eyes widened in fury. She snatched up a baby and said, "You want a bris? Have a bris!"

Then she walked out of the house into the snow, wearing nothing but her bare feet and dressing gown.

The smile remained glazed on Benjamin Cohen's face. He fully expected Sarah to return immediately, her teeth chattering and her feet blue.

After all, she left the door open. All the hot air was going out.

Five minutes later, Benjamin was still waiting, and the house was getting cold.

The baby started to cry.

"Oy," he muttered, climbing to his feet. He looked out the door and saw Sarah's bare footprints filling with snow. He shut the door. He picked up the infant. "Which one are you?" he cooed.

He dug a finger through the folds of the infant's blanket and got his answer with a warm wet spray in the face.

"Yakov! Bleah!" Benjamin sputtered. "Bleah!"

Chapter Three

Did you Bris Me?

The coffee was taking too long. In the old days, Mrs. Chaipul had just taken a handful of roasted beans, smashed them with a hammer, and thrown them into a pot of water to boil until everything was black and sludgy. Recently, however, she had purchased a newfangled device from Reb Cantor, the merchant. This "filter method" coffee had two advantages. The coffee tasted better, and you didn't have to chew it. The disadvantage was that after the water came to a boil, you had to pour it into the filter over the coffee and then wait forever for it all to drip through into the serving pitcher. Also, the coffee filters tended to fall apart after about ten uses, so she was often picking bits of paper out of her teeth.

First thing in the morning, she wanted coffee quickly and just as she was about to gnaw on a used filter, the bell over the door rang and Sarah Cohen ran into the restaurant wearing little more than a wool robe and carrying a bundle in her arms.

Two moments later, Mrs. Chaipul had Sarah seated at the table farthest from the door with her two bare feet soaking in a bucket of warm water and a cup of hot tea in her hands. Sarah's teeth were still chattering, while she alternately sipped and blew. A healthy color was returning to her cheeks, and her fingers weren't blue anymore.

With the baby curled snugly in her left arm, Chanah Chaipul finally managed to pour herself a cup of coffee, add three tablespoons of sugar, and take a long and welcomed sip.

"Tt-thank y-you f-for everyth-thing," Sarah sputtered. "I d-don't have any m-money w-with m-me, but-t…"

"Pff," Mrs. Chaipul said, waving her hand. "On the house.

Consider it a motherhood present. I planned to come by and check on the babies today anyway, so you're just making my day easier. The other one is all right, isn't he?"

Sarah nodded. She supposed that her husband, Benjamin, was taking care of the boy. Or at least that's what she hoped. She hadn't really taken the time to assign that duty to him when she'd run out the front door, but that had been implied, hadn't it?

"Good," Mrs. Chaipul said. "I've always believed that the first week is hardest for the parents. That's why they have the bris after eight days, so that nobody's throwing pots and pans at the mohel."

"He doesn't understand a thing," Sarah said. "My husband, not the babies." She was feeling warmer now, better.

"I know," Mrs. Chaipul nodded. "Men never do. They seem to think that after all your labor and lying about in bed for a day, you should be grateful to get back to the cooking and cleaning and taking care of the new babies."

"It's more than that," Sarah said. "I don't think he loves her."

Mrs. Chaipul glanced at the little sleeping bundle in her arms. "Feh. He's a man. You're lucky he loves anything beyond himself."

"No," Sarah said. "That's not true. He's a sweet man. But the way he talks, his son this and his son that… You wouldn't think he had a daughter at all."

"Ahh."

The bell over the door rang and Reb Cantor and Rabbi Yohon Abrahms kicked the snow off their boots and went to their usual stools at the counter.

Mrs. Chaipul's restaurant was the only kosher restaurant in the village of Chelm. It was a cozy place, with five tables, twenty chairs, and five stools in front of a counter. During the day, men liked to stop in and have a bite to eat on their way to or from the fields or their shops. Some of the men were unmarried, like Rabbi Abrahms. Others were wealthy, like Reb Cantor, and others had wives who were mediocre cooks, although Mrs. Chaipul made it a policy never to mention this. Two nights a week, Mrs. Chaipul opened her restaurant for evening meals, and sometimes she had whole families out for a treat or a couple celebrating a simcha.[2] The food was both magnificent and abundant. She kept two sets of plates and had two stoves, so that depending on her mood she could serve pastrami sandwiches as thick as a Megillah scroll or lay out a spread of bagels and lox, whitefish salad, and fresh cream cheese.[3] Her cast-iron matzah balls were legendary, her pea soup was delectable, and (fortunately for everyone in the village) she only made potato latkes once a year at Chanukah[4].

Given all this, the two men glanced around and were somewhat confused to see the two women conferring in the back, one of them wearing a red bathrobe.

"Pour yourselves some coffee," Mrs. Chaipul said. "I'll be with you in a minute."

"I'm interrupting," Sarah said.

"Nonsense."

"I didn't know where else to go. I wasn't really thinking. I was so angry at him. If I had thought about it I might have packed everything up and just left forever."

"So, it's good you didn't think," Mrs. Chaipul said. "Listen. Whether you admit it or not, every parent has a favorite child. Benjamin likes the boy. Chances are, you like the girl."

Sarah thought for a moment, and then nodded, "I do." Tears began to fill her eyes. "It's horrible. I really shouldn't, but I do."

"Sha, sha," Mrs. Chaipul smiled and rocked the baby. "You can't help it. It's something that happens. The trick is to have a favorite, but not play favorites. To know that you have a preference, but never ever to show it. If anyone asks you, you lie. If you do your job right, you will go to your grave and all of your children will be

---

[2] A simcha is a joyful excuse for a party. It can be large like a wedding, or small like when houseguests who have stayed too long finally leave and you have the house to yourself.

[3] The Megillah is read on Purim and contains the Book of Esther, which boils down to the quintessential Jewish story, "They tried to kill us. We survived. Let's eat."

[4] For all the gory details, see the stories "Mrs. Chaipul's Lead Sinker Matzah Balls" and "The Lethal Latkes."

convinced that each of them was your favorite. And may that time be distant and the children be many."

"I don't know if I can do many," Sarah said. "I'm not sure I can even do these two."

"You start with one," Mrs. Chaipul said, passing the tiny girl back to her mother. "Then you do the other. Don't think you can take care of them both at the same time. You will always have to take turns. Babies are like men; they are immature and selfish. They always want service."

Sarah giggled. She had noticed that Reb Cantor was tapping his spoon impatiently against the counter.

"The trick," Mrs. Chaipul continued, while ignoring her customer, "is to give them the service they deserve at the opportunity that suits you, and make them feel grateful for your beneficence."

"What do I do about my husband?" the young woman whispered.

"You take care of your children," Mrs. Chaipul whispered back. "And don't make any foolish choices just now." She leaned over and gave Sarah a kiss on the cheek.

"Now," said Mrs. Chaipul, her voice rising, "what can I get you wise gentlemen on this cold winter morning?"

Sarah Cohen sat very still. The baby was asleep in her arms. With one hand, she ate the plate full of eggs and toast and fried potatoes that Mrs. Chaipul placed in front of her. It was delicious. She hadn't had a meal served to her like this since she was a child. And Benjamin, who always was served his meals, still came to the restaurant almost every day? What a luxury. Every so often, Mrs. Chaipul came by with a kettle and poured some more warm water into Sarah's teacup and into the pot where her feet were still soaking.

After a while, Sarah began to feel restless. You can only eat so much breakfast and drink so much tea. She had a home to get back to and another child who was probably hungry. There was a bris to plan. And a husband to... She sighed.

"Excuse me," said a voice.

Sarah looked up and saw Rabbi Yohon Abrahms, the schoolteacher. He was a tall, skinny man with reddish hair and a reddish beard. Sarah realized how little clothing she was wearing, and she blushed.

"I was wondering if you might like to borrow my gloves," he said. He was offering a pair of black leather gloves to her. "I think they might fit on your feet. I have big hands, and… You can give them back to me when they are dry."

Sarah nearly burst into tears. She hadn't even thought about how she was going to get back home through the snow. In the back of her mind she had imagined that Benjamin might have come for her by now, but he didn't know where she was and she wasn't sure she wanted him to see her like this or talk to her here. It had been such a peaceful interlude, that to have him come to rescue her would spoil it completely.

"Thank you," Sarah said. She took the gloves.

The young rabbi nodded, backed away, and rejoined Reb Cantor at the counter. Mrs. Chaipul brought a towel and string, and held the baby while Sarah dried her toes and then tied the gloves to her feet.

Gathering herself up, Sarah wrapped the baby tightly in her blanket, stood proudly on her warmly gloved feet, and strode out of the restaurant, back into the snow.

"I wish I had a wife like that," Rabbi Abrahms said as he watched Sarah Cohen make her way against the wind back to her house.

"You like them crazy?" said Reb Cantor. "Maybe you should start courting one of the Shimmel sisters. They spend all their time with the goats."

"Sarah's not crazy," Mrs. Chaipul said, as she poured the young rabbi more coffee. "She's a mother, and mothers always want to do what's best for their young."

"Sure," agreed Reb Cantor. "Like taking them out of the house in bare feet in the middle of winter?"

"Sarah was in bare feet, not the children," Mrs. Chaipul said.

"Your point being?" Reb Cantor answered.

Mrs. Chaipul glared at Reb Cantor. "No more coffee for you this morning."

"You see, Rabbi Abrahms? You can marry anyone you want," the fat merchant laughed. "Everyone in Chelm is crazy."

* * *

People forget that Mrs. Chaipul wasn't born in Chelm. Like most institutions, she'd been there forever. Her restaurant was a landmark, and most of the village's children had been born into her hands. She was a workhorse, indefatigable. All day she cooked at her restaurant, and between breakfast and lunch and lunch and dinner she made visits to cottages and farms to tend to the sick and elderly. Somehow, in between all of that, she managed to revel in the production of huge banquet feasts. No event or simcha (or funeral) was considered important unless it featured one of Mrs. Chaipul's sumptuous spreads.

When she catered a bris, it was a work of art. She knew that love and tenderness were edible, so every bit of food and drink was presented with passion and care. The social hall was transformed into a banquet room. Tables were covered with white linen. The tablecloths were covered with silver platters. The silver platters were covered with delicacies.

She always liked to take a moment after the chaos of the setup and before the chaos of the eating. It was an interval of peace—when all the napkins were folded, the plates were stacked; all the glasses were in lines and the silver knives and forks and spoons were in rows. The room was quiet, the smell of warm bread floated in the air. You could feel the spirit of the world, breathing.

"Looks nice. Smells nice," she said to herself. "They're gonna love it."

Then, when she heard the crowd gathering outside, Mrs. Chaipul opened the doors, and stood back.

It was always a stampede. First came the little children, flying like chickens, then the old men who lived by themselves and needed both a full plate and a place at a table with friends. Then the young men and women would scurry in because they knew if there was smoked salmon, it wouldn't last long. At the end of the pack sauntered the craftsmen and their families. The baker, the carpenter, the shoemaker, the merchant, these were the closest Chelm had to a nobility or gentry class, and they felt it was beneath them to run to the food like a starving goat to a trough. Or rather, their wives felt it was important for them to set a good example, because if it was up to the men, they would have darted ahead just after the children. And lastly came the hosts. Not because they weren't hungry, but because they were usually too busy accepting congratulations or condolences, depending on the occasion. Mrs. Chaipul always made sure to set aside a plate of the best items for the parents, because the rest of the villagers in Chelm tended to eat like wild animals, devouring everything in sight.

On the morning of Yakov Cohen's bris, when the feeding frenzy was in full fling, Mrs. Chaipul raised her eyebrow. Mrs. Meier, the balanit ha mikveh, smiled and waved her fingers. Deborah Rosen, the washerwoman, grinned and held up a thumb. The ripple spread through the room as every married woman signaled every other married woman, and (after taking a last bite of nosh) they slipped away.

It is perhaps a telling fact that none of the men, younger women, or children noticed their absence. Benjamin Cohen, the tailor didn't even realize that his wife and daughter had been whisked away. He was too busy holding his boy in his arms, wincing at every slap on his back, and wondering how he was going to eat without waking up the child.

The women made their way quietly out of the social hall and through the streets to the mikveh.

A mikveh is a ritual-bathing place. With the exception of Reb Cantor, the villagers of Chelm did not have running water in their houses. For most, bathing at home meant shivering in a small metal tub with water heated on a stove and no privacy. While mikvehs in many communities were somber and religious communal baths, in Chelm the mikveh was a bit more festive.

Although balanit ha mikveh means female bath attendant, Mrs. Meier was much more than just the cleaning lady for the tub. She was also the swim instructor for women and children, as well as the kind of person who could listen to an entire conversation, hear every syllable, gasp, giggle, and curse, but breathe not a word.

In the mikveh, men and women were separated (naturally), but Mrs. Meier knew that Rabbi Kibbitz encouraged laughing, smoking cigars, and even splashing. She often grumbled to Mrs. Chaipul about the mess men left, and the ring of dirt, ash, and hair that required firm scrubbing and sometimes cleaning the water with a fine sieve.

Built in the distant and forgotten past, older than the village's current synagogue, the ritual bath of Chelm was a small, but deep, pool of water in the basement of the Meier's home. It was kept covered from the elements, but still kissed by the rain through a narrow pipe. Legend has it that the stones lining the walls and floors of the mikveh had been brought all the way from Jerusalem, so whenever a married woman came to visit Mrs. Meier, she left feeling quite holy. Reb Meier liked to laugh that not even the Czar of Russia had a finer indoor swimming pool, although Mrs. Meier swatted him every time he joked about her domain.

"Is everyone here?" Mrs. Chaipul said. She looked at the wives of Chelm, crowded around the narrow ledge of the bath.

"Don't push!" Oma Levitsky shouted. "At my age I don't think my heart could take a swim in the frigid water."

The assemblage giggled, but then they fell silent as Mrs. Chaipul gave them a long and icy glare.

None of them knew what Mrs. Chaipul was planning. A bris in Chelm was a typical event, but this? Some kind of ceremony for a newborn girl? This was something new, and no one wanted to miss a moment.

Sarah, for her part, wasn't so sure that doing something new to her daughter was such a good idea. She stood near the edge of the mikveh, her baby held protectively close. She nearly fell in when Mrs. Chaipul called her name.

"Sarah," Mrs. Chaipul said, "you are the daughter of Chaya, who was the daughter of Naomi, who was the daughter of Deborah…" It took quite some time for her to finish because, like most of the villagers of Chelm, Sarah's family had kept meticulously detailed written records of their births and deaths. "Have you brought your daughter?"

"I have," Sarah said nervously. "This isn't a baptism, is it?"

"No," Mrs. Chaipul shook her head, and allowed herself a smile. "This is a naming ceremony. When a boy is named at his bris, the cutting of the mohel seals it into his flesh. Fortunately, we don't have to do that with her."

There was an audible sigh of relief from the ladies.

"Instead," Mrs. Chaipul continued, "we will bless her with the water of life, and allow her name to seep in through her skin."

"It certainly seems like a baptism to me," muttered Oma Levitsky, who was never a fan of change.

"Well, it's not," Mrs. Chaipul snapped. "It's a new spiritual ritual, created by Jewish women for Jewish women."

"New shmoo. Let's get on with it then," Oma Levitsky grumbled. "My feet are getting cold."

Mrs. Chaipul ignored her. "Sarah, have you chosen a name?"
Sarah shook her head and whispered, "No."
The room fell silent.

"What do you mean, no?" Mrs. Chaipul asked.

"I don't know what to call her," the poor young mother wailed. "I've tried out every name I could think of. Twice! She could be any of them. She could be none of them. I don't want her to be unhappy or miserable or die at an early age because of the wrong name."

"Oy, this is going to take a while isn't it?" said Oma Levitsky in a whisper that reached everyone in the small humid room.

Mrs. Chaipul ignored the giggles and spoke gently, but firmly. "Sarah, I understand. The name that you give to your daughter will be perfect. Lower her into the water."

Sarah looked panicked. "I don't want to drop her! She doesn't know how to swim."

"You won't drop her. When she is in the water, you will say her name. You will give her that name."

Sarah thought for a moment. She had gone to Mrs. Chaipul because she was so sad that her son would get everything and her daughter nothing. Mrs. Chaipul had described the ritual she had learned from her mother, and it had sounded so lovely. But it was wintertime in Chelm and the mikveh was cold and the women were grumpy. And she still didn't know her daughter's name...

At last, Sarah nodded. She knelt down on the hard stone, unwrapped the blankets, and slowly lowered the baby into the water.

The tiny girl had been asleep, but when the water touched her skin, her eyes shot open. Everyone gasped.

She looked around the room. She took in everything. She did not cry or squirm. She looked into each and every face, into each and every soul. She seemed to understand.

The girl floated in the water, resting in her mother's hands, and seemed quite content.

"Rachel," Sarah whispered. "I name you Rachel."

"Mazel Tov!" Mrs. Chaipul shouted.

"Mazel Tov!" came the cheer from the rest of the women.

"Don't push me in!" yelped Oma Levitsky.

Now the baby began to cry, and her mother quickly yanked her out of the pool and wrapped her in a warm towel.

"Rachel," her mother whispered. "Sha, sha. Rachel."

Chapter Four

Out of the Frying Pan

Benjamin Cohen was trying to take the news calmly. He had managed to survive his son's bris without the help of his wife, who had sauntered back into the social hall just as the last of the bagels had been eaten. In Chelm, as in many other communities, when the food is gone, the party is over. Benjamin handed the newly circumcised Yakov to Sarah, who was getting quite adept at balancing a child in each arm. He gave Rabbi Abrahms his fee, and Reb Levitsky, the synagogue's caretaker, a small gratuity as thanks for cleaning up the mess. He handed Mrs. Chaipul her envelope for providing the nosh. He nodded his head to Sarah, and walked purposely out of the shul back through the darkening streets to their house.

When he got home, he hung up his coat, dropped a log into the stove, and began warming his hands. By then, Sarah had set the children into their crib and joined him next to the stove.

"What was the towel for?" he asked her. He had noticed that before she had set down the girl, Sarah had carefully unwrapped a towel from the sleeping infant.

"To dry her off," his wife answered.

"She got wet?"

"No." It was a single syllable, uttered with sarcasm.

"If she wasn't wet then why did you dry her with a towel?" Benjamin asked.

"Obviously she was wet! She was soaking wet."

"Her diaper leaked?"

"No." This time the word was three-syllables long and even more sarcastic.

Benjamin turned his head and glanced at his wife. "Maybe she fell into a pool of water?"

"Exactly!"

Benjamin Cohen rubbed his hands. He wasn't really cold, but it gave him something to do. "How is it possible for a baby girl to fall into a pool of water in Chelm in the middle of the winter?"

"I put her there," Sarah sighed as she reached for a frying pan. What with all the excitement, she hadn't fixed anything for dinner. "And her name is Rachel."

Benjamin raised his hands and cowered back, "Don't hit me!"

"What?" Sarah squinted. Her husband stepped farther away.

"Please, please. Whatever I said. Whatever I did, I'm sorry."

Sarah raised her hands in a gesture of disbelief, but Benjamin misinterpreted it and ducked his head, cowering behind his arms.

Sarah looked at the frying pan. She looked at her husband. She started to laugh. "You should know that, if I was going to hit you, I wouldn't give you any warning."

Benjamin peeked up and bit his lip. "Somehow that isn't comforting. This isn't funny."

She set down the pan. "No," she giggled. "It isn't. You're frightened of me?"

"You haven't been acting yourself recently," Benjamin said. He allowed himself to stand back up, but didn't come any closer. "We've been married for a long time, and I thought I knew you, but all of a sudden… You're different."

Sarah raised a finger and pointed. "You're different too. You think it's easy taking care of two children when you were only expecting one? You think it's easy carrying them around inside for months. Now they're on the outside, but you think it's easy trying to get back to normal when you have absolutely no idea what normal is supposed to be?" Her voice had been rising, and now it was practically a shriek. "You think it's easy worrying about the future and wondering how it's going to be for them?"

Benjamin said, "Me? How am I different?"

Sarah lifted her arm and made a fist. For a moment, she imagined smashing her fist down on the frying pan's handle, levering it off the stove, the frying pan flying through the air, and striking her husband flat in the forehead with a great CLANG! Then of course he would be bleeding and screaming or unconscious, and the babies would be awake and yowling. And she would run from the house and leave them all, never to return.

When she realized what she was thinking, she dropped and unclenched her hand, gasped, and collapsed into a chair. She put her elbows on the kitchen table, rested her head in her hands, and began to sob.

"This is what I mean," Benjamin mumbled, but he was careful to keep the remark quiet and unheard. He sidled next to his beloved, and put his hands on her shoulders. She shook them off and shrugged him away. He stood there, not quite sure what to do.

There was a knock at the door.

Benjamin looked at his wife. He looked at his children. He looked at the door. "I'll get it," he said.

He moved to the door and opened it.

Mrs. Chaipul stood outside. She had a basket in one hand and a cast iron cooking pot with a lid in the other. It was dark now, and snow was falling, making her shawl look like a white flow of ice.

"So, are you going to invite me in? Or you want I should freeze in the cold so you can have a statue in front of your house until spring when I thaw and melt into a puddle?"

Benjamin hesitated. "Sarah and I are having…"

Mrs. Chaipul peered around his shoulder. "I see. All right. Well, I brought you some dinner." She lifted the pot. "I also brought you some supplies." She raised the basket. "Inside is a paper parcel full of tea supplements. Give her one teaspoon in a pot of regular black tea. Only one teaspoon per day. It will help."

Benjamin reached out, took the basket and the iron pot, and felt their sudden weight almost rip his arms from their sockets. "These are heavy. What is it?"

"Food," said the old woman. "Left over from the bris. Your wife is going to be having a difficult time for a while. She's not going to be able to do everything she did. Not right away. This will see you through. Others will bring more."

"What's in the tea supplement?" he asked, a little concerned.

There were rumors, not loud ones, but rumors nonetheless, that Mrs. Chaipul was a bit of a witch. It wasn't something that you said. It was something you inferred.

Again Mrs. Chaipul squinted. "You remember when I tore my favorite silk scarf, and you repaired it so I couldn't even tell where it had been ripped?"

Benjamin nodded. "I remember. It was a beautiful scarf."

The midwife continued, "I asked you how you did that. You just patted my cheek and said, 'Trade secret!'"

Benjamin nodded.

Mrs. Chaipul patted his cheek. "Trade secret."

She turned and vanished into the snow.

Benjamin backed into the room and kicked the door shut with his foot. He lugged the stew pot to the stove and set it on top to warm. He hoisted the basket onto the table, opened it, and peered inside. Mrs. Chaipul knew how to pack a basket. In one compartment there were three salami, a piece of pastrami, and a piece of corned beef. In another compartment were two wheels of cheese and a jar of butter. In a third compartment were four loaves of bread, two cabbages, ten potatoes, four heads of garlic, six onions, and a walnut strudel. On the bottom, next to the strudel, was a folded paper bag the size of his fist.

"Who was that?" Sarah asked. Her eyes were rimmed red.

"Mrs. Chaipul," Benjamin said. He filled the teakettle with water from the fresh bucket and set it on top of the stove.

"You didn't invite her in?"

Benjamin shrugged. "She couldn't stay. She brought us some dinner."

"What are you doing?"

"I'm making you tea."

"I don't want tea," Sarah said.

Benjamin sighed. "I do," he said. "Will you join me?"

Sarah waved her fingers. "All right."

He waited until the water had boiled and then made the tea, adding a teaspoon of the fine brown powder from the paper packet. The stew he set to simmering on the back of the stove.

Benjamin sat down and put one mug in front of her, and another in front of him. He wondered what would happen if he drank the tea.

She lifted the mug to her lips and sipped it. "This is good."

He nodded, and then something struck him. Had Sarah just said that she had named their daughter Rachel?

Chapter Five

Not My Cup Of Tea

He wasn't quite sure he remembered it correctly, so at first Benjamin Cohen decided to ask his wife straight out.

"Did you say you named our daughter…" he began, but then he hesitated. He wasn't quite sure exactly what he wanted to say. Or more to the point, he was fairly sure he knew what he wanted to say, but he didn't quite know how to say it. It was a sensitive subject. He wasn't interested in starting another fight.

The pause however was enough.

"Yes," Sarah said in a testy voice, "I named her. While you were busy doing your duty as a father to our son, I took our daughter and I gave her a name. Do you have a problem with that?"

Never in human history has a sane or rational husband answered that question with a yes. Benjamin saw that Sarah's teeth were gritted and her hands were firmly on her hips. He decided that he was not going to be the first.

"No, no," he said hastily. "Of course not."

"Good," Sarah said. "Then it's settled."

They sat quietly for a moment. Their tea grew cold. Neither dared to move.

At last, Benjamin interrupted the silence. "Only, what did you name her?"

Sarah pounced. "I told you what I named her. Weren't you paying attention when I spoke? Don't you listen to anything I say?"

Benjamin wasn't sure what the right answer to that question was. He decided to dodge. "I forgot," he said. "It's been crazy in the shop. We haven't been getting enough sleep. The bris was overwhelming. Drink your tea and remind me what you named her."

Sarah sipped her tea. He wondered how long it would take and how much she should drink for Mrs. Chaipul's herbs to work.

Again they sat. If the Cohens had been wealthy enough to own a clock, they would have heard the seconds ticking away. Instead they heard the crackling of logs in the stove, then the sound of their breathing, and finally the quiet gurgles of their children.

Sarah sighed, "I named her Rachel."

"That's what I thought you said."

"You knew, so why did you ask?"

"I wasn't sure."

"So?" she said.

"So," he answered.

"Do you have a problem with Rachel?"

Even the best husband can only avoid conflict nine times out of ten. Benjamin knew he was far from the best. He decided to grab the bull by the horns.

"His name is Yakov," he said.

Sarah nodded. "Yes."

"Her name is Rachel?"

Again she nodded. "Yes."

"They're married!" Benjamin sputtered.

"Who are?"

"Rachel and Yakov."

Sarah looked aghast. Anywhere else in the world this sort of a remark would inspire smirks, giggles, or even guffaws. In Chelm, however, language is a very real part of life, and a statement of fact is often assumed to be the truth.

"How can they be married?" Sarah covered her mouth. "He just had his bris! He's not even bar mitzvahed. She's just a baby. I haven't taught her anything I know. When did you see the marriage broker? More importantly, who are they married to?"

By now Sarah's voice had risen, and Benjamin had to put a finger on her lips to keep her from waking the babies.

"They're married to each other," he whispered. "No!" she hissed back, amazed. "How is that possible? I didn't see you make a suit for him or a wedding dress for her. How is that possible?"

She gasped and pushed his hand away as another thought came into her head. "Why wasn't I invited to the wedding? They don't love their mother!"

Benjamin felt frantic. It was all spinning out of control. "Sarah, Sareleh, get a hold of yourself. If there had been a wedding, you would have been invited, but there was no wedding."

Sarah burst into tears. "My children are married to each other out of wedlock. I am a horrible mother!"

"No no no! You're a wonderful mother. They aren't married."

Her face suddenly grew somber. "You said they were married. Are you lying to me now? Didn't you just say they were married?"

"Yes, that's what I said," Benjamin tried to explain. "But it's not what I meant."

"You meant to drive me crazy. You meant to make me mad with worry? You want me to rip my clothes and pull out my hair?"

"No no. I love your hair, and if you tore your clothes then I'd be the one who would have to repair them. Drink your tea."

"What's with the tea?" Sarah said, suspiciously. "Why aren't you drinking your tea?"

"Tea?" Benjamin said. "Tea? Tea? What? What? Ok. I'll drink it." He picked up the mug and drank it in a gulp. "Now listen. Our children are not married. Yakov and Rachel are married."

"Yakov and Rachel are our children."

"But they're not married."

"You just said they were. You just did."

"Not that Yakov and Rachel. The Yakov and Rachel from the Torah! They are married to each other. How could you name our children after a husband and wife?"

"I didn't," Sarah said. "I named her. You named him. If anything, it's your fault."

"You knew what I was naming him. I didn't know what you were naming her!"

"Did you ask?"

"No."

"So?"

"So!" he answered. "So now they're brother and sister, and

husband and wife!"

"But not really," Sarah said.

This panicked Benjamin. "They're not really brother and sister? Who are they then? They can't be cousins, although I suppose if they were second cousins they could marry each other without any trouble."

Now it was Sarah's turn to put her finger over his lips. "Sha, sha. Stop it. Calm down. Here, have some more tea."

Without thinking, Benjamin took the mug from Sarah's hand, and drained it down.

"You know, Sarah," he said, "I love you."

Then his head thunked against the table and he began to snore.

Sarah covered her mouth, first in concern, but then to hide her smile. She reached out one hand and began brushing it through her husband's hair. Then she kissed her fingers, and touched them to his cheek.

"I love you too, Benjamin. Sometimes."

Chapter Six

The Invitation

Oma Levitsky stood patiently on the doorstep of the Cohen house. It was a dark and chilly morning. She was wrapped in a sweater, a shawl, and an overcoat, and she still wasn't warm. As the sun began to peek over the top of East Hill, she lifted her arm. Her sister, Sadie in America, had told her about a place called Miami that was warm and had fresh oranges all year-round. Sadie, of course, was a well-known liar, but still, keeping warm without sitting next to a fire was a dream worth imagining every so often. As soon as the first rooster crowed, she rapped her knuckles against the door in a gentle tattoo. There was no answer, so she rapped again. Now she heard stirring inside, so she shuffled back a half-pace.

The door opened and Sarah Cohen peered out. "Is anybody dead?"

Before she answered, Oma Levitsky thought about it. At her age it didn't pay to make any assumptions. "Not right here, not right now," she said.

Sarah blinked. She didn't think that Oma Levitsky had ever visited her house before, and she couldn't imagine what she was doing here just now and so early. "Would you like to come in?" she asked.

Chelm's oldest resident[5] shook her head and said, "No. I would

---

[5] It is always difficult and dangerous to make a claim like "Oldest resident" in a place like Chelm. First of all, many people who might be eligible for the title are superstitious and would hesitate to claim being oldest for fear that the evil eye would immediately strike them dead. Next, record keeping of things like dates was both haphazard and subject to the whims and calendars as interpreted by various kings, czars, popes, and rabbis. Finally, the records themselves were frequently illegible and often lost to fires, rain, mold, and hungry mice. That said, Oma Levitsky wasn't superstitious and didn't have any records to prove her claim,

like you to come with me."

"Wha?" mumbled Sarah. "It's still dark."

"Yes, I know. Are your children asleep?"

The younger woman nodded.

"Is your husband home?"

Again Sarah nodded.

"Then everyone will be fine. Get your coat."

"But I have to make breakfast," Sarah said.

"Oy," Oma Levitsky grumbled. "Look, the sooner you come, the sooner you'll be back. No one is going to starve because they missed breakfast."[6]

When Sarah heard this, she knew that whatever the old woman was there about was important, so she grabbed her overcoat, slipped on her boots, and tiptoed out the door[7].

She was just shutting the latch when she stopped. "I should write a note."

The old woman's lips pursed and rolled about as if they were two fidgety pink worms attached to her face. "If you must."

Sarah nodded. She opened the door, raced back inside, jotted on a scrap of paper, "I'll be back soon," and left it on the kitchen table. Then she ran back to the door, and gently pulled it closed. "Benjamin and I have been having some troubles of late," she explained. "I wouldn't want him to worry."

"A little worry never killed anyone," Oma Levitsky said as they began to walk south away from the village.[8]

---

but nobody else disputed the issue.

[6] As difficult as it is to believe that a woman, who was not only a Jewish grandmother, but a Jewish great-grandmother, would utter these words, Oma Levitsky did. She had noticed over the decades of her life, that in fact, no one had starved to death just because they missed breakfast. Now, if they were to miss lunch or dinner... That was another matter entirely.

[7] You should know that for three out of four seasons, keeping warm at night in Chelm involves burying yourself under many covers, while wearing all your clothes. So Sarah was already fully-dressed when she got up.

[8] Oma Levitsky enjoyed telling people all the things that would not kill them. She had only come close to being wrong once, when she and her second cousin, Eli, had sneaked into their grandmother's kitchen and eaten fifteen blintzes each.

They strolled in silence for a while, and then Sarah asked, "Are we going to the mikveh?"

"Near enough," Oma Levitsky said. "Listen, you like to talk, don't you?"

"Of course," Sarah answered. "Everyone in Chelm likes to talk. I can't think of anyone who doesn't like to talk, except for the Silent Man, and since he never says much of anything, who knows what he really thinks? Maybe he likes to talk, but just doesn't have anything to say."[9]

"When we get to where we are going, you need to be quiet," Oma said.

Sarah continued. "I think that we like to talk because there isn't that much else to do for entertainment. I understand that in large cities they have things such as musical concerts and theatrical plays, but it's so rare than any troupe of actors finds its way through the Schvartzvald to Chelm, that I'm not even sure they really exist or are just rumors."

"Did you hear me?" the old woman said as they reached the mikveh.

"What? No."

Oma Levitsky sighed. She was about to say, A little peace and quiet never killed anyone, but she wasn't sure that was entirely true. So she settled for the truth. "When we get to the last door, you will need to be quiet for five minutes. If you can't do that, you might as well go home now."

"How will I know it's the last door?"

"Because you'll be standing in front of it in absolute silence for at least five minutes."

"Can we still talk now?" Sarah asked.

Eli had asked, "Should I eat another one?" and Oma, a young and foolish girl, had said, "Why not, it won't kill you." He had just stuffed the delicious treat into his mouth, when their grandmother had come in, and shouted, "I'm going to kill you!" Eli had been so terrified that he vomited the blintz up, and spent the next week in bed with both a stomachache and a sore tuchas.

[9] The Silent Man of Chelm is famous for having been quiet for so long that even his wife forgot his name.

Oma Levitsky nodded, and led the way into the ritual bathhouse.

"Are we meeting someone?"

"Yes."

"Who?"

"You'll see."

They walked into the mikveh, through the bath area, and through a small door in the far wall. Beyond this was a short narrow passage with a low ceiling. It dead-ended at another even smaller door.

"Close that door behind you," Oma Levitsky said in a quiet voice.

Sarah did and the sudden blackness made her gasp.

"Shh," hissed the old woman. She knocked on the small door three times and then twice.

In the darkness, the five minutes of silence seemed like an eternity. Sarah found herself imagining horrible things, like being trapped underground in a mine with no air and no food and no light, being stuck there forever, and knowing that you'll never see the light of day again, that you'll never feel the cool fresh breeze or smell a flower blossom or hear your children laugh...

When the small door finally opened, the light from the room on the other side was so warm and bright that Sarah felt as if she'd gone to heaven.

Oma Levitsky stood aside, and let Sarah walk through the door first.

Mrs. Chaipul met her with a warm embrace. She gave Sarah a kiss on each cheek and then said, "You are the first woman in the entire history of the Council to make it through the entire five minutes in the Hall of Silence without once talking."

"Really?" Sarah smiled shyly, as she looked around. She wasn't sure if she was in a room or in a cave. The walls were smooth stone, but the space was very comfortable. The floor was carpeted. There were four low tables each with three brightly burning candles set in old-fashioned brass candlesticks. There were two sofas and a dozen comfortable chairs, all full of women. Sarah looked around and realized that she knew them all. Mrs. Chaipul, Mrs. Gold, Mrs. Stein, Mrs. Cantor, Oma Levitsky's daughter-in law... Nearly every woman over the age of forty was sitting quietly, smiling, and sipping a cup of tea.

"Shall we get started?" Mrs. Chaipul said.

"No, we should all wait until we die of old age," muttered Oma Levitsky as she creaked her way to her chair. "I'll go first. Did anyone bring mandel bread?"[10]

Soon everybody was talking all at once, and it took some time for Sarah to focus.

"We want you to join the Council," Mrs. Chaipul was saying.

Sarah found herself sitting in a comfy chair, surrounded by women she had known all her life. She held a cup of tea in one hand and a rock hard piece of mandel bread in the other. She lifted the cookie to her lips and tried to bite. Her teeth were stopped in their gums.

Oma Levitsky leaned over and whispered, "Dip it in the tea."

Sarah did, and several minutes later the pastry was soft enough to nibble.

"Usually women are not invited to join the Council until after their children are of age," Mrs. Chaipul was saying. "But in your case, we are making an exception. We know and understand that you are having a rough time. It is difficult enough to manage with one child, but to have two suddenly thrust upon you... When Rebecca Schlemiel had her boys we stuck to the rules, and that was probably a mistake. So, we're trying something different. Are you interested?"

Sarah's voice was quiet. "Mrs. Chaipul, I don't even know what you're talking about."

Mrs. Chaipul laughed. "First of all, child, here we do not call each other by our husband's or family's names. Please, call me

---

[10] Mandel bread is the Jewish version of the Italian Biscotti. It is a twice-baked dessert that is usually rated on its density. One theory is that Mandel bread is based on the bread of affliction in the bible. Another is that it is named after a man named Mandel, who was considered particularly thick and dense.

Chanah."

"All right," Sarah sputtered. "Chanah, I don't understand."

"Perhaps I should start at the beginning..."

"Oy," whispered Oma Levitsky, rolling her eyes. "Here we go again."

But even though they had all heard the story many times, the women in the warm cave fell silent as Chanah Chaipul spoke.

* * *

When my husband, Sam died, may he rest in peace, I was miserable. I did not yet live in Chelm, but far from here in a place I would rather not mention. My children were grown and had left our village to make lives for themselves in other cities, in other countries. I was nothing. A woman with a barren womb, old and ugly. What future was there for me? If I had grandchildren in the area, then I would have been too busy to notice, but the truth was that no one in our little shtetl valued me for anything except cooking, cleaning, and bearing children. At first I thought that my misery was sadness from Sam's passing. He had been in my life since I was a girl, and to have him gone, it was like losing an arm. The year of mourning passed, and although I stopped wearing black and torn clothing, the world I saw was still veiled in darkness.

One evening there was a knock at the door. I opened it reluctantly because there were often rumors of bandits and even Cossacks, but the knock was soft and undemanding. Through the crack in the door I saw the shape of a woman, all alone. She wore, as we all did, a shawl over her head. It was not considered seemly for a woman's face to be seen by strangers.

"May I help you?" I said.

She echoed my words, "May I help you?"

I had expected a request for alms. Widows are known to be either generous or stingy to travelers, and my reputation was kind.

"I'm sorry," I said, not really sure whether she had heard me. "Can I help you?"

Again, she repeated my words. "I'm sorry. Can I help you?"

Now I began to feel a little angry. Was she just stupid or trying to mock me?

"Would you like to come in or go away?" I demanded.

"I would like you to come with me," she said.

Now I was furious. "Why should I come with you? It's the middle of the night. I don't know who you are or what you want. If you need some food, I will give it to you. If you need some money, I will give it to you. If not, be on your way."

Then the shawl lifted, and I saw her face. She was neither old nor young. Her face was lined but still smooth. It is difficult to describe it even today. A smile lit her face. Her eyes were deep green, and they stared into my soul.

To this day I don't know why I followed her. Perhaps because there was nothing in my house to hold me back. She could have been leading me to my death or taking me into slavery, butthere was no one left in my house who would care. So I threw on my coat and my shawl, and I followed her.

She took me to a cave, not unlike this one, and we stood outside in silence for five minutes before crossing the threshold. She lit a candle. Inside it was empty. There were no chairs or tables, only rocks and puddles. It was clear though that people had met there, perhaps lived there at one time or another, but that was long ago. Now it was empty and deserted.

She set the candle on a rock, and we sat side by side while she told me "The Legend of the Council of Wise Women."

She told me that the Council of Wise Women was born when Sarah, the mother of the Jewish people, learned that her grandson, Jacob had brought home two wives. As sisters, Leah and Rachel had always fought and argued, and it was clear that as wives they were little inclined to do anything differently. Sarah herself felt deep regret at the way she had treated Abraham's servant, Hagar, and Hagar's son, Ishmael, so many years earlier. She was determined that her family should not be torn apart.

So she invited her daughter-in-law, Rebecca, and her two grand-daughters-in-law, Rachel and Leah, to her tent for a nice cup of tea. Once the cups were poured, they all sat in silence.

As you know, it is not an easy thing for people to sit in silence, let alone women, let alone three generations of related women.

Somehow, though, they managed, and when at last the silence was concluded, they were able to listen to each other and speak without bitterness or rancor.

This was the beginning of our tradition of silence, and from that day until this, the Council of Wise Women has passed from grandmother to granddaughter, across lands and around the world, until at last it reached me.

While I sat in the cave I listened to this woman's story with a certain amount of skepticism, but at the same time her tale captured me. What would it be like for women to come together to support each other and protect each other?

I didn't really believe her. It seemed like an elaborate facade, a pleasant fabrication, a lie. But for what? What could she possibly want from me?

"I never heard of this Council," I said.

"It has always been a secret," she said. "And as you can see the Council in this land has not fared well. Although we strive for knowledge and understanding, sometimes fear and suspicion rule instead. We are, after all, only human."

"So," I laughed. I looked around at the light flickering off wet rocks. "This so-called Council of Wise Women is just you and me sitting in this damp and empty cave?"

"No," she too laughed. "Only you..."

And when I looked back she was gone. I looked at the ground and I saw only my muddy footprints on the floor. For a moment I was frightened that, like a young girl in a fairy tale, I had been lured into a labyrinth by a witch. But the candle was still there, and I could see the exit from the cave back into the woods.

I sat on that rock for a long time, wondering if I had imagined it or dreamed it or invented it all myself. And at last I decided that it didn't matter.

If the Council of Wise Women didn't exist, then it should. And if it should exist, then why not make it so?

Before the candle stub flickered out, I lifted it off the rock and made my way back to my house.

The next morning I brought several of my friends into the

woods and led them to the entrance. I asked them to stand in silence, but they wouldn't listen. Eventually, I gave up and I brought them into the cave anyway and told them the story, but they just laughed.

Not a single woman in my old shtetl could hear what I was saying. For them, their lives with husbands and families and farms and businesses and just the hard work of survival was enough. They thought me a fool, probably out of my mind, since the death of my husband. Sometimes they would come with me to the cave, to humor me, but they would not just sit and listen. They could not.

At last I gave up. I sold my house and my small farm. They tried to dissuade me, but I saw no future there with them. I saw only loneliness and old age stretching before me in an endless succession of empty days and nights until at last I would die. And at my funeral, before they buried me next to my husband, they would probably laugh and say that I was crazy.

So I left and I traveled for a time. But everywhere I went I heard stories of the Wise Men of Chelm.

Ah ha! I thought. If there are wise men in Chelm, then perhaps there are wise women.

* * *

Chanah Chaipul smiled, and looked around the room. So many friends!

"The first person I met in Chelm was Hannah Meier, who happened to run the mikveh. An important woman in the lives of women. And her name was so close to mine! Was it a sign? I asked her if there was a cave nearby, and she brought me to this place. It was as empty and unused as the cave I had first discovered. I didn't dare speak and together we stood in silence for a long time."

"And then?" Sarah asked. "What happened?"

"Then," Hannah Meier giggled, "we redecorated."

Chapter Seven

Awake and Scream

The children were crying – two voices like wailing sirens, twirling in and around each other like ivy winding up a tree. They sounded like beasts, wild animals baying at the moon.

Still half asleep, still wanting to go back to sleep, Benjamin Cohen thrust out his left arm to nudge his wife to quiet the children. His fingers flailed in the empty space where her body was supposed to be. He squinted at the half-empty bed. For a time, he was confused, but then realized that she must already be up. He allowed himself a smile through the haze. What a good wife he had! She knew that he had his job and she had her job and that for their family to work they had to work together as a team. As his father had told him, "You can have a needle without a thread and a thread without a needle, but you can't sew without looping the thread through the needle." Then Benjamin sighed, blinked, and relaxed.

But the crying continued. The screaming got louder. Those babies were much more difficult to deal with than he had ever imagined. Poor Sarah. It was so hard on her. Other mothers were able to cook with one infant, but with two? Almost impossible.

Perhaps he should get up and help. But if she was already up that meant that she wanted him to rest, so if he tried to help he would actually be thwarting her. The last thing he wanted was for his wife to think he didn't appreciate the lengths she went to for his happiness and comfort.

Still those two certainly had a set of lungs. He wondered if all of Chelm was awake by now.

Benjamin stared up at the ceiling. It needed a coat of whitewash, but that was the sort of thing that could wait until after Passover — or even for another year.

It was funny, he thought, how much he had longed for a son, but now that he had both a son and a daughter, how much he longed for the peace and quiet he and Sarah had once shared.

He was about to call to her, to ask if she needed help, but a shout might be misinterpreted and he didn't want to start another fight.

It was hard to believe that two creatures so tiny could make such a horrible racket. In his mind he began writing a letter to his cousin, Shmuel in America. What name did he call himself now? Oh, yes.

"Dear Sammy,

"How are you? Me, you ask? I am exhausted. Did I mention that I have twins? Yes, a boy and a girl, Yakov and Rachel. They don't seem to need to sleep during the night. I suggested to Sarah that she wake them up during the day, but she gave me one of those looks of death. You know the ones that can curdle milk? But oy, the racket these two make! It's like living with two roosters who can't tell the difference between dawn and dark. Right now they sound like…"

What did they sound like? He thought for a moment and then picked up his imaginary pen.

"…like a pair of feral cats biting each other on the tails."

And then there was quiet.

It was as if by defining the nature of the sound, by actually capturing the essence of the din in language, he had managed to give it full expression, so that now silence crept through the house.

Perfect unbroken silence.

Again, Benjamin sighed. The twins were asleep, Sarah had accomplished her task, and he could go back to his rest. All was well with the world.

Except, of course, he couldn't sleep. The tiny brown patch on the ceiling that needed whitewashing was driving him crazy. Now that the babies were quiet he could hear the sounds of birds outside, which meant that it was time to get up anyway.

It was crazy making. Like someone describing a loaf of bread on Passover — a delicious fantasy of contentment forever out of reach.

Why couldn't he just make his mind calm? He had work to do,

orders to fill, hems to raise, patches to sew, suits to make.

He began to sit up and then lay back. He couldn't even get up. If he got up now then Sarah would see it as a comment on the length of time it took her to settle the children. It would invalidate all of her efforts.

Feh!

"Dear Sammy,

"Having children is like having a portion of your mind removed. Even worse, you can see that bit of mind on the floor. It's just out of reach, and every time you try to grab for it to put it back into your head, it skitters away like a frightened dog with a bone."

Benjamin wondered how long he should wait, pretending to be asleep, before he could get up without creating a confrontation. Even then, what should he say? He was not a good liar. If Sarah asked, "Did you sleep well?" he could answer, "Yes…" But he would have to stop himself before continuing on with the truth, "…until those two yowling brats woke me up!"

Benjamin bit his tongue. How could he even think such a thing about two innocent babies? Better to say nothing to Sarah, to shrug and kiss her on the forehead.

At last, he felt he had no choice. He rose and washed himself, got dressed, and went into the kitchen to see what was for breakfast.

Nothing was for breakfast.

On the table was a note, "I'll be back soon."

Were they out of eggs? Benjamin opened the cupboard and saw four eggs and a half-loaf of bread.

He scratched his beard. He hadn't heard the door open. Perhaps he actually had drifted off? This thought made him smile. The idea of being so angry at being awake that he actually fell back asleep but was still dreaming that he was awake!

Just then the door opened, and in came Sarah.

"Good morning, Sarah," he said, cheerfully.

"Oh!" She seemed startled. "Good morning, Benjamin. You seem to be in a good mood." She began to take off her coat.

"Well enough," Benjamin answered. "I slept."

"You slept?" Sarah said. "What about the children?"

Benjamin hesitated. Looking back, this probably saved him from a huge knock down fight. He forced a smile. "The children?"

Sarah's eyes widened in panic. "Yes, the children! Where are the children? What happened to the children?" Her voice was rising to a hysterical pitch.

She ran into the children's room and caught herself just before she screamed.

There they were, lying in their crib, fast asleep.

Benjamin, his own level of fear only slightly slower than their mother's, followed and whispered a silent prayer of thanks.

"The children," he said, "they are right there."

Sarah turned and looked him straight in the eyes. "You took care of them? You? You took care of them?"

Benjamin bit his tongue. He put his hand on his chest. He stalled, trying to think of an answer that wasn't a lie, and that wouldn't provoke.

"I'm their father," he said at last.

This seemed to satisfy their mother. Sarah came back to herself, gave him a quick kiss on the nose. "I'll have your breakfast in a few minutes."

When she was back in the kitchen, Benjamin breathed another sigh of relief.

He leaned over and looked at his babies. How sweet. They were holding each other's hands, and were sucking on each other's thumbs.

Was that a good thing? Were they supposed to be doing that?

He decided not to ask, and in the process, also completely forgot to ask Sarah where she had been so early in the morning.

And for a moment, over oven-toasted bread and fried eggs, peace reigned in the Cohen home.

Chapter Eight

Dressing Up

Every year the villagers of Chelm held a Purim parade and it caused trouble for months. Many people around the world consider the Chelmener to be fools, but they are not. They are, however, very specific and honest. So, when you dress them up in different costumes, they often become frightened and confused. One year the entire yeshiva[11] class dressed as Mordechai, and they very nearly got into a fistfight about which Mordechai should have the honor of riding Haman's horse. And there had always been something unsettling about seeing Reb Cantor, the merchant, shimmying down the street dressed as Queen Vashti...

Rabbi Kibbitz, the wisest man in Chelm, had seriously considered canceling the Purim parade, but as in most communities, it is easier to start a tradition than to stop one.

Instead, he declared that only children between the ages of five and seven would be permitted to march. Not only did this make the parade safer, it made it cuter.

In the Cohen house, this was good news and bad news.

Rachel and Yakov Cohen had turned five a few weeks before the holiday, which meant that at last they were eligible for the pageant.

However, their father, Benjamin Cohen was the best (and only) tailor in Chelm, which meant that their costumes had to be more than a pinned up sheet and a false beard.

The twins' costumes had to be magnificent. If they were anything less, Reb Cohen reasoned, it would reflect badly on his

---

[11] The religious school for boys. In Chelm, the yeshiva is the only school. As Rabbi Yohon Abrahms, the school teacher often tells the boys, "Your parents don't pay me enough money to do this job!"

abilities as a clothier.

His wife, Sarah, had offered to make the children's outfits, but he declined.

"How would that look if I let you do the work?" Benjamin said.

Sarah thought about that for a moment. "Are you questioning my abilities with a needle and thread? You think I bring every rip and tear to you?"

"No. Not at all," he reassured her. "You bake the best strudel, you keep the house clean. You are a wonderful mother. I, however, am a professional needleman. Cutting and sewing is what I do all day long. In the tailor's guild, I am an officially ranked threadbearer!"

Again, Sarah waited before she spoke. "You're very good with the men's clothes," she admitted. "But, honestly your women's clothes are a bit boring. Every woman in Chelm wears the same dress. A Purim queen needs a gown that is extraordinary, powerful, beautiful, and elegant. I don't know if you can do that."

Benjamin knew a challenge when he heard one. "All right," he said. "I'll make the fabulous dress, and you make the suit. But we can't tell anyone because it would ruin my business, so you have to make me proud."

Sarah gritted her teeth, sighed, and agreed. "Done." They even shook hands on the bargain.

Reb Cohen slapped the table. "Now, who wants to be Mordechai?"

"I do! I do!" said Rachel, looking up from her reading.

"I was kidding." Her father smiled at her. "You're a girl."

"Papa, it's a costume parade. We are supposed to dress up as someone who we are not. I am not Mordechai, but I would like to be. Mordechai was kind, patient and wise. Those are good qualities, don't you think?"

"Yes, yes," Reb Cohen said. "But your mother and I have agreed that I will make the dress and she will make the suit. Don't you want me to make you a beautiful dress?"

"No." Rachel shook her head. "Not really. I have plenty of dresses already, but I do not have a nice suit."

Just then Yakov looked up from the drawing of a goat he was making with a stick of charcoal on the wall.[12]

"Papa, I'll wear the dress," Yakov said. "I want to be Esther."

"But you're a boy!" Reb Cohen sputtered.

"Esther was brave," Yakov said. "And you always tell me I should be brave."

"But brave as a boy, not as a girl," said their father. "And wise as a girl, not as a man."

The children looked at each other and then at their father. "Papa," they said simultaneously, "it's just a costume."

"Besides," Yakov said. "I already have a lot of boy clothes, but I don't have any dresses."

Benjamin Cohen winced. He looked at his wife for support, but she was covering her mouth with laughter.

So it happened that Sarah Cohen spent her days learning how to make an extra small man's suit for her daughter, and Benjamin Cohen spent his evenings trying to make a ball gown for his son.

They did it in secret. Neither was willing to concede to the other that he or she was a better clothing designer.

It wasn't until the morning of the Purim parade that their efforts were revealed.

Benjamin Cohen was eating his breakfast of hamentashen and eggs when there was a knock at the door.

He opened the door and looked down to see that Rabbi Yohon Abrahms had shrunk in half. The schoolteacher had been the tallest man in the village, but now he was probably the shortest. And strangest of all, he was wearing a gorgeous white and purple suit that fit perfectly his miniature size.

Reb Cohen gasped. "Rabbi Abrahms, what happened? Did you get stepped on by an elephant?"

"It is I, Mordechai," the diminutive schoolteacher's voice squeaked. "Do you have any hamentashen?"

At first this puzzled Reb Cohen, because Rabbi Abrahms first

---

[12] You should know that Yakov loved drawing so much that his parents had given him a portion of the wall to devote to his art. Every few months the wall was washed and repainted.

name was Yohon. Then he remembered what day it was.

"Doodle," he said. "That is a great costume."

Just then the beard was pulled from the young child's face. "Papa, it's me! Didn't Mama make me a wonderful suit? I sneaked out of the house early this morning to surprise you."

The tailor grinned as his daughter hugged him and then ran past him into the house. "Mama! Mama! It worked!"

No sooner had he shut the door and turned around when a tiny version of his wife Sarah walked into the room. Benjamin was stunned. Her face was veiled and she looked as lovely as she had on the blessed day they were wed. But she too had shrunk. And she was wearing the Parisian-style gown that he had made for the Purim carnival!

"Papa, don't I look beautiful?" came Yakov's voice from his wife's mouth.

The poor man covered his mouth in horror, and then yanked at his hair as his son lifted the veil.

"Ack! Ack!" Benjamin Cohen sputtered. Even though he had made the costume himself, he hadn't thought through all the implications until that moment. And none of the thoughts he was thinking were making any sense at all.

Sarah Cohen, the full-sized real woman who was both his bride and the mother of his children, stepped from the bedroom, poured him a glass of water and waited until he'd drunk it all down.

"I think," she said, "that our contest was a tie. They both look fabulous."

"Agreed," Benjamin said, once he had come to his senses. "But isn't there something wrong with our boy dressed as a girl and our girl dressed as a boy?"

"No." Sarah shook her head. "If Yakov wanted to dress as Haman and Rachel wanted to dress as Vashti, would that be wrong?"

Benjamin shrugged. "Of course not."

"Exactly. It is all just pretend. Haman is wicked and Vashti is vain, but they are only costumes. And of course you know that as soon as they take off the costumes, they again become Rachel and

Yakov."

Indeed, Benjamin could see that with the false beard and veil removed, his children were already fighting and arguing as usual.

"So be it," the tailor conceded with a sigh. For that, his wife gave him a kiss on the cheek.

He was also pleasantly surprised that the day after Purim he had three orders for new white and purple suits, and his first ever commission for a wedding dress.

Part Two

The Old Woman

Chapter Nine

Dying to Get Out?

Oma Levitsky knew she was going to die. She kept saying so. No one else in Chelm believed her. She'd been predicting her own imminent death for years — decades even. In fact, whenever her name came up, the conversation often went like this.

"So, Oma Levitsky says she is going to die."

"Nu?[13] What else is new?"

"She says it's going to happen soon"

"Ah, feh. She'll live forever. She's older than the trees. She's older than the rocks."

It wasn't true. She was old, but she was no Methuselah. She didn't know exactly when she was born, but claimed it was at least a hundred and eighteen years ago. Of course time in Chelm is flexible, so even that was a bit of a guess. Rabbi Kibbitz once asked her what was the earliest date in history that she remembered, but Oma never paid much attention to current events, so it was a waste of time.[14]

On the other hand, what else did she have to waste but time?

She had raised children and grandchildren and great grandchildren and even great great grandchildren. She had watched them grow and love and marry. She had buried many of them.

The worst thing about living so long, she would tell anyone who might listen, is burying all your friends and family.

She hated going to funerals.

---

[13] "Nu?" is a rhetorical question somwewhere between "So?" and "You know I'm right!"

[14] Although, when she was young and beautiful, she had flirted with Rabbi Kibbitz's great grandfather, who had founded the village of Chelm, but one didn't talk about such things.

The funerals didn't make her feel sad. They left her feeling lonely. When the first of her children had died, that had been sad. She hadn't wanted to live another day. But she had, partly because she had other children to care for, partly because suicide was a sin, and partly because she wanted to see what would happen next.

It was this curiosity more than anything else that she believed kept her going. So many of her departed acquaintances had reached a point in their lives when they stopped caring. She had noticed that not long after that they were gone.

She didn't have to vow to keep caring, to stay interested, and to keep meddling to stay alive. She reveled in it!

It was why she loved going to weddings. At weddings, like at bar mitzvahs and brisses[15], the world was just beginning. It was often the best place to pick up gossip and to learn what was truly going on.

"Did you know that the bride is expecting?" one gossip would whisper.

"Of course she's expecting," another would reply, looking around carefully to make sure they were alone. "Did you know it's not his?"

The hens would cackle and Oma Levitsky would hear it all, because she could become invisible.

Oma Levitsky could sit so still for so long that she blended in with the furniture. It was how she learned nearly every secret in the village. She would hobble into a room, relax into a chair, close her eyes, and vanish.

She was never asleep, although her breathing slowed nearly to stopping. Then she would allow her ears to travel around the room, listening for what was important and divisive.

"Did you hear that Reb Stein's wife threw out his toothpick collection?"

"Didn't he have a golden toothpick that had once been used by the Czar?"

---

[15] There are, of course, arguments about how many letters "s" should be in the plural of the word "bris." Some sources suggest using the spellings, "britot" or "brits." These often provoke discomfort in men from England. We're going with brisses, because in Chelm the belief is, "The more the merrier."

"Yes! It even had a bit of food still on it. Reindeer gristle, I think."

"Ecch. That's disgusting."

"Exactly what his wife said."

Perhaps the only person in Chelm who knew about Oma's secret power was Chanah Chaipul, who was one smart cookie. And the only reason Chanah had found out was because Oma had gotten careless.

Usually, when she was "collecting wood," as she called her habit of learning all the juicy bits about other people's lives, Oma would wait outside a door for someone else to let her in. Because of her age, it was difficult to walk, and closing doors behind her was always a major task.

It was wintertime, and Oma slipped into Chanah's restaurant to learn the fate of one of the Shimmel sisters, who had run off to Moscow and just sent a letter back home. Rather than draw attention to herself by taking twenty minutes to close the door, she had left it slightly ajar and made toward a corner table where she quickly blended into the woodwork.

When the wind suddenly slammed the door shut, everyone jumped, and even Oma Levitsky twitched.

That twitch was enough for Chanah Chaipul, whose eyes were as sharp as a hawk's. She brought the old woman a pot of tea, and then forgot about her. Two hours later, after all the news had been told and everyone else had moved on about their days, Chanah was cleaning up when she came across the full pot of tea.

"That's odd," Chanah muttered to herself.

"It's cold too," Oma Levitsky muttered back. Usually when she sneaked into the restaurant, she managed to come and go without ordering anything. But, if she was going to have to pay for the tea, she might as well enjoy it.

The teapot had flown through the air. Oma Levitsky had snaked out one thin arm and snatched the pot before it could smash against the wall. Barely a drop was spilled. The look on Chanah's face had been priceless.

"Would you mind warming this up?" Oma had asked, sweetly.

Ever since then, when something of importance was being discussed, Chanah Chaipul would wander through her restaurant, dusting off each chair and stool, so that at least she would know how many people were sharing in the knowledge.

It had been a wonderful life, Oma thought. So many sunrises and sunsets. So many births and weddings. So many funerals. So many good meals. So many flowers to sniff. So many secrets to learn and to hold.

And now she was going to die. Soon. For real.

It wasn't that she was moving slower. She wasn't sure it was possible to move any slower without standing still. It wasn't that her bones were more brittle. Long ago she had accepted the fact that her limbs were like twigs and her skin was as thin and soft as the last leaf on a tree in the dead of winter. She still enjoyed eating. She still enjoyed squinting at the sunset, absorbing the lingering rays of light.

She was still curious, and she still cared.

But something had changed. The world was still moving, but she sensed she would not long be with it.

And there was still one more thing to do.

Chapter Ten

Gesundheit

Oma Levitsky sneezed. It was a little bit on the sloppy side, one of those sudden ker-choos that take everyone by surprise, especially if you happened to be sitting across the table from the sneezer. Fortunately, Oma was alone, so the embarrassment was less, but that in itself proved to be a problem.

After the sneeze, she reached for a handkerchief to wipe up and found that she could not move her hand.

That was strange. She hadn't given much thought to reaching for something since she was a child. Again, she sent her mind out in the direction of her pocket to pluck a thin piece of cloth, and found that nothing happened. She tried her other hand. Nothing. She tried wiggling fingers and toes. Still nothing.

Oh dear.

Her eyes darted around the room. That was something. She couldn't turn her head or lick her lips, but her eyes still worked. She saw that the kettle on the stove still wasn't boiling. Her pot of tea, full of fresh leaves, was on the counter beside the stove, waiting. A piece of toasted bread spread with fig jam waited on a plate not two feet from her hand, which was resting like a limp piece of meat on her lap.

She reviewed her situation. She was sitting at her kitchen table, with her knitting lumped in a pile in front of her. It was the morning after the Sabbath. There were no major or minor holidays on the horizon. No one would notice she was missing for days, not until one of the Shimmel sisters came by for her milk delivery. In the meantime, if she couldn't move, she couldn't eat or drink, and soon she would be gone.

That's what I get for thinking so much about death, she thought to herself. I'm not dead yet, but I might as well be.

If she could have laughed, she would have. How many times in her life had she said, "It's just a little sneeze, it won't kill you."

Now she pictured her gravestone, "Here lies Lotte Levitsky. She sneezed herself to death. Gesundheit."

She wondered if anyone in the village of Chelm would even remember her real name. They had all called her Oma for so long...

Killed by a sneeze? How fantastic. She remembered a story her father had told her about a sneeze that had deposed a king.

It had happened in the old days, her father hadn't been too specific. Every year the king was required to prove his fitness by slicing a sheet of parchment in two with a sword. As far as tests for rulership go, it wasn't the most difficult, but it wasn't as easy as being born into the position. It required three important qualities of character — the use of a sharp blade, a sudden decisiveness, and a steady hand.

The long-ago king held the parchment in one hand, the sword in the other, and in the middle of his swift downward cut, he sneezed.

The parchment rippled but didn't cut.

The King's eyes followed the movement of the parchment, the blade followed his eyes, and he lopped his own left hand off at the wrist.

Even as his life's blood spurted around the throne room, the king had argued for a second chance, but by the time one of his servants held up the severed hand, which still gripped the parchment tightly, the poor man toppled forward dead.

A good king must be persistent, her father had concluded, but also needs quite a lot of self-control.

What would papa think of her now? Would he be proud that she had shown so much self-control over the years, or would he cluck his tongue and shake his head that she had slipped at last? What did it matter? Her beloved papa had been gone for almost a hundred years. By now, he would have said, she was old enough to make up her own mind.

She tried to smile at that thought, and found that her lips could move, just a bit.

She tried wiggling her tongue and found, much to her relief that it could still wag a bit. She concentrated. The more she thought, the more it moved, until at last it slipped out between her teeth and moistened her lips.

How long had it been? An hour? Two? More. Suddenly panicked, she looked across the room. At the back of the stove, the slow steam rising from her soup pot was still simmering, thank goodness.

Then her eyes glanced at the teakettle. It still wasn't boiling. Only a moment had passed. A long moment. She could hear the water beginning to rumble around inside it.

This passing away nonsense was going to take quite some time, wasn't it? She wanted to talk about it, to tell someone. It wasn't so much that she had regrets or was afraid, but rather the opposite.

It was strange, but just now dying felt somewhat exciting. So many memories were beginning to flood back. She remembered her mother taking her into the garden on the first day after the spring thaw and showing her how to dig up the carrots that had grown sweeter over their long winter's rest. She remembered her husband's first gentle kiss on her cheek the morning after their wedding. He had been so tender. They had both been so frightened.

Thought after thought came and went. Was this what they meant by seeing your life flash before your eyes?

Now she heard the water in the kettle begin to boil. Her eyes looked up and saw the steam shooting from the spout. Then the whistling started, and thinking about anything else became impossible.

Fifteen, maybe twenty years ago, the teakettle her mother had given her as a wedding present had finally dissolved into rust, and she had gone to Reb Cantor the merchant. The fat man had shown her "the latest thing" which was a whistling teakettle.

"You'll never boil a pot of water dry again," he had insisted. "It will be a cheerful reminder every morning."

Feh. It was a horrible sound, not natural at all. It reminded her of the scrape of metal against rock, shrill and sharp.

Frequently she didn't bother to close the little lid that made the noise. At her age, who cared if the water bubbled a few minutes longer? But this particular morning she had.

Phooey. The whistling noise grew louder and louder as the pressure of water was forced through the tiny hole and shot up toward the roof. And of course it went on and on and on. It wouldn't stop until all the water had boiled from the kettle, and since she had filled the kettle nearly to the top that was going to take quite some time.

The whistle was like a reminder that she still had one more thing she had to do before she died. How could she have waited so long? She was a perfectionist, that's why. She had been waiting for the right person, and now it was too late. The whistle was like a death toll, reminding her that her work was unfinished, that it was always going to be unfinished.

Now she wanted to die. Right now. Just to stop the noise. To stop the reminder. How disappointing, to have survived for so long, to have experienced so much love and beauty and bravery and magnificence, only to have her last moments spoiled by an extravagant purchase.

She closed her eyes and waited for the end. The whistling continued, pushing all other thoughts from her mind.

And then it stopped.

Wonderful, she thought. I'm dead at last.

Then she heard the sound of water pouring, and smelled the warm aroma of freshly moistened tea leaves.

Her eyes flickered open and she saw a little girl dressed in white, holding the kettle with a dishtowel.

"Are you an angel?" Oma Levitsky said, her voice a faint croak.

The girl giggled. "No. I'm Rachel Cohen. I was walking past your house and I heard the whistling and thought you might need some help."

"You can't be Rachel Cohen," Oma muttered. "Rachel Cohen is just a baby." But perhaps the girl was. The older you got, the more quickly it seemed that time passed. It was such a shame. Long days of boredom were wasted on the young.

Without saying anything, the remarkable little girl was moving about the house as if it were her own. She put away dishes. She folded the knitting. She cleaned Oma Levitsky as if the old woman was a little child.

And when the tea had cooled, she gave Oma small sips from a cup and fed her toast.

The tea was delicious, perfectly brewed with just the right amount of honey. In no time, the toast was gone.

"My mother will want to know where I've been," the girl said.

"Don't go," came Oma's quiet voice.

The girl squeezed the old woman's hand. "I won't leave you alone for long." She ran the backs of her fingers over the old woman's wrinkled cheeks. "I'll be back soon."

How long had it been since she had been touched with such tenderness? How wonderful to feel the warmth of a child again.

Oma Levitsky heard the door close. It was good to have something to look forward to.

Chapter Eleven

A Moving Problem

No one in Chelm knew what to do about Oma Levitsky. Mrs. Chaipul, who was the closest thing the villagers had to a doctor, had examined her thoroughly.

"She's an old woman," Mrs. Chaipul had said, serving a schmaltz sandwich to Reb Cantor, the merchant. [16] "Things break down over time. She's already lived longer than Moses. All things considered, she's remarkably healthy. You, however, that's another story. If you don't cut back on the fatty food, she'll probably outlive you…"

"Feh," said Reb Cantor. He ate quickly, paid his bill, and left the restaurant. He had an important meeting to attend.

Privately, Chanah Chaipul was concerned. She knew quite a lot about the human body and its limits. Chanah knew that her old friend was unlikely to get better. She also knew that willpower and determination kept most people alive, especially someone like Oma.

"Can you move?" Chanah had asked while examining her.

"Just my head," Oma had answered. "And even that not much."

"Does it hurt?"

"No," the old woman had croaked.

"Are you in pain?"

"No!"

"Are you suffering?"

"Just this conversation."

Chanah had smiled. "What do you want to do?"

"Aside from wipe my own bottom when I go to the bathroom?

---

[16] Shmaltz is congealed rendered chicken fat. Usually, it's used for cooking, but some people find shmaltz so irresistibly delicious that they smear it on bread, douse it with salt, and eat it raw. Often these people die young, clutching their hearts.

I'd like to dance naked in the woods in the middle of summer. What do you think I'd like to do? Walk about! Do my life. Right now I feel a bit like a useless old bag. I know that some people have called me that for years, but now I'm beginning to see their point."

It was good that Oma was so talkative. For the time being, her spirits were high, but who knew how long the feisty lady could stand being inactive.

* * *

Reb Cantor walked across the village of Chelm, through the round square, to the Rabbi's study. Already, most of the important men in the village were gathering to discuss what should be done.

"Is everyone here?" Rabbi Kibbitz asked as he peered through the forest of bearded men.

"Reb Schlemiel and Reb Cohen said they'd be along shortly," Reb Cantor said as he shut the door. "So, I think we can begin. What are we going to do about Oma Levitsky? Does anybody have any ideas?"

The room was quiet for a moment. Then Reb Levitsky, the synagogue's caretaker, stood. "I don't know what all the fuss is about," he said. " Of course I'll take my mother in."

"Phooey," said Reb Stein, the baker. "You and your mother never get along."

"That's not true," replied Reb Levitsky. "I love my mother."

"Loving your mother is one thing. Living with her is another," answered Reb Stein. "I remember the day you left her house you grew six inches. Very literally. You used to be stooped and crabby, and then, all of a sudden you were much taller and much friendlier."

"I've changed," Reb Levitsky said, defensively. "I've grown up. Besides, she would be living in my house, not the other way around."

"Your wife can't stand your mother either," Reb Gold, the cobbler, pointed out.

"That's not true! My wife loves my mother."

"Love and tolerance are often two different things," Rabbi Kibbitz said. "There are many people I tolerate who I cannot love.

There are some people I love who I cannot tolerate. I remember that when you were a young boy every single thing that you did drove your mother crazy. One time she dragged you into my office and demanded that I tell you to stop getting your trousers dirty."

"Which, as I recall, is exactly what you did!"

"Of course I did." The elder rabbi shrugged. "What was I going to do, try and explain that it was perfectly normal for a young boy to get mud on his cuffs? She never would have listened to me again."

"Did she ever listen to you?" asked Rabbi Abrahms, the schoolteacher. "She never listens to me."

"No, she never listens to me either," Rabbi Kibbitz agreed. "Nevertheless, Martin, the entire village was relieved when you finally established your own home."

"My mother is not an ogre!" Martin Levitsky said, throwing up his hands.

"Except with you," all the men in the room said simultaneously.

Reb Levitsky's head fell into his hands, and he began rubbing his temples. "I know! I know. I don't know what else to do, though. She has no one else. I'm the only one left."

"That's what we're here to discuss," Reb Cantor said, patting the poor caretaker's back. "Just so long as she doesn't come and live with me, everything will be fine."

All the rest of the men agreed.

* * *

At that exact moment, back in Mrs. Chaipul's restaurant, a gathering of women were having exactly the same conversation.

"If that old woman moves into my house, I'll rip out my hair, cut out my eyes, poke holes in my ears, and bite off my tongue," wailed Chaya Levitsky. "I love my mother-in-law, but whenever she comes to my Passover Seder nothing I do is right. My matzah balls are too salty, my plates aren't clean enough, and my brisket is too moist. Too moist? Whoever heard of a brisket being too moist? But I put up with it, because I know it is just one meal a year. I can't imagine what it would be like to serve her breakfast, lunch, and dinner. Have you seen what she does to mandel bread? I'd rather tear out my own heart and serve it on a platter."

Mrs. Chaipul, who was just about to bite into a chopped liver sandwich, set down her meal untouched. "Really? I do think you are exaggerating."

"No," said Shoshana Cantor. "With you she's different, because you are still a newcomer to Chelm."

"Thirty years or more I've been living here," Mrs. Chaipul said.

"Nevertheless," Shoshana Cantor said, "you're still new. Those of us who are native, she treats with a certain level of..."

"Contempt!" inserted Chaya Levitsky.

"I was going to say..."

"Lack of respect!"

"No, I was trying to..."

"Utter disregard for our feelings or preferences?" Chaya shouted.

"No!" Shoshana said. "Will you let me finish?"

"Why?" Chaya snapped. "My mother-in-law never lets me finish. If she moves into my house I will be finished. I might as well walk into the Uherka River and drown."

Mrs. Chaipul snorted. Except after heavy rains, the river was notoriously shallow. "You'd have to get down on your hands and knees and bury yourself in the mud to accomplish that."

"If that's what it takes to get away from her nagging, then that's what I'll do!"

"There, there," Eleanor Stein said. "We'll think of something."

* * *

Meanwhile, only a stone's throw from the restaurant and the rabbi's study, the problem was already being handled...

* * *

Moving Oma Levitsky wasn't the problem.

Rachel Cohen had simply asked Reb Schlemiel, the carpenter, if he still had that chair with wheels he had built several years earlier to ferry a bride with a broken leg to and from her wedding. He did, and Rachel borrowed it.

Oma didn't have so many belongings either. A small trunk of clothes, a box of memories, and her cookware were all she really cared about. Physically, she was a skinny old woman, who didn't weigh more than a hundred and ten pounds. The six year-old girl and her mother had no trouble lifting the old woman into the chair. Six-year-old Yakov was kept busy running back and forth with the luggage and frying pans.

The muddy streets of Chelm weren't the problem either, although they were a challenge. In the springtime, after the snows melted and the ground began to thaw, all of the roads and paths in and round the village were sloppy and viscous.[17] Young Rachel Cohen, however, had also asked Reb Schlemiel to loan a number of boards, so the chair was pushed through the village on a moveable wooden ramp. Progress was slow. The carpenter only had three boards wide enough, long enough, and flat enough to support the wheeled chair. Every ten feet two boards would be pried from the muck, lugged past the stalled chair, and dropped back into the mud. Progress was slow, difficult, and dirty, but not impossible.

The big problem was The Soup. People thought of it in capital letters. For as long as anyone could remember, Oma Levitsky had kept a pot of chicken soup simmering on the back of her stove. It was always cooking and never empty. She was always adding ingredients to the pot, bits of chicken, pieces of vegetables, a little bit of salt, some pepper, a bucketful of water from the well... The Soup was a bit like a river, never the same twice, but always the same river. The Soup was spoken about with pride and in whispers. As far away as Smyrna, everyone knew that the best soup in the world came from Oma Levitsky's pot. If you were a new bride and had trouble with your broth, you only needed to ask, and she would give you a measure or two to add to your stock, and the magic would spread. It was this magic that caused the whispers.

Superstition is a belief in something supernatural that isn't true. In Chelm, the villagers had many superstitions that they knew were superstitions. Knocking on wood brought luck (or avoided bad

---

[17] Everyone joked that mud season in Chelm lasted from the day after the last frost until the day before the first snow, but it wasn't quite true. In the late spring there was pollen season, in summer time there was also dust and dirt season. And in the autumn there was dead leaf season. All of which were mixed into and on top of the mud.

luck). If you dropped a dead chicken on the floor, you had to twirl it around your head three times to shake off the dirt. If you bit into a baked potato and found half a bug it meant that if you ate it you would have a good dream. Nobody really believed that knocking on wood was magic, but the superstitions were kept more for the sake of continuity and to avoid spitting pieces of potato out on your plate.

Oma Levitsky's chicken soup, however… Maybe that really was magic.

Even in Chelm, everyone knew that chicken soup could heal the sick. It was a well-accepted medical practice. It wouldn't bring you back from the dead or sew on a missing finger, but if you had a cold or an ache, you would feel better. It didn't matter who made the soup or how good it tasted, a bowl of chicken soup would improve your health.

The Soup was more than that. Oma Levitsky's soup was so good that everyone enjoyed it. You could be dying without a tooth left in your head, preparing yourself for whatever came after life, and you would still eat and enjoy every spoonful, every drop of The Soup as it slipped between your lips, across your tongue, and down your throat. It lightened the spirit. It cleared the mind. It brought contentment into even the heart filled with despair. A sip of The Soup wasn't always a permanent fix, but it served well as a momentary reminder that the world was full of peace and joy and wonder. Since every soup in the village of Chelm had been touched by Oma Levitsky's soup, there was a certain suspicion that the magical powers of all their soups were derived from this mystical source. The villagers wondered, for example, if the reason the old woman had been around so long was that she was constantly tasting and drinking from her own broth.

The unspoken fear in the village was that moving The Soup would kill its power.

Even Oma Levitsky wasn't sure what would happen.

"We could bring it to a boil, and cover it with a lid" she croaked. "Then we could pick up the pot and run as fast as we can to get it onto another stove."

Given that she was speaking these thoughts while waiting for Sarah Cohen to schlep two mud-soaked boards so they could roll her another ten feet, moving quickly, let alone running, with a boiling hot soup pot seemed neither advisable nor likely to prove a success.

"We could just leave it," Sarah panted. "Assign someone in the Council to watch and tend it."

"Nonsense," the old woman hissed. "If that's the plan then take me back to my house right now. It's not that I don't trust anyone else on the Council, but I don't trust anyone else on the Council."

Sarah Cohen looked back and realized that they were almost exactly halfway between Oma's house and the Cohen home. It would take just as much time to bring the old woman back and leave her there as it would to shift her ahead. For a brief moment she even considered tipping the wheeled chair into the mud and walking away, and she wondered (not for the first time) whether it was a good idea to bring a crotchety old woman into her house with two rambunctious youngsters and a husband who was also set in his ways.

"I have an idea," little Rachel said.

Her mother sighed. Rachel was full of ideas. At six years old she had already taught herself to read not only Hebrew and Yiddish, but also English and German. She was the one who had come up with the idea of moving Oma into the Cohen home. She would give up her room and sleep with her brother. She had remembered the carpenter's chair and had devised the moving ramp. They were all wonderful and practical ideas. Nevertheless, it rankled a bit to depend on a six year old for practical advice. And Sarah still hadn't told Benjamin that Oma was moving in.

"What's your idea, Bubeleh?" the old woman asked.

"A toboggan," Rachel said. "We'll put a big pot on a metal sledge, fill it full of coals, set the soup pot on top, and have a horse drag it through the street to our house. The Soup will still cook. It probably won't even spill a drop."

Sarah and Oma looked at each other in astonishment. It was such a simple and elegant plan that neither of them could find a single flaw.

With delight, Sarah scooped her daughter up. "I'm sure you already have a horse in mind, don't you?"

"Not actually a horse, Mama. But the Shimmel Sisters have a very strong and patient ox."

"Run ahead and ask them."

Rachel giggled. "I already have."

Sarah gave her daughter a squeeze.

Oma Levitsky sighed with relief. She knew that all would be well.

Chapter Twelve

She's staying where?

The first thing Benjamin Cohen noticed when he opened the door to his house was the smell of chicken soup, a wonderful, rich, happy smell that filled his home. With one foot inside and one outside, with his hand still on the doorknob, Benjamin closed his eyes and remembered the chicken soup his mother had made for him when he had been sick. As a boy, he'd had a bad cough, the kind that he knew, now that he was a parent, was more than troublesome or worrisome. It had been fearsome. That was in the days before Mrs. Chaipul lived in the village, and a doctor had to be summoned from Smyrna. Benjamin remembered the sad look on the doctor's face as he whispered to his mother and father. He also remembered the false cheerful smiles his parents had given him when they brought him the soup and the whispers while his mother made sure he ate every drop. Which he had. And a few days later, he had been up and running around the house while his father grumbled about wasting good money on a foolish doctor.

Benjamin blinked his eyes. His parents were long gone, and now that he was a father with children of his own he had a new appreciation of the pain and suffering they had been through on his behalf. He whispered a brief prayer of thanks to their memory, and then finished getting into the house.

It had been a very strange and bewildering day. He had been deeply immersed in the fine stitching for the tallis he was making his son.[18] Never mind that Yakov was only six years old. True, his

---

[18] A tallis (or tallit) is a prayer shawl with fringes. Around the world some are plain, some are striped, some are quite ornate. In Chelm, they make the fringes extra long because they tie them into "memory knots" to celebrate every joyful occasion. Rabbi Kibbitz nearly lost his mind when his tallis became so small

bar mitzvah was seven years away, but as Benjamin's father had taught him, good work takes time.

Besides, Benjamin had a fear that he had never told anyone. He was afraid that he would be dead before his son turned thirteen. He knew it wasn't rational. It was one of those thoughts that came to him while he was out in the woods looking for mushrooms. The day had been cool, the soil had been moist, and he'd suddenly imagined his own funeral, with everyone gathered around sobbing. Sarah was dressed in black, holding little Rachel in her arms. And Yakov, who looked to be about ten years old, stood next to his father's closed casket with a frown of despair quivering on his youthful lips. It was like being in a dream, except he was awake, and he almost tripped on a tree root.

Benjamin had tried to get rid of that horrible thought. It was just a thought. Nonsense and nothing more. But the more he tried to dismiss it, the firmer it took hold. He had said a prayer. He had said another prayer. He had made the sign against the evil eye. He had knocked wood. Nothing helped.

He thought about discussing it with the old Rabbi, but something kept him silent. Maybe because he could already imagine what Rabbi Kibbitz would say...

"Don't worry about it," the wise old man would smile. "I used to think that my mother, may she rest in peace, would die also."

"But she did, Rabbi," Benjamin would answer.

"True," Rabbi Kibbitz would shake a finger, "but not when I thought she would. It was years and years and years later. Oy did I feel silly. Every day she would wake me up and say, 'See, I'm not dead yet!'"

Benjamin also thought about talking with the new Rabbi, who had recently moved to the village to become both the schoolteacher and Rabbi Kibbitz's apprentice. Rabbi Abrahms seemed like a nice

---

and full of knots that he couldn't put it over his shoulders. Reb Cohen the tailor solved the problem by cutting the tallis in half, adding more fringes, and sewing a new piece of cloth in between. The resulting garment was so bulky and unwieldy that Reb Cantor suggested it could be used as a weapon. Rabbi Kibbitz didn't mind. He lugged it out on special occasions, and used a backup tallis for ordinary days of prayer.

enough fellow, but he was even younger than Benjamin himself. What sort of wisdom could a childless bachelor with short whiskers have to offer in such a situation?

Instead, Benjamin had begun to work on the tallis, so that if the horrible thought actually came true, at least Yakov would have one final gift from his father. Making the prayer shawl helped, too. Whenever Benjamin was worried or upset, he would take out his finest needle and silver thread and get to work. It focused his mind wonderfully, and he always felt relieved when he carefully folded the silk and put it back in its box.

That was why he'd been late to the meeting in the Rabbi's study. He had heard Reb Cantor's knock at the workshop's door, and had told the merchant he'd be along shortly, but you can't rush fine work.

By the time Benjamin Cohen arrived, everyone else was leaving. "What's going on?" he'd asked the departing men.

"It's already settled," Reb Stein said, hurrying off.

"It's a done deal," Reb Cantor agreed, following the baker.

"I'm sorry," said Reb Schlemiel, the carpenter. "I had no idea what the boards were for. Please forgive me."

Benjamin shrugged. "I don't know either, so of course I forgive you."

By then, Benjamin and Rabbi Kibbitz were alone.

"What did I miss?" the tailor asked.

Rabbi Kibbitz looked furtive. "Nothing happened here. If I had anything to do with this, I would tell you."

"Okay," Benjamin said slowly. "So I guess I should go."

"Wait," Rabbi Kibbitz said. "Is there anything you want to talk to me about? Anything you want to tell me?"

Was the old man a mind reader, Benjamin wondered? He hesitated and mulled the idea of talking about his impending doom. The tallis was coming along. It was still going to take years to finish, but when he was done, it would be a masterful gift from a father to a son. He wasn't sure he wanted to interrupt the progress.

"No," Benjamin said. "Everything's fine."

"Good luck then," the Rabbi had said, sounding somewhat

relieved.

"Thanks," Benjamin had replied with a shrug. "And for you."

By the time he left the Rabbi's study, Benjamin had already decided that he was done working for the day, so naturally his feet had begun to take him home, picking his way through the spring mud. Coming home early would make a nice Shabbat present for Sarah.

He nearly fell back in surprise when he thought that he saw his daughter riding away from his house on the back of an ox. Rachel seemed to be laughing, her face bright with joy in the fading sunlight. The ox was pulling a toboggan, and running after the ox were the three Shimmel sisters.

Clearly another delusion. Benjamin slapped his cheek, trying to snap himself out of it. He'd been having so many strange thoughts recently. What was going on? He had arrived at his house, opened the door, smelled the welcome...

At last, he shook himself out of his dreams and stepped inside, ready to hug his family and laugh over his foolish vision.

Which was why he nearly had a heart attack when, from a chair in a dark corner of the room, an old woman suddenly spoke.

"I hope you don't mind," her voice wheezed.

Benjamin staggered back clutching his chest. Death had come for him! But Yakov's tallis wasn't done yet! He'd barely embroidered enough cloth to make a yarmulke!

"Didn't mean to startle you," said the whispering crone.

Benjamin came to his senses just after his head smacked against the still-open door. Now he rubbed the back of his head.

"Oma? Oma Levitsky?" He squinted. The light in the house wasn't very good, but it was still too early to light candles.

"Very good," the crone hissed. "I would get up to greet you, but that's part of the problem."

Just then, Sarah bustled into the room.

Because the tailor was a wealthy and respected man, his house had four rooms: one for each child, a room for the husband and wife, and the main room, which was where everyone spent nearly all their time when they were awake. It was a kitchen, dining room, family room, play room, den, and library all in a very compact space. This space was now even more crowded with several extra chairs and end tables.

Now that Benjamin had a moment to recover, he realized that the old woman was sitting in a chair that he didn't even recognize. Where did this other furniture come from? Was he even in his own house?

But it must be his house because Sarah was there and why would Sarah be in someone else's house?

Usually when he came home from a hard day, if no one was around and looking, Sarah came over and gave Benjamin a warm and loving embrace. It made him feel welcome and taken care of. She hadn't been doing it very much lately. He wasn't sure if that was because things were good or things were bad.

This evening, things must be very bad, because Sarah was already across the room reaching for him. His arms came up automatically, and they would have hugged, but then the old woman coughed.

Sarah and Benjamin stopped, waved their fingers about for a moment in embarrassment and then dropped their hands to their sides.

"Benjamin, you know Oma Levitsky," Sarah said.

"Yes, we've met."

"Wonderful," Sarah smiled. "Then it's settled."

"That's good," Benjamin answered. "What's settled?"

"Oh." Sarah paused. "Oma has moved her things into Rachel's room. Rachel has moved her things into Yakov's room. Dinner should be ready soon. We're having soup!"

"Ah," Benjamin nodded. "That would explain the ox."

Sarah's eyes twinkled. "Exactly. You always were quick with the scissors." Then she withdrew to their bedroom to prepare for the Sabbath.

"You know," Benjamin mumbled as he took off his coat, "I still have no idea what's going on."

"Yes you do," said the old woman. He had forgotten about her for a moment, and again jumped as she spoke. "Believe me, if there was any other way..."

Enlightenment dawned in Benjamin's mind like an egg cracked into a frying pan. "You're planning on living here?"

"We'll just have to make the best of it," Oma was saying. "After a while, you won't notice. I can make myself invisible."

Benjamin Cohen, the tailor of Chelm, wasn't sure if that was a good thing.

In fact, the more he thought about it, the more Benjamin Cohen thought that having Oma Levitsky sitting around the house was just about the worst thing that had happened to him.

He glared at the old woman, took a deep breath, and without another word, walked into the bedroom, and buried his head in his hands.

"Benjamin?" Sarah said. Her voice was soft and startled him. He'd forgotten she was there. "Are you all right?"

He didn't answer. What could he say? He was miserable. It felt as if a heavy fur hat was pressing down on his head. He was having a hard time breathing. He wanted to lie down in bed and never get up. Was that all right? Better to stay quiet. Perhaps it was just another foolish dream.

"Benjamin?" Sarah put a hand on his shoulder.

"Did I miss a conversation?" he muttered. "Was I out of the room when we discussed a significant change in the way our home operates? Maybe we were talking about something else and I dozed off and you didn't notice?"

Sarah chose not to answer. She knew he might be upset, but she didn't know how upset.

"Was there a letter in the Yiddish newspaper that explained it all, and I missed that edition? Or did everyone in the village conspire behind my back so that I would be the last one to find out? No wonder everyone ran out of the Rabbi's study as soon as I arrived. No wonder Rabbi Kibbitz wished me luck. They were all laughing at me."

"No," Sarah said, quietly. "That's not it."

"Then why?" he demanded. "Why is that woman here?"

A thin croaking voice slipped through the cracks in the door, "I can hear you!"

Benjamin's eyes shot a look of fury at the door that might have set the wood afire. "Why," he whispered, "is she here?"

"I can still hear you!" Oma Levitsky's voice hissed.

With that, Benjamin jumped to his feet, took one step toward the door, both his arms flew up into the air, his hands clenched into fists.

Sarah leapt back, startled at the rage and violence of her husband's swift movement.

Her gasp brought him back to himself. His eyes were wide. His heart was racing. It was as if he had turned into an animal. He spun around, wild-eyed, and looked at Sarah, who shied away from him.

He sat back down on the bed. Again he buried his head in his hands. Again he closed his eyes. He took deep breaths, and imagined that he could hear the sound of the blood coursing through his veins.

After a time, Sarah sat down on the bed, a little further away.

"It was Rachel's idea," she said, softly. It didn't matter if Oma heard, because she already knew. "While everyone else was arguing and worrying, Rachel knew that the poor woman was sick and needed help. By the time she talked with me, she had already discussed it with Yakov, and the two of them agreed that they could share their room. She had already discussed it with Oma, who told her that she didn't eat much and would be little or no trouble. Then Rachel came to me. She said that you wouldn't mind. I assumed that she had already talked with you about it, because I, of course, would have begun the conversation with you, rather than the other way around. I told Rachel that it wasn't fair for her to give up her room and to live with Yakov, but Rachel said that it would be no bother. She said that she knew it would be hard at first but that after a time we would become used to it. She also said that it wouldn't be forever. Oma Levitsky is an old woman.

"So, you see, of course I agreed. And I agreed to work quickly, because, if we did not, Reb Levitsky would feel obliged to take his mother into his house, and we all know what a disaster that would be."

Wonderful, Benjamin thought. My six year old daughter is

taking good care of the synagogue's caretaker, the oldest woman in Chelm, my wife, and my son — everyone but me. Me, she knows. Me? I'll be fine, she thinks. And of course I will have to be. What else can I do? I can't kick the old woman out because then everyone will say I am cold and heartless. I can't even complain to my wife in private because the old woman has the ears of a bat.

Just then there was a soft tapping knock at the door.

"Papa," came his daughter's voice. "May I come in?"

Benjamin Cohen loved his children. He would do anything for either one of them. He worked his fingers to the bone to provide for them. And he did his best to set a good example, teaching them how to behave in a world that was not always kind or polite.

His daughter was a gem. She had bright blue eyes and a smile that lit up his world. She had been growing so fast he couldn't believe it. As much as he worried about his son, Benjamin had no similar concerns about Rachel. His biggest worry was that she might be too smart to find a husband. Fortunately, that was years and years away.

"Not now," Sarah said. "Come back in a bit."

"No," Benjamin coughed. "It's all right. Come in."

The door slowly opened and Rachel shuffled in. In her hands she had a small bowl.

"Papa, you're hungry," she said. "I brought you some soup."

Benjamin nodded his head. "Set it down on the end table."

Rachel carefully lowered the bowl onto the table, reached into her skirt pocket, and pulled out a spoon.

"Here," she said, handing it to her father. "Please, eat some soup now. It's not too hot."

Benjamin took the spoon. He looked at his daughter. He looked at his wife. "Leave us for a moment."

"Are you sure?" Sarah said. You won't hurt her, she silently prayed. Please…

Benjamin nodded and seemed to read her mind. "We'll be fine."

Sarah straightened her blouse and slipped out into the kitchen, leaving the door ajar behind her.

For his part, Benjamin didn't care if the door was open or closed.

It was clear that privacy had fled his house the moment the old woman had arrived.

"You told your mother I would be fine?" he asked softly.

Rachel nodded her head. "But I knew you would be angry," she said. "You often are."

Benjamin's eyes widened. He bit his lip. "Then why didn't you ask me first?"

"Because you would have said no."

Again, truth from a little girl. "Of course I would have said no. Your mother is right; it isn't fair to you to live with your brother. It isn't fair for your brother either. It isn't fair to your mother..." His voice trailed off before he could finish with the last thought. And it isn't fair to me.

Rachel nodded. "It wouldn't be fair to Oma that she live in a house where she is neither wanted nor loved. Please eat your soup."

"Oh ho!" Benjamin said. "This is Oma's Soup? The Soup that will make me feel better?"

Again Rachel nodded. "Yes. It will."

"What if I don't want to feel better?"

For the first time since the conversation began, it seemed as if Rachel had no ready answer. She paused, puzzled. Then she asked, "But Papa, why wouldn't you want to feel better?"

Because by being angry, I know I am me, Benjamin wanted to shout. Because this is my house and my home and I already have more children than I expected. What do I need with another body needing to be fed? Because this is my life and I don't like feeling like everyone else is in charge but me. Because at least if I feel this way I know that it's real and true.

Benjamin found that he could not move. He couldn't budge. He couldn't open or close his fingers or move his head or speak.

The feeling only lasted a moment and then came the thought: is this what it is like for Oma Levitsky? To be trapped and frozen, unable to change...

His shoulders slumped. He lifted the spoon, looked at it, lowered it into the bowl, filled it with broth, and lifted it to his lips.

Benjamin didn't taste the first spoonful. He wasn't even sure he had really swallowed it. In fact, he didn't quite remember picking up the bowl and putting it into his lap, and eating every drop.

Then it was gone. He looked down at the empty bowl and smiled. It was one of the good china bowls, one of the bowls that he had accidentally erased the pattern from so many years before. Sarah never let Rachel touch the truly good china, but these scarred bowls she was permitted to climb up on a chair and take down from the shelf.

"Papa?" Rachel asked. "Do you feel better?"

Benjamin nodded. He wasn't sure if it was because of The Soup or because he had decided that his life was hard enough without making it harder by putting up a fight.

"Papa," Rachel said. She took the bowl and put it on the end table. Then she sat down on the bed beside him. "Can Oma Levitsky stay with us?"

The answer came in an instant. "Of course, little one," Benjamin said. "Oma Levitsky is staying here. You were right as always."

With that, Rachel jumped up and wrapped her arms tightly around him. "I knew you'd be fine!"

And Benjamin Cohen, the tailor of Chelm, felt himself enveloped in the warm and most comforting fabric of a child's loving hug. It wasn't the kind of clothing you could wear all the time, but when you put it on it felt so good.

I'm insane, he thought to himself, but what else am I going to be?

It didn't matter so much as he held her in his arms.

Chapter Thirteen

Too Nice

To everyone's surprise, the arrangement seemed to be working out. Oma Levitsky had settled into the Cohen house without a single cross word or complaint. This in itself was considered by many to be a miracle.

Each morning, Sarah Cohen helped the elder out of bed and got her dressed. Meanwhile, Rachel prepared the morning tea and cut Oma's toast into bite-sized pieces. Her brother Yakov followed his sister around like a puppy and did whatever he was told.

For his part, Benjamin Cohen was optimistic but wary. Ever since the children were born, but before the old woman moved in, he would wake with the birds and wonder if he should nudge his wife to get up and make breakfast. Mornings had been fraught with anxiety because if he did anything the wrong way, then Sarah would get upset. If he got up without waking her, then she would get upset. Even if he did nothing, sometimes she would get upset. This new routine was much nicer. Now, he lay in bed, pretending to be asleep, but listening to the birds and for the sound of his daughter summoning him to breakfast. A moment after that, he would rise, put on a clean suit, and dine with the family. No Emperor in Austria had it so good.

Everyone kept waiting for something bad to happen.

In Chelm, as in most of the world, fortune is often balanced with misfortune. You might be wealthy but ill, healthy but poor, well fed but badly clothed, and so on. The small village was subject to horrible fluctuations of the weather from the frozen winter just past, to the sweltering summer yet to come.

But for now, even the weather was beautiful. The skies were blue and clear in the mornings. Light rain fell every day, but not for long—just long enough to keep the farmers happy. When the skies cleared, the school children had enough time to play outdoors in the dry warm afternoon before washing up in time for supper and studies. The nights were cool, perfect for sleeping under a light blanket or sheet, with a soft breeze coming in through the window and tickling the nose. Each day was more splendid than the next!

So much pleasantness was making people nervous.

In Mrs. Chaipul's restaurant, customers were knocking on the wooden tables and making signs against the evil eye whenever she said, "Have a nice day."

It was driving her crazy.

"Why can't you just enjoy things?" she asked Reb Kanfer one morning.

Reb Kanfer was a potato farmer, a kind and thin man who loved the smell of the soil and the feel of the dirt. He was one of the best potato farmers in Chelm, a village well known for spuds of the highest quality.

"It's simply not right," he said. "I have worked my farm my whole life, since I was a child. Never have I had such ease digging. Never has the earth been so loose and yet so rich. Never have the worms wriggled with such vigor and never has the rain fallen in such perfect amounts and regularity."

"My bread is rising faster and baking quicker," agreed Reb Stein, "I'm using less fuel than usual. And it tastes, if anything, better. I'm not doing anything differently. In fact, I've been sleeping late. Do you know that as a baker, I have always been told that it is my duty to rise in the middle of the night to get all my work done? Now I'm not so sure."

"Everyone in the village has ordered new shoes," said Reb Gold, the cobbler. "It's never happened before. I can't keep up. I have a waiting list and will be busy through the end of the year."

Realizing what they had just said, all three men rapped on the tables, crossed their fingers, uncrossed their legs, made circles with their thumbs and forefingers, and threw salt over their shoulders.

"What are you doing that for?" Mrs. Chaipul shouted, with exasperation. "You're just wasting salt!"

"It's like in the story of Joseph when he was in Egypt," said Reb Cantor. "The Pharaoh dreamed of seven fat cows and seven skinny cows. These days feel like the fat cows!"

Mrs. Chaipul squinted at the merchant. "Are you saying you've had a prophecy?"

"No, far from it." Reb Cantor lifted his palms. "But when I get word that each of my three ships arrived safely in port with all of their cargo intact and incredibly profitable, I start to worry."

The fat merchant shrugged. He folded his hands. He waited patiently for Mrs. Chaipul to go into her back storeroom. Then he too rapped on the table, crossed and uncrossed everything, made the sign against the evil eye, and threw salt over his shoulder. And just for good measure, he said half a dozen prayers and on his way out, paused and dropped seven kopeks into the tsedakah box near the restaurant's front door.[19]

The pleasant days turned into pleasant weeks and the pleasant weeks turned into the nicest summer in anyone's memory.

The crops were growing well. The cows were getting fat. Even the Uherka River was flowing deep and quick and full of fish, something not even Oma Levitsky remembered ever hearing about!

When the rain stopped, the sun came out, and the mud hardened.

Oma asked Rachel to take her to the river to see the fish for herself. Sarah helped the paralyzed woman into Reb Schlemiel's famous chair with wheels, but Rachel herself pushed her new friend through the village.

It wasn't easy going for a six year-old girl, but Oma was light and the dry dirt streets were firmly packed.

On the slight slope that led down from the village to the riverbank, Rachel felt the wheelchair start to get lighter and move faster. Delighted that she was getting some momentum, she pushed harder and harder, and soon she was running behind the chair.

---

[19] Tsedakah is charity, usually anonymous. That morning, Reb Cantor's gesture was meant as a sacrifice to ward away misfortune, but usually he gives because he knows he is very fortunate and others are less. When given correctly, tsedakah isn't supposed to make you feel better; it makes others' lives better.

At first, Oma Levitsky was frightened to be moving so fast. What if they hit a rock and the chair toppled over? But the breeze on her face was exhilarating, and the giggles of laughter from the little girl were so delightful that she closed her eyes and felt for the first time in her life like she was flying.

Faster and faster the chair went. It began to pull away from Rachel, and rather than try and slow it to a stop, the small girl grabbed the chair with both hands, hopped up, and stood on the wooden crossbar near the bottom across the back that held the legs together.

The chair was rolling and she was riding it down the hill. There was a slight turn to the right, and Rachel leaned and the chair turned, hugging the curving road, its wheels gently but firmly in place in the deep ruts worn by centuries of horse and ox carts.

The Schlemiel twins watched in amazement as the old woman and the young girl zipped past.

"Was that a ghost?" Adam asked.

"I don't think Oma's dead yet," Abraham answered. "Besides, Rachel Cohen was with her, and I know she's not dead yet."

Then, both boys looked at each other with the same frightened thought.

Chapter Fourteen

How do we stop?

At first, the downhill ride on the wheelchair was almost breathtaking. With the old woman sitting and the young girl hanging onto the back of the chair, it was as if the two of them were piloting some fantastic flying machine that was skimming just over the ground on the hill down to the river. Rachel Cohen felt her hair waving behind her. Oma Levitsky had a broad smile on her face as they moved faster than she had in decades.

"Rachel?" Oma said.

"Yes!" the girl yelped back with glee.

"How do we stop?"

Rachel sighed. She had already had that thought and didn't have an answer. In fact, during the first few moments of the ride, she'd mulled it over pretty thoroughly, and decided that rather than worry she should just enjoy the ride while it lasted.

The chair that Reb Schlemiel the carpenter had made was perfect for pushing on a flat road, but it didn't have any brakes. It was clearly an oversight on his part. Even ox carts had brakes. However it wasn't the carpenter's fault. Rachel hadn't asked him to add a brake, so why would he even think about it? The roads in and around Chelm were usually muddy or snowy, not hard-packed and smooth.

If Rachel had knocked the chair over sideways early on, they would have stopped, and chances were that Oma wouldn't have gotten hurt in the process. But now it was too late. They were moving too fast for a tumble. There really was only one place they could stop and hope for the best.

"We'll stop in the river," Rachel shouted.

Oma nodded. "I was afraid you'd say that."

Well, the oldest woman in Chelm thought, it's been a good life. If I'm going to go, which let's face it, everybody is, I might as well go quickly rather than waste away for years confined in a wheelchair...

The chair rounded a curve and Rachel leaned into it to keep them from spilling over. Wheels that swiveled in the front would be a good idea too, she realized.

Now they were racing along the edge of the road on the last slope down to the Uherka River.

The Uherka was a tributary of the Bug River that ran through the great Black Forest called the Schvartzvald.[20] Ordinarily, the Uherka was a shallow muddy stream. It was the sort of pathetic waterway that inspired jokes about walking across dry-shod. Even Bulga the Fisherman was rarely able to catch more than a minnow in its weak flow.

The winter snows, however, had been deep, and the spring melt from the mountains had filled the river almost to overflowing its banks. The water was frothing white and moving fast.

"Rachel?" Oma asked.

"Yes?"

"Can you swim?"

"Am I too thin?" Rachel asked, puzzled. It was hard to hear Oma's voice with the wind and the speed.

"No! You look fine the way you are. Never forget that," the old woman snapped. "Can. You. Swim?"

As she looked down the bank to the rapidly approaching river, Rachel Cohen considered the question. She had paddled around in the mikveh, but to swim the way a fish or an otter did?

"No," she admitted. "But, I suppose it's time to learn."

Oma sighed. Then she shouted. "Okay, so listen quickly. Three things to know about swimming. First, don't breathe under water.

---

[20] Schvartzvald means "Black Forest." There are many Schvartzvalds in the world, but the one that surrounds Chelm is the blackest and most forested, full of wolves, demons, and Cossacks. It is said that you can get lost forever if you wander ten feet from the road. Because of this, few people visit Chelm, and the village is mostly left alone.

Take a deep breath before you go under. Then blow bubbles while you're under the water. It's easier than trying to hold your breath. Second, cup your hands while you paddle. It will move you quicker. Third, get your shoes off quickly and kick your legs as fast as you can. Fourth, don't worry about me."

This puzzled the young girl. "That's not three, that's four. Why shouldn't I worry about you?"

"Because I can't swim either. Even if I wasn't paralyzed from the neck down, I'd sink like a stone. No point in both of us dying."

It was this talk about dying that woke Rachel up from the dream-like delight she'd enjoyed during the wild ride.

Without wasting a single effort, while still hanging on to the chair with one arm, she untied the belt from her waist, looped it around Oma Levitsky, and cinched it to the chair.

"What are you doing?" Oma sputtered as the belt pulled tight against her stomach.

"Dam!" Rachel yelled.

"Young girl," Oma said, her voice stern, "we may be about to die, but that is no reason to curse…"

But then the road ran out and they were tumbling into the water.

The river was icy cold. Oma barely remembered her own advice, and caught a mouthful of water as she filled her lungs with one last sweet deep breath.

You know, she thought to herself, I never really appreciated walking until I was in this chair. I never really appreciated breathing until just now. I wonder what else I've been taking for granted.

Her head went under, she closed her eyes, and began saying prayers, thinking about all the friends she would see again in the world to come — if there was such a thing.

Then she had a thought. I came down to this river to see the sights. I am not going to miss these few last minutes with my eyes closed!

Oma Levitsky opened her eyes under the water and was amazed at the number of fish she saw. They were all around her. Silver and gold skins, flashing their tails. One had whiskers and an ugly face.

A giant turtle floated by. An otter darted through the water after the whiskerfish. There were eels in the river, slithering like giant snakes. She shuddered. She'd never been a huge fan of snakes.

Then a fat fish, the size of a whale, swam closer to her. It stared right into her eye. And it winked. It opened its mouth and seemed to ask, "Oma? Oma Levitsky. Are you all right?"

I must be dead and dreaming, Oma thought. There's no such thing as a whale in a river.

The whale's mouth opened again. "Oma? Can you hear me?"

Phew! Its breath was horrible.

Oma sputtered and coughed. "Would it hurt for you to eat a little less garlic?"

The fish grinned. "She's alive!"

More fish cheered and clapped their fins together.

Oma Levitsky shook her head, not believing what she was seeing. She rubbed her neck, and sat up.

"What's going on?" she said, as she rose slowly to her feet.

All the fish gasped. Oma blinked, and was amazed as suddenly before her eyes the fish transformed into the villagers of Chelm. Everyone was standing on the bank of the still rushing river.

"She can walk!" Reb Cantor, the giant fat whale said.

"It's a miracle!" little Doodle shouted.

"Of course I can walk," the old woman said. Then she remembered. She remembered the stroke and the paralysis. She remembered the wheeled chair. And she remembered the wild ride to the river.

"Rachel? Where is Rachel Cohen?"

The little girl pushed her way through the crowd, ran up to the old woman, and threw her arms around her. "I'm here," she said. "I'm here."

The two stood together, both in tears for a long time.

Eventually, Reb Cantor explained that the wooden chair had floated, and that after the first dunking, Rachel had managed to swim well enough to keep both her and Oma's heads above water. The Schlemiel boys had run ahead to a beaver dam downstream, and when the chair reached the blockage, they'd managed to pull

Oma and Rachel out of the water. The wheeled chair, which had saved their lives, had been destroyed, but everyone was safe.

"I can make you a new one," Jacob Schlemiel said, helpfully. "This time, as Rachel suggests, I'll put on a brake."

"I don't need a chair with wheels," Oma snapped. "I can walk by myself!"

"How fortunate," Rabbi Kibbitz said.

"Rachel?" Oma staring sternly at the young girl. "I thought I told you not to worry about me."

"I wasn't worried," Rachel said, looking up with bright blue eyes.

The old woman's face softened. She smiled. "Of course you weren't."

With that, Oma Levitsky began to dance. She held her hands up to the sky and she moved her feet forward and backward, first shuffling, and then turning, and then twirling.

The villagers of Chelm laughed and clapped and danced along with her.

At last, when no one was paying attention, Oma Levitsky lowered herself down and sat on a rock. Rachel came and sat down beside her.

"Rachel," Oma said. "Will you remember something?"

"Of course."

"Stir the pot three times a day. Add one of each vegetable that you can find once a month. Strain it, but be certain the pot never empties. Boil it, but be certain it never boils dry. And kiss it as often as you like, because every taste of life adds richness and flavor."

"I understand," Rachel said.

Oma smiled. "I know you do, child."

And then she laid her head on Rachel's tiny shoulder and closed her eyes.

The villagers found them there, the young girl not moving, with tears running down her cheeks.

While Rabbi Kibbitz laid the old woman's body down and began saying prayers, Sarah Cohen took her daughter and hugged her tightly.

"Rachel, Rachel," her mother whispered. "It's not your fault. It was her time."

"I know," Rachel said, her voice quiet. "But I miss her already."

Chapter Fifteen

Saying Goodbye

Rachel Cohen stood on a chair in front of the stove. She reached down, scooped up two handfuls of sliced carrots, and then dropped them into the pot. She picked up a bowlful of chopped onions and dumped them into the pot. She looked at the parsnips and sighed. Rachel hated parsnips. These were the last of last year's parsnips, and she'd been hoping they would go bad before her mother could serve them. Nevertheless, Rachel had scrubbed them clean, cut them into slices, and now she scooped them up and dropped them into the pot.

She hesitated, looked around, and saw that she was alone. Then, just as Oma had taught her, she blew a kiss onto the still surface of the pot. Almost instantly, the liquid began to boil, and the scent of the water subtly changed to broth.

Rachel looked over her shoulder at the empty wheeled chair, and chewed on her lip. Then she turned back to the pot, and gave it three stirs with the wooden spoon. She stepped down off the chair, moved it back to the kitchen table, went outside, and rinsed her hands off in the splash barrel.

She turned away from her house, and walked through the empty village to the graveyard.

Everyone else in Chelm was already there. Rabbi Kibbitz had said the prayers. The shovelfuls of dirt had already been thrown and the grave was full. Yet no one had left.

When Rachel arrived, there was a quiet stirring and a few murmurs as she made her way to the graveside. Her parents and brother were already there. Her mother was in tears, squeezing young Yakov's hand.

Her father had his hands on his wife's shoulders. His face was serious as he watched his little girl heft the shovel and throw dirt onto Oma Levitsky's grave.

Then Rachel cleared her throat and spoke. "I'd like to say something."

There was a mumble and a grumble and more than a few coughs. In Chelm, funeral speeches were rare, almost unheard of. It was generally felt that the life of the deceased was eloquent enough, and that if you expected a litany of praise after someone died, you were likely to start hearing as many lies as truths.

But how could you say no to a six-year-old girl who had just lost her friend?

"Go ahead," Rabbi Kibbitz said, nodding his head. "We're listening."

Rachel smiled and nodded back.

"Oma Levitsky is dead," she began. Her blunt words caused a minor disturbance and much head turning and nudging. "And I miss her.

"She was, as we all know, the oldest person in Chelm."

There was another pause as everyone in the village tried to figure out who was the new oldest person. It was, they realized, a mixed blessing. On the one hand it was an honor. On the other... It meant that you were probably next on the list.

Rabbi Kibbitz blinked, did some calculating and realized that he was probably it. This, however, wasn't the time to ask around and make sure.

"Oma Levitsky was a crotchety old busybody," Rachel said. "She knew everything about everyone. She knew all the secrets."

There was a brief laugh, and then the cemetery grew quiet. Even the birds seemed to be listening.

"She knew all of your secrets, and many of you were afraid that someday she might tell."

If it was possible for people to be even quieter than silent, then the villagers of Chelm had finally managed it. Even the littlest babies made no sound.

"But Oma Levitsky is dead. She did not tell those secrets to anyone. She kept them, and held them, and said nothing. Your secrets are safe. They will never be spoken. It was enough that she knew. She took those secrets with her, and she brought them to heaven. "

There was a sigh of relief as the villagers began to breathe again. A few were wondering whether it was such a good idea to have their secrets arrive in heaven before they did.

Rachel continued. "Oma Levitsky was the master of the kvetch.[21] She spent her life searching for perfection, and rarely found it. Almost nothing and no one measured up to her incredibly high standards, and she had a habit of letting you know. Sometimes she said things straight out, but more often than not she could express her dissatisfaction with a sigh, the flicker of an eyebrow, or the slightest shake of her head. Even after she was paralyzed, she could criticize."

There were chuckles and smirks now, as the villagers remembered. They were amazed at how observant and eloquent Rachel Cohen was for a six year old. And how tactful. Every single person in Chelm had at one time or another, in fact many times, been the victim of one of Oma's subtle or not so subtle recriminations.

Suddenly Rachel turned and pointed a finger at Reb Levitsky, Oma's only living relative in the village.

"You. Your mother is dead," she said to him. "She judged you harshly, because she loved you more than anyone else in the world. But she is gone, and you are free."

Martin Levitsky didn't dare move. His wife stood beside him, too shocked to speak.

Rachel went on. "From time to time, you may hear her voice in your head—criticizing, attacking, excoriating, denouncing, maybe even condemning you. That's not her." Rachel shook her head. "That's not your mother's voice. It's you. That's you talking to yourself. You don't get to blame her for that, because she's dead. The dead can't talk to us. We can only talk to them. Your mother is dead, and she loved you."

Martin Levitsky felt a tightness in his throat and across his heart.

---

[21] Kvetching is complaining. In Chelm it is a competitive sport!

In his mind, he heard his mother speaking.

"I love you, Martin. I am going to miss you."

Then the voice faded and the tightness in his throat and across his heart loosened. He listened. And it was quiet. For the first time in his life, she had nothing to say to him. Tears of relief and joy and sorrow began to flow down his cheeks. He smiled, pursed his lips, and nodded to Rachel.

"Oma Levitsky," Rachel said, her voice growing louder and spreading out. "She made The Soup. She loved and fed and healed and knew each and every one of us.

"But she is dead. And she doesn't want us to remember her only as Oma Levitsky. She had many names, and wants to be remembered for all of who she was. For the life that she lived as a girl. As a young woman. As a wife. As a mother. As a grandmother. As a great grandmother. As a friend.

"Goodbye Charlotte Esther Kotel Levitsky. Goodbye Oma. We'll miss you. I'll miss you."

Rachel took a small rock that she had strained from the bottom of Oma Levitsky's soup pot, and she set it on the grave. Rachel's mother and father and brother encircled her in their arms as the young girl cried.

There was not a dry eye in the cemetery. One by one, the villagers said goodbye and made their ways back to their homes.

"You know," Rabbi Kibbitz said to Mrs. Chaipul as they unlocked the door to her restaurant, "I can still smell Oma's soup."

Mrs. Chaipul lifted her head and sniffed the air. Then she smiled. Remarkable. What a remarkable girl.

Part Three

The Boy

Chapter Sixteen

The Rosh Rush

Every day after yeshiva, Yakov Cohen wandered into his father's shop. Young Yakov was nine years old and, except at school, was always surrounded by women: his mother, his twin sister, and all the girls and ladies they spent their days with. All of the men, he knew, were defined by their work. With the new year approaching, Yakov reasoned that he could be a big help. He'd wander in the front door, tell his father he'd arrived, and then sit in a chair, waiting and watching.

Many people look forward to dipping apples in honey on Rosh Hashanah. Others make sweet cakes for a sweet year. Reb Stein, the baker, makes his challahs round to signify the annual cycle of ending and beginning.

But for Benjamin Cohen, the tailor of Chelm, the New Year always presented problems.

First, the seasons were changing. Regular customers were coming in for new clothing appropriate to the switch from Chelm's hot and humid summers to its cold and rainy autumns.

Then there were "The Sprouts," youngsters whose new suits and dresses needed to be altered drastically because of sudden and unexpected growth spurts. Fortunately, Benjamin knew when a short 12-year-old boy was about to become a gigantic 13-year-old young man, and always hid enough extra fabric in the garment to let hems out seven or even eight inches.

Then there were "The Expanders." These were usually older men and women who had gained weight, so that when they tried on their best outfits, the squeeze was tight - if not impossible.

There was another category that Benjamin called "The Dwindlers" who actually lost weight. But, in a Jewish village where food was delicious and occasionally plentiful, they were rare.

For weeks before the holidays, there were huge rushes of urgent repairs. The tailor was in his shop from dawn until dark, and often later.

Benjamin Cohen didn't mean to ignore his son. He absolutely wanted Yakov to learn to measure and snip, estimate and clip, hem and sew.

But the Rosh Rush was no time to teach.

So, mostly, Yakov sat around waiting and watching.

On the morning before the New Year, Benjamin was finishing a pure white cotton underskirt for the merchant's wife. He was rushing. He got careless, and he pricked his finger with the needle.

"Ow!" he yelped.

Immediately, Yakov leapt into action. He snatched the white skirt from his father's bleeding hand, and ran from the shop.

"You fool!" his father yelled. "What are you doing? Where are you going?"

Yakov didn't answer. He dashed across the village, careful to keep the skirt from dragging in the dirt. He raced up the steps to the merchant's house and pounded on the door. With cotton, Yakov knew, you have to quickly rinse off the blood. The Cantors had the only indoor hand-pump in the village.

Reb Cantor's youngest daughter, Gittel, opened the door.

"Where's the fire?" she asked, with a smile.

"May I use your water pump?" Yakov panted. "It's urgent!"

They say that anything that can go wrong will go wrong. This is even truer in Chelm.

Gittel immediately leapt to the wrong conclusion.

"Our house is on fire!" She ran past Yakov screaming, "Our house is on fire." Her mother, father, brother, and two sisters fled the house and joined her in the street.

Yakov, however, was on a brave mission to help his father. He sped through the (imaginary) flames, into the Cantors' kitchen, to their sink, and began pumping furiously.

Mechanical hand pumps usually need to be primed with water to speed the flow. Yakov didn't know that, so he just pumped and pumped and pumped.

Meanwhile, outside, the Cantor family's wails and shrieks attracted attention. There is nothing more urgent than a fire in a village with houses made of wood, sticks, and straw.

Everyone in earshot grabbed a bucket and made a line that weaved from the well all the way to the Cantors' house.

In the kitchen, Yakov finally managed to get a dribble, and then a thin stream, of water. He held the bloodied skirt under the flow. It wasn't enough, so he kept jerking the handle, up and down. Because he was yanking so hard, Yakov was getting hot, and he imagined that the flames were getting closer.

When Benjamin Cohen, his left index finger wrapped in gauze, heard that his son was trapped inside a burning building, he raced to the merchant's house and tore at his hair. (Fortunately, his wife and daughter were off in the woods searching for mushrooms, so they didn't share his panic until much later.)

"What have I done?" he moaned. "I've cursed my son!"

At that moment, Yakov stumbled out the front door.

"My boy!" Benjamin rushed forward.

"Stand back!" shouted Rabbi Yohon Abrahms, the schoolteacher, (and leader of the fire brigade,) as he splashed Yakov with a bucketful of water.

Panting and drenched, the young boy fell into his father's arms.

"Are you all right?" Benjamin asked. "I'm sorry. I am so sorry."

"I'm hot and I'm wet," Yakov said. "But I didn't see any flames."

"The fire is out!" Gittel Cantor said.

The entire village cheered. Yakov was lifted from his father's hug and hoisted onto the schoolteacher's shoulders.

"Papa!" Yakov shouted. "I got the stain out!"

"What stain?" Benjamin called back as the crowd carried Yakov away.

"The blood stain!" Yakov shouted. "Catch!" He threw the skirt to his father.

Benjamin almost caught it, but he stumbled, and dropped the cleaned white skirt in the muddy street. Sighing, he bent down and pried it from the muck. It had been a lovely piece of work.

He knocked on the merchant's door.

Shoshana Cantor, the merchant's wife, who had been searching her house for signs of damage, answered.

"Is there another fire?" she asked.

"No," Benjamin Cohen said. "I finished your skirt, but it got a little dirty."

He squeezed out some of the water before handing it to her.

Shoshana Cantor held the limp soggy garment between two fingers. "This is a little dirty?"

"I'm sorry," the tailor said. "I'll buy you a new one."

"Forget about it." The merchant's wife waved her other hand. "My husband often buys me clothes that are just too nice. It's good to wear something that I don't have to worry about keeping clean. Besides, your son just saved our home from a fire. Consider it a fair trade."

"Thank you," Reb Cohen said.

He turned to go back home and realized that his son was safe and his work was done. The Rosh Rush was finally over! A feeling of lightness and joy began to fill his heart. He started to hum, and naturally his feet began to move.

Shoshana Cantor watched the tailor hop from her doorsteps, dance into the road, and slip in the mud. He splashed flat on his tuchas.[22]

"Are you all right?" she called.

"I'm wonderful!" Benjamin Cohen grinned, as he jumped to his feet, and danced all the way home.

---

[22] A tuchas is slang for the posterior. Usually considered cute, although sometimes a source of humor.

Part Four

The Girl

Chapter Seventeen

Learning to Learn

At nine years old, Rachel Cohen was having her first moral dilemma.

She lay in her bed, listening to her parents fight and knew it was all her fault. Her brother had just become a hero, who had nearly died in a fire. And her mother was berating her father for not trying to save her boy.

"What did you do to help!" her mother was hissing. "Rabbi Abrahms organizes a bucket brigade and all you do is stand around and moan? You couldn't even grab a bucket? You couldn't run into the burning house to save your own son?"

Her father was ominously silent. What could he say? His wife was right. He had been so upset that he had frozen into helplessness. He should have done something. Still, he was angry with her for accusing him.

"Sarah, keep your voice down," he hissed back. "The children…"

"Don't you tell me to keep my voice down," Rachel's mother snapped. Then immediately she lowered her voice, and the young girl could hear no more.

As Rachel lay in bed and stared through the dark, she realized that she needed to talk to someone, but whom? Her mother and father and brother were out of the question. If Oma Levitsky was still alive, she would know what to do. Rachel sighed and bit back a tear. One of the rabbis? She shook her head. No, it would have to be Mrs. Chaipul.

Once the choice was made, her mind eased and within minutes she was fast asleep.

* * *

After the Fast of Gedaliah and before the Fast of Yom Kippur,

Mrs. Chaipul's restaurant was always packed. The owner-cook-waitress-and-dishwasher was running from table to table, grumbling about the busy-ness but secretly happy about all the business.

When Rachel Cohen pushed open the door and made her way to the counter, the morning customers paused for a moment, took stock of the tiny girl, and then went back to eating, drinking, and schmoozing. So many new people. It seemed as if the villagers were becoming used to new and unusual people appearing in the restaurant.

The high stools around the counter proved to be a slight embarrassment. Rachel was short for her age. When she'd been to the restaurant with her parents they always sat at a table. She evaluated the situation, and wasn't quite sure whether climbing up the stool would work or if it would tip over.

Suddenly a pair of hands grabbed her waist and boosted her up into the high seat.

She looked up and saw Rabbi Abrahms' smiling face.

"I hope I didn't startle you," he said.

"Only a bit," Rachel answered. "I'm not old enough to have a heart attack, though."

The Rabbi smiled awkwardly. Boys he was used to, because he taught so many at the yeshiva, but girls... They were a different story altogether. He shrugged and wandered back to the table he was sharing with Reb Cantor and Reb Stein.

Mrs. Chaipul appeared behind the counter in front of Rachel. "You want coffee?" she said as she plopped a mug on the table. Then she looked up and nearly dropped her coffee pot.

"Tea, please," Rachel said. "I don't have any money, but I'll gladly help out."

"Don't you have any chores?"

"I'm all done with my chores." Rachel grinned. "I'm very efficient."

It only took Mrs. Chaipul an instant to evaluate the situation. She poured the girl some tea, brought her toast and a fried egg, and as soon as she was done eating, put her to work clearing dishes from tables.

It wasn't until after lunch that they finally had a chance to sit down at a corner table and rest.

"Oy," Mrs. Chaipul muttered, "my feet are killing me."

"This is hard work," Rachel admitted. "I always thought running a restaurant would be fun, but now I'm not so sure."

The girl was remarkable. She'd had every table cleared and wiped almost as soon as a customer rose. She'd moved a chair in front of the sink and washed all the dishes. And not once had she spilled, bumped, or broken anything.

"Now you know why they call it 'running a restaurant.'" Mrs. Chaipul sighed. "What do you have on your mind?"

"The other day, I almost killed my brother," Rachel said.

"Really?" the caterer said. "I know when I was younger I wanted to kill my brother."

"I'm serious," the small girl insisted. "Yakov was driving me crazy. He is always moping around the house after yeshiva, complaining about his schoolwork. Even when I helped him finish, he wouldn't stop kvetching. I told him to go somewhere else because he was driving me crazy. He said, 'Where else can I go but home?' I suggested he go to Papa's shop. Yakov was completely against it until I told him that Papa probably wouldn't want him anyway. Then, of course, he had to go right away. You know the rest."

"I'm not sure I do," Mrs. Chaipul said. "I understand how you reverse convinced him to go to your father's shop, but what's this about almost killing him?"

"If Yakov hadn't been in the shop, he wouldn't have taken the skirt to the Cantor's house, and he wouldn't have been there when the fire started," Rachel said.

"True," agreed Mrs. Chaipul. "But then the Cantor's house might have burned to the ground, and who knows how far it would have spread. So you did something good."

"My parents are fighting about it!" Rachel said. "My mother says that my father should have been the one to take the skirt to the Cantors. Then he would have been at risk and not my brother. I don't know what to do. I was trying to do something good, but other things happened as a result."

"I think I understand." Mrs. Chaipul nodded. "Clearly you have too much time on your hands. You're hired. You finish your chores early enough to help me for hours at a time. You help your brother with his school work?"

Rachel nodded. "Yes. It's quite easy. I'm not sure why he can't do it himself."

"Have you thought about going to school?" Mrs. Chaipul asked.

Rachel laughed. "To the yeshiva? With all the boys? Is that even allowed?"

"No, it's not allowed," Mrs. Chaipul admitted. "But it's not disallowed either. Just because no girls have ever gone to the yeshiva doesn't mean they never could."

"Really?" Rachel's face brightened. "You think I could go?"

"It can't hurt to ask." Mrs. Chaipul shrugged. "I'll talk with Rabbi Abrahms about it."

Chapter Eighteen

It Hurts to Ask

Like many junior rabbis, Rabbi Yohon Abrahms had to cobble together a variety of different jobs to make a living. In addition to teaching the youngsters at the yeshiva, he was the rabbi on call for sick visits during bad weather, the designated mohel performing circumcisions whenever Rabbi Kibbitz's hands were too shaky, and also the mashgiach traveling from farm to farm making sure all the animals destined for consumption were kept (and slaughtered) according to the kosher laws.

It was in this capacity that Mrs. Chaipul found the young Rabbi, hard at work examining goats in the Shimmel sisters' dairy barn.

"I have a new student for you," Mrs. Chaipul said, talking to his back as he knelt down in the straw to examine a kid's hindquarters.

"Nu?" he said, smiling at his small joke.

"Yes, new," Mrs. Chaipul said, growing agitated. She liked to look people in the eyes when she spoke, especially when she was about to make an important request. "Not old. Unknown, uncertain, untested."

Rabbi Abrahms nodded. The young goat looked fine. He moved on to its mother. "Is Bulga the Fisherman finally going to learn his Aleph-Bets?"[23]

"That would be an old student," she snapped.[24] "This is

---

[23] It was a well-known fact that Bulga the Fisherman was stridently and vehemently opposed to formal education of any kind. "I know how to fish, how to sail, how to fix my boat, and how to swim," he said. "What do I care what some dead rabbi said to another dead rabbi a thousand years ago."

[24] For her part, Mrs. Chaipul knew that Bulga was actually quite literate, and had a preference for the French love poetry. It's a long story....

someone new."

"Nu?" giggled the Rabbi, who believed that, if a joke that was funny once, it would be even funnier with repetition.

"Yes, new!"

"Has another family come to the village?" Rabbi Abrahms asked. He nodded his head and patted the nanny goat. She was fine, too. He scooched over and began examining the billy, who was eating hay from a bale.

"No," Mrs. Chaipul said. "An old family with a new student."

This puzzled the young rabbi, who knew every family in the small village and wasn't aware of any new youngsters who ought to be entering his school. "So, who is it?"

"Before I tell you, I want you to listen," Mrs. Chaipul said. "For you to listen, I want you to pay attention. For you to pay attention, I want you to look at me and not the bottom of an old goat."

Rabbi Abrahms bit his tongue as he suppressed the urge to compare looking at Mrs. Chaipul's face to examining the bottom of an old goat. "I'm almost done," he said. "You have no idea how difficult it is to get these animals to cooperate. By nature they are skittish and frisky. As much as you may want my attention, they don't particularly like it."

"All right!" Mrs. Chaipul said, impatiently. "She can read. She can write. She's brilliant. She understands things that I don't, in ways that I can't understand."

Now Rabbi Abrahms was confused. "The goat?" he asked. "This is a male goat. The kid and the nanny are the females."

"Not the goat," Mrs. Chaipul said. "The girl."

"What girl?"

"The new student."

"I don't have a new student," said the rabbi.

"You will," said the caterer. "And she's a girl."

"She's a girl? Of course she's a girl. If she was a boy, she'd be a he. But, Mrs. Chaipul, girls are not students."

"This one is," Mrs. Chaipul said. "Or rather she will be."

"She will? No, I don't think so. I don't have girls in my yeshiva."

"Not yet."

"Not ever!" The young man was having a difficult time focusing on the goat and the conversation simultaneously. "There aren't any girls in the school. There never have been any girls in the school. And there never will be any girls in the school."

"No, that's not true," the old woman shook her head. "Maybe, there haven't been any girls in the school. But that doesn't mean that there never will be any girls in the school."

"My dear lady," said the rabbi, trying to keep his focus on both issues simultaneously. "There is not a single yeshiva in the world that admits girls for a very simple reason: they don't need to learn the things that men do. They need to learn the things that women do. Secondly, I'm not sure I'm permitted to teach them. Thirdly, I have a school that is filled with boys and young men. I shouldn't have to tell you what a difficult task it is keeping their focus on their studies, without adding the distraction that a young girl would bring. You understand? Good. Now, let me go about my business."

Mrs. Chaipul stared at the young rabbi's backside, and for a moment considered placing her foot firmly into it. The moment passed, and she spoke again.

"Listen, I spoke to Rabbi Kibbitz and he said it was up to you whether girls could attend yeshiva. Let me respond to your other reasons. Girls distract young men, whether they are in the same room or not. The fact that it has never been done before does not mean that it should never be done. If that was true, then we would still be living in tents and bringing animals for sacrifices. Times change."

"No," the young rabbi said. "No. No."

Mrs. Chaipul rarely faced such obstinacy. Of course the one time Rabbi Abrahms had dared to criticize her soup, she had handed him her apron and walked out of her restaurant.

She softened her voice. "Listen, this girl already knows everything a girl her age needs to know as a woman, but she needs more. She is hungry for knowledge. She has already read all of her brother's books and probably does his homework for him. She speaks more languages than I do. She's brilliant."

"She does her brother's homework?"

"I don't know that for certain, but I would imagine so."

"Who is it?" Rabbi Abrahms said. If there was one thing he couldn't stand, it was someone who didn't do their own homework. "Tell me."

"Rachel Cohen, who else?"

"Rachel OWWW!"

He should have known, but it came as a surprise. When Rabbi Abrahms heard Rachel's name, he made two mistakes. First of all, he turned to look at Mrs. Chaipul, and second, he squeezed the billy goat too hard in the wrong place.

The goat kicked the rabbi in the chest, knocking him backwards into Mrs. Chaipul, who fell on top of the poor man with a screech.

The goat returned to its business, noshing on hay. Mrs. Chaipul leaped up and began examining the rabbi, worried that he might be dead.

Rabbi Abrahms, dazed, imagined that Sarah Cohen was kneeling down beside him, begging for him to take her daughter into the yeshiva.

"Yes, yes," he said. "Of course. Of course I'll take her."

"You will?"

"Did you ever doubt I would?" he said, his head still spinning. "Sarah, I could never refuse your request."

The smile on her face was so broad that he sat up and kissed her right on the lips.

"What in the name of cabbage are you doing?" Mrs. Chaipul said.

Rabbi Abrahms blinked. He saw the old woman pulling back from him in surprise.

"Have you lost your mind?" she said. "Were you kicked in the head?"

Completely embarrassed, Rabbi Abrahms wiped his mouth and quickly began making excuses. "I thought you were my mother," he lied. "My mother always took care of me when I was hurt."

"Your mother's name was Sarah?" Mrs. Chaipul said. "And you called your mother by her first name?"

"It was a nickname," the flustered man said. "We all called her that. I don't know why. I was just a child! I am so sorry. Please don't tell anyone."

Mrs. Chaipul squinted at the young rabbi's face. His cheeks were flushed. His eyes were wide. She knew he was fibbing. Nevertheless, she also had him exactly where she wanted him.

"So, it's ok with you that Rachel Cohen starts school after Yom Kippur?"

Rabbi Abrahms saw that the old woman had her feet set and her arms crossed. She was determined.

"She can read and write?"

"Beautifully."

"She won't be a distraction?"

"You have the Schlemiel twins in your school, how much more of a distraction could one little girl be?"

True, he thought. Abraham and Adam Schlemiel were troublemakers to the core.

"All right," he agreed. "She can come. We'll try it."

"You'll make it work," Mrs. Chaipul said. "And I'll keep quiet about everything else."

Mrs. Chaipul spat on her palm. Rabbi Abrahms spat in his hand. They shook. The deal was sealed.

She helped him to his feet. He brushed himself off.

She left the barn, pleased with the results, but feeling a little mournful that she now had a secret that Oma Levitsky would never know.

Rabbi Abrahms sighed and hoped he had done the right thing for the right reasons and would not get run out of Chelm. Then he went in to tell the Shimmels that their animals were perfectly kosher.

Chapter Nineteen

School Girl (Part One)

The villagers of Chelm were not known for their athletic prowess. In running races they tripped, in swimming competitions they dog paddled, in archery contests they were banned. If there was an Olympic sport in which they excelled, it would have been gossip. Any tidbit or morsel of interesting information about anyone in the village would spread like a wildfire across a dry field, circle about, make the rounds, become public knowledge, and often transform into something completely separate from the truth.

For example, when Shoshana Cantor, the merchant's wife, made a trip to Odessa to visit her second cousin, before she even reached Smyrna a rumor started that she was having an affair. By the time she returned home a month later, Reb Cantor himself was pulling out his hair believing that his wife was married to someone else and actually had five children by this phantom. It took them six months of counseling (him with the Rabbi and her with Mrs. Chaipul) to resolve their differences. And still the next time he went off on a buying trip, a rumor spread that he was out to kill her former lover, and the whole process began again.

On Yom Kippur, the solemnest day of the year, when every man, woman, and child old enough to stand (and some who weren't) were in the synagogue praying and atoning for sins, the chatter was incredible. A day of silent reflection, meditation, and contemplation, it was not to be.

Everyone was talking about what would happen when Rachel Cohen went to school.

"None of the boys will be able to learn anything," hissed Reb Stein, the baker to Reb Gold, the cobbler. "The next generation of young men will graduate school illiterate."

"I'm worried for her safety," Reb Gold answered back. "Boys and young men are not always in control of themselves."

In the women's balcony, the whispers were similar.

"I think it's shameful," muttered Bella Shimmel to her sister, Bertha. Bella, of course, had recently returned from Moscow with a new husband in tow, so she was trying her best to be a model of propriety.

"Disgraceful," Bertha Shimmel, who enjoyed grumbling about almost everything, agreed.

"I wish I could go to school," mumbled Peninah Shimmel, the youngest of the three.

Her sisters stared at her in horror. "Why?"

"I don't really like goats and cows. I would like to learn about other things."

"Shameful," Bella said.

"Disgraceful," Bertha agreed.

Chastened, Peninah returned to her prayers.

Even the two rabbis on the bimah were distracted, exchanging quiet remarks with each other while the congregation chanted. [25]

"Are you sure this is a good idea?" Rabbi Kibbitz asked.

"You're the one who authorized it!" Rabbi Abrahms answered, holding the Torah scrolls high.

"Yes of course I authorized it," Rabbi Kibbitz said. "When Mrs. Chaipul asks me for something I almost always say yes. You, however, I expected to say no."

"I wanted to say no," the junior rabbi hissed as he set the scrolls down.

"I understand," the senior rabbi whispered. "I have compassion. In the old days, when I refused one of Mrs. Chaipul's requests, whenever I went into the restaurant, my eggs were over-salty and my corned beef sandwiches were full of gristle. And the pickles.

---

[25] A Bimah is a podium or a platform from which the Torah is read. In Chelm, the floor of the shul slopes downward, so the bimah is actually at the same level as the rest of the congregation. When he first arrived, Rabbi Yohon Abrahms suggested raising it higher, but Rabbi Kibbitz said that the Torah was made for everyone, and besides, he got dizzy from heights.

Ecch."

The elder rabbi paused and caught his breath. It was Yom Kippur. He was hungry, and knew he shouldn't be talking about food. Even horrible food.

"But there's never been a girl in the yeshiva!" Rabbi Abrahms said loudly.

Of course that was the moment the room went absolutely silent, and the young rabbi's words echoed and reverberated. He hadn't meant to make his discomfort so public.

Now every pair of eyes was on him. He couldn't say the truth, that he had momentarily mistaken Mrs. Chaipul for Sarah Cohen, and that he would do anything for Sarah Cohen.

He smiled nervously and glanced at Rabbi Kibbitz, who waved his hands and shrugged, as if to say, 'This is your problem, you deal with it.'

Rabbi Abrahms sighed, and decided to make the best of things. He gave a speech. It wasn't exactly his turn to do the sermon, but he knew that, with any luck, by the time he finished most of the villagers would be asleep and his words would be forgotten.

"On this Day of Atonement, we are asked to make amends. To correct the imbalances that exist in this world of ours. People, as you know, are imperfect. They often say and do things they don't mean.

"When we ask the Almighty to forgive us, he does so immediately and completely and willingly. However, he says that his forgiveness is not enough. We must also ask forgiveness of those whom we have offended. A wrong is not righted until the wrongee is the rightee."

There was coughing and shuffling of feet.

Rabbi Abrahms continued. "For hundreds and hundreds of years we have reserved education and instruction for our sons. What need do women have, we said, for knowledge and learning? Their work is in the home and with the family. It is the man's place to shape and change the world."

Now most of the villagers were nodding their heads and nudging each other with elbows. A few sat still and silent, poking their cheeks with their tongues.

"So, why should this change?"

"Yes!" Reb Stein jumped to his feet. "Why should this change?" The baker looked around awkwardly. He hadn't meant to say anything. It wasn't right that he should. Except he was starving. For most people, the Yom Kippur fast was difficult, for him it was nearly impossible. On a typical morning, he woke up hours before dawn to mix the dough, and he always baked a special loaf of bread for himself, which he ate and enjoyed warm from the oven with butter melting as soon he slathered it on. During Yom Kippur, he woke up as usual in the middle of the night, but instead of firing up his ovens, was forced to lie awake in bed, staring at the ceiling, thinking about bread, and growing hungrier by the hour. By the end of the day he was usually so crazy from starvation, that as soon as the sun set, he would rush to his bakery and selfishly devour the loaf of sourdough rye that he 'accidentally' left on the counter every year. Only then he would go home for his family's break-the-fast dinner.

"I'm sorry," he said. "I have no children in the school, and I really have no say in this." He sat back down in his chair and buried his nose in his prayer book.

Once again everyone was looking at Rabbi Abrahms.

At last he spoke. "Change happens. Change is inevitable. Even though we have resisted change for so many years..."

He was lost. He knew he was lost. So he kept talking...

"This change is an experiment," he said. "Some experiments work, and others do not. I will welcome our newest student into my school, and do everything I can to educate and teach her. But if the experiment does not work, or the price is too high, then we will have to say it is unsuccessful and that the lessons and examples set by our ancestors were justified."

"You mean," asked Reb Gold, "if there's a problem you'll kick her out?"

Rabbi Abrahms blinked. He cleared his throat. He would not have put it so bluntly, but that was exactly what he'd been thinking.

He glanced up to the women's balcony, and saw Sarah Cohen

sitting sternly next to her daughter. Rachel was in the front row, leaning forward with a hopeful smile on her face and her bright eyes gleaming.

"On this Day of Atonement," Rabbi Abrahms said, "all problems are in the past, and the future is yet to be written. May our futures be happy and healthy, rich, and full of wisdom for all of us."

Sarah's face softened, and she hugged her daughter as Rachel began to cry.

Rabbi Abrahms watched the tears running down the young girl's cheeks as the entire village of Chelm answered, "Amen!"

He hoped they were tears of joy, because he knew that for this girl he would truly do his best to make sure this new experiment was a success.

"Amen." He nodded and sat down.

"Amen," bellowed the booming voice of Bulga the Fisherman. "That was the shortest sermon I've ever heard."

Rabbi Kibbitz looked at his colleague with pride. Then he realized that on Yom Kippur a short sermon meant that there was still a long way to go before sunset. He sighed.

"Everyone rise," he said, feeling his stomach rumble.

Chapter Twenty

School Girl (Part Two)

It was still dark. Rachel Cohen was pretending to be asleep, but really she wasn't sure if she had slept at all. She heard her mother padding softly in the kitchen and thought about joining her, but remembered her mother's words the night before.

"You sleep late. I'll make breakfast by myself. You have a big day tomorrow."

So she lay in bed and looked into the darkness, smiling and feeling a tightness in her stomach.

If Oma Levitsky had still been alive, Rachel would have run to her and confided all the swirling feelings as they passed through her mind. For a moment, the young girl closed her eyes and sent a prayer to her dead friend.

She felt her mother's hand on her shoulder, and a brief brushing kiss on her cheek. "Wake up little girl. Wake up little school girl."

The sun was up! Rachel smelled the fresh baked rolls her mother made on special occasions. She sat up in bed and grabbed her mother, wrapping her in a warm hug.

Sarah Cohen enjoyed the embrace and returned it gratefully. "If your brother was this easy to wake up on a school day then my life would be so much more pleasant," she whispered.

Rachel pulled back and told her mother, "But for him school is a normal and every day thing. For me this is all new."

"True," her mother nodded. "On his first day of school he barely slept the night before. And I suppose he jumped up too, but it was so long ago that it's difficult to remember. Come, get dressed. I have to wake the beast."

As soon as her mother left the room, Rachel ran to her dresser and pulled on her clothes. She smiled as she heard her mother warning, "Yakov, you've got to get up because if you don't, I'm going to throw you into the Bug River!"

Her father was sitting at the table reading a week old copy of the Yiddish newspaper, so she gave him a quick peck on the cheek.

She went to the stove and poured herself a cup of coffee and added a lump of sugar.

Her father peered over the top of his paper. "Coffee?"

"Am I too young?" Rachel asked. "Mrs. Chaipul lets me drink it when I help her at the restaurant."

Benjamin Cohen shrugged. "Most women drink tea. But then again most women don't go to school."

He wasn't sure what he thought about the whole idea, but he was going along with it mostly to preserve happiness and harmony in his home. That way, he could take the credit if everything worked out, but if something went wrong with the schoolteacher's "experiment," Rabbi Abrahms would take the blame.

"Papa, I have a question."

Benjamin rolled his eyes playfully. "Not even in school and you already have a question."

"But I always have questions."

"Yes you do. Which is why you are going to school. What's your question?"

"Rabbi Abrahms said that in order to be forgiven and be written into the book of life we must ask for forgiveness from those whom we have offended. Do you think that it's too late to be forgiven for this year?"

Benjamin Cohen blinked at his nine-year-old daughter. He hadn't even finished his first cup of coffee. This was why the girl should go to school, so she could bother the rabbis with these sorts of questions. He was a tailor, not a thinker of deep thoughts.

He almost said as much, but one thing his children had taught him was a modicum of patience, and to occasionally look past the obvious and search for the truth behind a seemingly innocent remark.

"What do you mean?" he asked. A safe counter-question, he felt.

Just then Sarah dragged Yakov into the room by the boy's ear.

"I warned him that I would do this if he gave me any trouble," she explained. "This is an important morning and he's futzing around like he's got all day."

"Ow! Ow! Ow!" Yakov yelped. "Mama it hurts."

Benjamin lifted the newspaper up to hide the smile on his face. It wasn't that he enjoyed cruelty, but he knew how difficult it was to budge Yakov in the morning, and he appreciated every day that Sarah did the job.

"Sha!" Sarah let go of the ear. "I was barely pulling. If you didn't keep fighting me it wouldn't have hurt at all."

Yakov rubbed his ear. It felt red. He glared at his sister. "This is all your fault."

Rachel nodded. "You're right. It is."

Yakov frowned. His sister drove him crazy. Why couldn't she just argue with him like a normal person? All his friends told him about the fights they had with their brothers and sisters. The only time Rachel would fight with Yakov is when she was certain she would win.

"No," Sarah said, kissing her son on the top of his head. "Your ear hurts because you were moving too slowly."

Yakov grinned. At least he could fight with his mother! "It wouldn't be a special day if it wasn't for her."

Sarah bent down and grinned right back at her boy. "But I still would have pulled your ear."

Yakov folded his arms and sulked while Sarah stirred a skillet of eggs.

When everything was ready and on the table, the family sat down and three of the four attacked their food as if they hadn't seen a meal in months.

Maybe it was the changing of the seasons. With Yom Kippur just past, the days were getting shorter and the air was getting colder. Sunrise was coming later, and the memory of fasting was still close.

"Can I say something?" Rachel asked in a small quiet voice.

"What's stopping you?" her brother answered.

"You haven't touched a thing," her mother said. "Eat while it's still hot."

"I'm not hungry," Rachel said.

"You need energy for school," her father told her.

"What do you need energy for? To sit around all day?" her brother countered.

"I need to ask for your forgiveness," the little girl said at last.

For a moment not a fork moved.

"What happened?" her mother asked.

"Did someone hurt you?" her father said.

"No," said her brother. "I will not forgive you. What did you do?"

Rachel covered her mouth and then spoke to her brother through her fingers. "I almost killed you."

"I almost kill you all the time," Yakov replied. "You don't hear me asking for your forgiveness."

"Quiet!" Benjamin said. "Rachel, what are you saying?"

"If I hadn't suggested that Yakov go to work with you in the shop after school, he wouldn't have been at the Cantor house when it caught on fire. It's all my fault. He was driving me crazy, and I convinced him and you and everyone else that he needed to get out of the house."

"That wasn't your idea," Yakov said. "It was my idea."

"No." Rachel shook her head. "I let you think that it was your idea."

Yakov looked at his parents. "Mamma, will you tell her to stop taking credit for my ideas!"

Sarah nodded. She was sure that both of her children were right. Prior to joining his father in the tailor shop, Yakov had been driving her crazy at home, too. At the same time, they were at an age that whenever Rachel told Yakov to do something he would do the exact opposite. Was that what had happened?

"That's your sin?" Benjamin said. He picked up a roll and began buttering it. "Look, I don't care whose idea it was. I'm glad Yakov's working with me. He's a brilliant helper. The other day he showed me this amazing way to cut cloth in a perfect circle using the marking wax, a piece of string and a straight pin."

"Like Leonardo Da Vinci?" Rachel asked.

"Exactly!" Yakov said.

Benjamin's eyes narrowed. "Who is this Leonard fellah, and was he the one who put this foolish idea into your head?"

"It's from a book, papa," Yakov said. "Rachel told me about it and I thought that if it would work for painting it would work for cutting cloth."

Benjamin accepted this, knowing that he really didn't want to know anything else. "In any case, everyone's all right. Nobody got hurt. So, yes, I forgive you even though I don't think you did anything."

"Mama?" Rachel asked.

"Of course. What your father says goes double for me," Sarah said. Privately, she was thrilled that Yakov wasn't hanging about the house, and it was so good for the boy to work with his father.

"Brother?" Rachel asked.

Yakov crossed his hands and shook his head. "Nope."

"Yakov," Benjamin warned. "You tell your sister you forgive her."

"Papa, it doesn't count if he doesn't really mean it," Rachel said. "Please, Yakov. I'm sorry. I won't do it again."

"You'll stop taking credit for my ideas?"

Rachel nodded. "I promise."

"All right," Yakov shrugged, and was surprised when his sister jumped up and gave him a hug. "Eww! All right. All right. Enough. Let me eat."

* * *

"I'll walk with you to school," Sarah Cohen said to her daughter.

Rachel smiled. Yakov had already run ahead. Their father had gone to his shop. Rachel was helping her mother clear the table.

"You don't have to," Rachel said.

Sarah shrugged. "What else am I going to do, mope around the kitchen and wonder whether you arrived safely?"

Rachel laughed. "It's just on the other side of the square. I walk myself to the well every day. What's the difference?"

"The difference is that this is your first day of school," her mother said. "The difference is that you're the first woman in the history of Chelm to go to school. The difference is that you shouldn't be alone. And I want to come."

"All right," Rachel said, softly. She gave her mother a kiss on the cheek, and began drying the plates as her mother handed them to her.

* * *

Chelm is a small village, but even a small village can take pride in its educational system.

Before the school was built, all the students had been educated in the synagogue, but they complained about the cold and the drafts. So they moved the teaching to the rabbi's study, which was fine until the village grew and soon young boys were sitting on bookshelves and dangling their feet out the windows.

So, a door was cut in the rear of the synagogue and the one-room school building was attached to the back wall.

The one-room yeshiva was a simple affair. Twenty feet wide by thirty feet long, there were ten benches in five rows with an aisle down the middle and skinny tables in front of each bench for reading and writing. At the front were bookshelves and a long, wide table for the teacher. Light came mostly from the windows on the left and right walls, but there were also sconces to hold lanterns and candles, because in the winter natural light was brief and often quite dim.

That first winter, Rabbi Kibbitz said, school was a pleasure. Each bench held two students, and the heat from the synagogue drifted in, keeping everyone warm.

Then came the spring thaw, and on the first warm day when at last the windows were flung open, the flaw in the yeshiva's design and placement became pungently obvious. The windows on the right side of the yeshiva opened directly into the row of three outhouses behind the synagogue.

Indoor plumbing was not unheard of in the rest of the world, but in Chelm, the privy was the best and least expensive solution to the disposal of necessary, but unwanted, waste. Because of the vast depth of the holes, the physics of heat absorption and the heavy demands made on the three privies, the solids and liquids deposited there never froze during the winter.[26]

That first warm day, when Rabbi Kibbitz cut the paint and opened the windows on the right side of the yeshiva, the stench drifting in from the latrines drove him and his twenty students out of the schoolroom, gasping.

School was closed for a week, while everyone debated and argued and tried to chase down the general contractor, who had traveled from Pinsk to build the school. No one knew what to do. It was intolerable.

At last, Bulga the Fisherman spoke. "When I pull something stinky up from the sea," he said, "I throw it back over the side."

Reb Cantor, the merchant looked aghast. "You want us to pick up all that... stuff... and throw it somewhere else?"

"No," Bulga said.

"Good, because that wouldn't work."

"But sometimes the smell remains, so I turn my boat about. Then I sail away."

"You can't move three holes in the ground."

"No," Bulga said, "but we could turn the school house around."

The elegance of this solution was so profound, it struck the gathered elders silent. If the building was turned then the wind wouldn't blow in, classes could resume, and all the young boys would get back to their studies and out of their fathers' way.

At last, Reb Stein, the baker, raised what he thought was an obvious objection. "It's a building. It's attached to the synagogue. How are we going to move it?"

That was a stumper, until young Doodle, the village orphan, spoke up. "Passover's coming."

"Yes, Doodle," Rabbi Kibbitz said.

"Time to make the matzah!" Doodle said.

"Oy," Reb Stein said. "Don't remind me. Everybody always complains. 'Reb Stein, how come I can't get a rye bread the week

---

[26] Visitors from Smyrna joked that the villagers of Chelm had a special prayer they said every time they went to the outhouses during services: "Phew... Oy! Pheeeew!" You may laugh, but at the time it was no joke.

before Passover?' Because I've got to make the matzah. For the matzah to be kosher, I have to clean the whole bakery. I have to make these bland crackers in advance, otherwise nobody will have enough. Then they say, can't you just put a little salt in them, and I say no. Then, they want to have their challahs the day after Passover. It's impossible. Impossible."

"Wait a minute," Rabbi Kibbitz said. "That's it! Doodle, you're a genius."

Reb Stein glared. "You want to cover the windows with matzah? They're absorbent, but I can't promise that they'll keep smell out."

"No," Rabbi Kibbitz said, "But that's a good idea too. When we were slaves in Egypt, our ancestors built the cities of Pithom and Rameses.[27] They moved huge stones with nothing more than the strength of their backs. We are modern men. Are you telling me that we can't move a little school room?"

Nobody told the rabbi that they didn't have a clue how to move a little schoolroom, so naturally he thought they all agreed with him.

The next day, Reb Schlemiel, the carpenter, cut the side walls of the school away from the back of the synagogue building. All the benches and tables and books and shelves were carried out.

Then, every man and boy in the village gathered around the school. They bent down. They wedged their fingers under the edges.

Mrs. Chaipul, shaking her head with dismay, counted. "All right. One. Two. Three. Lift!"

And lift they did. Staggering under the weight, they backed slowly away from the holy house of worship.

"Careful," Mrs. Chaipul said. "Careful. Don't drop it. Now, everybody turn to the left."

It was a simple enough command, but what she neglected to remember was that roughly one-third of the men and boys were facing the other third across the building. Their left was the other

---

[27] Actually, the ancestors of the villagers of Chelm built the small stone post office outside of Pithom. Uncovered in 1845 by Prof. James Bakker, it is notable for the discovery of the world's first laundry list: "two dresses, one breechclout (remove stain), two robes, one shirt (no starch)."

side's right. The building refused to turn.

"Okay, so don't go left. Go right."

Again there was no turning.

"Oy, men," Mrs. Chaipul muttered. " I give up."

Now, you and I know that she was talking to herself trying to think up a way to communicate to the stubborn half of the species how to do what she wanted.

But, what the groaning and struggling males heard was, "Oy! Men... Give up."

And they dropped the building right there and then.

It settled with a loud thud, fortunately missing everybody's toes.

"It's not done," Mrs. Chaipul pointed out.

The windows of the yeshiva had not been moved away from the stench. In fact the building itself had only been shifted five feet away from the synagogue, and three feet closer to the outhouses.

"I don't care," Rabbi Kibbitz said, grabbing his back. "I'm done!"

"It's not going to work," she said.

"Maybe you should lift the yeshiva while I give the directions," the aching rabbi snapped.

"What about Succoth?" Doodle said.

Rabbi Kibbitz squinted at the boy. "You want us to cut a hole in the roof?"

"No," Doodle said. "But you could move the doors on the outhouses."

The rabbi put his hand on the young boy's shoulder. "You couldn't have come up with that idea yesterday?"

The next day, Reb Schlemiel got his tools, wrapped a towel around his head, and shifted the doors on all three outhouses. It took him a week to recover.

For a time, there was talk about shifting the school back to reattach it to the shul, but everyone was afraid they might miss and damage the synagogue, so it was left where it was. New walls were constructed.

The next year, the population of the school doubled. Everything got crowded, and when winter came, the villagers realized that the building wasn't heated.

A combination of body heat and a jury-rigged stove kept the students warm, and the arrival of Rabbi Yohon Abrahms kept Rabbi Kibbitz from quitting and moving to Miami, where he claimed to have relatives.

This was the school that Rachel Cohen was about to attend.

Chapter Twenty-One

School Girl (Part Three)

Mother and daughter were smiling and holding hands as they rounded the village square[28] and approached the synagogue. Sarah Cohen felt a wide grin stealing across her face. Rachel Cohen felt the same grin widening on hers. It was everything they could do to walk calmly, and even that pretense was abandoned as the two of them glanced at each other and began skipping around to the left of the small and ancient synagogue.

Across the square, Shoshana Cantor and her daughter Rivka watched with lips pursed into frowns of disapproval. The merchant's wife and eldest daughter shook their heads and clucked their tongues. "Silly," Shoshana muttered. "I hope she doesn't get hurt."

Rivka glanced at her mother. "They would hurt her?"

Shoshana shook her head. "Not physically. Probably." She tapped her head with her forefinger. "Here…" And she then patted her chest. "…and here. Men have no idea."

Neither did Rivka, and even though she knew Rachel Cohen was doing something silly and foolish, she still felt a pang of jealousy as she saw her head toward the yeshiva.

Just before they reached the door, Sarah gave a tug on her daughter's hand to stop her.

"Sweetheart," she said. "No matter what happens I am proud of you."

Rachel nodded. "Thank you, Mother."

"You have no idea how much this means to me."

"I think I do," Rachel answered. "For hundreds if not thousands of years, men have assumed that knowledge was their domain. It's

---

[28] In Chelm, you should know, the village square is actually round.

not fair, and it's not true. Women can be just as wise as men, if not wiser."

"How did you…" Sarah caught herself.

She had never talked with Rachel about the Council of Wise Women. She hadn't told her daughter about the cave and the secret meetings, about the warm discussions and rock-hard mandel bread.

Rachel had been the topic of much conversation. Many members were opposed to her attending the school, and if Chanah Chaipul hadn't been firmly in favor of the experiment, Sarah wasn't sure she could have resisted the powerful opinions against educating her daughter.

"It will just give her ideas," Shoshana Cantor had argued.

"She already has ideas!" Mrs. Chaipul had answered. "She needs to know what to do with them all."

"Do you really think that putting her in with a room full of boys will help? Or will it just give the boys ideas?"

Eleanor Stein, the baker's wife, had rolled her eyes. "If they're boys, then they have no ideas. If they're young men, they already do. Either way no one wins."

"Enough!" Sarah said, waving her hand.

"What?" Rachel asked. "Mother, are you all right?"

"I'm fine," Sarah said. "I just forgot where I was."

"You were about to let me go to school."

Sarah nodded. "Yes, I was." She bent down and kissed her daughter once on each cheek. "Learn a lot, and tell me everything."

Rachel nodded seriously. "I will, Mama. I will."

She waited a moment, until her mother had turned away, and headed back around the side of the synagogue. All alone, Rachel took a deep breath, put her hand on the knob, and pulled it open.

She had expected to see the entire class full of boys turning their heads and staring at her as she made her grand and confident entrance. She had planned on walking calmly down the aisle and taking a seat next to Adam Schlemiel.

Instead, she came face to face with a large white sheet and two signs. The one pointing to the left read, "Boys." The one pointing to the right read, "Girl."

If this was a reading test, it was an awfully simple one.

Rachel went right and followed the sheet around a corner and down a narrow aisle on the right side of the school building.

The sheet was hung from a rope and as she walked, she found that it overlapped another sheet, and then another. She could hear the whispers and rustles of the boys on the other side of the curtain.

It was a mechitzah, Rachel realized with a sigh.[29] She wasn't going to be a part of the school, she was going to be apart from the school. For a moment she thought about turning around and leaving, but that would be the same as giving up. It would be admitting that women weren't strong enough to study, which was exactly what Rabbi Abrahms and the boys suspected, expected, and perhaps hoped for.

She gnawed on her bottom lip and continued the long walk up the aisle to the lone desk that had been brought into the school so that she would not have to sit at the tables with the boys.

She arranged her dress and sat down. She could see part of the front of the room, part of the black board, and through the window next to her she could see the backs of all three of the synagogue's outhouses.

Rabbi Abrahms walked over, poked his head around the curtain and said, "Ah. Well. Rachel. Good of you to join us at last."

"Am I late?" Rachel asked. Her family was not wealthy enough to have a clock, like Reb Cantor.

"You're not early," Rabbi Abrahms said.

"How do you know?" Rachel asked. "Is there a clock?"

Rachel heard guffaws of laughter from the boys' side of the mechitzah.

Rabbi Abrahms frowned. His face became stern. It was hard enough taking back talk from the boys. Now he was supposed to take it from a girl?

"There is no clock," he said through clenched teeth. "Whoever is

---

[29] A *mechitzah* is a curtain in a synagogue to prevent virtuous men from being distracted by the beauty of women. In Chelm, they know that this is impossible, so they put the women in a balcony out of reach. Mrs. Chaipul isn't happy about it, but she knows when to pick her battles, and when to doze off during services.

last to arrive is last. Is late. And receives the consequences."

"And what are those?"

"To clean the erasers."

Just then, young Doodle stumbled up behind Rachel, and looked about confused. "Have you seen everybody else? I was trying to find my seat, but it seems to be gone. May I share your desk?"

"Doodle!" Rabbi Abrahms shouted.

Doodle jumped.

"You're late! You know what that means?"

Doodle grinned. "I get to clean the erasers."

"Yes!" shouted Rabbi Abrahms. "But first come around here and take your seat."

"Where would you like me to take it?" Doodle asked.

"Just get over here and sit down!"

Doodle winked at Rachel, took two steps, and then tripped. His hands flailed out, he grabbed onto the white curtains and as he fell, the entire wall of white sheets fell with him in a fluttering wave.

There was a gasp from the boys, as those who weren't buried in white cloth, looked across the room at Rachel Cohen. Embarrassed despite herself, Rachel felt her cheeks grow red.

"You did that on purpose!" the Rabbi said.

"It was an accident," Doodle answered.

"It took me three days to put those curtains up."

"Do you want to cancel classes for three days to put them back up?" Doodle asked.

"Yes!" shouted Abraham and Adam Schlemiel simultaneously jumping to their feet. "No school for three more days!"

All the boys cheered loudly.

"No!" barked Rabbi Abrahms. "Sit down. All of you. The curtain is down. It stays down. School is not canceled. We are going to do some writing practice. Take out your pens and begin to write what I tell you."

Rachel felt the blood rush away from her face. A pen. She had no pen. She had assumed that school was about reading and talking and discussing and answering questions. Why hadn't she realized that she was supposed to do writing as well?

What should she do? What could she do?

She raised her hand.

"What is it, young lady?" the Rabbi snapped.

"I don't have a pen."

"You are unprepared?" Rabbi Abrahms' face widened into a grin, as he pounced on the infraction. "Why that... What is that on your desk? Isn't that a pen?"

Rachel looked down and saw a chicken quill.

"Yes, it is," she answered. "But it wasn't there before."

"Do you think chickens grow on trees?" the rabbi asked.

"No," Rachel shook her head. "They come from eggs."

"Exactly!" Rabbi Abrahms said, raising his finger to the sky. "Chickens come from eggs!"

"Rabbi?" Doodle asked. "How do you spell chickens? Does it matter if there are two or three chickens? Are they hens or roosters?"

"What?" the Rabbi's head swiveled.

"I took the paper and ink out of my desk," Doodle said, "and I started writing everything down, just like you said. But I don't know how to spell chickens."

Rabbi Yohon Abrahms felt his ears burn with anger. He stood in front of Doodle's bench. "You don't have a desk."

"Oh," Doodle looked. "My mistake."

Rachel Cohen gasped quietly. She lifted the lid of her desk and looked. Inside was a new bottle of ink, a stack of blank white paper, a straight ruler, and a ripe red apple.

She took out the ink and the paper, and set it on her desk. Her eyes darted to Doodle, and she saw him wink again. Then Rabbi Abrahms collected four erasers, grabbed the poor boy by the ear, and pulled him down the aisle.

"If anyone says anything while I am gone, then I will have you writing the entire book of Numbers word for word! From memory!"

The schoolroom was dead quiet. A moment later Rachel heard the sound of erasers clapping together.

Rabbi Abrahms stormed back into the room, scanned the students, and said, "All right. Let's begin at the beginning. Who knows what I'm talking about?"

There was a giggle from the boys.

Rachel raised her hand.

"Yes. You."

"Genesis?" Rachel asked.

"Exactly!" Rabbi Abrahms said. "In the beginning…"

Chapter Twenty-Two

Swatches of Time

Sarah Cohen kept her head high as she turned away from her daughter and walked around the side of the Synagogue. She tossed a jaunty wave across the square to Shoshana and Rivka Cantor. They smiled and waggled their fingers back. She walked quickly and purposefully through the village, avoiding the narrow lane that would take her past her husband's tailor shop.

Chelm was a small village, and making your way home without stopping for a chat with a neighbor (and everyone was a neighbor) was almost unheard of, but Sarah made it safely to her house, through the front door, and shut it behind her without saying a word to anyone.

The house was quiet. Empty. Her children, both of her children, were in school. Her husband was at his shop. There was cooking to be done, and cleaning. But now it was so quiet.

As much as Sarah had wanted Rachel to go to school, to learn and grow... Now that her daughter was gone, she realized how much she was going to miss her. From the day Rachel had been born, they had never been apart for more than a brief time. Rachel was so sweet and kind and bright...

That was the problem, wasn't it? Her daughter was a genius, and it was impossible to keep her in the kitchen. Not impossible, perhaps, but certainly not a good idea. It would have been a waste. Look at how much she had done for the women of Chelm simply by being the first girl to go to the school. Yes, it was only her first day, but even that little crack in the door was enough to get a toe and then a foot and then... Who knew what would be next?

Sarah took a deep breath, and let it out. She poured herself a cup of tea from the still-warm pot, and sat down at the table. She took a sip. Quiet was good, wasn't it?

She folded her arms in front of her on the table, dropped her head on her forearms, and began to sob.

* * *

In his shop, Benjamin Cohen was whistling and humming a tune his father had taught him.

"Stitch it in, stitch it out. Never mind. Don't you shout."[30]

He had smiled with a mixture of pride and uncertainty when he saw Sarah walking Rachel past his shop to school. It was something unusual to have such a famous daughter. He hoped that it wouldn't cause trouble for his son, Yakov. Yakov was a good boy. His heart was in the right place. He was learning how to sew and cut and measure and to think like a tailor. But Yakov knew he wasn't as sharp as Rachel. Rachel was good at everything she set her mind to. If Rachel had wanted to become a tailor, she would have been one of the world's best. If Rachel wanted to be… anything, she probably could. But what good was that in a woman? Would it make her a happy and good wife? Probably not. Would it make her a better mother? Who knew? For untold generations, since the creation of the earth, it was Eve's job to be Adam's helper. Now Benjamin had a feeling that everything was going to change, and he wasn't sure that was such a great idea. Where would it leave a fellow like Yakov if his wife was smarter and better educated than him?

Benjamin looked up from the seam that he was closing. He had expected Sarah to walk past by now on her way back from taking Rachel to the yeshiva. He had hoped that she might stop into the shop, and perhaps they could sit and talk while he worked.

Probably though she had work of her own to do at the house, so he bent his head and applied his needle, and whistled and hummed the tune his father had taught him.

"Stitch it in, stitch it out. Never mind. Don't you shout."

---

[30] Actually, it was a poem in Yiddish about a goat and a beggar's boot. The author heard the poem recited to great laughter at a wedding by one of Reb Cantor's great grandchildren, and made the mistake of writing it down on a napkin that went through the wash.

* * *

Chanah Chaipul was pouring coffee into Reb Cantor's cup.

"There they go," the merchant said to the cobbler and the baker, as they watched the Cohen women skipping along. "Look at them."

"What do you think of the whole thing?" Reb Gold asked.

"I still don't like it," Reb Stein said. He made the sign against the evil eye.

"We all know Rachel is very bright," Reb Gold said. "But school? For a girl?"

"I'm glad to see people so happy," said Reb Cantor. "What harm can it do?"

"What harm?" Reb Stein shrugged. "My nephew, Muddle, went to school for years and he came out knowing less than when he began."

"This was the same Muddle who liked to drink tea by putting the leaves in his mouth and sipping hot water?"

Reb Stein looked at Reb Cantor, and nodded.[31]

"But Muddle was a student with Rabbi Kibbitz," Reb Gold pointed out. "The children have a new teacher now."

"I like Rabbi Abrahms," Reb Cantor laughed. "But what can that young man possibly teach them?"

Mrs. Chaipul coughed and cleared her throat. Gossip she didn't mind, but speaking ill of people so quickly after Yom Kippur seemed to be in particularly bad taste.

The three men glanced at her, shrugged sheepishly, and fell quiet.

At last Reb Stein spoke, "So, how about those floor mats I ordered for the bakery?"

"Yes!" said Reb Cantor, latching onto the lifeline. "I finally did get a big order of woven cloth mats from India. They have wonderful colors."

"What's the point of a pretty floor mat?" wondered Reb Gold. "It's just going to get muddy and dirty."

"Ahh," said Reb Cantor, raising his cup for a sip, "but the women who buy them for their houses love them, and they keep

---

[31] For Muddle's most famous adventure, see the story of "Muddled Challah."

the men from walking on them, so then they have to come back to my shop and buy another mat that isn't so nice! It's wonderful for business. SPLURT!"

Reb Cantor was so surprised when Mrs. Chaipul thwacked him on the back of his head that warm coffee spewed across the table into the faces of Reb Gold and Reb Stein.

"Oh, I'm sorry," she quickly said, passing dry napkins to the dripping men. "I thought I saw a mosquito about to bite you."

"It's all right," said Reb Gold. "Now I can tell my wife I don't need a bath this week."

"I'd better get back to my baking," Reb Stein said, leaving a coin for his bill. "The rye sour needs to be fed."

When the other two were gone, Reb Cantor looked at Mrs. Chaipul, who had poured herself a cup of coffee and sat down at the table with him.

"Are you all right?" he said.

"I'm fine. You?"

"Good. Good," Reb Cantor agreed amiably. "It's just that I know you took a keen interest in this school girl business."

Mrs. Chaipul shrugged. "It's not business, it's knowledge and learning."

"You know as well as I do, Mrs. Chaipul, that knowledge and learning can be good for business."

Mrs. Chaipul sipped thoughtfully. "Or it could be bad for business, especially if the women involved have enough knowledge and learning to figure out that when you sell them a pretty floor mat it's next to useless."

Reb Cantor shrugged. "I didn't say they had to use them on the floor. They can hang them on the walls. Or use them for a small blanket for a baby. They are lovely and well made. I don't sell schlock or dreck."

"That's true," Mrs. Chaipul admitted. "I am worried. I want for Rachel Cohen to succeed. But that is going to change the way things go around here. People don't like change, but it happens anyway. Sometimes when things change, they blame. And I don't want Rachel Cohen to take the blame."

"So, you're going to volunteer to be the scapegoat?" Reb Cantor suggested.

"I will if I have to," Mrs. Chaipul said. "Still, I would prefer it if nothing went wrong."

"In Chelm?" Reb Cantor snorted.

Mrs. Chaipul ignored him and continued, "And knowing that a smart and learned merchant like yourself is on the same side as a smart and unlearned little girl — well, that would mean quite a lot to me."

"Consider it done," Reb Cantor said.

He spat in his palm. Mrs. Chaipul raised an eyebrow, and then spat in hers. They shook hands. Mrs. Chaipul wiped her hand off, and then passed the napkin to Reb Cantor. "We really need to change that particular method of sealing a deal. It's not sanitary."

"I agree. One change at a time, though. Okay?"

"Done," Mrs. Chaipul nodded.

Reb Cantor cleared his throat and lifted his palm. Mrs. Chaipul grabbed his arm and said. "All right. All right. Enough's enough!"

They both laughed.

Reb Cantor patted her hand. "Yes, I agree. In the meantime, I think you can relax and stop worrying. This is Chelm. What could possibly go wrong?"

Chapter Twenty-Three

The Contest

Everyone thinks the people of Chelm are fools. No, don't deny it. They call them, "The wise men of Chelm," but that is with a wink, not respect. Especially in Smyrna, the village just to the north of Chelm, the townsfolk view their neighbors to the south with scorn and disdain.

"I heard that the rabbi of Chelm had a toothache," said the blacksmith of Smyrna. "He put a bandage on it!"

And then everyone laughed. Such is what passes for humor in Smyrna.

One day, however, Smyrna at last had the opportunity to prove once and for all how foolish Chelm really was.

The Czar was planning on building a new road, and he decided that it should run through the town that would use it most wisely.

So there was to be a contest between Chelm and Smyrna. Three questions were to be answered by the wisest men from both towns.

On the appointed day, groups from the two villages gathered in the courtroom before the regional magistrate.

"Have you chosen your representative?" said the magistrate to the delegation from Smyrna.

Rabbi Sarnoff, the eldest sage of Smyrna, stepped forward and nodded his head sagely.

"And Chelm?" asked the magistrate.

"Me!" squeaked a small voice. A little girl pushed to the front of the group.

"Who," said the magistrate with disdain, "are you?"

"Rachel Cohen," said the girl. She curtsied politely.

"This is your wisest man?" the magistrate asked.

"She's a girl," said Rabbi Sarnoff. "Obviously she is not a wise man."

"Not at all," said Rabbi Kibbitz, the chief rabbi of Chelm. "Rachel is the newest student in our yeshiva. The first girl! We didn't think it would be fair to the people of Smyrna to have them compete against our wisest."

A ripple of laughter washed through the room. Fools from Chelm! Even the magistrate smiled.

"Very well," said the magistrate. "We will ask three most important questions to each of you. Whoever answers best will have the honor of choosing where to build the road."

The magistrate turned to the young girl. "Who were the parents of all people?" He smiled, happy he had given her such an easy question to begin.

"I don't know," said Rachel.

"Child," said the eldest rabbi of Smyrna, "don't you remember Adam and Eve?"

"I meant to say," said Rachel, "I don't know their names. They were monkeys."

"Monkeys?" laughed the magistrate in surprise.

"Yes," nodded Rachel. "I read a book by a man named Charles Darwin, and he believes that people are descended from the apes…"

The rest of the girl's answer was drowned out in the laughter that filled the court. At last, the magistrate raised his hand.

"First round to Smyrna," said the magistrate. He turned to the rabbi. "This question has two parts. What is the smallest number?"

"One," answered the rabbi of Smyrna instantly.

The magistrate nodded. "That is correct."

"Wait," said Rachel Cohen. "Isn't one-half smaller than one? Isn't a quarter smaller than a half?"

"Ahh," said the magistrate, "but those are not numbers."

Rachel Cohen frowned, not sure she understood. The rabbi of Smyrna had studied mathematics once, and thought the girl might have a point, but he kept silent.

"And the largest number?" asked the magistrate.

Rachel Cohen thought for a moment and then said, "The

Almighty."

"Infinity," said the rabbi.

"But the Almighty contains everything," Rachel explained. "Therefore he contains all the numbers, including infinity."

"A basket may hold eggs," said the rabbi, "but would you say that the basket is the eggs?"

"Round two to Smyrna," said the magistrate. "The last question. You will write down your answers, and then I will read them aloud."

Everyone in the chamber fell silent while paper and pens were brought.

"Why," said the magistrate, his words slow to draw out the suspense of the moment, "are we here?"

The eldest rabbi of Smyrna began scribbling furiously.

Rachel Cohen thought for a moment, and then wrote down a few words. She folded her paper and handed it to the magistrate.

"Are you sure?" he asked her quietly.

The young girl nodded confidently.

Half an hour later, the rabbi from Smyrna was finally finished. He handed the magistrate a sheaf of paper.

The magistrate read both answers to himself, and then nodded thoughtfully.

"Read them aloud!" someone shouted.

The magistrate raised his palm and waited for the crowd to settle.

"The rabbi from Smyrna writes, "'We are here to live, love, laugh, eat, drink, walk, work, study, play music…' He goes on in this vein for seven pages, and then finishes with, 'But most importantly we are here to worship the Almighty.'"

A whisper of admiration rustled through the courtroom. The eldest rabbi from Smyrna nodded, obviously pleased with his answer.

"The young girl from Chelm takes a slightly different view," said the magistrate. "She writes, 'We are here to decide where the road should go.'"

Everyone laughed. In comparison to the wisdom of the eldest

rabbi, Rachel Cohen's answer seemed quite frivolous. How silly!

"But I'm right," Rachel said loud enough to quiet the room. "We are here to decide where the road should go!"

Holding his belly, which ached from laughter, the magistrate nodded in agreement. "Indeed, child. Indeed. It is most difficult to decide when faced with such brilliant opponents. Tell me, child, if you were to choose, where would you have the road go?"

"I think the road should go through Smyrna," said Rachel Cohen without a moment's hesitation.

The magistrate grinned. "And rabbi?"

"Through Smyrna," said the rabbi, quickly taking advantage of the child's obvious mistake.

"Then it is decided," said the magistrate, "the road will go through Smyrna."

In Smyrna that evening there was much rejoicing. Not only would the new road bring prosperity, but also the Smyrnans were now certain that the villagers of Chelm, entrusting their future to a child, were the most foolish on the planet.

In Chelm, however, the celebration was even more festive. The answers young Rachel Cohen had given were thoughtful and true, and the magistrate had obviously decided in her favor because the road was going to go through Smyrna.

"Tell us Rachel," Rabbi Kibbitz asked at last, "why did you choose for the road to be built through Smyrna?"

"That's easy," Rachel Cohen said, pleased that she'd been allowed to stay up past her bedtime. "Chelm is a small, quiet, and peaceful village. A new road would bring hundreds of travelers. Our village would become noisy and crowded, with strangers everywhere. We have everything we need now, and if we happen to need something else we can always go to Smyrna."

Everyone in Chelm cheered at the wisdom of her words.

The moral of the story: Wisdom or foolishness, it's all a matter of perspective.

Part Five

The Council

Chapter Twenty-Four

A Plague on Your Village

The way she told the story later, Bella Shimmel knew there was trouble the moment she set foot in Smyrna.

The streets were empty. There was no one about. Not a single man, woman, or child. Not even a dog running or a cat prowling.

However, the truth was that Bella didn't really notice right away.

She was taking a cart full of cow's milk and goat's cheese to the cheesemonger. Her ox, Sevastopol, named after her grandfather's birthplace, was a balky and fusty old creature. If the animal wasn't coddled, caressed, and occasionally jolted into action, he would stop and gnaw at every blade of grass on the road from Chelm. Even in the cobbled streets of Smyrna, Sevastopol would root and nibble around for the occasional dropped piece of fruit or vegetable.

Bella spent so much time prodding and cajoling Sevastopol back into motion, that she didn't really pay attention to her surroundings, so when she finally lifted the latch at the cheesemonger's shop, she was startled to find the door locked and bolted shut.

"Hallo?" Bella called. "Mr. Leider? Yoo hoo!"

She peered through the window and saw that the store was deserted. The shelves, normally stocked high with cheeses, were nearly bare.

Had he moved? Quit? Given up? Passed away? Bella hoped not. The Leiders had been good people to trade with. Reliable customers who purchased everything that the Shimmel Sisters' Dairy could deliver.

That hadn't always been true. Mr. Leider had once been a hard sell. Then again, everything had been difficult after their father died. When Mr. Leider learned that Papa had left his farm to his daughters, the cheesemonger told them that he was reluctant to do business with women.

"One of you should get married. Then I will talk with your husband," Mr. Leider had said to the three sisters when they had shown up at his door with their first delivery following Papa's burial. He had shrugged at Bertha, Bella, and Peninah. "I'm sorry."

If any one of the three sisters had been alone, she might have turned around and gone home, milk unsold, and cheese unbought.

But together, the Shimmel girls gave each other courage enough to stay, if only for a moment.

Bella had asked if the milk or cheese tasted any different.

"No," Mr. Leider assured them, "it is still just as tasty."

Peninah had asked him if the demand for their cheese or milk had diminished.

"Not in the least," Mr. Leider said. "Your dairy is still magnificent. People were asking about your goat cheese when I told them that your father had passed on."

So, Bertha had asked, hands on her hips, what was the problem?

Mr. Leider had shrugged. "No man, no money. It's not my idea," he explained. "It's just the way things are in business. You don't talk with men about childbirth and we don't talk with women about money."

Bertha had pointed out that the sisters had been making all the deliveries for nearly eight years. Mr. Leider hadn't dealt with Papa in all that time, and probably wouldn't have even known that Papa had passed on, if they hadn't first told him. Furthermore, from what they understood it was only after their father stopped making the cheese himself, about ten years ago when Bertha took over that job, that Mr. Leider decided that the Shimmel dairy goat cheese was tasty, solid, and good enough to sell in the shop.

Bertha's tone grew angry, "Papa always said that you…"

Bella kicked Bertha, who yelped, "Ow!" and glared at her sister.

"In other words," blurted Peninah, "our Papa was a poor farmer and a bad cheesemaker. The only reason you like our cheese and our milk is because we've been in charge for so long!"

"Ahh, but the business relationship," Mr. Leider explained, "was with the man. You girls may own the cows. You may own the milk and the cheese. You do not, however, own the business. That is the way of the world. My wife, she runs the house. Me, I run the business. We don't interfere in each other's domains."

It was a defining moment for the Shimmel Sisters' Dairy Farm.

The three sisters had been feeding and milking the animals, and making cheeses since they were little. Their mother had died when Peninah was born, so, except when they were out on deliveries, the girls had spent most of their time on the farm on the outskirts of Chelm.

The Shimmel sisters had traveled through the world, but truly hadn't dealt with it very much.

In Chelm, nobody thought anything about the sisters' role in running their father's farm. And no one had said anything about them not owning the land, animals, or the business after he was gone. But nobody talked with them about it either.

Instead, the Chelmener had gossiped. Bertha, at twenty-nine, was well and truly an old maid. Bella, the pretty one, was nineteen, unmarried at the time, and a risk to every man who walked passed her.[32] And young Peninah lived alone only with two older sisters to care for her. Why hadn't their father arranged for marriages? It wasn't natural.

When Papa's mourning shiva was over, visitors to the farm dwindled.

Bertha, Bella, and Peninah went about their chores feeling quite isolated, not sure what to do.

Then, one day, Mrs. Chaipul wandered out to the farm, and over a cup of tea had reminded them that they had missed their regularly scheduled delivery of milk and butter to her restaurant for the days when she wasn't serving meat.

As soon as the villagers saw that Mrs. Chaipul approved of the Shimmels, everything went back to normal.

---

[32] Men in those days were not known for virtuous thoughts and self-control. Several years later, the villagers had been relieved when Avi Weiss married Bella Shimmel. But for some reason they all forgot about Avi, and only referred to the three Shimmel sisters.

But outside of Chelm, it seemed that being a man still counted for more than being a good cheesemaker.

"Excuse us for a moment," Bella had said to Mr. Leider.

"Take your time," the cheesemonger said. He took a clean towel and began polishing and rotating his cheeses.

The girls gathered just out of his earshot, conferred for a moment, and then came to an agreement. They knew that crying had always worked wonders on their father, so they decided to try it on the unsuspecting cheesemonger.

"You're still here?" Mr. Leider said as they caught his attention. "What can I do for you?"

Young Peninah sniffled. Bella allowed her lower lip to purse in and out, in and out. Even Bertha found her right eye twitching.

"Are you all right?" Mr. Leider said. "Is there some kind of mold in the air?"

Then as one, all three Shimmel Sisters burst into tears. It was as if a dam had burst and the floodwaters flowed. The three women bawled and howled like infants. They sniffled and snuffled, leaking droplets from their eyes like a particularly runny cheese on a hot summer's day

"What? What? Was it something I said?" The poor cheesemonger was frantic.

Bertha, pretending to cry with both hands over her face, peeked through her fingers at Mr. Leider's wide-eyed terror. She almost laughed, but turned the sound into a sob, like a goat with a sore on its lip.

Bella was a better actress. Gasping between torrents of tears, Bella told Mr. Leider that without his order, no one else in Smyrna would buy from them, that their milk would go sour, their cheeses would get moldy and rot, and they would starve to death. But that wasn't the worst part, because without their care, all the animals on the farm would grow skinny and then sickly and then die from neglect.

It was too much for the poor Smyrnan. He threw his hands up in the air. "Enough!" he cried. "Stop. Stop. I'll buy the cheese."

"But is our cheese good enough to buy?" Peninah asked, still bawling.

"Yes, of course. It's the best cheese I sell."

"And the milk?" Bella gasped. "Isn't it fresh and tasty?"

"Like no milk anyone else brings to me," Mr. Leider assured her. "I tell my customers all the time that I don't know how you girls do it all with your father so sick... I mean while he was still alive."

"So," Bella asked, "you'd be willing to pay a premium price for it?"

"Yes, yes, of course! I will pay you double what I've been paying you and consider it a bargain, just please stop crying."

And as if their reservoirs had suddenly gone dry, all three sisters ceased their weeping, spat into their palms and held their hands out to be shaken.

Mr. Leider knew when he was beaten. He shook hands with each of them, and then muttered to himself, "This is why you shouldn't do business with women!"

"I miss papa too," said young Peninah softly, wiping the tears from her cheek.

Since then, the Leiders had bought every drop of milk and every wheel of cheese, and the Shimmel Sisters had provided the finest, best-tasting, and freshest dairy to all of Smyrna.

However, to make sure that they didn't renegotiate, Mr. Leider made the request that only one sister at a time visit his shop for deliveries.

Bella knocked again at the door. "Hello? Mr. Leider? Mrs. Leider? Are you all right?"

There was no sign on the door, no notice in the window, and no sound from the house. It was very strange.

That was the moment Bella noticed that the streets of Smyrna were completely empty and that the only other creature in sight was her ox, Sevastopol, who was nibbling on a bit of thistle growing from a crack in a wall.

It was one of the eeriest sensations she had ever experienced. Bella didn't know what to do. She couldn't go back to Chelm, her milk would sour...

She hammered on the door.

An upstairs window shot open.

"Go away!" came a voice.

"Mr. Leider?" Bella asked.

"Go away!"

Bella could just see the tip of Mr. Leider's long skinny nose peeking out through the open window. "Mr. Leider. It's Bella Shimmel. Is everything all right?"

"No, we're sick." There were sounds of coughing.

"Who's sick? Can I get you something?"

"Everyone is sick."

"Your wife is sick as well?" Bella said. "I'm so sorry. Perhaps I could get you some soup…"

"No," the old man stammered. "Everyone in Smyrna is sick! Go away. Go away!"

The window slammed.

Bella's eyes widened. Everyone in Smyrna was sick?

The street was quiet and empty.

"Come, Sevastopol," Bella clucked her tongue at the ox. "We'd better go."

Chapter Twenty-Five

The Cold

"They have a cold?" Shoshana Cantor asked. It was difficult for her to keep the sarcasm from her voice. "They all have a cold? The entire town has a cold?"

Sarah Cohen shrugged her shoulders. "Bella Shimmel was almost hysterical, and you know how high strung she can be."

The Shimmel sisters were famous for the extremes of their behavior. Beautiful Bella was prone to hysterics, and though she was finally married, you really didn't want her lingering around your husband. Bertha was solid with a face like a rock. And eleven-year-old Peninah, everyone still thought of as the baby. All of which is a long way to say that, if Bella was upset, it was nearly impossible to say whether it was because a problem was big or inconsequential.

"But a cold?" Shoshana Cantor repeated. She had her feet up on an embroidered ottoman footstool.

The women were gathered together in the Council cave. A small fire was burning beneath the chimney hole. Outside the first snow of the year was beginning to flurry down. Inside, it was warm and cozy.

"When my husband has a cold, I have to do all my work and all his work," said Eleanor Stein. "I have to prepare all the dough, fire up the ovens, shape the loaves, wait around for them to rise."

"Okay, okay," Hannah Meier interrupted. "We've all baked bread. You don't have to give us all the details."

"One loaf, two loaves you've baked," Eleanor Stein said. "But not two hundred."

"Two hundred loaves?" Shoshana Cantor began calculating the price of the baked bread in comparison to the cost of the flour she knew her husband provided the Stein's.

"Sometimes more, sometimes less," Eleanor said. "It depends on the day."

"A day?" Shoshana was surprised. There were only about eighty families in Chelm. How much bread could anyone eat? "So, you sell bread to the people of Smyrna?"

"Naturally," Eleanor said. "Whenever I go to the market for my shopping, I take a cartload to the Gossanger's Grocery. They buy the bread from me and sell it to the Smyrnans."

"Really?" Shoshana leaned forward as she sipped her tea. "How much do you get wholesale?"

"Enough!" Chanah Chaipul said, waving her hands to dispel the foul spirits. "No business. Let the men talk about money and trade. We are here to figure out what to do for the people of Smyrna."

Deborah Shikker looked thoughtful. "We could send them handkerchiefs."

"Why would we send them handkerchiefs?" Rebecca Schlemiel asked.

"So they can blow their noses," Deborah said.

"We could sell them the handkerchiefs," said Shoshana.

"Enough with the business," Chanah said. "This is about a mission of mercy, not a mission to make money."

"There's no reason not to combine them both," Shoshana said glumly.

"What else?" Chanah asked.

Sarah raised her hand.

"What are you doing?" Hannah Meier asked.

Sarah glanced at the mikveh attendant. "I'm raising my hand."

"I can see that," Hannah said. "Why are you raising your hand?"

"My daughter says that Rabbi Abrahms has the children raise their hands when they want to be called on. She says he does it to maintain order."

Eleanor snorted a bit of tea out her nose. "Are you crazy? Order? Here?"

All the other women were giggling. The idea of raising your hand before butting in was patently absurd.

"Sweetheart," Hannah said, putting a gentle finger on Sarah's wrist, "talking in the Council Chambers is a bit like making a stew. If you've got an idea, throw it into the pot. We'll stir it around for a while, let it cook, let it simmer, let it blend. Then, when all the ingredients are tender, we'll serve the stew."

"You're making me hungry!" Shoshana said.

Hannah rolled her eyes. "You're always hungry."

"All right," Sarah said, gathering her courage. "All right. What are the men doing?"

"What do you mean?" Chanah asked.

"What do our husbands want to do? My husband says it's not our problem. He says that he has enough to do here in Chelm without worrying about Smyrna."

"My husband says the same thing," Deborah agreed.

"Isaac thinks we should quarantine the whole town," Shoshana said. "He'll send his wagons around, instead of through."

Chanah leapt to her feet. "Wait a moment here. What are you all doing?"

"Talking," Deborah said.

"Reaching for a piece of mandel bread," Shoshana said guiltily.

"No. This is not about the men," Chanah said. "This is about the women. What do we want to do? The men of Chelm are useless."

There was a moment of quiet and general agreement on this subject.

"I wouldn't want to get rid of them, though," Hannah said. "Not all the time anyway."

"That's not the point," Chanah said. "The point is that in these circumstances, the men are not helping."

"It's just a cold!" Shoshana said. "Give them a week of rest and they'll all be back on their feet."

"No," Chanah said. "Maybe it's just a cold, or maybe it's influenza."

There were a few gasps, and then Sarah asked, "What's influenza?"

"It's a cold," Shoshana said.

"That you can die from," Chanah said. "It spreads like crazy. Everybody gets sick. They can't eat. They can't drink. And what they can eat and drink they can't keep down or can't keep in."

"No need to get all detailed in your descriptions," Chaya Levitsky said. "Some of us would like to eat mandel bread without feeling nauseous."

Chanah waived her hand. "Believe me, I haven't even begun to get into revolting descriptions. I've treated the influenza. It spreads like crazy. I've seen the bedsores and smelled the..."

"Are you trying to make me sick to my stomach?" Chaya said. Now that Oma was gone, her daughter-in-law had taken up the role of the crotchety Levitsky.

"No," Chanah said, apologetically. "I'm just trying to explain that if we don't do something then people in Smyrna could die. Men, women, and children."

The Council fell silent.

At last Eleanor said, "Look, I know we're not supposed to talk about the men right now, but my husband says that the reason we shouldn't do anything is because of the danger of contagion. If we try to help, we could all get sick."

There were some nods and grumbled agreements.

Then Chanah spoke. "What kind of a world do you want to live in? One where we are all safe, but our neighbors are all dead? We have to help each other; otherwise we are no better than the animals. And even animals will help a sick friend."

Again there were nods and grumbled agreements.

"If my mother-in-law were alive," Chaya said, "we could send them some soup."

Once again there were nods and grumbled agreements.

"Yes!" Sarah put up her hand, realized what she'd done, pulled it down, and blurted. "The Soup! We'll make them The Soup."

"Look, Sarah," Chanah said. "Chicken soup is a wonderful thing, and I think we should consider it, but Oma is long dead. May she rest in peace."

Oma's soup had been almost magical. Everyone knew it. Everyone agreed.

Everyone echoed, "May she rest in peace."

"My daughter has been making The Soup," Sarah said.

"Your daughter," Shoshana said. "Your daughter this. Your daughter that. Your daughter is going to school. Your daughter is conferring with the governor. Your daughter is making The Soup. Enough with your daughter."

The cave got very quiet, except for the crackling of the fire.

At last, Sarah said, very slowly and through gritted teeth, "Rachel has been making The Soup since Oma passed away."

"It's not the same soup," Shoshana said, dismissively.

"Of course it's not," Sarah shot back. "It's her soup now."

"Oh, so now she's a soup maker as well as a genius! Has she found a husband yet?"

"She's not even ten years old!"

"ENOUGH OF THIS!" Chanah shouted. Heads jerked around. "Sarah, has Rachel really been keeping Oma's Soup alive?"

"I think so," Sarah said. "She stirs it every day. She tends it, talking to it like it's young child. And sometimes when she thinks I'm not looking, she kisses it."

"Your crazy daughter is in love with some soup," Shoshana said. "No wonder she doesn't have a husband."

Sarah jumped up. "At least my crazy daughter's got a brain."

"Don't you insult my daughters?"

"Will you two stop!" Hannah said. "Fight about your families later. We have to save Smyrna. So far we've got two ideas. Send them handkerchiefs and send them soup. What else?"

Deborah raised her hand tentatively.

"What already?" Hannah said. "Stop with the raising of hands."

"Tuck them into beds?" Deborah whispered. "Kiss their foreheads. Read them stories."

"Okay," Hannah said. "Now we're up to five ideas. Let's keep going..."

Chapter Twenty-Six

The Chicken Soup Bucket Brigade

It was the first chicken soup bucket brigade in the history of the world. Every villager from Chelm, man, woman, and child helped out.[33]

A long sparse line snaked from the kitchen of the Cohen house, through the village square, between East and West Hills, and up the Smyrna road, through the Schvartzvald to a square in the center of Smyrna. Here, the buckets of soup were emptied into a kettle set over a fire, supervised by Mrs. Chaipul to warm up, and then dispatched to every home in Smyrna in bowls covered with new clean handkerchiefs. Then, the bucket was sent back to Chelm, where it paused by the well, was refilled with water, and returned to Oma Levitsky's magical Soup pot.

The process was complicated, the work was hard, and the challenge was great. No one had to schlep anything very far, but it wasn't as simple and quick as passing water to put out a fire.[34] You had to collect your bucket from the person behind you, and walk it carefully without spilling up to the next person up the chain. Then, if you were lucky, the empty bucket was ready and waiting to be returned to Chelm. If not, you had to hustle back for the next load on its way to Smyrna.

Fortunately, Rabbi Kibbitz had abandoned all his objections to

---

[33] With the exception of a few infants, who were strapped in slings to their mother's backs.[*]

[*] Oh, and Tante Kanfer, who upon realizing that she had inherited the position as the oldest Chelmener from Oma Levitsky, had taken to her bed and hadn't risen since…

[34] Schlep. To carry. To lug. To move a burden. Usually accompanied by a certain amount of kvetching.

the project when Mrs. Chaipul had explained that she was perfectly willing to shut down her restaurant and leave Chelm forever if he didn't agree to help out. Once the Rabbi conceded, he convinced the rest of the elders, which is to say the rest of the prominent men in the village, that it was in their best interest to help as well.

He conferred with Rabbi Yohon Abrahms, and they developed a quick and easy method for kashering the milk buckets from the Shimmel farm.[35]

Reb Cantor hitched his horses and wagon and began riding through the countryside collecting chickens and onions and garlic and mushrooms and anything else he could find for The Soup's pot.

While the Chelm contingent was getting organized, Mrs. Chaipul took the first buckets to Smyrna.

Reb Shikker, the accountant (and town drunk) insisted that he come with her, and once her improvised kitchen for reheating the soup (because you can't give a sick person cold soup) was established in the grand plaza in the middle of Smyrna, she learned his reason.

Some of the residents of Smyrna had locked their doors before they had gone to bed, and Reb Shikker, as it turned out, was a natural-born locksmith. He unlocked the doors, and opened them for Mrs. Chaipul to carry in the warm broth.

When they had a moment to catch their breaths, Reb Shikker confided to Mrs. Chaipul that, long ago, he had been a thief. He had broken into houses in fine cities like Minsk and Smolensk, and taken anything and everything he could carry. Then, when he had met his wife, he had given up the life of crime, and since devoted himself to paying back all the people from whom he had stolen. Mrs. Chaipul listened to his story somberly, and told him that if he had repaid the money then he had surely fulfilled his obligation, because without his skills many families in Smyrna would have had homes with broken doors or windows.

From dawn until dusk and all through the night the buckets

---

[35] Kasher - to make a pot or utensil that isn't kosher, kosher. Usually, this can be quite an involved process, but whatever Rabbi Abrahms did was efficient, and nobody asked about it.

were passed from man to man to woman to child to woman and so on, up and down the road between Smyrna and Chelm. Fortunately the moon was full, or else no one would have dared to venture into the Black Forest after dark. As it was, in the middle of the night, the children were sent home and the schleps for the adults got longer and longer.

For her part, Rachel Cohen kept adding ingredients and stirring The Soup in Oma's pot. Every time some well-meaning woman offered her advice, Rachel did her best to smile and consider, but shooed the helpful lady out of the house before following the recipe for The Soup that Oma had taught her.

Three hours before dawn, when her mother came in with a bucket full of water and a sack of freshly chopped leeks, she found Rachel standing over the pot fast asleep.

"You have to go to bed Rachel," Sarah said.

"I can't, Mamma. I'm the only one who knows how to make The Soup."

"Won't the pot take care of itself?"

"I don't know, Mamma. I'll be fine. If Yakov can stay awake, then so can I."

"Yakov went to bed an hour ago. Oma Levitsky's soup was so strong and powerful that it can rest for a moment or two while you rest."

"I'm fine, Mamma. I have to be. After all, I have to taste The Soup, so I should be healthy enough."

"At least have some bread," Sarah insisted.

Rachel agreed, but when her mother picked up the next full bucket and brought it outside to pass to her husband, who would then pass it up the chain, she set the crust down and began to sob.

Rachel knew the truth: the soup in the pot was not Oma Levitsky's Soup. Not anymore. Some time after the first ten buckets had been sent to Smyrna, Rachel had looked into the pot and realized that she had scooped out the last drop and that the pot had boiled itself dry.

"Where is that water?!" she shrieked, and was relieved that Adam Schlemiel had arrived at that moment with the first bucket on its way back.

"It's right here," he said. Fortunately, he had already filled the bucket with water.

"Get me more!" Rachel yelled as she snatched it out of Adam's hands. Then she ran inside and dumped the bucket into the pot where it hissed and quickly started to boil. "Get me more water!"

The poor boy shook his head at the rudeness, but raced to his task.

Soon the pot was full to the top with boiling water and fresh ingredients. Rachel was stirring and blowing and tasting and kissing the broth.

The soup was delicious. It was warm. It was thick.

But it wasn't Oma Levitsky's Soup.

After that, Rachel was more careful. She made sure that the cauldron was never emptied. She sent Adam back and forth to the well twice for every bucket that went out. She kept Reb Cantor busy filling her order for meat and bones and vegetables.

The buckets kept moving from Chelm to Smyrna and back. The bowls of soup were hurried from Mrs. Chaipul's reheating to the sick townsfolk.

Rachel was terrified that it was all a waste of effort. She was petrified that because of her inattention, because of her mistake, the people of Smyrna would not get well. She didn't dare tell anyone, though. If they knew, they would hate her. They would say that she had lied on purpose. They would say that she was just trying to show off. That was what Gittel Cantor always said. Rachel didn't mean to be smart or be the one that Oma entrusted with The Soup and The Soup's pot... And the fact that the pot had gone dry was proof enough that she shouldn't have been trusted. Keep soup in the pot. That, if nothing else, was the main point that Oma had emphasized, that the pot should never be empty. The Soup was like a sourdough starter that had been passed down from generation to generation. Until Rachel Cohen had lost her focus and now... Who knew?

Rachel stared into the pot. It was getting low again.

She left her post long enough to rush to the door. "More water!"

she shouted. "More chickens!"

Adam Schlemiel was standing there, right outside her door as she yelled in his face. "The well is empty," he said. "There is no more water."

"What?" Rachel yelped.

Reb Cantor was standing beside Adam. "There are no more chickens either."

"What?" Rachel gasped.

"No chickens in the whole village," the merchant said. "No onions, mushrooms, or garlic. No carrots. We've used everything."

"But The Soup," Rachel said. "There's only a bucketful left!"

"We'll send it to Smyrna," said Reb Cantor. "We'll bring water back from Smyrna. And chickens. And everything else."

"That will take too long," Rachel wailed. "The pot will be dry. It can't be empty. Oma told me!"

Rachel burst into tears and collapsed on the ground.

"Go get her mother," Reb Cantor ordered.

Adam Schlemiel took off like a shot.

Huffing and grunting Reb Cantor bent down, picked up the sobbing youngster and brought her back into the house. By the time he had crossed the threshold, the ten year-old girl was asleep in his arms. He set her on her bed, and tucked her in.

On his way back out of the house he peered into the pot. There wasn't much left. He gave it a stir and sighed.

Sarah Cohen and Doodle burst into the house.

"Where is she?" Sarah said.

Reb Cantor nodded his head toward Rachel's bedroom. Her mother rushed off to her daughter's side.

"I guess I have to go to Smyrna now," Reb Cantor grumbled.

"No," Doodle told him. "It's done. Every house in Smyrna has gotten soup. The villagers are on their way back home."

"Really?" Reb Cantor's face brightened. "Did it work?"

"I don't know." Doodle shrugged. "Mrs. Chaipul and some of the other ladies are staying in Smyrna to check up on people."

"We did our best, didn't we Doodle?" The poor merchant was himself exhausted. He had been rushing about without stopping for food or drink.

"Yes we did," Doodle said. "Go home. I'll stir The Soup."

Reb Cantor handed the young boy the spoon and tottered off to his rest.

After a time, Sarah Cohen passed through the kitchen and patted Doodle on the shoulder. She greeted her husband as he returned home.

For twenty-four hours the villagers of Chelm slept, except for one.

Doodle stood at his post, stirring the dregs of The Soup and adding water as needed. When he heard a noise from Rachel's room, he stopped long enough to fill a small bowl with broth, which he brought in to her room and set beside her bed.

A short time later, Rachel emerged. Her face was shining and her eyes were bright.

"I didn't hear the rooster," she said.

Doodle shrugged. "All the chickens are dead."

"Did you make that soup?" she asked. "It was pretty good."

"No." Doodle shook his head. "I just stirred it. It's your soup."

"Yes," Rachel agreed. "It's my soup. Have you heard anything from Smyrna?"

Again the boy shook his head. "No. Nothing."

Rachel peered into the pot. "Can you see if there's more water in the well?"

"Of course," Doodle agreed.

He returned shortly with a full bucket. Rachel was so pleased that she gave him a kiss on the cheek. She was resolved that the pot would never boil dry again.

By late in the afternoon, word finally arrived back from Smyrna.

It was good news! The townsfolk were recovering. Their fevers had broken. They were eating and moving about. Many were out of bed already. The ones who weren't were expected to do fine.

Only two people had died, ancient Rabbi Sarnoff and Mrs. Leider, the wife of the cheesemonger.

In a town the size of Smyrna, with an epidemic of influenza that virulent, only two deaths was, in Mrs. Chaipul's estimation, a miracle.

The sad news, however, hit Rachel hard. She had met Rabbi Sarnoff, and had respected his wisdom and kindness. She insisted on traveling with Mrs. Chaipul to Smyrna for the funeral.

As they walked along, Rachel told Mrs. Chaipul how the pot had been emptied and that the soup she had served wasn't really Oma Levitsky's. She said through her tears that it was her fault that Rabbi Sarnoff and Mrs. Leider had died.

"Nonsense," Mrs. Chaipul snorted. "Sarnoff was old and poor Agnes Leider was always sickly. It was their time. Because of you, everyone else lived."

Rachel tried hard to believe her, but wasn't sure.

"One thing you should know," Mrs. Chaipul warned. "The Smyrnans don't remember what happened. All they know is that one day they were sick and a few days later they were better. They don't remember us coming and feeding them. They are wondering about all the new handkerchiefs, but they are calling that a miracle."

"Didn't you tell them the truth?" Rachel asked.

Mrs. Chaipul shook her head. "No. Why should I?"

"To get the credit?" Rachel said.

"There is no credit for taking care of your neighbor. Besides, if I had told them, they would have just laughed in disbelief. They think that we Chelmener are idiots. It would drive them crazy to believe that we had anything to do with their recovery. Better to let them think that the handkerchiefs came from heaven."

Rachel considered this for a moment. "They think that we Chelmener are fools, but that Smyrna's sneezes have a divine blessing?"

Mrs. Chaipul smiled. "What can I say, child? People are people. When you look around Smyrna, I want you to take notice of all of the people that you and your soup kept alive."

"I didn't do it by myself," Rachel insisted.

"No," Mrs. Chaipul said. "And that you tell me so just now lets me know you are going to be just fine."

She took the young girl's hand, and together they made their way to the great synagogue in Smyrna to pay their last respects to the famous Rabbi Sarnoff.

Part Six

The Village

Chapter Twenty-Seven

An Icy Wind

At first, the knocking at Rabbi Abrahms' door seemed far away, like the tapping of a woodpecker deep in the forest. Then it grew closer, like the furious hammering of a carpenter trying to finish building a box before sunset. Finally, it came closer still, like the vicious pounding of the Czar's secret police on the door to his very own house. It was as if they were standing right outside!

Rabbi Abrahms sat up in bed with a start. His heart was racing from the terrible dream. It took him another moment to realize that the pounding hadn't stopped when he'd woken up. Someone was at the door. Someone wanted him. It was dawn. That was when they always came.

He looked around the small one-roomed house he lived in. It wasn't very cozy. There were no hangings on the walls or rugs on the dirt floor. But he had a stove to make tea and porridge, a chest of clothes, a shelf of books, and a table that doubled as a writing desk. It wasn't much, but it was his. He would miss it in prison.

Sighing, he pulled on his pants and shirt before he got out from under the warm covers. He stomped his feet into his boots, and grabbed his long coat from his chair.

"All right! All right! I'm coming."

Whoever was thumping couldn't hear. Rabbi Abrahms wondered whether they would take him away, or just shoot him where he stood. He considered diving out the window at the back of the house, but if they were going to arrest him, there would be a guard there, and he had never been much for physical heroics. Better to die well than die like a klutz.[36]

---

[36] A klutz is a bumbler, someone who, if they found a diamond in the road, would run to sell it, trip, and drop it in the river. In Chelm, there are many klutzes.

At last he yanked open the door, and nearly got hit in the face by Reb Cantor.

"Yow!" Rabbi Abrahms said, dodging the blow.

"Oh. You're awake," said the fat man, huffing and puffing from the effort.

"Who died?" Rabbi Abrahms asked. It was what you always said when someone woke you for no good reason. He hoped it wasn't Rabbi Kibbitz.

After Rabbi Sarnoff died, Rabbi Abrahms had applied for the job of Senior Rabbi in Smyrna. If Rabbi Kibbitz too passed on, then the young school teacher would become the only rabbi for two towns. That would be too much at once.

"Who died?" said Reb Cantor with a moan. "My business."

"You won't tell me?"

"My business!" cried the merchant.

Rabbi Abrahms scratched his head. "Listen, I know it's none of my business, but when you knock on my door to tell me someone died then it becomes my business too. Don't you think?"

"My business!" yelped Reb Cantor. "My business has died!"

Finally it dawned on the young rabbi that the merchant really was talking about his business, and not a person.

"I'll get my hat," he said. "Let's go for a walk."

* * *

It was a cold day for a walk. The sun was barely peeking above the horizon. The leaves had all fallen from the trees, and the wind blew fiercely out of the Black Forest. The ground was frozen. The Uherka River was a solid block of ice.

Rabbi Yohon Abrahms the schoolteacher and Reb Isaac Cantor the merchant huffed and puffed their way up to the top of East Hill, barely able to catch their breaths[37].

When at last they stood on the summit, they paused and marveled at the sudden warmth from the bright red sun on their faces. They closed their eyes and willed themselves to absorb the

---

[37] Remember there are only two hills in Chelm? The road from Smyrna runs between them. East Hill is sometimes called Sunrise, while West Hill is also known as Sunset.

sunlight, hoping that they might be able to store it somehow, like a quick harvest of new potatoes.

Still with his eyes closed, the junior rabbi of Chelm spoke. "So, what's the problem that was so urgent you had to terrify me out of bed in the dead of night?"

"No one is buying Chanukah presents this year," the merchant said. "They are saving all their money for food and clothing and firewood."

Rabbi Abrahms nodded. "It is a difficult time. People are worried."

While Chelm had never been a wealthy community, rarely had its larder been so empty. The villagers had given every single chicken they owned and much of their stored vegetables to make The Soup that had saved the town of Smyrna. That the Smyrnans had neither noticed, nor repaid the Chelmener's compassion was not an issue. A gift given freely does not expect a return. But without chickens or eggs, onions and carrots, food was scarce and the villagers were frightened.

"Yes, of course they're worried," Reb Cantor agreed. "I'm worried too. I have a warehouse of tchotchkes that I've been collecting to sell for Hanukkah.[38] It's become almost a third of my business, and no one in Chelm is buying anything."

"What about Smyrna?"

Reb Cantor shook his head. "They're still recovering from the influenza."

"All right," Rabbi Abrahms shrugged. "So this year you don't sell your stuff. It's not all perishable, is it? It will keep in your warehouse. Next year, when we have new chickens and new carrots, we'll buy new presents."

The merchant shook his head. "There is no such thing as next year."

This comment took the young rabbi of Chelm by surprise. "Is the end of the world coming already? I haven't even washed my dishes!"

---

[38] A tchotchke is a gewgaw, a bauble, maybe a little nicer than a piece of dreck, so you could give it as a gift, but why would anyone want to keep it?

"No, you don't understand. If I don't sell my stock this year, then I won't have any money to buy things for next year, and my business dies."

"So what if you don't buy things for next year? Hold them in your warehouse, and you will be able to sell it next year, won't you?"

"Oy." Reb Cantor dropped his head to his chest in frustration. "So it is clear that you don't understand about fashion. People don't want to buy last year's shmattas, even if they're brand new."[39]

"They'll buy them if they're old?"

"Of course! Thrifty people buy used things all the time."

"So, again, what's the problem?" said Rabbi Abrahms. "Pretend that these things in your warehouse are used."

"But they're not used. They look new. People can tell! If they see me selling something new but I say it's used, they'll think something's wrong and they won't buy."

"You're making my head hurt," the poor young rabbi said.

"Mine too!" said Reb Cantor. "Forget about fashion for a moment. I'll make it simple. If people don't buy my stock now, I won't have any extra money. I won't be able to eat breakfast at Mrs. Chaipul's restaurant. I won't buy a new pair of shoes from Reb Gold. I won't be able to afford the new dresses for each of my daughters, for which the tailor has already bought the cloth. And I won't be able to contribute my usual amount to the yeshiva, which means that the school teacher will have to take a cut in pay."

"Why didn't you say so?" Rabbi Abrahms blinked. "What are we going to do?"

"That's what I've been trying to ask you. I don't know!"

At that moment the sun went behind a cloud and both men felt chilled to their marrows.

They quickly turned around and were quiet as they walked back down the hill toward the village.

Times had been good in Chelm. Over the past few years the village had grown accustomed to the merchant's wealth. His free

---

[39] A shmatta is a rag. Why would anyone want to buy a new rag? Because the old one is worn out. Sometimes a rag man is someone who collects old rags to resell. Sometimes a rag man is someone in the clothing business...

spending and generous contributions had become dependable and expected. The villagers had grown lazy and comfortable, and if there was one thing they should have remembered, it was that when you became complacent, disaster was just around the corner. Better to be hungry and work hard, than full and relaxed. Even while they had spent their energy and food rescuing the Smyrnans, the villagers of Chelm had been secretly glad that at least the calamity wasn't happening to them. They were wrong. They had fallen asleep, and now there was a sudden hammering at the door!

At Rabbi Abrahms' house they both rushed to the stove to warm their hands.

"You could have a sale," Rabbi Abrahms suggested.

"Everything is already on sale!"

"A bigger discount?"

"But no one is buying!" the older man sputtered.

"Then give it away," said the younger man. He reached for a log, opened the stove, and threw it in.

Reb Cantor stared at his friend. "Are you insane? I paid good money for all that nonsense. I have dried figs from Turkey. I have silk from China. I have fourteen beautiful chess sets from Morocco. I have cotton underpants from America! How can I give that away?"

"You call those things tchotchkes? What do you call the good stuff?"

"Expensive."

"You could give them a way quietly, one item at a time." Rabbi Abrahms spoke carefully, because he really could use a new pair of cotton underpants, but that wasn't his reason. "What good is it all sitting in your warehouse? If you don't think that you can sell it this year, then give it away and you will be repaid in good will."

"Feh." The merchant opened the door to the stove and spat inside. "I can't feed my family with good will. That's magical thinking. It won't work. My job in this community is to bring things in and take things out. I've got lots of things here, but nothing is going out. We barely have enough to survive as it is! If the Governor's tax collector, may he rot, decides to visit our village this winter, we will be destitute! The flow of money is like the flow of water over a mill wheel. As long as it keeps moving, the wheel turns. When the water freezes, the mill stops, and no one gets any more flour. Do you get it?"

Rabbi Abrahms was used to Talmudic arguments with Rabbi Kibbitz, but never had he heard such wisdom from the merchant. "I understand. At least we will all starve together."

"You know, Yohon," the merchant said, "that is small comfort to me. Skinny people like you are used to being hungry. As a fat man, whenever I miss a meal I already think I'm starving. The idea of really starving does not particularly appeal. This whole conversation is making me hungry. What's this?"

Reb Cantor was looking through a pile of papers on the rabbi's table.

"It's nothing. The Smyrnans wanted me to write something about what it has been like to live in Chelm."

Reb Cantor chuckled over the page he was reading. "Did we really do this?"

Rabbi Abrahms looked over his shoulder. "Nail the moon into a rain barrel? Yes. Rabbi Kibbitz told me that his father tried."

Reb Cantor flipped a page. "Oh, I remember this. That time we hired those poor fellows from Smyrna to carry us through the snow. The looks on their faces were priceless."

Rabbi Abrahms shrugged. "I had a cold that day."

"You write well. These stories are pretty funny."

"Not to the Smyrnans," sighed the young man. "As I recall, the fellow who carried you hurt his back so badly that Mrs. Chaipul had to walk on it to fix him."

"I bet I could sell these stories," said the merchant thoughtfully. "Put a few drawings in. Print a thousand copies or so. Offer the book with different bindings... Will you sell this manuscript to me?"

"I thought you didn't have any money."

"I'll pay you in warm underwear," said the merchant. "In advance. Then, when the book sells, you'll get some royalties."

"You're going to marry me off to a princess?" Rabbi Abrahms said.

"What? No. A royalty is a payment to the author on the sale of a book to a publisher. I'll be the publisher and sell the book. You'll get the royalty."

"That's good, because I don't know that I want to marry a princess." the rabbi laughed. "You think this will solve all our problems? Why would anyone buy a tale of Chelm?"

Now the merchant grinned. "People like to laugh. And if there's one thing I've learned in my life it is that people love to feel superior. The Smyrnans already think they're better than us. When your book comes out, they will gladly pay good money to be certain that it is true!"

Rabbi Abrahms looked doubtful. "Can I still use the manuscript for my job interview?"

"Of course!" the merchant said. "Publishing takes time. You'll have the job long before this book comes out next year."

"Yes, but what happens if it doesn't work?" Rabbi Abrahms asked. "I thought you said there was no next year."

"That was before," Reb Cantor smiled. "When you know nothing but fear, there is no future. As soon as we have an idea, the entire world becomes possible. Whether it works or not, we'll find out later."

"Do you still have those warm red long johns from America?" Rabbi Abrahms asked. "I want five pairs."

"It's a deal!" said the delighted merchant.

Chapter Twenty-Eight

Cabbaged

"The Winter of the Cabbage" was how they referred to it years later. Someone would wonder when a certain event occurred and the answer would come, "Oh, that was during The Winter of the Cabbage." For a moment they would savor this thought as if it was a fond and nostalgic memory, and then both the listener and the teller would queasily shudder.

They called it The Winter of the Cabbage because that was all they had to eat. There were no potatoes, no carrots, no beans, no turnips. There were no parsnips, no rutabagas, no sweet potatoes, and no dried beans. There was cabbage and only cabbage and plenty of cabbage. It had been a bumper cabbage harvest that year. Reb Cantor the merchant had an entire warehouse filled with cabbage that he had been planning to export to Miami, but, because all the other winter vegetables were ingredients that had been used in The Soup to heal Smyrna, the only thing left for the Chelmener to eat were the cabbages.

So they ate cabbage.

They had cabbage for breakfast, cabbage for lunch, and cabbage for dinner. They ate it baked, boiled, fried, rolled, and stuffed. What did they stuff it with? They stuffed it with cabbage.

Reb Stein, the baker, devised a way to dry cabbage out, turn it into a fine powder, and bake it into a flat bread he called "kroit krackers." Nobody much liked it, but with enough butter or schmaltz they claimed it tasted at least as good as stale matzah on the last day of Passover.[40]

The children were miserable. For that matter, the adults were

---

[40] Not that they had much butter or schmaltz. But you could dream…

miserable too. Reb Cantor offered a prize of fifty cabbages for the first person who could make a decent tasting cabbage cake for dessert but there was no winner, only many many many failures.

Esther Gold devised a way to make cabbage pops that looked like lollipops. They were round, translucent, stuck on a stick, and came in many different colors. But they still tasted like, you guessed it, cabbage.

Reb Shikker devised a cabbage vodka that was both potent and brutal. If you drank too much, your head felt like it was (yes, yes) a cabbage. Fortunately, it was difficult to choke down more than a sip or two.

In her restaurant, Mrs. Chaipul served cabbage sandwiches, cabbage tea, cabbage coffee, and cabbage soup with cabbage dumplings and cabbage balls.

The villagers of Chelm ate Cabbage until it was coming out of their ears.[41]

When Rabbi Abrahms traveled to Smyrna for his fifth interview for the position of chief rabbi, the synagogue elders sniffed as he walked into the room.

"Do you smell cabbage?" sniffed Reb Zalman, the fishmonger.

Rabbi Abrahms shuddered and answered them truthfully. "I couldn't smell a cabbage right now if you stuffed one up my nose."

It was a strange answer, but it must have been the right one because they offered him the position for a trial period of six months. Much to their surprise, he asked for his first month's salary to be paid in advance in potatoes. After a brief backslapping and handshaking celebration with the selection committee, Rabbi Abrams immediately drove his wages back to Chelm.

When the load of potatoes arrived in Chelm it caused quite a stir. As word spread, the villagers dropped everything they were doing and ran to the round square.

"What's going on?" said Mrs. Meier, who was shortsighted and getting hard of hearing.

"Rabbi Abrahms is riding on a donkey cart with a heap of potatoes," said Shoshana Cantor. She started to drool. "A pile of

---

[41] … and everywhere else.

potatoes. A hill of potatoes. A mountain of potatoes!"

Everyone in Chelm stood in the square, salivating so much that the frozen ground began to grow slippery from the ice.

"Friends!" shouted Rabbi Abrahms standing on the cart. "I've got good news and I've got bad news! Which do you want to hear first?"

Then, as now, such a question presents an impossible dilemma. If you hear the good news first, then you know all that follows is downhill. On the other hand, if you hear the bad news first you may be so heartbroken that the good news makes no difference.

"You choose!" shouted young Doodle.

"I am going to have to leave Chelm!" said the Rabbi sadly.

"So, what's the bad news?" heckled Adam Schlemiel, who had never really gotten along with the schoolteacher.

Rabbi Abrahms scowled. "That was the bad news. As of tomorrow I am officially the Temporary Interim Acting Provisional Short-Term Tentative Chief Rabbi of Smyrna!"

"That's wonderful news!" said Rabbi Kibbitz.

"Well, it is subject to review and confirmation following a six months probationary period, of course," said the young rabbi modestly. "But thanks to your help and training I think I can safely hope that I will manage to convince them that it should be permanent. Probably. Of course I'll have to stop teaching at the yeshiva…"

"That's wonderful news!" shouted Adam Schlemiel.

"That's horrible news!" moaned Rabbi Kibbitz, who realized he would have to go back to teaching.

"Look," said Mrs. Meier crossly, "are you going to tell us the rest of the news or not?"

"Oh," said the younger rabbi. "I brought potatoes."

This, everyone cheered.

"How many?" Reb Cantor shouted.

"Enough so that everybody in Chelm can have one and a half!" Again everyone cheered.

Except Rachel Cohen, who gasped.

Now, if you've ever been in a crowd where all are rejoicing save one, you know that the smallest sigh can reverberate and resonate until it overwhelms the most joyous outburst.

"That's horrible," said Rachel, her voice little more than a whisper.

Her brother nudged her. "What's wrong?" Yakov said. "Do you have cabbage sickness?"

Cabbage sickness was something that nearly everyone in Chelm had experienced at one point or another throughout the long winter. Its symptoms were headaches, nausea, dizziness, and flaking skin. Unfortunately, Mrs. Chaipul had learned the hard way that the only cure for cabbage sickness was more cabbage.

"No," Rachel said, trying to keep her voice down and the panic from her lips. "One and a half potatoes aren't enough."

"Not enough?" Her kind brother sighed. "All right," he said. "I'll give you some of mine."

By now everyone in the square was watching and listening to them argue.

"That's not the point," Rachel said. "Spring is still months away. There won't be any more new food until after the first harvest. After we eat our potatoes we'll have to go back to eating cabbage."

"So?" Yakov asked. "What's the difference? Cabbage is disgusting."

The villagers muttered their agreement.

"Cabbage is revolting!" Adam Schlemiel added.

There was a cheer.

"It's putrid!" his brother Abraham agreed.

Another cheer.

"If I have to eat another cabbage I think I'll explode!" shouted Doodle with glee.

There was much applause and back slapping.

"That's my point!" Rachel yelled. "You see? If we eat those potatoes then we won't want to eat any more cabbage!"

"Again, so?" said Yakov. He turned and addressed his friends and family. "Who wants to eat more cabbage?"

If it wasn't in the middle of winter it would have been so quiet that you could have heard the crickets chirruping.

"You see?" Yakov said. "We're all tired of cabbage."

"Yes," Rachel agreed. "And so am I. But after we're done with the potatoes, what will be left?"

"Cabbage!" said Doodle with more excitement than he meant. (Truth was that despite his complaints, Doodle still liked eating cabbage. He had learned, however, to keep this fact to himself.)

"Exactly," said Rachel. "The cabbage isn't so bad now because that's all we have to eat."

"It's pretty bad now!" heckled Abraham Schlemiel.

Rachel ignored him and continued, "But after we eat the potatoes... I don't think it will be easy to go back to cabbage."

"I don't care!" Reb Shikker moaned. "I'll take my chances. I'll eat my potato and a half and then starve!"

"No, no," said Rabbi Kibbitz, "she's right."

And with that, everyone in Chelm knew the potatoes were not on the menu.

There was a general gasp of despair from the crowd. Rabbi Abrahms tried to apologize, but his voice was drowned out in the sudden outpouring of sorrow. Children began to cry. Women tore their hair. Grown men began to wail.

"Good news and bad news," Adam Schlemiel muttered. "More like great news and horrible news."

The potatoes were returned to Smyrna, where Rabbi Abrahms donated them to feed the poor.

And in Chelm, the next day, they had a rather sad feast to celebrate the junior Rabbi's departure: cold cabbage soup, cabbage latkes, cabbage brisket with sautéed cabbage, and seventeen kinds of coleslaw and sauerkraut.

Rabbi Kibbitz, who had thoroughly enjoyed his retirement from the teaching of youngsters, broke down in the middle of his farewell speech and leapt at the throat of his friend shouting, "How can you do this to me?"

No one realized how strong the old man was until they had to pry his fingers off Rabbi Abrahms' neck.

They finally calmed him down by pouring him an extra-large shot of Reb Shikker's cabbage vodka.

Rabbi Kibbitz shuddered, and then passed out cold.

The evening wound down quickly after that, and everybody went home.

On her way out of the social hall, Gittel Cantor turned to Rachel Cohen, and hissed, "You glomp! This is all your fault."

Rachel paled at the insult. A glomp, she knew, was the worthless stump of… a cabbage.

Chapter Twenty-Nine

Kvetchfest

Everyone in Chelm was miserable and crabby. It was cold. The snow that had fallen just after Chanukah had turned to ice. Food was still scarce, and the menu was limited. The brief promise of potatoes and the pungent reality of cabbage had turned everyone grumpy.

But even worse, the departure of Rabbi Yohon Abrahms was felt in ways no one had imagined.

Chelm is the sort of place that gets into your bones and is impossible to escape. If you're born in Chelm, you stay in Chelm, you live in Chelm, and you die in Chelm. The young folk especially feel this rootedness as a heavy burden. Ambition in a Chelmener is rare. While many dream of Moscow, Vienna, and Pittsburgh, few of these fantasies last beyond bar mitzvah age.

If you, by some chance or misfortune, move to Chelm, the pull is if anything even stronger. After all, Chelm has everything a person could ever need — food, shelter, and companionship. The people are warm and kind. The food is – when not exclusively cabbage – delicious, and the small houses are well built and cozy.

Now, visitors and travelers might look at the collection of eighty or so houses and shrug. They might look at the tiny Bug River and roll their eyes. They might observe the plain clothing and calloused fingers of the residents and smile at the obviously rural but primitive quaintness.

"There was nothing there," they would say with a laugh as they reported back to their friends. "There was no majesty, no grandeur. There was no zest of human experience. There was no art."

Such arrogance. Such dismissiveness. Such a mistake.

Because in Chelm there is majesty, grandeur, zest, and art in its fullest, richest, and most ephemeral expression — the complaint.

Kvetching, you might argue, is nothing more than grumbling or whining. It is little more than an animal's moan of discomfort. Feh. This may be true of the ordinary everyday griping that goes on in your home or community.

Not in Chelm.

In Chelm, kvetching is food. It is drink. It is sun, it is water, it is blood.

And the annual Kvetchfest is the single most important gathering outside of the holy days. Weddings and births are celebrated with joy, bar mitzvahs with pride, and deaths with mourning.

Kvetchfest is celebrated with both dread and glee.

Twenty-eight days after the Winter Solstice, the doors to the social hall are flung wide, and the villagers file in. Then the doors are shut, and no one is allowed to leave until all who wish have spoken their minds.

The rules are simple. One person, one complaint, no pauses. As long as you keep talking, you can gripe, and everybody has to listen.

A judge and three referees are appointed to arbitrate whether a long breath is a pause in the kvetch or just a necessary gasp for air.

Every man, woman, and child is entitled to complain about whatever they like with neither consequences nor punishment.

Awards are given for any number of categories including brevity, length, vehemence, most expressive, loudest, softest, most mundane, most elegant, most superficial, and of course, best kvetch of the year.

Votes are rarely needed for best kvetch, because every year some individual shines above and beyond the ordinary mumble and grumble. One person is declared King or Queen Kvetch. They are given a worthless gold-painted wooden crown that is both uncomfortable and too heavy, and for the next year they are entitled to speak their minds freely about any subject, at any time, without fear of repercussions.

(Interestingly enough, it is rare for any individual to win the kvetching contest more than once in their lifetime. It seems that receiving a year's license to vent and spew is less of a privilege than an onerous burden. By autumn, the King or Queen has completely exhausted his or her bile, and they often abstain from competition for several years. The one exception to this had been Oma Levitsky, who was blessed (or some might say cursed) to wear the crown of Queen Kvetch seven times.[42]

At Kvetchfest, children complain about homework. They raise a stink about their brothers and sisters, cousins, and even parents. They snivel and moan about tight shoes, foods they can't stand and yet are forced to eat, and especially about early bedtimes.

Adolescents and teens usually take a different approach. They often spend weeks writing and rewriting, honing and practicing their bellyaching, hoping to turn their whining into the golden freedom to say whatever they like.

By the time Chelmener are adults, they very rarely prepare. Most of the greatest kvetches are impromptu, inspired by and fired with the emotions of the moment.

It isn't easy to win. Standards are high.

Many a runner-up has been applauded for their twitchy fussing about their burning need to visit the privy. Physical ailments are always popular but rarely unique enough to score high. Circumstantial mishaps make good fodder for secondary awards, but broken furniture or faulty wagon wheels must be more than temporary inconveniences.

A true winner must take complaining to a higher level that includes the physical, mental, and spiritual.

Everyone remembers the year Shoshana Cantor declaimed in no uncertain terms that not only had her merchant husband neglected his home and family, but the inconsiderate schmendrick had simultaneously brought her both fattening chocolate and a dress that was too small. Worst of all, she had added, masterfully bridging the pause that everyone expected to be the end of her entry, the dress had obviously been used — you could see the sweat stains

---

[42] Bulga the Fisherman came in a distant second with three lifetime wins, most of which harped on all the time he had to spend outside of Chelm in order to make his living.

and smell the stink of its previous owner — and even worse, the chocolate was infested with disgusting bugs, so she couldn't even eat it![43]

Shortly after she moved to Chelm, Mrs. Chaipul entered the contest and was declared the clear victor with her brief, honest, and heartfelt statement, "My husband is dead, my restaurant has no customers, my children don't care, and I have not a single friend among you."

The cheers the surprised woman received completely wiped the sorrow from her heart. She realized that she had found herself in a community full of friends, and she tried to decline the honor.

You didn't always have to be articulate to win. Once, Reb Kanfer, the potato farmer, had simply held up a spud that was so obviously disgusting and deformed that his victory was assured.

The Winter of the Cabbage was expected to produce the greatest and most competitive Kvetchfest ever.

It was not a disappointment.

* * *

The weather was miserable. It was both unseasonably warm for late winter and raining, which meant that the snow on the ground was melting, turning to slush, and then freezing back into slick slabs of ice. Every so often it would pour, then sleet, then hail. For a few minutes, as if taunting and teasing, the sun would come out promising the warm glow of spring to come, and then quickly dart behind a black curtain of clouds for a frigid downpour.

In other words, it was a perfect day for Kvetchfest.

Shortly after yet another breakfast of boiled cabbage and cabbage pancakes, the villagers sloshed and slogged their way through the streets to the synagogue's social hall.

They gathered, shivering and shoving, in front of the wood stove, huddling together for warmth until the stench of wet wool blended with the never-ending stink of cabbage shvitz.[44] A cloud of

---

[43] Reb Cantor, for his part, took the hint, made his journeys shorter, and always brought his wife both a selection of pristine gowns in the correct size and a variety of well-preserved desserts, some of which were less fattening than others.

[44] Shvitz: to sweat. Often profusely. In big cities, some people actually pay money

steam floated up to the ceiling, and everything in the room looked a bit hazy.

At last, Reb Cantor, who was acting as chief judge, banged his gavel, which one of the Schlemiel twins had doctored. The head of the mallet flew up and struck the merchant in the forehead.

"FLERSHUGEN!"

The loud curse drew silence and then cheers from the villagers. Mrs. Chaipul checked for bleeding, and Reb Schlemiel brought out the spare gavel.[45]

"All right already!" Reb Cantor bellowed. "Let the kvetching begin."

And, as was traditional, everyone started yelling at once, until once again Reb Cantor was forced to pound on the table, although this time he made sure to lean away from the hammer. "One at a time! One at a time!"

Eventually the referees decided on the rules of order. Sometimes the referees opted for a line, which usually provoked a number of complaints because of confusion and cutting. Sometimes they drew lots or went alphabetically. This time they went with numbers.

Rabbi Kibbitz had already prepared a huge deck of numbered cards. He shuffled, cut, and began handing them out.

"Come on, come on!" demanded the crowd.

"Four hundred and twelve?" someone toward the back wailed. "I didn't know there were that many people in Chelm!"

Reb Shikker elbowed Mrs. Chaipul. They were both acting as the other two referees. "There aren't that many people in Chelm," he whispered. "The rabbi didn't pass out the cards in order. Watch what happens when Reb Cantor starts..."

Finally the cards were distributed, and Reb Cantor stood.

"Number one? Who has number one?" He looked around the room. "Number one?"

Reb Shikker, Rabbi Kibbitz, and Mrs. Chaipul giggled softly.

---

to go into a hot room and shvitz.

[45] This sort of trick happens annually, and usually whoever is the chief judge knows enough to duck when he hammers, but this time the poor merchant forgot.

"Come on, come on! Who is number one? You don't want to go? Number two? Number two. What is the matter with you people?"

By now the referees were all chuckling.

"Three?" the merchant shouted. "Four? Five? Ten? Twenty? Fifty?"

"Hey," came a shout from the middle of the hall, "You skipped me! I'm number forty-three!"

All three referees were rolling on the floor as Mrs. Meier, the balanit ha mikveh, made her way to the front of the room to lodge the first official kvetch of the evening.

At last she stood in front of the chief judge and the referees, who were gradually regaining their composure.

"So?" Reb Cantor said.

Mrs. Meier glared at him. "Aren't you going to ask me what's new?"

"Can't we just get started!" the Merchant demanded.

"You have to ask me what's new!" she hissed back.

"Fine," he said, slamming the gavel, which snapped in two, nearly spearing him in the cheek. "What's new?"

"What's new?" Mrs. Meier inhaled deeply and then gave the traditional opening reply. "Nothing's new. You should ask me what's old. And I'll tell you what's old. At the mikveh, everybody who comes out of the bath drops their towels onto the floor and leaves them there. They don't hang them up! They don't put them away! I'm an old woman and bending down to pick up every single towel and washcloth not only hurts my back and my knees, but it makes me crazy! What, do I look like your mother? Pick up your towels!"

Mrs. Meier paused for a breath, and then smiled. "I'm done."

The room erupted in crazy cheers and applause. The two hundred and forty-fifth (more or less) annual Kvetchfest had begun.

One after another the men, women, and children of Chelm made their ways to the front of the room to litany their woes and out their bursts.

Old men complained of failing eyesight, falling out hair, aching joints, painful kidney stones, and hemorrhoids.

Old women complained about too much cooking, too much

cleaning, bunions, warts, thinning hair, hot flashes, and always being taken for granted.

Young men complained that the girls acted as if they didn't exist. The young women complained that the young men only had one thing on their minds.

Children complained that their parents expected too much of them. Parents complained that their children were lazy and had no idea how difficult life had been when they were children themselves.

Cabbage, of course, was a major source of inspiration — its smell, flavor, and effects on the intestines were bemoaned again and again.

Doodle was an early favorite for best kvetch with his florid description of how disgusting the texture of over-boiled cabbage was. "It reminds me of the rotting skin of a dead chicken after it's been partially chewed by a fox and then regurgitated."[46]

Reb Cantor, when it was his turn, surprised everyone by not complaining.

"I'm sorry," he said with a shrug. "It's been a good year. My family is well. The problems with my business are being resolved. Everyone is in good health. And I actually don't mind cabbage."

There was a moment of silence and then the booing and hissing began, quickly rising to a deafening roar.

Reb Cantor grabbed the broken gavel and hammered on the table.

"What kind of a village is this?" he screamed, "where a man can't be content and happy?"

The referees looked at each other, nodded, and agreed that even though it wasn't much of a complaint, it would do.

* * *

Interestingly enough, the Cohen family all had numbers in a row.

Reb Cohen rose first. "My wife doesn't appreciate me. My scissors are always dull. The light in my shop is too dim, and it's difficult for me to thread my needles."

---

[46] Again, Doodle didn't mention that he actually liked this taste…

Sarah Cohen went next. Her eyes were red with anger. "My husband doesn't realize how much I appreciate him. I spend all day at home by myself because my daughter is in school, my son is in the shop, my husband is in the shop, and we don't have any more children. I cook and I clean and I do laundry and then I cook and I clean some more. Do I get a kind word? No. Do I get any affection? No! I get whining and complaining and kvetching not like this little stream of feh that he gives to you. No, I get the full-blown description of how my cooking isn't as good as his mother's and my hair isn't so nice, and why don't I take better care of myself? By the way, how come his favorite shirt isn't cleaned better? There was a stain on the back toward the bottom that didn't come out. And really, really, he thinks I should smile more? But what do I have to smile about? To work and work and work and work until I die?"

Sarah stopped abruptly. Usually the complaints at Kvetchfest are general, and rarely are they as violently heartfelt as the list she had just uttered.

She looked at her husband, who was smiling. He was egging her on!

Honestly, Benjamin believed Sarah had a good chance of winning, but if she stopped now, he wasn't so sure.

Sarah realized that Benjamin thought it was all an act; that he hadn't heard a word she'd said. She burst into tears and, grabbing her coat, ran from the room.

That was a good finish! Benjamin rose to his feet and heartily applauded his wife. Reluctantly, the rest of the villagers joined in the ovation.

Then it was Yakov Cohen's turn. He smiled and waved.

"You're not going to like this," he said.

"Is that your complaint," Reb Cantor asked.

"No, just a warning." Yakov took a deep breath. "The people of Chelm dress like peasants. And yes, I know that mostly we are peasants. But we don't have to look like everything we wear is made from a potato sack. And yes, much of the clothes that we wear are made by my father from potato sacks. But there is such a thing as dye. Not every coat has to be black or brown. Not every shirt white.

You can wear other colors. Red. Orange. Purple. Blue. Green. Imagine! And you can wear different colors at the same time. A black coat and a white shirt. Boring. A black coat and a pink shirt! Amazing. A black dress? Another black dress! No. A blue dress. And a red hat! Maybe a scarf. Maybe a small piece of jewelry."

Again there was a moment of nervous silence as the villagers looked around the room and realized that indeed all of the clothing they were wearing was black and brown (and a little white).

"You're not supposed to advertise," said Reb Cantor.

"I'm not advertising," said Yakov. "I am complaining! Just because we're peasants doesn't mean we have to dress like dirt!"

Then, Yakov unbuttoned his tasteful black overcoat and revealed a spectacular lime green vest, a royal purple shirt, and a cardinal red tie.

Almost blinded, Reb Cantor staggered back, and fell off the dais.

After the applause died down, Rachel Cohen made her way to the front of the room.

"So, what's new?" Reb Cantor asked. He was getting tired.

"What's new?" Rachel answered. "This is not new. Everyone thinks I am smart. That I am smart enough to go to school."

Mrs. Chaipul shifted uncomfortably in her chair. "Is that a complaint?"

"Not at all," Rachel said, softly. "I like school."

Rabbi Kibbitz cleared his throat. "Rachel, do you need a few minutes to think your complaint through? We can come back to you."

"No! I'm just getting warmed up." Rachel's usually smiling face curved into a frown. She pointed out at the villagers. "You all think that I'm smart and your daughters are dumb. You think that I am the smartest girl in Chelm so that I should go to school, but that all the rest of the girls aren't bright enough, so that they shouldn't. All the girls in Chelm think that I'm too smart to talk to. All the boys think that I'm too smart to talk with…"

"Hey!" Doodle muttered, "I don't."

"…so nobody talks to me. Nobody wants to be my friend. And the saddest part is that your daughters are not all stupid and your sons are not all bright. Everyone in this village deserves an education. But because I made some trouble, I'm getting one, and because they didn't, the rest of the girls aren't. And they all hate and resent me for it. So what does it matter how smart I am or how much I work or how much I know if nobody likes me?"

Then, like her mother, Rachel burst into tears and ran from the room.

Again Benjamin Cohen jumped to his feet and began clapping and cheering. Again the villagers reluctantly joined him.

Kvetchfest continued for another three hours.

In the end, Peninah Shimmel was declared the winner for her complaint that her mother was dead, her father was dead; her sister Bella had escaped the farm by running away to Moscow, getting married, and dragging her husband back to Chelm; but Peninah was still stuck mucking out the goat pens with her other sister, Bertha, who was a grumpy old maid who only loved making stinky cheese. Not only that, Peninah hated everything about goats and milk and especially cheese, which was how she spent every single waking moment of her life!

Bertha was called upon to recite the traditional words, "Not that you need a license to kvetch, but…" and then drop the heavy, ugly crown on Peninah's head with a thud.

The young Queen of Kvetch burst into tears that blended joy and pain.

All in all, it had been an exhausting day, and everyone went home feeling worn out but refreshed, as if they'd been run through a wringer and hung out to dry.

By the next morning, the temperature had dropped. The rain had stopped. The sun came out. And the ground was frozen into a shimmering landscape of ice.

Chapter Thirty

Loud Discussions and Quiet Whispers

During the week following Kvetchfest, there were two topics of conversation racing through the village of Chelm. One was heated and contentious. The other was whispered, bewildered, and sad.

In house after house, home after home, parents and children, mostly the girls, were arguing over whether or not girls — all girls — should go to school.

It may be difficult in our society, where the education of women is taken so much for granted, to imagine the commotion that this debate caused in the village of Chelm. It was a complete overthrowing of the ancient order.

Most of the women in Chelm knew how to read. In fact, many of them could read and write and speak in several languages. They read prayers and wrote letters. But after that, in the realm of wider knowledge of the world, or deeper knowledge of Talmud, they were not only ignorant, but ignored.

"School is for men. It's a man's place," grumbled Reb Stein, the baker, as he ate his breakfast at Mrs. Chaipul's restaurant. "The yeshiva should be for concentration and learning and discussion and exploration without distraction and frivolity. I knew that letting that girl in was a mistake."

"I completely agree," echoed Reb Gold, the cobbler, waving about a piece of rye toast. "The lessons we received from Rabbi Kibbitz were wonderful. They informed my very being. They provided me with enlightenment and understanding."

"For example?" asked Mrs. Chaipul, who had been standing behind the counter, drying the same plate for more than fifteen minutes.

"I'm sorry, what?" Reb Gold said. The men were all so used to

Mrs. Chaipul's listening in on their conversations that they had forgotten she was there. Nevertheless it seemed unseemly for her to interfere in this particular discussion.

"What did he teach you?" she demanded. "What did you learn?"

The thin cobbler stared into her eyes, which were dark brown and furious. He looked away. He swirled the coffee in his cup.

"What about you?" she said, turning toward the baker. "Did he teach you anything? Anything at all that you can remember?"

"Yes!" declared Reb Stein. "The Rabbi taught me that a man's place in the home was as the leader. That a woman's role is to serve her husband."

As soon as he realized what he had just said to Mrs. Chaipul, the baker shied away physically. She was probably the most independent, stubborn, and pig headed woman that any of them had ever met. Then he gathered his courage and leaned back in, as if challenging her to dispute him.

She smiled and poured more coffee into his cup. "Is that why your wife comes in every month to pay your bill?"

"Exactly!" exclaimed Reb Stein. "I give her the money so that she can take care of me."

Reb Gold was snickering, and Mrs. Chaipul thought about a devastating fact she knew about his family situation, but decided that betraying a trust and demolishing the man in front of his friend was more than was necessary.

Reb Cantor, who had just come into the restaurant and was still in the process of removing his coat moaned, "Now my youngest daughter wants to go to school."

"Of course she does!" Mrs. Chaipul said. "And of course she should. Gittel is a brilliant girl, and should be encouraged."

"She could find a husband and get married," said the merchant, taking his place beside his friends.

"Can she get married without a husband?" joked Reb Stein.

"She can't get married and still go to school?" Mrs. Chaipul said. She set a mug in front of the fat merchant, but held the coffee pot up and away, as if she was unsure whether to fill his cup or pour the hot black brew over his head.

"Of course!" Reb Cantor said. "Of course she can do both!"

Mrs. Chaipul nodded, and gave him his coffee.

The merchant, relieved that he had remained dry and unscathed, resumed his diatribe. "It's not whether she can do both. It's whether she will do both. A woman without education has few choices. She can marry or she can become an aunt. A woman with an education may have more choices, but marriage may not be the one that she picks."

"And what is so wrong with that?" Mrs. Chaipul said.

"Children!" the merchant said, slamming his palm on the table and sending coffee flying. "AAAH! You see. When women know too much, when they learn too much, they don't want to have children any more, and the entire species will wither and die. Ow! This hurts."

While the baker and cobbler were scrambling out of the way of the flying coffee, Mrs. Chaipul raced behind the counter, dipped a clean rag into a bucket of cold water, and dashed back to cool, clean, and comfort her scalded customer.

"Even women with education want to have families," Mrs. Chaipul said, soothing the merchant. "It is still part of who we are. Children are a pleasure and a burden, a blessing and an obligation, but they are the best part of us that we are able to leave behind."

Reb Cantor nodded. "I feel much the same way. I told Gittel that of course, if Rachel Cohen could go to school then so could she."

At that moment they all looked to the kitchen in the back of Mrs. Chaipul's restaurant, where they knew Rachel was probably busy working.

Their voices dropped into a low whisper.

"Is her mother still…" Reb Stein asked.

"Yes," hissed Mrs. Chaipul.

"Have they…" asked Reb Gold.

"No," breathed Mrs. Chaipul.

"Poor girl," muttered Reb Cantor, and they all nodded.

Just then, Reb Cohen, the tailor, opened the door and walked into the restaurant.

"Good morning everyone!" he said with a smile. He saw them all staring at him. "Did I interrupt?" He shrugged off his coat and hung it on a hook.

"No, no," said Reb Gold.

"Of course not," said Reb Stein.

"I just spilled some coffee," said Reb Cantor.

"Would you like your breakfast?" asked Mrs. Chaipul.

And for a moment, the subject was closed.

Because no one knew what had happened to Sarah Cohen. Rachel and Yakov's mother, Reb Cohen's wife, had vanished.

* * *

It was one of those things that people didn't like to talk about. It made them uncomfortable, and if they were to admit the truth, a little bit frightened.

Sarah Cohen was gone.

Following her outburst at Kvetchfest, Sarah Cohen had fled from the social hall, ran to her house, packed a bag, wrote a note, and departed from Chelm without saying a word of goodbye.

Sarah's daughter, Rachel, had found the scrap of paper, after she too had left the ill-fated celebration of complaining in tears. Rachel had planned to commiserate with her mother about their mutual woes. When the almost-ten-year-old girl had reached the house, found her mother gone, and discovered the note on the table, it was a hard blow.

"I can't stay," the paper read. It was her mother's handwriting, Rachel was sure of it. "I'm sorry. You are a good family. It's not your fault. Don't forget to stir The Soup."

Automatically, with the note in her hand, Rachel picked up a spoon and gave the weak broth in Oma Levitsky's soup pot a stir. Then, almost without thinking, she tore the paper into small scraps and dropped them into the pot.

Later on, after the fright and the chaos, when her father asked her why she had done it, she had explained that The Soup needed salt, and the tears her mother had shed on the note would add to the seasoning.

Benjamin Cohen was heartbroken. He moaned and wailed. He

cried. He tore at his hair. The howls had frightened his children, who then joined him in his screams and tears.

Reb Shikker, on his way home from Kvetchfest, had heard the ruckus and at first had been convinced that a wild bear had invaded the Cohen home and was ripping its occupants apart.

He darted back and forth in confused circles for a few minutes, trying to decide whether it was more heroic to charge in and attack the bear or hurry away and find help.

Fortunately, the choice was made for him when Reb Levitsky and his wife happened along. Chaya Levitsky ran for Mrs. Chaipul. Martin Levitsky convinced Isaac Shikker that the two of them would be able to chase the bear out, and at least one of them would survive.

When they opened the door and saw the three sobbing Cohens, they shouted, "Where? Where?"

"Gone! Gone!" Benjamin sobbed.

They saw that Sarah was missing and immediately assumed the worst.

"Did it take her?" Martin Levitsky said.

"She's gone!" Benjamin agreed.

When Mrs. Chaipul arrived, she was informed that a bear had taken Sarah Cohen.

This was the first that Benjamin, Yakov, and Rachel Cohen had heard about the bear, and they immediately began to scream and shriek even louder.

It was a horrifying and horrible three hours, until at last young Doodle managed to convince everyone that there was no bear.

"What do you mean there is no bear?" Reb Shikker said. "I heard a bear tearing Sarah apart."

"But Sarah Cohen wasn't here when you came inside!" Doodle insisted.

"No," agreed Martin Levitsky. "The bear had taken her by then."

"Then how did you hear a bear?" Doodle asked. "Besides, there are no bear tracks in the snow."

They all looked out the door, where the snow was packed flat by the tramping of dozens of curious neighbors.

"I circled the village," Doodle said. "There are no bear tracks anywhere. There was no bear."

"Maybe the snow covered the tracks?" Isaac Shikker said. He had been rather looking forward to telling his children the story of how he had single-handedly (with Reb Levitsky's help) chased a bear from Chelm.

Doodle shook his head. "No. The only tracks I saw were a single set of women's boot tracks heading away from Chelm along the Smyrna road."

Mrs. Chaipul had given each of the Cohens a sleeping draught, but Benjamin Cohen, who had been listening to this conversation from his bed, rose and made his way to the door. "So, she's alive?"

"Yes, sir," Doodle said.

"May she be safe," the poor man said, before collapsing in a heap.

They helped him back to his bed, and one by one left the house. The whispers, however, had only just begun.

* * *

The next morning as he made his way through the restaurant, Benjamin Cohen smiled at Mrs. Chaipul, nodded to his friends, and sat at the counter.

A few moments later, Rachel made her way from the kitchen, bringing her father his favorite breakfast. It was called a winkie. Take a piece of challah and cut a hole out of its middle. Then slather it in butter and place it in a hot frying pan. Finally, drop an egg in the middle of the hole to cook. When the egg was done, her father always said it looked like an old man, winking up at him with a sly grin.

Unfortunately, there still weren't any real eggs nor any real bread, so Rachel had made the winkie out of cabbage colored with turmeric.

She set the plate down and patted her father's head. Mrs. Chaipul had already poured him some coffee.

"Yakov isn't coming today?" she asked.

Her father shrugged. "He likes making himself breakfast. He adds all these French herbs to his cabbage. I can't stand it. I like the way Rachel makes my breakfast."

Rachel smiled. "Thank you, Papa."

She leaned over and kissed his cheek.

The other customers and the owner of the restaurant shifted around, uncomfortable and embarrassed, and the rest of the meal continued in silence, which in itself was something of a miracle.

Part Seven

The Other Woman

Chapter Thirty-One

A Visitor

The knocking on the door woke Rabbi Yohon Abrahms with a start. He sat up in bed; his heart racing. Were they here? Had they come at last? Then he realized that the sound wasn't a pounding knock. It was a sharp hammering of metal on wood.

Where was he? He looked around the room. It was dark. He was confused. This was not his room. No?

Yes, it was his room, but not in Chelm.

Now, he was in Smyrna, living in the Chief Rabbi's house – his house, sort of, for now. And there was a metal knocker on the thick oak front door; he remembered that now. It was a funny knocker, a brass replica of a fur cap. You lifted the brim and rapped it against a brass plate.

The relentless tapping of brass on brass continued. Were they here? Had they finally come for him after so many years?

In Chelm, he could not have escaped easily. His house was too small, but in Smyrna there was a backdoor that was used for deliveries. It went into a narrow alleyway that curved to the street behind the house. If his pursuers were thorough, they would be there too, waiting. And it always looked worse if the suspect fled. Shot while attempting to escape. In Moscow he had read that phrase in the newspaper so many times.

Perhaps it wasn't them. Perhaps it was just a Jew of Smyrna in need of council, or comfort. He couldn't be afraid all the time, could he?

Actually, he could. He had been afraid for years. Why stop now?

Sighing, he reached for his robe, and tied it around his waist. Then, he realized it wouldn't do. His robe was warm but threadbare. It had the patches and stains of a bachelor's schmatta.

Sighing again, he grabbed the great fur coat he had inherited along with the house from the late Rabbi Sarnoff. He buttoned it up, pulled on some boots and carefully felt his way down the stairs.

He could have lit a candle, but he was still used to Chelm, where a candle at night was only used to read by, and never wasted on such a short trip.

The tapping continued, and then stopped. He listened, and then realized that whoever was downstairs might have given up, which almost certainly meant they were not the Russian secret police, but someone in need.

"I'm coming," he called, hurrying along. "I'm coming."

Rabbi Sarnoff's fur coat was too big. The dead man had been about the same height as the young rabbi, but Sarnoff had been fat, so the hem of the robe was long in the front.

Rabbi Abrahms stepped on the hem and fell down the last three steps of the stairs before thudding to a stop against the front door.

"Ow!" he pried himself up off the floor, grateful he hadn't broken anything more than his pride.

He unbolted the door, turned the lock, twisted the knob, pulled it open, and peeked out through the crack.

It was nearly dawn, and there wasn't much light.

There was a woman. She was wearing a coat and a shawl with a hood, but he knew who she was the moment he saw her.

"Sarah?" he said. "Who died?"

Sarah Cohen looked up from under her hood. "No one died," she whispered. Her cheeks were slick with what looked like glass. He realized that her cheeks were covered with frozen tears. "May I come in?"

"Of course," he nodded. He opened the door wide and stepped aside. "Be careful, it's dark." He shut the door. "Let me light a candle."

"Is there a fire?" she said.

He realized that she was cold, shivering. "Of course. Come, quickly. You must be frozen." He led her into the grand dining room where there was a wrought iron stove covered with beautiful tiles. It heated the whole house, but used a fortune in coal. He opened the door and poked the coals, saw they were still lit, then opened the flue, and added more coal. "Would you like something to drink? I can warm tea on the stove."

She nodded and moved closer to the heat.

He wanted to put his arms around her, to warm her body against his, but he pushed that thought aside. She was a married woman, and he was not her husband. Perhaps to save a life, such a thing would be acceptable, but now that she stood near his fire, it was inappropriate. He cursed the luxury of the late Rabbi's house.

Limping, he made his way to the kitchen, found two earthenware mugs, and filled them from the cold samovar. He brought them back to the grand dining room, and set them on top of the stove to warm.

"So," he said. "How's the family?"

She did not answer.

"Are the children well?"

A smile flickered over her face. "Healthy and well and growing every day."

"And Benjamin?" he asked. "Your husband?"

Her eyes stared at him, and then moved back to the warm glow of the coals through the narrow slits in the iron stove. "I have left him."

Yohon Abrahms' heart began to pound. He felt his face flush and was glad for the darkness. "Oh," he said, at a loss for words. "Really?"

It was a stupid thing to say. Of course she had left him. She was alone in the middle of the night in another village at his door and inside his house. Nevertheless, she heard his question and nodded.

What should I do? He wondered. What should I say?

I am the Acting Associate Interim Temporary Chief Rabbi of Smyrna. It is supposed to be my job to help people in need. And she is a person who needs my help.

A thousand thoughts raced through his head: You should go back to your husband. He hasn't hurt you has he? If he has hurt you then you can leave. You can't leave your children. Who is at your house? Are you well? Have you lost your mind? What happened?

Did you do something? Did you say something? Why are you here? Couldn't you have spoken to Mrs. Chaipul? Will you stay with me?

He couldn't speak. He was frightened. His heart was pounding louder than the secret police at the door. He was afraid that she would hear it.

He reached past her for his mug just as she reached for the same mug, and their hands touched.

He felt the jolt, and he knew that she felt the jolt too, and neither one of them pulled back. His hand closed on hers as she moved closer.

He put his arms around her. Her back was to his front. He felt her relax against him as if the weight of the world had been lifted from her shoulders.

* * *

They stood together in front of the stove for a long time. The mugs full of tea on the stove grew hotter and hotter, but the man and the woman did not move. He held her, and she was held. It was enough.

"This is wrong," he whispered at last.

"This is nothing," she answered back.

"You have no idea what is going on in my mind," he said.

"I am sure that they are the same thoughts that I am having," she said.

"Oh my," he said.

And they both laughed.

And then they were quiet. By now the frozen tears on her cheeks had evaporated. Her feet were thawed. Her belly was warm in his embrace. Just touching her sent a shiver through him.

"What happened?" he said, trying to keep his voice calm.

She gave a slight shrug. "He didn't notice me. You did. He never appreciated me. You did. He's a tailor. You are the chief rabbi of Smyrna."

The Temporary Acting Interim Possibly-to-be-finalized-at-some-future-moment Chief Rabbi of Smyrna, he thought. But instead he said, "He's your husband."

"In name only for many years."

"He's the father of your children."

"Yes, he is," she nodded, and he felt her hair smooth against his cheek. "But for him I am nothing but a cook and a laundress, a cleaner and a shopper. I am a tool that he uses, like he uses his scissors. When he needs me I am treated well, when I am done, he sets me down gently and goes about his other business. I am lonely. I have been lonely. Are you lonely?"

The question echoed through him like a bell resounding in an empty cathedral. Yes, he thought, but he dared not speak.

It was quiet, and on top of the stove, the tea in the mugs began to boil.

"Do you want me to go?"

This time, he spoke. "No," he said.

"Do you want me to stay?" She turned her face and looked up into his eyes.

Her lips were so close to his.

I am frightened, he thought. My job is conditional. She is married, and this is a scandal. If people find out, I will be gone. I will lose my position in Smyrna; I will never be able to return to Chelm. And who will hire me? How will we live? A poor rabbi and a fallen woman?

And yet...

Her lips touched his.

At that moment, the mugs on the stove burst with a crack, sending tea and hissing clouds of steam down the black iron sides.

For a time they did not notice.

Again he spoke. "Tonight you will stay. I will give you my bed, and I will sleep on the couch in my study. In the morning we will see what the dawn brings."

"I won't go back. I can't go back."

"Not tonight," he said, agreeing. She nodded.

"Let's get you settled," he said. "Be careful on the stairs."

"You have an upstairs?" she said.

"I have six rooms," he bragged. "A kitchen, the grand dining room, a study, my bedroom, and two children's bedrooms."

"You have children?" she turned and stared at him with panic in her eyes.

"No," he laughed. "Not me. The rooms were for the other rabbis, the ones before me, the married ones."

"Oh," she said. "So, why don't you stay in one of the other bedrooms?"

"I'd rather stay downstairs for now. You understand?"

She nodded, and then kissed his cheek softly before walking boldly up the stairs.

He felt like his cheek had been touched by an angel.

His smile felt so genuine, he wondered if it could be as wrong as he imagined.

* * *

Outside in the early morning darkness, the milkman was on about his deliveries. He saw the woman standing at the rabbi's door. He watched her go inside.

On his return rounds, as he came back down the street, the milkman glanced down at the snow and saw that the woman's footsteps went in, but did not come out.

He smiled and clucked his tongue.

Chapter Thirty-Two

Council Meeting

The noise in the cave was deafening. The Council of Wise Women was meeting, and no one seemed happy about it. Usually, the carpets on the floor helped to muffle the echoing resonance of chatting women and clinking teacups. Today however, everyone was talking all at once, and no one was listening. There was a frantic edge to the conversation, and the walls seemed to be booming with panic and disappointment.

Trying to regain some semblance of order, Chanah Chaipul had been tapping her teacup with her spoon for a good ten minutes, and no one had noticed. At last, she stopped, mostly because she was afraid she'd break the porcelain, and while that might get everyone's attention, the white and blue cup from Vienna was one of her favorites. This was perhaps the first time that she'd ever wished that the Council had a gavel. Years ago, they had decided that gavels and gongs and other such methods of getting attention were male options, and unnecessary in a roomful of responsible women. Today though, the lines between gossip and agenda were blurry.

Chanah felt about in her mouth with her tongue for any crumbs of cabbage mandel bread that might be lingering. Usually by now the women would have run out of steam and the meeting could begin. Then she put her fingers between her lips and blew a shrill whistle, loud enough to stop Napoleon's army in its tracks.

Hands leaped to ears. Tea and cookies flew through the air in startled reaction. It was a wonder no one broke a dish.

When the echoes died, Esther Gold blinked and asked, "What was that?"

Chanah shrugged. "Something useful I learned from my poor

dead husband, may he rest in peace," she said. "Now, I think we need to talk."

"So, what were we just doing?" asked Chaya Levitsky.

"What she means," said Deborah Shikker, "is that she thinks it's time for her to talk and us to listen."

Chanah waited for this grumbling to pass. "We need to decide what to do about allowing the girls to study in the yeshiva."

"You don't want to talk about Sarah Cohen? About how she deserted her children and husband and then disappeared?"

The words were sharp and angry. No one was really sure who had said aloud what they all had been thinking.

Chanah shook her head. "No, I don't. That's not our business. Education is."

Shoshana Cantor jumped to her feet, which wasn't so easy for a woman as large as she, and with a pointing finger sputtered, "This is all your fault. If you hadn't encouraged that girl to go to school, none of the others would be wanting to. Now it's a problem that we all have to deal with."

There was more finger pointing and accusations. Chanah allowed these to be aired without argument. Finally she spoke. "Yes, I felt that Rachel Cohen would benefit from an education. As I recall, most of you agreed at the time. Frankly, I knew that something like this might be a possible outcome, but I didn't think it would happen so soon, nor did I think it would occur without our direct and initiating involvement."

"What did she just say?" asked Esther.

"I'm not sure if she's apologizing or trying to blame us," Deborah answered.

"Neither," said Chanah. "It is clear that Rachel Cohen is her own woman..."

"Woman?" Shoshana said. She was leaning against a wall, unwilling to sit still. "She's not even ten years old. Her family is a mess, and because of her, my family is also a mess."

Chanah looked Shoshana in the eyes and said, "Are you still blaming your family troubles on a ten year old girl?"

It was a well-known fact that in the Council of Wise Women,

Chanah Chaipul and Shoshana Cantor were dedicated and friendly opponents. They respectfully disagreed on almost every issue and matter of small or large importance. What always seemed remarkable to the other women on the Council was their ability to set aside personal opinions, avoid lasting animosities, and actually listen to and talk with each other.

For a moment, Shoshana had a defiant look in her eyes, and then she exhaled and shook her head. "No. It's not the girl's fault. It's mine."

The cave that served as the Council chambers fell silent, except for a loud gnawing sound. When she noticed all eyes staring at her, Bertha Shimmel muttered an apology, and set down her plate of mandel bread.

"I don't want my daughters educated," Shoshana said. She looked around the room at her friends and neighbors. "Is that wrong? Is that horrible? I don't want them to know more than me. It was good enough for my mother; it was good enough for my grandmother. It was good enough for me. But now they want to know more. They want to understand more. They want to learn more. And they will be smarter than me. They will learn from the men and not from the women. And they will have new ideas and new pieces of knowledge. And I won't be able to argue with them because I won't know. They will understand things that I was not allowed to. They will think things that would never have occurred to me. And they will tell me that I am wrong and they are right and I will not be able to refute them. Because they will be educated, and I am a fool."

Chanah nodded her understanding. "Knowledge does not make someone wise."

"No," agreed Shoshana, "but it may make them more stubborn and certain and unwilling to listen to those who they believe — rightly believe — do not share their knowledge.

"We live in Chelm. We are all wise here in our different ways. Until recently, though, book learning and knowledge acquired by studying was part of the men's world. We women were able to cherish our subtle knowledge passed through words and whispers and gentle guidance. Men were living in the world of the mind and sometimes the soul. Women were living in the real world — in harmony with nature and the spirit. The men were always convinced that they were superior, and we allowed them to think this. But now? If we adopt their ways and set aside our own, who can claim victory?

"The inheritance I received from my mother and her mother and her mother will not stand against the arguments of men. You and I know that. In the past, we have solved problems by nodding and agreeing and letting the men think what they like, certain of our own truths.

"But I'm not certain any more. Or rather I am still certain, but my daughters may not be. Will not be…"

Chanah scanned the room and looked at the women she considered her sisters. Many were nodding. Many were thoughtful. Several had tears.

"I'm not sure it's either-or," Chanah began. "I'm not sure that it's a battle between men's and women's knowledge and wisdom. But I'm also not sure that you're wrong. It's like in the Garden of Eden, when Eve ate of the fruit…"

Shoshana shouted, "Don't go to the Torah! Don't start with that."

Chanah Chaipul felt her heart racing. Allowing Rachel to go to school hadn't seemed like such a big deal. Clearly she was wrong. There were factors she'd never considered. Implications she hadn't imagined.

"The world is changing," Shoshana said. "The boundaries are shifting and the old truths are not uncontestable nor intact. If my daughters want to go to school now, there is little or nothing I can do to stand in their way. Either I become their opponent or I become their enabler. If I encourage them, I move them further away from me. If I hold onto them and try to shield them, they will resist and blame me, as girls always will do.

"It's too late to discuss whether or not the girls will go to school. The door has been opened. They will. You and I both know that. Now, the question now is how will we continue to teach them what we know to be important?"

Chanah felt her eyes filling with tears. "I don't know," she said. "I don't know."

"Maybe we should ask Rachel Cohen," said Hannah Meier.

Shoshana's face spun in anger. "Don't say her name to me," she spat. "Her whole family is a scandal and a wreck. Her mother is missing. Her father is a shell, and her brother is insane. You think that they are an example to look to in times like these?"

"Actually, I do," Hannah said. "But I'm not willing to fight with you about it just now. You are my friend, and I would much rather give you a hug."

With that, the older woman took the younger woman in her arms and supported her head on her shoulder as the sobs began and spread throughout the room.

"Oy," sighed Esther. "I hate cry fests. They always make my tea salty."

Chapter Thirty-Three

Shabbat Dinner

Twilight. The Sabbath candles were being lit throughout Chelm. In the Cohen household, Rachel took a long twig to the stove and held it in the flames until it caught. Carefully cupping her hand the way her mother had shown her around the flickering end, she walked slowly across the kitchen to the two candles waiting in their silver candlesticks. Her father and brother watched her slow steps. The quiet in their home was thick.

Benjamin Cohen was astonished at the beauty of the ceremony. Most weeks he was hurriedly finishing up work and rushing to shul to welcome the Sabbath with other men in prayer. He remembered Sabbath candle lightings with his mother when he was a child, but had never before seen them lit in his own home. Every week, Sarah had done this, but she was gone now, and he needed to be here with his children.

Rachel touched the fire to one wick and then the other. When she was sure that both had caught, she carefully blew out the twig and set it leaning against the bottom of the right candlestick, the way her mother had.

She closed her eyes and waved the softly flaming light toward her face. Then in a soft sweet voice, she sang the blessing.

She opened her eyes and watched as her father chanted over the wine, and then her brother over the challah. When the bruchahs were done, the family held hands.[47] Her father held her hand and her brother's, and she held her brother's in a family circle. Well, really a triangle, she thought, but not a perfect one. Mama was missing.

---

[47] A bruchah is a blessing. They're called a bruchah because they all begin with the word, "Baruch," which means Blessed. Also spelled Bracha or Berakhah.

They stood for a moment, until Benjamin Cohen squeezed and then let go.

Rachel went to the stove for the chicken stew that Yakov had made. Yakov began slicing challah. Their father sat in his seat staring across to the empty chair on the other side of the table. His lips moved in prayer.

Rachel served the warm stew, and for a few moments, they ate in silence. At last, she could take it no more.

"Do you think she's all right?" she said, softly, staring into her spoon, not daring to look up at her father or brother.

There was no need to say who she was. Sarah Cohen, mother of Rachel and Yakov and wife of Benjamin, had been missing for two months. For two months the family had said little of it.

"This is delicious stew," her father said.

"Do you think she's dead?" Yakov asked, suddenly angry.

"No," Benjamin answered his son, just as quickly. "No, she's all right. I know that she is."

"How can you know?" Yakov said. "Why haven't you looked for her?"

Benjamin felt himself getting angry. "I'm a tailor," he answered. "I am not a detective. I have asked people. I have placed advertisements in the newspapers. I have two young children at home, and work that must be done. What more can I do?"

"You put ads?" Rachel said. "What did they say?"

Benjamin caught his sorrow and looked away from his daughter as his eyes filled with tears. "'Sarah, come home. We miss you. I'm sorry.' I would have written more, but you pay by the word, and it's expensive, and I wanted it to run for as long as it takes and as much as I can afford."

"That's nice, Papa," Rachel said.

"Do you think she went with another man?" Yakov demanded.

Benjamin's nostrils flared in outrage. "How can you say such a thing?!"

"I have wondered too." Rachel was nearly in tears. "Haven't you thought of it?"

Benjamin looked at his children and realized that it was time to talk, to tell them the truth as best he could.

"I did at first," he said. "How could I not? But then I thought, no, how could she. Once, several years ago, I asked her if she ever had thoughts about another man."

"Who?" Yakov demanded.

The tailor wondered if it was right. Do I talk about this with my children? This should not be their problem. But if I keep quiet now and they find out later... Besides, she denied it.

He spoke softly. "Rabbi Abrahms. The schoolteacher. It's silly." Benjamin found himself laughing with quiet nervousness. "Your mother seemed... different... around him. But I asked her if there was anything and she laughed.

"She said, no. And she kissed my cheek, and I believed her. How could I not? So you should too."

"Do you still?" Rachel gently asked.

Benjamin's heart was breaking. Still, he was determined to be honest. "Yes. No. Sometimes. Of course. But what does it matter?"

"It matters," Yakov said. "Of course it matters! Mama could be in Smyrna with Rabbi Abrams."

"If she is, she will see the advertisement and read it." Benjamin shook his head. "What matters to me is that your mother was so sad, and I didn't know. And she must have been like that for a long time, but I did not know, or I could not see, or hear. What matters to me is that she is so far away, and I don't know where. What matters to me is that she isn't here now. That she is far from you two. And from me. And I miss her."

The tears filled their eyes, and then fell into the stew. The flames on the candles flickered shadows of gold across their cheeks.

"Papa, it's not your fault," Rachel said at last.

"Whose fault is it, then?" Benjamin snapped back. "What kind of a husband am I that my wife is suffering for so long and I do not know? How can she hate me so much without my understanding or even glimpsing? Where have I been? Who have I been? What kind of a man am I that I lose my love and can not say goodbye?"

"You are a good man," Rachel said, putting her hand on her father's.

He nearly yanked his hand away, because his daughter's touch reminded him so much of his wife's touch, but he caught himself and allowed her fingers to rest on his.

His sadness was secondary. He needed to comfort his children.

"I thought she left because of me," Yakov said at last.

"What?" Benjamin's head turned and stared at his son. "No. That's not true."

"I thought that she was angry with me for being different from all the other boys," Yakov said, quietly looking at his spoon. "I like to cook. I don't like to study. I'm not as smart as my sister. I like to make beautiful clothing. I thought she was ashamed."

Benjamin put his hand to his chest. "Yakov, my son. You are perfect in every way. Even your flaws are perfect. And you don't have that many. Your mother would never leave because of you."

"I thought it was me," Rachel whispered.

"What?" Benjamin's head swiveled. "You too?"

Rachel nodded. "Because I am different too, and all the fuss I've been causing about school, and because I work, and because I left her alone."

"No, no," their father insisted. He reached his hand out and took his son's hand, and held his daughter's hand. "Your mother loved you both. She was proud of you both. You were… You are… You two are her children, her pride and her love."

"Then why did she leave us?" cried both children at the same time. Their tears began to stream down their young faces.

"That's what I'm trying to tell you," Benjamin insisted. He too was crying. "It's my fault. I wasn't paying attention. I was the one who left her alone."

No one was listening to anyone else. They were all too busy being miserable and tearful. The stew grew cold, and the candles burned down.

"What if it's her fault?" Rachel whispered at last. "Mama's."

"Why does it have to be anyone's fault?" Yakov shot back.

"I don't know," Rachel said.

"You hear that, Papa?" Yakov said with a bitter laugh. "For once there is something that Rachel doesn't know."

"Stop it," Benjamin insisted. "Don't be cruel to your sister."

Yakov was about to answer with automatic anger, but then he nodded.

"Listen." Benjamin rubbed his forehead for a moment, and then spoke. "When I look at you two, I see that your mother is still here. Rachel, you have her eyes and her face and her smile and her touch. Yakov, you have her kindness and generosity. Rachel, you have her insight and determination. Yakov, you have her laughter and her heart. You both have your mother and are your mother. Am I making sense?"

"Not much," muttered Yakov.

"Yes, of course," Rachel answered, shooting her brother a look.

"What?" Yakov said.

"What about you, Papa?" Rachel asked. "Are you all right?"

"Don't worry about me, my children. I am an adult," Benjamin said, hoping that his words would ring truer than they felt. "I will be fine. I am keeping my heart open in hope and waiting. The truth is that your mother would not want you to be sad and miserable."

"Then why did she leave?" Yakov shouted. "Why did she leave?"

"I don't know," Benjamin whispered. "She said that I didn't understand. And she was right. I didn't. I don't.

"But I say to you, my son and my daughter, the sadness and anger that has infected your mother is not your responsibility. She is the adult and you are the children. Even if you are remarkable children, which you are, you are not the cause and you do not, you must not, accept or hold the blame. One day you will find yourself laughing and happy, and you may think to yourself, 'I shouldn't feel this way because... because my mother is gone.'" Benjamin shook his head. "No, do not think that. Or if you do, know and hear this. What I tell you is true. Your mother loves you. She loves her children. Even if she can't be there to share it, she wants happiness for you."

After a moment, Benjamin looked at his daughter. "Do you understand?"

Rachel nodded.

"Yakov, do you understand?"

"Yes, Papa," Yakov said. "She wants happiness for you as well."

For a moment, Benjamin's heart stopped. Then it started again. "You are a kind boy," he said, smiling. "And you," he turned to his daughter, "are a wonderful cook! I said it before and I will say it again, this is a delicious stew. I'm starving."

Instantly, Yakov's face froze with anger. His lips went white.

"What did I say?" Benjamin asked.

"Papa, Yakov made the stew," Rachel said. "He prepared it in the morning before going to the yeshiva and the shop."

Benjamin looked in the bowl. Even cold the stew tasted better than anything he had ever eaten. Chicken and rosemary, garlic and potato, even a bit of cabbage that didn't make him feel at all sick or nauseous. Aside from cabbage, food was still scarce, where had Yakov found all the ingredients?

"You made this?" he said at last. "I didn't realize."

Yakov nodded, biting his tongue not to start shouting at his father on the Sabbath.

Benjamin Cohen looked his son in the eyes and said, "This is the most delicious food I have ever eaten. Thank you. I am so glad that you are such a wonderful cook."

"Me too," Yakov agreed. "Let's eat it before it gets any colder."

For the children, the silence was quickly filled with the clinking of spoons in the bowls, the slurping of broth, and the dabbing of challah to scoop up the last drops.

For the father, with the empty seat across the table, the silence was never filled.

Chapter Thirty-Four

School Daze

Rabbi Kibbitz had his head determinedly down on his desk. He refused to lift it. He refused to look up. He pressed his forehead on the draft of Rabbi Abrahms' manuscript, and covered his ears with his hands.

Still, the noise in the small classroom was deafening. It sounded like a whole herd of unmilked cows at feeding time — low and constant, but frequently interrupted by a loud bellow or bark.

The school children were driving him mad.

It had been bad enough when he'd been dragged out of retirement to fill Rabbi Abrahms' shoes as the only school teacher in the village. Was it too much for a man of his age to ask that he be able to go back to sleep after morning prayers, instead of trying to pound nails of knowledge into the thick wooden skulls of young boys? Clearly it was too much, because there was nobody else to do the job, so he had taken it back. Instead of lounging about in his cozy bed, or shuffling over to Mrs. Chaipul's restaurant for an endless cup of tea and hours of chess or conversation, he had found himself once again trapped in the stifling room trying to pass his hard-earned wisdom to the witless and unwilling.

Then all of the other young girls had come to school.

Rachel Cohen by herself would have been enough of a delightful student to keep a scholar and a teacher engaged in the struggle for understanding for decades. A ten-year-old who can ask insightful questions and can explore the possible answers without judgment was like finding a boulder of gold in the middle of the Uherka River. His conversations with her had been the one redeeming aspect to his entire de-tirement.

But now, with the sudden influx of a giggle of girls...

He tilted his head up and peeked an eye open.

Adam Schlemiel was standing on one foot, on a chair, which was balanced on another chair, which was perched on top of his desk.

Rabbi Kibbitz closed his eye, tilted his head back, and pounded his forehead against the manuscript. All he wanted to do was relax and sleep.

* * *

Three weeks earlier, when Mrs. Chaipul had barged into his study with her flock of women behind her, the senior rabbi of Chelm had looked up, smiled, and simply said, "Yes."

That had stopped her cold. "Yes?" she said. "You can't be bothered to say, hello?"

"Hello." He nodded in agreement. "And, yes."

Mrs. Chaipul's mouth had been opened, mid-inhale, in anticipation of a long-winded speech. Instead she coughed.

"What do you mean, yes?" The caterer's voice was of a slightly higher pitch than normal. "I haven't even said anything yet."

"You didn't say hello to me, either," the rabbi pointed out. "All I said was yes."

"And you keep saying it!"

"Yes," he agreed. "And you still haven't said hello."

Mrs. Chaipul cleared her throat, looked at the other women, shrugged, and said, "Hello."

Rabbi Kibbitz smiled and waited.

Finally, Mrs. Cantor nudged her.

"All right!" Mrs. Chaipul spoke. "We have come to ask…"

"Yes," said the rabbi.

"You don't even know what I'm going to say!" Mrs. Chaipul shouted.

"But I do," the rabbi answered with a smile on his face. People were strange and confusing creatures. He knew in his heart that most of the time he was clueless about their minds, their opinions, their reasons, motives, and desires. It was so rare that he actually knew what was going on that he was enjoying himself. "You have come to ask me to admit all the girls of Chelm into the yeshiva."

"Yes!" Mrs. Chaipul agreed. "We have come to ask you to admit all the girls of Chelm into the yeshiva."

She stopped. Repeating the rabbi's words back to him was hardly satisfying. She had prepared a long speech with a list of justifications and explanations.

"All right then," the rabbi said.

"What do you mean, 'All right'?" Mrs. Chaipul bellowed.

"I already said yes." The rabbi covered his mouth to hide his smirk.

"But the girls need an education," Mrs. Chaipul said.

"Yes," the rabbi agreed.

"It is not fair that the boys should have access to knowledge that the girls do not."

"Yes," the rabbi nodded.

"Modern times demand modern thinking!"

"Yes."

"You can't keep them out!"

"Yes... I mean, no. I mean, of course the girls are welcome."

"What?" Mrs. Chaipul sputtered. "What? What?"

By now, Rabbi Kibbitz had both hands firmly over his lips and was struggling hard not to burst out laughing. "I am giving in. I accede. You win. The girls and boys will learn together in Chelm."

"In the same room?" said Mrs. Gold.

"We only have one teacher," said the rabbi. "We only have one room."

"What about a curtain?" asked Mrs. Meier, the balanit ha mikveh. "What about a mechitzah?"

"It won't work," the rabbi shook his head. "Rabbi Abrahms tried it with Rachel Cohen, and it fell down the first day. If the girls are going to study with the boys then they will have to sit with the boys."

"But that will lead to pregnancy!" shouted Mrs. Shikker.

"Not in my classroom," said the rabbi firmly. "What they do after school is up to their parents to control."

There was a long and tactful silence.

One by one the women of Chelm thanked the elder rabbi and made their way back to their houses to tell their daughters the good news and gently break the controversial news to their husbands.

At last, only Mrs. Chaipul was left.

"Yes?" Rabbi Kibbitz said.

"Now it's a question?" she sputtered. "You don't already know the answer?"

"I might," he chuckled. "You want to know why I didn't argue or make a fuss?"

"I want to know why you didn't argue or make a fuss!" Mrs. Chaipul said, almost simultaneously before stopping herself with a blush.

The rabbi grinned. "I was going to lose. No matter what I said, there was no way I was going to win. So, rather than fight, I thought I would say yes."

Mrs. Chaipul pursed her lips. She frowned. Several thoughts, some of which were fairly unkind, crossed her mind, but she let them pass. At last she spoke quietly. "Are you sure about this?"

"In truth, no," the rabbi answered seriously. He shook his head. "I think we might be making a big mistake. In Chelm and everywhere else in the world, boys go to school, and girls stay home. In ancient times, some learned rabbis used to educate their daughters, but it didn't take. I'm a practical man. None of the men in Chelm want this. All the women in Chelm want this. I'm the one who's going to be stuck in the classroom, while Rabbi Abrahms lives in a big house in Smyrna and teaches nothing but boys. The consequences to me will be dire either way.

"How about you, Chanah?" he asked her. "Are you sure you want the other girls in the school?"

She shook her head. "No. But I do agree with you. I don't know if it's a good idea either."

"Will you teach with me?" he asked her.

"What? Are you insane? What do I know about Torah or Talmud?"

He shrugged. "What do I know about cooking or healing?"

"That's different."

"Not really."

"No, I won't teach with you." Mrs. Chaipul said firmly. Then she sighed. "Look, it's your job. I already have two full-time jobs, running the restaurant and taking care of the sick."

"I know," he nodded. "But I had to ask. Consider it. Let me know if you change your mind."

"All right," she said. Then she smiled. "Yes."

"Does that mean you'll help?" he brightened.

"No," she shook her head quickly. "But I will consider it."

* * *

There was a crash and a scream in the yeshiva as Adam Schlemiel plunged to the ground, gashing his cheek open on the corner of a table.

Rabbi Kibbitz slowly lifted his head. He reached out an arm and grabbed Doodle by the shoulder.

"Run and get Mrs. Chaipul," he said. "Tell her I need her. Again."

The young boy raced off.

Sighing, Rabbi Kibbitz opened the bottom drawer of his desk and removed the yeshiva's first aid kit.

"All right, all right," he said, pushing his way through the crowd. "Adam, are you dead? No. Good. Because when your mother finds out, you're going to wish you were."

Chapter Thirty-Five

Rabbi to Rabbi

Rabbi Kibbitz stared at the brass door knocker in the shape of a fur cap, and smiled. It would be good to see Rabbi Sarnoff again, it had been too long… Then he remembered, and his spirits fell. Rabbi Sarnoff was gone, passed away during the influenza epidemic. In his place, in his very house, lived Rabbi Abrahms, and that was who the elder rabbi of Chelm had come to see.

Rabbi Kibbitz sighed and rubbed his forehead. Time was merciless. It ate everything and moved on. The problem with getting old was that everything familiar went away and was replaced by the new and the different. It didn't pay to become too comfortable or settled because something was bound to change or someone was bound to die. It saddened him that he would never again see his old friend — that they could not play chess, argue about law, or laugh about their duties. It was good that Rabbi Sarnoff lived on in the memory and in the minds of all those whom he had touched. But you still missed the real person to shake hands or clap on the back.

Well, he was here for a purpose and he might as well get on with it. He lifted the knocker and tapped on the door — continuously and without pause because it was early, and he knew that Rabbi Abrahms was a heavy and late sleeper.

A shape moved in the upstairs window, so Rabbi Kibbitz stopped his knocking to wave.

Strange. It looked like a woman, but the figure darted back out of sight before the old man could be sure. Very strange.

He waited on the front step and was about to start knocking again when the door jumped open.

"Who died?" Rabbi Abrahms said, blearily.

It was a traditional greeting from a rabbi when disturbed at unusual times of day, and Rabbi Kibbitz answered with the quick and efficient, "Nobody new today."

Rabbi Abrahms blinked awake in the early morning dawnlight. He was dressed in Rabbi Sarnoff's warm fur coat and little else. "Rabbi Kibbitz?"

"The very same!"

"Is everything all right?"

"Of course not," said the old man, shaking his long-bearded head. "If it was, then I would have visited you in the afternoon rather than in the morning. But before we get into that, you should invite me in."

The younger man blinked away the rest of his sleep. Then he looked over his shoulder. "Right. Yes. Of course. Please. Come in." He stepped aside, letting his elder into the house and shut the door behind them.

For Rabbi Kibbitz, it was like stepping back in time for a visit with his recently deceased friend. Nothing had changed. Absolutely everything was the same. Even the chessboard in the corner was still set from the last game they had been in the middle of playing.

"So, how are you settling in?" Rabbi Kibbitz asked as he hung his coat on the rack, which was exactly where it had been for decades. It even seemed to hold all the same coats that Rabbi Sarnoff had worn.

"Eh," Rabbi Abrahms said. "It's not easy filling another man's shoes."

Rabbi Kibbitz looked down and realized that quite probably Rabbi Abrahms really was wearing Rabbi Sarnoff's shoes. "Don't they pay you?" he asked.

"Some." Rabbi Abrahms shrugged. "But I took the first month's salary in potatoes to start, and most of the rest is deferred until after my appointment is finalized. Something about the terms of the rabbinical trust. I have enough for coal and food and a few books. To be honest, I was better paid in Chelm. But that's not why you're here. Can I offer you some food? In the kitchen, I have some kugel and some kiggle and some kasha and some knishes. It seems to be a theme."

Suddenly, with the offer of refreshment, Rabbi Kibbitz found himself salivating. His mouth was watering at the thought of eating anything — especially anything without cabbage. "I'd better not. It would spoil my appetite for lunch."

"Are you sick?" Rabbi Abrahms said, suddenly concerned. Rabbi Kibbitz was a large man, a big man, almost a fat man. He had never been known to turn down a nosh, let alone a free nosh. But the women of the sisterhood had been after him for years to lose weight, and he did look a little haggard…

"No, I'm fine," Rabbi Kibbitz said, trying to suppress an urge to shout, Yes, bring me one of everything because I'm starving for anything that doesn't have cabbage in it! "Perhaps just some tea," he managed in a soft whisper. "I know where the samovar is, I can…"

Rabbi Kibbitz began to move through the dining room toward the kitchen. He was used to helping himself at Rabbi Sarnoff's house because his late friend had bad gout and difficulty walking.

"No, no," Rabbi Abrahms said suddenly, cutting off the way. "I'll get it…"

They both stopped suddenly as the door to the kitchen slowly swung open, and a tray with two steaming cups of tea floated into the dining room, carried by a slender woman shrouded in scarves.

While the two men watched in silence, she drifted to the table, set the silver platter down, lifted each cup and saucer, and then the sugar bowl, and then the tiny milk pitcher, and placed them all on the table. Without saying a word, she arranged the tea service, laid napkins down, set spoons on top, lifted the tray, and drifted back out of the dining room into the kitchen, the door slowly closing behind her.

* * *

"Was that a ghost?" Rabbi Kibbitz said. "Because I don't remember Rabbi Sarnoff being that skinny."

"No, no," laughed Rabbi Abrahms nervously. "I have a housekeeper."

"They pay you enough for a housekeeper, and you're complaining about money? Here I thought I might be able to tempt you with an offer to return, but I don't have enough in the budget for hired help for the hired help. You know, I thought I saw a woman's shape in the upstairs window when I knocked."

"She does a lot of work cooking and cleaning," Rabbi Abrahms said. "But she's not paid."

"Ahh!" Rabbi Kibbitz said. "A sisterhood volunteer! I know the kind. Probably a widow! They are always attentive to a fault. Be careful she…"

Rabbi Kibbitz paused. He might be old. He might be from Chelm. But he was not a complete idiot. He knew that when it came to human relationships, when you put one plus one plus one together it only occasionally added up to three.

"Shall we have some tea?" both men said at the same time. Then they laughed nervously.

"Maybe I should get myself dressed," Rabbi Abrahms said. "You sit. I'll be back in a moment."

He excused himself into the kitchen.

Rabbi Kibbitz sat at the long table, pulled the tea cup close, and added six teaspoons of sugar. It had been a long time since he'd had sugar in his tea and he wanted to make the most of it. He heard whispering in the kitchen. He blew on his tea, sipped, and smiled.

He remembered so many years ago, after his wife had died, how the widows from the sisterhood had literally lined up to serve him and bring him food. It had been both wonderful and tragic. Wonderful because the attention and the warmth was flattering. Tragic because at the time, and to some extent even now so many years later, he could never imagine any of them replacing his beloved in his heart or home. He had accepted the food and the conversation and the house cleaning with gratitude. He played dumb on everything else. And eventually, the years passed and the widows remarried. From time to time they would remember him with a casserole, but even that had faded away when Mrs. Chaipul had opened her restaurant. Now he was getting old… He snorted. Getting old? He was old. He felt old. But the loneliness didn't bother him so much. Except at night.

Rabbi Abrahms came back into the dining room, nicely dressed and with his beard combed. He sat across the table, picked up his tea, and sipped.

"So, my good friend from Chelm," Rabbi Abrahms said, assuming the role of the acting temporary interim chief rabbi of Smyrna, "what brings you here so early?"

"Two things," Rabbi Kibbitz said, pleased to get down to business. He reached into his large pocket, brought out the manuscript, and set it on the table. "I wanted to return this to you."

"My book!" Rabbi Abrahms said, brightening. "Did you like it?"

Rabbi Kibbitz laughed, "Of course I liked it! Who wouldn't like to read about his own life's adventures written in stunning prose? Who would have thought that anyone would be interested in reading about the life of Rabbi Kibbitz of Chelm?"

Rabbi Abrahms face fell. "You hated it, didn't you?"

"No, no!" Rabbi Kibbitz said, quickly. "It made me laugh. How rare to be able to see yourself in the mirror of another person's mind and feel both honored and amused. You made me into a funny guy. I had no idea I was such a clown."

Now Rabbi Abrahms was really worried. "Please don't sue me. I'm planning on giving most of the money the book makes to Chelm, so that the school can afford to hire a new teacher. Really. Honest. I swear."

"Sue you?" Rabbi Kibbitz said. "Why would I sue you? Feh. If people read your book and believe that I and everyone else in the village of Chelm are fools, so much the better. They will always underestimate us, and Reb Cantor the merchant will be able to drive much harder bargains. No. I liked it."

Rabbi Abrahms had been shifting back away from the table, ready to run in case Rabbi Kibbitz started throwing cups and saucers. He stopped. "You're not kidding? You really did like my book?"

"Yes, I loved it. Have I ever lied to you?" Rabbi Kibbitz drank some tea, then added more sugar. "Mind you, I'm not sure how Jacob Schlemiel will feel if he ever reads it, but I think he's already told his boys about their curse, so it shouldn't matter too much."

"I'll write him an apology," Rabbi Abrahms said.

"Nonsense. He'll be fine. I only have one problem."

Rabbi Abrahms tensed.

Rabbi Kibbitz continued. "Why did you spell my name Kibabibitz? There's too many letters. At first I thought it was a mistake, but you did it throughout the whole book."

"Ha!" Rabbi Abrahms laughed nervously. "It was funnier. It was a mistake at first, but when the printer saw it the first time, he almost fell out of his chair laughing, so we kept it. Also, it helps to make the book a little more fiction than fact, so that in case you did actually decide to sue me I could say that I wasn't really writing about you but about this other fellow, Rabbi Kibabibitz. Look, I'm sorry. It was Reb Cantor's idea. If you really need me to change it, I can't because the book is already being printed and sold and is in its fourth edition. It's wildly successful in Poland, and I hear that the book sellers in Pinsk can't keep it on the shelves."

"Really? It's already out?" said Rabbi Kibbitz. He bobbed his head. "How about that? Well, then you should ignore my corrections in the margins, and Mazel Tov. If the book is doing as well as it seems then maybe when you donate the money to the education fund, I will be able to offer you the position of school teacher with enough salary to truly hire a housekeeper."

"That would be wonderful," Rabbi Abrahms agreed.

"So, how about it?" Rabbi Kibbitz said.

"How about what?"

"Will you take the job?"

"What job?" Rabbi Abrams asked.

"School teacher of Chelm. And junior rabbi of course," Rabbi Kibbitz said. "I'm going crazy. They're making me crazy! I liked being retired. I can't stand going to school in the mornings. And I know that the students don't like it either. Boys and girls together? Oh, you don't know that. That's the latest news. After we let Rachel Cohen come to yeshiva, the dam burst and we had to let them all in. And they're all crazy. Girls and boys alike. I can't get them to sit still and listen. I don't know how you did it. You are a good schoolteacher. I'm a lousy one."

"Girls?" Rabbi Abrahms said. "You mean just Rachel Cohen or

more than her?

"Yes, more," Rabbi Kibbitz said. "More and more and more and more. All of them. And all the boys, too. Even the ones who used to skip school now come just to see the girls. It's a mess. It's a zoo. It's about as bad as you imagined it when we first talked about it before Rachel started. But what can I do? We opened the barn door and the whole herd of horses got in."

"You mean they escaped, don't you?"

"No," Rabbi Kibbitz shook his head furiously. "They all show up every day! Not to listen to me, but to talk with each other. To chitter and chatter and clatter and natter and it's making me crazy.[48] Come back to Chelm. Take your job. We'll hire you a housekeeper. Please! I'm begging you."

Rabbi Abrahms looked at his old friend and realized that he was serious. "But I have a job here. I'm the man in charge."

"Do you like it?" Rabbi Kibbitz said, bluntly.

Truth was that Rabbi Abrahms missed Chelm. Smyrna was too big. The synagogue was too large. The congregation was gigantic. There were more people on the board of directors than could fit into the small schoolroom in Chelm. In addition to prayers and teaching and studying, he had meetings to go to three, four, even five times a day. The life cycle duties alone, officiating at all the brisses and bar mitzvahs and weddings and funerals were almost a full-time job. Plus they wanted him to be the mashgiach, and make sure that all the butcher shops in Smyrna kept kosher law. And all the sick visits were exhausting. It was a wonder that Rabbi Sarnoff had lived to be eighty.

"I can't desert them," Rabbi Abrahms said, tactfully avoiding the truth. "They need somebody."

"But do they need you?" asked Rabbi Kibbitz. "I understand what you're saying. Smyrna does need a rabbi. But Chelm needs you in particular. The village of Chelm wants and needs Rabbi

---

[48] Actually, Rabbi Kibbitz kept using the Yiddish word, *meshuggah*, which means crazy. The author of the book didn't want to use that word here, because there's a superstition in Chelm that if you use the word meshuggah more than twice in a row it means that you're actually crazy. Crazy, right?

Yohon Abrahms."

Rabbi Abrahms rubbed his chin nervously. His heart felt warm, but his mind was concerned. "They haven't really offered me the final position yet."

"It's been months!" Rabbi Kibbitz said, outraged.

"I know!" Rabbi Abrahms agreed.

"What are they waiting for?"

"They say that I still need to prove myself," Rabbi Abrahms sighed. "But I think they're still interviewing other people."

Rabbi Kibbitz frowned and then loudly smacked his hand against the manuscript on the table. "You and I both know that, even before your book, people around the world thought villagers from Chelm were fools, but we have nothing on the idiocy of the townspeople of Smyrna! Here they have hired the youngest, the strongest, the smartest, the kindest, the gentlest, the sweetest, and the most honest rabbi in the entire world! And they're looking for somebody better? Feh. I would spit, except it would mess up the floor, and your housekeeper would have my head."

He sighed and stood up. "All right. I can't hire you away, so I have to go."

"Won't you stay and play some chess?" Rabbi Abrahms said.

Rabbi Kibbitz laughed. "Since when do you play chess? I thought you were a cribbage man."

"I am," the younger rabbi blushed. "But I have this chess set here, and I thought I should learn."

"Stick to your own games," Rabbi Kibbitz said. "Learn the new ones only when you want to, not because you think you should. Let me know what happens. The offer is open. I have a cabbage stew waiting for me in Chelm."

The two men rose. They embraced. Rabbi Abrahms helped Rabbi Kibbitz on with his coat, and they walked to the door. "It was good to see you. Are you going to be all right teaching in Chelm?"

"I'll be fine," Rabbi Kibbitz shrugged. "Worst that happens is I bore some poor child to death, and they arrest me for murder. But I don't think that's likely, because nobody listens to me anyway. It was good to see you too. Tell me one thing."

"What?" Rabbi Abrahms said.

"Have you heard from her?" Rabbi Kibbitz asked. His face was somber and serious. "Have you had any news about her?"

Rabbi Abrahms felt his heart skip a beat. "Her? Her who?"

Rabbi Kibbitz laughed. He couldn't help himself. "Your wife, of course!"

There was a crash from the dining room. It sounded like the entire platter of teacups had just fallen to the floor and shattered.

Both men jumped at the noise.

Then Rabbi Abrahms spoke. "No. No news. Thank you for coming, my friend. I had better go and help out with that mess."

Rabbi Kibbitz looked puzzled. "Isn't the housekeeper supposed to clean up the mess that she makes?"

"No." Rabbi Abrahms gave his friend another long hug. "Not this mess." Then he went inside and shut the door.

Rabbi Kibbitz stared at the brass door knocker and shook his head. One plus one plus one rarely equaled three.

Chapter Thirty-Six

The Student and the Dissident

As soon as the door was safely closed, Yohon Abrahms ran back to the dining room.

Sarah Cohen was standing there, beside the table. Her hands were filled with broken teacups. Blood was dripping from her fingertips. Her empty eyes lifted and stared at him with growing anger.

"You're married?" she said. It was little more than a whisper.

He couldn't speak.

She wore a slender silk dress that she had found in Rabbi Sarnoff's cedar chest. The scarves she had used to mask her face from Rabbi Kibbitz had fallen around her shoulders.

"You're married?"

He nodded his head. Yes.

He watched her squeezing a broken teacup in her hand. He stepped forward and took it from her. He set it on the table. He led her into the kitchen and lifted and pulled the hand pump until the water began to flow clear into the basin. He held her hands under the cold water, rinsing away the dirt and the bits of broken china. The basin turned pink and then red.

He sat her at the kitchen table, where they had usually eaten their meals together. From a cupboard next to the kitchen sink, he took the small box of ointments and bandages he had brought with him from Chelm. He smeared her hands with a salve that Mrs. Chaipul recommended for cuts, and then gently wrapped each palm and finger with light gauze, which he carefully tucked in under itself, so it wouldn't unwrap.

He went back into the dining room and looked at the wreckage. Everything was broken. It could wait.

He returned to the kitchen, took two sturdy mugs from the shelf, and filled them with hot tea from the samovar. He added milk to his, and two teaspoons of sugar to hers, which he set on the table in front of her.

Sarah Cohen had been silent the whole time. At last, when she spoke, she asked the question again. "You're married?"

"Yes," he said, staring into his tea.

"Were you going to tell me?"

He shook his head. "No."

Her eyes widened and her nostrils flared. "Why not?"

He sighed and rocked in his chair as if he was davening just a bit.[49]

Then he told her…

* * *

When I was a rabbinical student there was a coffee shop in Moscow that we would frequent. It was not a reputable place. There was music and poetry most evenings and always arguments and shouting. But we went there because, for the price of a cheap cup of coffee you could sit for hours and read or play cards. The coffee was awful, the pastries were stale, and we didn't dare ask if they were kosher or not. We went there because there were girls. Single girls, who would come in and play guitar or smoke cigarettes.

The owner was a thin Ukrainian woman who always had a cigarette dangling from her lips. The ash would grow longer and longer and we would sometimes take bets about whose coffee it would fall into. It was part of the charm.

The first time I saw her, I was struck by her beauty. She had straight dark hair, intense eyes, and a smile and laugh that filled the room with joy. Every man in the room was envious of the journalist who had brought her in on his arm. But he said something stupid, and she slapped him in the face, and he left in anger.

And then she looked at me.

My friend Izzy and I had been listening to a scrawny hirsute

---

[49] Davening is a rocking motion that Jewish men frequently make while praying. Some see it as a form of physical meditation. Others do it to stay awake.

poet with bad teeth spewing a horrible rant about the government and bread.

There was a smattering of applause, and then a pause, and I leaped into it. I stood up. I walked to the front of the room. I had never done anything like this before. I cleared my throat and from the center of my heart I spoke to her.

I translated the Song of Solomon directly into Russian. I told her the entire psalm as if I had written it myself because at that moment the words of the wisest one were my own.

The room was silent. Not even a teaspoon clinked in the sugar bowl.

When I was done, they clapped, as if I had done something remarkable, which I suppose I had because it was rare to command that level of attention in this place of agitation and dissent.

When I was done, she walked to me. She kissed me on the lips and held her body against mine.

I had never touched a woman, except for my mother. It was electric. It was sudden. It was real. All of my studies, all of my life, none of that mattered inside that kiss. And I kissed her back, as if I knew what I was doing.

From then on, we spent almost every moment together. I neglected my studies, and she neglected her painting. She was an artist, of course. A painter, who worked with colors. She showed me her pictures, but I didn't really like them. She laughed and said that I was the only man she had ever slept with who hadn't complimented her work.

Yes, we slept together. And two weeks later I asked her to marry me, and I still can't believe that she said yes.

She didn't believe in marriage. She had told me this. But she did this for me because she knew that I did.

We told no one. Not our families. Not our friends. We went to a rabbi on the other side of Moscow and gave him some money. It was done.

I thought I would feel different, but I didn't. I still felt consumed and impassioned.

I went back to my studies and she went back to her painting, and in the afternoons we would meet at the coffee shop and smoke cigarettes and play cribbage for hours before sneaking away to her studio in the attic of a four-story apartment building where we lived as husband and wife.

The days and the weeks passed, and I remember every single moment. We met near the end of winter. We married on the third day of spring. We picked mushrooms in the woods and cooked them in soups and stews because we had no money. When the attic grew hot in the summer, we rejoiced and roamed about in our small stuffy garden as naked as Adam and Eve.

Then, one morning in late summer, I woke to hear pounding at the door downstairs. It sounded like drums. She lay next to me and I brushed her hair with my fingers. Then I heard the front door open, and footsteps, like marching, like running, like a horse galloping up the stairs.

The pounding this time was closer. The door in the floor of our attic was shaking with violent angry continuous pounding.

"Did you pay the rent?" I asked her.

But her face was white as a sheet.

The door burst open and in they came. Three large men ran up the stairs. They took her. They laughed at her nakedness, ogled her beauty. One of them struck me with a leather sack as I stood to object, and I flew backward across the room, stunned by the blow.

They made her dress, and they dragged her away. I couldn't move. I couldn't stop them. One of them showed me a pistol, but he didn't even have to draw it.

I was naked and alone and bleeding, and she was gone.

We had known that the secret police were always a risk. But we laughed at their stupidity. Everyone spoke against the government. Everyone had a litany of complaints. Everyone dreamed of a day of revolution and rule by the people. We thought we were safe because we were all alike. We thought we were safe because we were young, and we knew in our hearts that we did not mean it, and that we did not matter. We were not the ones who would rush to the barricades. We were the ones who liked coffee and pastries and cards and poetry.

But she had painted a canvas showing a man having relations with an animal, with a pig. It was a horrible and disturbing and ugly painting. It was so ugly that it was the best painting she ever made. Naturally a gallery owner hung it on his wall. Naturally it caused a stir in the newspapers. Naturally the secret police looked at it, and when they did they saw that the face of the smiling man was the face of the Czar himself.

The gallery was burned to the ground. They took her away.

I asked. I looked. I tried to find her. She was gone. No one knew where. I couldn't find her. It was as if she never existed.

I went back to my studies. I graduated. Years passed. I read in the newspaper one day that a village was looking for a mohel.

And so I came to Chelm.

* * *

Sarah had listened without speaking and when he was done, she asked, "Did you ever see her again?"

He shook his head.

"She could be dead," she said.

"Maybe," he whispered. "But I don't think so. And I don't know. So, technically I'm still married."

"What was her name?"

"Malka. Malka Abrahms."

Sarah nodded. She stood. She leaned over and kissed him on his cheek.

He closed his eyes and felt the soft brush of her lips.

"I'm sorry," she whispered. Then she went back into the dining room and began cleaning up the mess.

With his eyes still closed, Yohon Abrahms touched his jacket and felt the pocket. There was the onionskin letter from Moscow in its thin envelope that he had received three weeks earlier. As if reading with his fingers, he remembered the words his friend Izzy had written.

"There is a rumor of a general pardon this spring. They say that there are just too many people in prison, so they're letting them go to save money. I don't know if Malka is still alive, but I thought you should know."

Part Eight

The Council (Again)

Chapter Thirty-Seven

Unleashing the Wind

Chanah Chaipul cursed when she saw the crocuses blooming in the center of Chelm's circular village square. The early morning sky was crisp blue and spring was coming. The tiny flowers were pink and purple and red and yellow, arranged in four wavy rows years and years before as a signal.

"No no. Not today," Chanah muttered. "I have a brisket and fourteen chickens that need…"

She stopped and glanced at the well. Three women were already there. Esther Gold, Eleanor Stein, and Nora Goodman were filling their buckets and chatting away eagerly. When they saw Chanah in the square, they pointed at the crocuses and then waved their hands in front of their noses.

Chanah sighed and shook her head. "Everything will have to wait."

She waved back. She finished her short walk to her restaurant, opened the door, went to the counter, and jotted a note, which she set in the window. Then she went into the back room to make sandwiches.

* * *

"Closed until lunchish," Rabbi Kibbitz muttered. "What is lunchish? When is lunchish?"

Reb Cantor smiled. "After you are hungry for the midday meal, but before you are completely famished."

"Oh," the tired rabbi yawned. "Would you mind if we went to your house for coffee? I am all out."

"I would say yes," the merchant said, "but my wife seems to have gone out early today, and Ramunya the servant girl makes coffee that tastes worse than the mud from the Uherka River."

"Your wife is gone?" said Reb Stein, who had just arrived. "Mine too." Then he read the restaurant's sign. "Closed until lunchish? What does that mean?"

While Reb Cantor explained, Rabbi Kibbitz's mind slowly turned.

"Were there crocuses blooming in the square this morning?" he asked.

"I don't come that way," said Reb Cantor.

"Yes," said Reb Stein brightly. "Four beautiful rows of flowers."

Rabbi Kibbitz paled. "Oy."

"Rebbe, are you all right?" Reb Stein asked.

"I'm all right," the oldest man in Chelm said. "It's just..."

"You're hungry. Come to my house," said Reb Cantor. "We might not have coffee, but even Ramunya can boil water for some tea."

The Rabbi grabbed the merchant's hand. "You have real glass windows in your house, don't you? They're tight, aren't they?"

Reb Cantor shrugged. Every so often he worried that Rabbi Kibbitz was getting too old for the job. "They shake in the wind, but they let the light in."

"Well, it's better than nothing," the rabbi muttered.

"Will he be ok?" Reb Stein whispered.

Reb Cantor shrugged.

"Sourdough bread this week," the rabbi muttered. "I hate sourdough bread."

"It's challenging enough to bake bread with cabbage. I wasn't going to make sourdough," Reb Stein said. "I have a new batch of baker's yeast."

"Like you have a choice!" the rabbi shot back, angrily.

"I guess children really are making him crazy," Reb Stein said to Reb Cantor. "Get him to lie down."

"You'll see!" the rabbi shouted as Reb Cantor led him away. "Sourdough bread. You'll see!"

* * *

There was a feverish knocking at the door of the Council Chambers.

Chanah Chaipul opened the door and saw Judith Chiribimbam's grinning face.

"It's springtime!" Judith said, brightly. She was practically singing. "The crocuses are in bloom! Time for the bottom burps!"

"You don't have to be so cheerful about it," Shoshana Cantor muttered.

Judith Chiribimbam was rarely seen at the Council of Wise Women. She was a farm woman, who prided herself on her strength and independence. She usually tested new farm hands by offering to beat them in an arm wrestling contest. The ones who refused were never hired. The ones who were defeated rarely stayed on the farm for more than a season.

"I love this day," Judith said, as she barged into the room. "It's such a powerful ritual. Such a magnificent release. We acknowledge our choices, the automatic decisions and tensions we have created for an entire year, and then let them go! Then we are empty vessels, free of all inhibitions."

Judith's voice had risen to a feverish pitch. Then she paused and shrugged. "For a moment anyway. Then, of course we will probably go back to our old habits. But that is another thing entirely."

"I still think it's disgusting," Shoshana Cantor grumbled.

"Then why are you here?" Judith asked. Her feet were planted and her hands were on her hips.

Shoshana climbed to her feet, put her hands on her own hips, and stared at Judith. "Because after a winter of cabbage, cabbage, and more cabbage, I am so fat and bloated and full of gas that if I don't do something about it I will plotz."

Judith grinned. "Good to hear it, sister!" she said, as she enveloped Shoshana in a bear hug.

"I'm not your sister," Shoshana muttered, embarrassed by the affection. "Don't squeeze so hard. I don't want to start early!"

Judith let go of Shoshana just as Bertha Shimmel burst in the door. "Am I late? I had to move all the finished cheese to the cellar and seal it up. Then I had to set out the special cheese on the shelves and open all the windows of the curing shed. I'm not late, am I?"

"Of course not. Don't you think you would have known?" Judith said, wrapping Bertha in her arms. "How have you been?"

"Lonely," Bertha admitted. "It's been hard since Bella got married to the cheesemonger from Moscow and Peninah spends half the day in the school." She pried herself loose from Judith's grip. "Other than that, fine. How about you?"

"Bella's married? Mazel tov!" Judith said. "I had another child."

Bertha stepped back. "No. Really? You look wonderful. A daughter?"

"Thank you," Judith beamed. "Of course!"

With four, now five, daughters, Judith Chiribimbam was the only woman in Chelm who never expressed longing for a son. She liked to say that any daughter of hers was worth two sons on the open market. It infuriated her husband, but she had placated him with the promise that they could keep trying as often as he liked until he got what he wanted, or one of them died.[50]

"My latest daughter is another ray of sunshine, and strong too. She has teeth already!"

Chanah couldn't help but chuckle. Then she clapped her hands three times.[51]

The nearly full Council Room fell silent. Judith began wriggling her tush…

"Stop!" Chanah said. "Wait. We have to change our plan for this year!"

"What?" Esther Gold said. "Why?"

"After The Winter of The Cabbage," Chanah said, "if we perform the ceremony in the cave, I'm not sure we'll survive. Instead, we will go up to East Hill and begin there."

"Good thinking," Shoshana said.

Judith nodded. "For once I agree."

The women began filing out of the Council Chambers, walked through the cave tunnel, past the mikveh, and out into the mid-

---

[50] Like Judith, her husband was a stranger in Chelm. In fact, no one was really sure what he looked like, or if his name was Reb Bam, Reb Bimbam or Reb Chiribimbam.

[51] It was better than banging a gavel or whistling.

morning air.

"Are you all right?" Judith asked Bertha. "You look concerned."

"I don't know what will happen to our special cheese," the goat farmer answered. "It's taken decades to perfect, and the hills are to the north and so far away from our shed."

"We'll just have to find out," Judith smiled.

Bertha smiled back. The two women linked elbows as they skipped out of the village.

* * *

Rabbi Kibbitz was peering out the window of Reb Cantor's house.

"What do you see?" the merchant asked.

"A parade of women."

"Really?" The fat man sidled up to the window. "My wife is there. Mrs. Chaipul, too. All the women in Chelm?" He reached for the lock to open the window.

"Stop!" the rabbi said, grabbing the merchant's sleeve. "Don't open the windows."

"I was just going to call for my wife, and ask her where she's going and when she's going to have breakfast ready."

The rabbi ignored his friend. "Do you have a cellar?"

"Yes."

"Hurry!"

* * *

A small fire was burning at the top of East Hill. There was a circle of logs for seating around the fire pit. Hannah Meier sat on one of the logs and prodded the flames. A cast iron kettle squatted on a pile of stones just next to the fire.

Chanah grunted and sat next to her. "We'll wait a few more minutes for everyone to get to the top and catch our breaths."

"Oy," moaned Shoshana. "I need new shoes."

"Will anyone please tell me what is going on?" asked Perel Dov.

Perel was the newest member of the Council. Her oldest son had just been bar mitzvahed, and she was still a little confused about this strange ritual.

Judith sidled next to Perel and stuck out her hand. "Hi, I'm

Judith."

Perel introduced herself, reached out, and was amazed at how firm Judith's grip was.

"Tell me, Perel," Judith said. "Do you ever fart in front of your husband?"

Perel blinked. She was still wincing from the pain of the handshake. "Pardon?"

"Look, everybody farts. It's a fact. What goes in has to come out. But we women are not supposed to fart in front of our men. This we are taught from an early age.

"Men fart all the time. They poot and twee and blat and flap their behinds at every opportunity. Then they scratch and laugh about it. They make jokes about it. They boast about it. Rarely do they apologize, and those who can will always blame the dog.

"We women have to sit and keep mum. Even me. I do almost everything like a man. I can even pee standing up. But I don't fart in front of my husband. I just can't do it.

"So I hold it in. And I hold it in. And I hold it in. Sure, some of that gets let loose during the course of my daily business. But something about holding it for so long creates a tension. It creates anxiety. Sometimes it even creates anger.

"Women need to let go. And so we, the Council of Wise Women, have created this magnificent ceremony where we unleash the wind!"

Judith's speech had been so enthusiastic that it was actually greeted with a round of applause.

"Well, I guess that's my signal," Chanah muttered. She raised her voice. "Everybody stand up."

"What's in the pot?" Perel whispered.

"Warm moist towels," Judith whispered back.

Chanah lifted her finger. The wind was blowing from the South, away from Chelm and toward Smyrna. For the first time since she'd seen the crocuses she allowed herself a small smile.

"All right, everyone. Line up and turn toward Chelm."

She had picked an open stretch of soft moss for them all to stand in, so that their feet could connect to the soil and not to the rocks.

The women arranged themselves in a ragged line. Several, who realized that they stood behind others, hustled to squeeze themselves in between.

"Underthings down!"

It was like watching a very strange army maneuver. Like a wave of flags being lowered, undergarments of all kinds fell from beneath the dresses of the gathered women.

"Bend over."

As one, the row of ladies bent at the waist. Some set their hands on their knees. The more flexible ones touched the moss with the palms of their hands.

"Skirts up!"

In Chelm, and throughout the land, a woman's modesty goes without saying. There are parts of the body that are never ever displayed. Most of the women involved closed their eyes at this point, because anyone observing this part of the ritual was likely to be struck dead with shock, as one after another their pale behinds were revealed to the open air. Some bottoms were smooth, some were shiny, some were pitted, some wrinkled, some red, some pink, some dry, and some were better not described.

"Judith," Chanah Chaipul said, "would you like to do the honors of releasing the wind?"

Judith's eyes twinkled. "It would be my pleasure. Ready? Aim! RELEASE THE WIND!"

* * *

"Is that thunder?" Reb Cantor said. As long as they were in the basement, he was proudly showing the rabbi his cellar stock of fine French wines. "It was such a clear day. I didn't see a cloud in the sky."

Just then the earth began to shake, and dust fell from the ceiling beams.

"An earthquake?" the merchant screeched. "We'll be crushed." He began to run for the stairs.

"Wait!" the Rabbi begged. "Don't go upstairs yet. Please. Wait!"

But it was too late. Reb Cantor banged through the door at the top of the stairs, and then staggered backwards, barely catching himself on the doorframe.

"Feh! What is that horrible smell?"

In the basement, Rabbi Kibbitz pinched his nose and held his breath until he passed out cold on the floor.

* * *

The explosion was heard in Smyrna. That much was confirmed a week later. They said that an echo of it reached as far as Moscow, but no one could prove it.

What is known was that, at the moment Judith shouted "Release!" the natural winds changed direction and all of the released winds blew backwards towards Chelm.

The breeze was so strong that the small fire went out, which was fortunate because the gas did not explode.

The gale, however, flowed invisibly over the long line of half-dressed women, and every single one of them fell unconscious, dropping face first onto the moss, which cushioned their cheeks.

Birds dropped from the trees as the breeze drifted past.

For a week, cows gave nothing but rancid milk, and for a month (as Rabbi Kibbitz had predicted) all of Reb Stein's breads were sourdough, no matter how much he scrubbed his bakery.

In the center of the round square, the patch of crocuses turned yellow, then brown, then black. All of the newly formed petals drifted to the ground like ash.

Whether it was a minute or an hour later, one by one, the Council of Wise Women of Chelm blinked their eyes and stumbled to their feet. Many of them immediately fell back down because their undergarments were around their ankles.

"I feel amazing!" Perel told Judith. "I think I lost five pounds!"

"Isn't it wonderful?" Judith agreed, wiping tears from her eyes. "Better out than in."

"A towel," Hannah called. "Does anyone need a towel?"

When she returned to her farm that afternoon, Bertha Shimmel was thrilled to see that the cheese wheels set in the open air shed had already developed a thick rind. Later, the special spring cheese from the Shimmel Sisters' Dairy was described in the Smyrna newspaper as, "…their best effort—powerfully pungent, wincingly ripe and runny with faintest hint of cabbage."

Chapter Thirty-Seven

A Fresh Breeze

There was something new in the air. Bella Shimmel sensed it at dawn as she milked the goats. In the several weeks since the unprecedented releasing of the wind, she and everyone else in Chelm had been breathing exclusively through their mouths. Perhaps that was it. She cautiously sniffed the air. A fresh breeze? A clearing of the lingering stench of intestinally digested and re-released cabbage? Whatever it was, it felt good to be able to inhale through her nostrils again.

Benjamin Cohen, the tailor, felt it too, as he rose for his morning prayers. All winter, he had been tied in knots around the abrupt departure of his wife, Sarah. His stomach had been tight, and in the morning, his pillow was often damp from what seemed to be an endless supply of soundless tears. He had taken great care to keep a dry pillow under his bed, so that his daughter Rachel wouldn't discover his secret, if she should decide to wash his bedclothes on a whim. Today, though, the pillow was dry, and there was no need to change it.

As was his habit, he dressed quietly and made his way through the brightening streets of Chelm to share the morning minyan.[52] For the first time in months, his step was light, and he almost felt like dancing. A smile played across his face, and even as he grinned, he felt a tinge of sadness that perhaps he had changed somehow

---

[52] A minyan is a gathering of ten men who have been Bar Mitzvahed. According to Rabbi Abrahms, you need at least a minyan for a prayer gathering to be official and count. According to Rabbi Kibbitz, since it's a well-known fact that two Jews have at least three opinions you only need seven. According to Mrs. Chaipul, any time you get more than five men over the age of 13 together it's a disaster waiting to happen.

without understanding why.

Hanna Meier awoke with such palpitations that for a moment she considered telling her husband to hurry and get Mrs. Chaipul. Then, when she realized what it was that she had been thinking about, she blushed down to her very core. Then, she woke him anyway. It had been years since she had felt that way, and before they were done, he was completely exhausted, and stayed in bed an extra three hours while she, humming to herself, made him a huge breakfast that she brought back and ate with him in bed.

All through the village of Chelm, children were bouncing, jumping, and giggling. Their mothers shouted at them to finish their cabbage broth, but without any real anger or conviction, because they too felt the inexplicable joy.

A delegation of men converged on Rabbi Kibbitz's study after prayers, and expressed their confusion.

"I don't understand this, Rabbi," said Reb Gold, speaking on behalf of all the men. "Yesterday I was miserable to the point of constipation. I felt no optimism or hope about the future. Every day ahead looked as bleak as the next. The sun would be shining in the blue sky, and I could only see the clouds to come. And now I am happy. I have done nothing different. Yesterday I was shouting at my wife and children. Today I am as glad to see them, as they are to see me. We hugged and tickled each other. I laughed. I haven't laughed in what seems like forever. What's going on?"

The rabbi's eyes twinkled. He held his hand to his mouth in a gesture of pretended thoughtfulness that was really designed to mask the grin hidden beneath his thick white beard.

"I think perhaps," he said, "we should all gather together in the village square to find out if this phenomenon is widespread, and discuss its consequences."

"A brilliant idea!" spurted Reb Shikker. He covered his lips in astonishment because he usually felt quite dour until after his morning coffee.

Chelm, as you know, has a round square. It is one of the unique features of the village. "You can't corner a Chelmener!" is one of their favorite expressions. The Smyrnans, of course think that it is

another indication of the foolishness of their neighbors, but when
they visit from time to time, they do walk away with the feeling
that the circle in the middle of Chelm fits perfectly, the way a hole
in the middle of a wheel allows the axle to function. On the south
arc of the round square is the Synagogue. On the north arc is Mrs.
Chaipul's restaurant. To the east is the bakery, and to the west is the
merchant's house. In the center is a small hill, on top of which the
village well is sunk.

From time to time, youngsters imagine holding their wedding
feasts outside in the round square. They dream of poles on the
top of the hill ribboning streamers of silk out in all directions, like
a giant spoked chupah.[53] Won't it be wonderful! The bride and
groom, and the whole village will pray and then eat in the open
air. Mrs. Chaipul, and every other wise woman, listen patiently
to the bride's wishes, and then make alternative plans to hold the
feast in the social hall, because the weather in Chelm is notoriously
fickle, and an outdoor celebration is almost certainly doomed to a
sudden deluge of rain, a blizzard of snow, a wailing of hail, or a wild
whipping of wind, regardless of the season or how clear the skies
had been a moment before.

None of this seemed to matter on this particular morning
because the mood of the day seemed to call for action rather than
reflection.

The men talked, and a plan was formulated. At the Rabbi's
suggestion, they began bringing tables from the social hall to the
square. When the school children arrived, they were thrilled to hear
that classes were canceled, and their only assignment was to start
schlepping chairs.

Mrs. Chaipul and the women were already in the round square
with piles of wooden boxes and baskets of white linen tablecloths,
which they ingeniously clipped to the table with a series of small
clamps that the caterer had commissioned from Jacob Schlemiel,
the carpenter.

It was mid morning by the time everything was ready. With the

---

[53] A chupah is a four-poled wedding canopy, sometimes made from a tallis. It
may keep the sun out of the bride's face, but it won't stop the rain.

exception of the streamers, the scene resembled the thwarted vision of so many brides. Circling the well hill were dozens of tables and hundreds of chairs.

Old men and women sat firmly in their seats. Young children raced to and fro. Bulga the Fisherman had brought out his fiddle, and Judith Chiribimbam had forced her husband to go home to retrieve and dust off his clarinet. Now the two of them were noodling away at a bright Klezmer tune.[54]

Reb Gold, however, was still feeling anxious in his exuberance. He wandered through the assemblage looking for some sort of reason, some sort of order, some kind of comprehension. The Council of Elders needed to make a decision, have some kind of a ruling.

"Where is Reb Cantor?" Reb Gold asked. "Where is Reb Stein? Why aren't they here?"

"Shh," Rabbi Kibbitz said.

"No," Reb Gold said, nervously. "It's not right. Something's wrong."

"Shhhh," Rabbi Kibbitz insisted. "Listen."

"I can't hear anything!" Reb Gold said, his voice rising higher. "Everyone is yelling and laughing and talking all at once. It just doesn't make sense."

Then, Rabbi Kibbitz clapped his hands three times, and much to his (and everyone else's surprise) the entire square fell into a hushed silence.

(Later on, they realized that moment of quiet was the true miracle of the day. Never in the history of Chelm, never in the history of the entire Jewish people, has a gathering of more than six fallen quiet so quickly and remained quiet so long.)

Rather than risk a conversation, Rabbi Kibbitz himself said nothing. He held the index finger of his left hand to his lips. His right hand, he lifted and cupped behind his right ear.

Shhh, he was signing. Listen.

For a moment all they heard were the birds in the sky, and the various wheezes and coughs that even the most attentive people

---

[54] Klezmer is Jewish jazz. Hot stuff!

can't hold in.

Then there was a change. A rumbling, faint at first — it sounded like distant thunder. Then banging. Then clattering. Then stomping and stamping and hoof beats and wheels.

Then, from between the two hills to the north of Chelm, four wagons appeared, each drawn by two horses.

Were the Cossacks coming? Wouldn't it just be the luck of the village to collect in an expression of happiness only to have it dashed and burned by the evil of soldiers!

But before such anxiety could spread, the figure driving the horses on the lead wagon was recognized as Reb Cantor, the merchant. The men behind him were strangers, but they did not seem to be chasing him, so much as simply following his lead.

The four covered carts vanished for a moment as they wended their way through the streets, between the houses, before entering the round square, and performing a complete lap, encircling the gathered people.

When at last the carts stopped, one at each of the four points of the compass, Reb Cantor leaped from his seat with a nimbleness that startled everyone. He ran to Rabbi Kibbitz and Mrs. Chaipul.

"Is everything ready?" he panted.

"I think so," the Rabbi said.

Mrs. Chaipul nodded. "As ready as ever."

"May I?" Reb Cantor said.

"Absolutely," the Rabbi said.

With a broad smile on his face, Reb Cantor climbed up on the nearest table, which sank down somewhat into the ground and creaked under his immense weight.

Mrs. Chaipul rolled her eyes and made a note to send him a bill for the cleaning of the tablecloth.

"My good villagers," shouted the merchant, "I declare the winter of the cabbage over! Cabbage is done. From today we will eat no more cabbage forever!"

Everyone cheered and clapped and pounded the tables. The din was as loud as the quiet had been silent. It went on and on and on...

Until a shrill voice screeched, "But I like cabbage!"

Everyone looked about to see who had spoken. It was Doodle, the most foolish boy in the village. While all around him people began to roll their eyes, Doodle said the next thing that came into his mind. "If we won't eat cabbage, what will we eat?"

There was a gasp at the truth at the heart of this question. Ever since the great chicken soup bucket brigade, the villagers of Chelm had little or no food, except for the abundance of cabbage. There had been no money for domesticated animals. An egg in Chelm would have been worth its weight in gold, a chicken its weight in diamonds. The spring plantings weren't even in the ground. It would be late spring and early summer before even the smallest vegetables could be harvested. Even Reb Cantor the merchant had been bankrupted in the giving of life to the ungrateful people of Smyrna.

"Doodle, I'm glad you asked," said the merchant, unfazed. "Our beloved former school teacher Rabbi Yohon Abrahms wrote a book about all of us, and he donated all the proceeds to the village. I took his profits and my profits and I have brought food! It is lunch time!"

With that, the covers were swept off the four wagons, and a majesty of comestibles was revealed.

There were piles of dried fruit, stacks of potatoes, baskets of winter greens, barrels of sour kosher pickles, but even more significant, there was meat. Seventeen different kinds of salami, forty-two pastrami, and six hundred pounds of corned beef!

"I even brought buckets of mustard!" Reb Cantor kvelled.[55]

There was a gasp and a loud slurping sound as every man, woman, and child in Chelm began to drool profusely, streams of spittle sluicing down their cheeks and falling from their chins in cascading waterfalls.

Even Reb Cantor, who had dined well that morning as he'd gathered his supplies in Smyrna, found himself reaching into his pocket for a handkerchief.

---

[55] Kvelling is swelling with pride, like a Mother over a child's drawing. Usually considered a good thing, you want to avoid kvelling too much or it festers like a pimple.

"But what about the bread?" screeched Reb Shikker. Again he covered his lips, disturbed by his own impudence. Then he stood firm on the realization as he yelled, "You can't make a sandwich without any bread!"

Reb Cantor laughed. "Well, you know, it's so close to Passover, that I thought bringing bread to Chelm would be a mistake. It's so much work to look for all the crumbs…"

Shouts of outrage and hisses of disdain rose through the crowd.

"Besides," the merchant continued, realizing that his joke might prove fatal, "Bread doesn't transport well." He scanned the crowd, panic rising in his eyes. "You need to have fresh bread with sandwiches, and who better to provide us with fresh bread than our own Reb Stein, the baker!"

Just then, gasping from the effort, out of the bakery came Reb Stein, pushing a gigantic wheelbarrow full to the top with warm crackling rye bread. He grunted and wheezed and sputtered to a stop beside the table Reb Cantor was standing on.

"I've been baking all night," he puffed. "I nearly forgot how. Am I late?"

"Almost," said the merchant. "But not quite."

Almost as one, the villagers realized that the scent in the air had been the long-forgotten smell of freshly baked bread – that warmed the heart and filled the soul with promise.

"Wait! Before we get started, one more thing," shouted Reb Cantor.

"What?" came a shout. "Wait?" came another. "Why?" came a third.

"A blessing from Rabbi Kibbitz of course"

All eyes turned to the old Rabbi, who smiled. "While you were setting up, I already said the blessing. Let's eat."

Someone surely would have been trampled if Mrs. Chaipul hadn't been ready with the carving knives, and the boxes full of plates and silver, and the glasses of water. Instead, like a general in charge of a battle, she appointed captains who quickly constructed, served, and distributed the thickest, juiciest, fattiest, and most delicious sandwiches in the history of Chelm.

Again, when everyone was served and eating in full-mouthed celebration, the round square was nearly silent.

Until Doodle opened his mouth and asked, "Excuse me, but is there any sauerkraut?"

Fortunately nobody choked.

"What?" Doodle said. "I like sauerkraut on my corned beef sandwiches."

Mrs. Chaipul sighed, pushed herself reluctantly away from the table and went to her restaurant. From somewhere inside her kitchen, she managed to find the last of the pickled cabbage from winter. She gave it to Doodle, who piled it eagerly on, and joined with his neighbors in the contentment of desire fulfilled.

Chapter Thirty-Nine

Something Fishy

Time is unstable. Sometimes it drags, and every moment seems longer than a lifetime. More often though, the days and weeks and months speed by in a blur of similarity. In Chelm, as in the rest of the world, time moves at a different pace   for different people. One year, two years, almost three years go by and each family has a different experience. In the Schlemiel household, for example, the three years included robbers and trials, romance, and a double bar mitzvah. Much to the surprise of all the villagers, in those same three years, Rabbi Kibbitz and Mrs. Chaipul were actually finally beginning to think about planning their own wedding.

In the Cohen household, each day of those three years was much the same. Benjamin woke for morning prayers. Rachel made breakfast for her brother and herself. Their father came home from the synagogue, walked them to school, ate his morning meal in Mrs. Chaipul's restaurant, and then went to his shop to cut and snip and stitch and sew. After school, Yakov joined his father in the shop while Rachel dashed home to quickly stir The Soup and then hurry to her job at Mrs. Chaipul's restaurant to help with the evening meal. Sometimes the family ate dinner at their home, but more often they took a table in the back corner of the restaurant, laughing and joking and making conversation with the other customers. Some evenings, Benjamin stopped back at the synagogue to pray, while the children returned to the house and went to sleep. Sometimes at night, lying in bed, Benjamin would stare at the ceiling, in anticipation of another day like the one he had just finished, and allow himself to think the dark and lonely thoughts that during the day he tried so hard to keep at bay.

There were, of course, variations. On the eve of the Sabbath,

Yakov would leave the tailor shop early. He would buy a challah from Reb Stein, and prepare a chicken for the oven and a pot of cholent for the stove. Rachel would return from Mrs. Chaipul's restaurant to make the home ready for the day of rest. The seasons passed with their intricate calendar of celebrations, feasts, and fasts.

It was early springtime. Yakov and Rachel were twelve, nearly thirteen. Mrs. Chaipul had already negotiated the catering for the boy's bar mitzvah feast with Benjamin. Yakov's one request was for fresh smoked salmon, which his father was glad to oblige, provided he didn't have to stop work to go to Smyrna to buy it. Mrs. Chaipul knew that Bulga the Fisherman was fresh out of salmon, so one bright morning she journeyed to Smyrna to visit the fish market and place her order.

It was a busy day, and the fresh breeze made all the women in the small market cheerful and chatty. As a visitor from Chelm, Mrs. Chaipul recognized many of the other customers, but wasn't on intimate terms with any of them. Still she nodded and smiled and laughed at the overheard jokes.

There was, however, one woman who stood slightly apart with a scarf covering her face.

While she waited, Mrs. Chaipul speculated about the stranger. Was she ugly or deformed? Was she shy? Did she have a husband who demanded that his wife keep herself covered at all times? That was something that she'd heard about. Reb Kimmelman, who had traveled the world, said that it was common among the Muslims, and that in Jerusalem he had even met some Christians who hid their wives away like treasure. It was difficult to imagine what that would be like. The woman seemed neither old nor young. She might be any size from skinny to plump. How strange to live in a box made out of cloth, like a gift wrapped and hidden from sight.

When the woman stepped forward to whisper her order to Reb Zalman, the fishmonger, Mrs. Chaipul started. The voice was familiar.

"Sarah?" Mrs. Chaipul said softly.

The veiled woman stopped moving. She stood perfectly still for a long moment, but neither turned nor acknowledged the quiet word.

Mrs. Chaipul was compassionate but stubborn. She repeated herself, and insisted, "Sarah Cohen?"

Totally still, the veiled woman held her pose. She might be waiting for her fish. She might be deaf. Was she just rude? She might be ignoring Mrs. Chaipul. She might have heard. It was impossible to tell.

At last, the man behind the counter handed her a package wrapped in paper. The veiled woman took the fish and placed it into a sack. She backed away from the counter and turned to walk away.

The way she was moving, it was clear that she intended to make no eye contact with Mrs. Chaipul. Then again, she was making no eye contact with anyone else in the market either. Was it personal? Was it intentional? Was it her habit? It was impossible to tell.

For a moment, Mrs. Chaipul considered stepping in her way and causing a confrontation, but what good would that do? If the woman truly was a stranger she would be embarrassed. And if she was Sarah Cohen, then what?

Besides, it was her turn in line and Reb Zalman was laughing and asking, "So what kind of fish do the villagers of Chelm need? I'm all out of cabbage-fish!"

Everyone laughed.

During that moment, the veiled woman slipped by, stepped out of the shop, turned, and vanished into the streets of Smyrna.

Mrs. Chaipul ignored the jibe and told the fishmonger how much salmon she needed and when she needed it by. Then she ordered some pickled pike and a few trout for a special fish fry she wanted to have at the restaurant.[56]

While the shopkeeper was weighing and cutting her fish, Mrs. Chaipul got an idea.

She turned around and asked the woman in line behind her,

---

[56] Bulga the Fisherman never understood why Mrs. Chaipul insisted on buying fish from the market in Smyrna. "I can sell the fish directly to you!" She always patted his hand and replied, "But then I can't complain about the freshness because you'll take it personally."

"Who was that?"

The Smyrnan woman's eyes brightened with the anticipation of juicy gossip. She had a round face, green eyes, and a black mole on her left cheek with a little hair twirling out of it. "Hmm? Who was who?"

"You know who I mean," Mrs. Chaipul said. "The woman with the veil. I'm just curious. Is she well? Does she have a facial disease?"

"Well enough." The woman with the mole chuckled. "You seemed to know who she was. Why don't you tell me?"

All the other Smyrnans were listening now.

Mrs. Chaipul realized that they were looking for information in exchange. Well, two could play at that game. "I'm not sure I was right. She reminded me of an old friend, but when I whispered her name she didn't answer. I didn't want to embarrass her. I'm sure I was mistaken, but I am curious about who she is."

"Ahh," said the woman. "Perhaps she didn't hear you, because I was standing behind you and I didn't quite catch what you said her name was."

Just then a woman near the back of the line said, quite loudly, "That was the new rabbi's housekeeper."

The woman with the green eyes cursed, realizing that she'd missed the opportunity to trade.

"Ahh," nodded Mrs. Chaipul. "So, she lives somewhere in Smyrna?"

"Oy yes," said the woman at the back. "She lives with him and keeps his house."

All the Smyrnan women dissolved in laughter, except for the mole-woman, who frowned with disappointment, since she was unlikely to learn anything new from Mrs. Chaipul.

"Really?" Mrs. Chaipul was surprised. Their new rabbi was Yohon Abrahms, of course, and as soon as the next thought came to her she had to ask. "Are they married?"

The fish store was filled suddenly with commentary.

"Not that I know."

"We don't think so."

"My husband says that's why, after three years, the synagogue board still hasn't offered him the permanent job."

"I heard he was already married."

"He's got two wives?"

"No!"

"I wish I had two husbands."

"Feh. What would you do with them?"

"If he really had two wives wouldn't the synagogue's board have fired him by now?"

"She may be his housekeeper, but of course it's not really his house. It's Rabbi Sarnoff's house, but Rabbi Sarnoff is dead, so really it belongs to the synagogue."

During the chaos, the fishmonger gave Mrs. Chaipul her order and took her money.

Mrs. Chaipul nodded to the woman she'd begun the conversation with. She thought about offering a salve that would probably remove the mole, but women were often touchy about such marks, and decided to let it pass.

The Smyrnan put her hand on Mrs. Chaipul's arm and asked, "So, what was your friend's name?"

Mrs. Chaipul smiled and replied, "I'm sorry. I can't hear you with all this noise. I really must hurry back to Chelm."

She left the shop, stepped into the fresh air. Not a cloud in the sky. She sighed and began walking as she tried to remember the way to Rabbi Sarnoff's house.

Chapter Forty

Visiting

After she banged it three times, Chanah Chaipul stared at the brass door knocker in the shape of a small fur hat.

The door knocker bothered her. Rabbi Abrahms never wore that kind of hat. In fact, he'd always made fun of the style, claiming that "Rabbis who wear hats with so much fur aren't thinking hard enough to keep their heads warm." Three years after Rabbi Sarnoff's death, the knocker should have been tarnished, or even better been removed and replaced with one associated with the new rabbi. Maybe a knocker in the shape of a book?

The thick oak door opened, and Rabbi Abrahms, dressed in Rabbi Sarnoff's long coat and warm fur hat, just like the knocker, poked his head out. "Yes, my dear, what can I…" He stopped as he recognized her. "Mrs. Chaipul! What a pleasant surprise."

"Are you going to invite me in?" she asked.

"Of course, come in," he said as he stepped aside. "Did someone die?"

"No," Chanah said, "but it took you long enough to ask."

The young rabbi smiled. "In Smyrna, I've learned, even such important news is delayed with meaningless polite conversation."

Chanah shrugged and looked around. Inside the house was just like the door knocker. Nothing at all was different from when the old rabbi of Smyrna had been alive. All the paintings on the walls were in the same places. The books on the shelves looked undisturbed. It was like a Rabbi Sarnoff museum, and the door had been opened by a skinny Sarnoff impersonator who was nearly lost inside the dead rabbi's large coat.

"Are you at least wearing your own shoes and underwear?" she asked.

Rabbi Abrahms blinked. He had forgotten how direct the women of Chelm could be. "Yes. Of course I did have to buy shoes last summer because the soles in Rabbi Sarnoff's finally wore out. Would you like some tea? The samovar is somewhat low. It may take some time."

"I didn't come to see you," Chanah said.

Again the poor young man blinked. "Do you need directions? I know that Smyrna is a much bigger place than Chelm and its streets can be confusing…"

She waved her hand dismissively. "I'm not lost. Are you?"

He sighed. He'd forgotten this about Mrs. Chaipul, too. She reminded him of his Aunt Ruth, who, when he was a child, had visited his home every year for Passover, and proceeded to tell him that nothing he did was right. Every time he was around Mrs. Chaipul he felt like a misbehaving boy. "I'm right here," he said. "This is my house. You knocked on the door."

Chanah shook her head. "It doesn't look like your house. It still looks like Rabbi Sarnoff's. How come you didn't redecorate?"

He shrugged. "At first it seemed disrespectful. Then I was lazy. Then there wasn't enough money. And by the time I thought about it again, I'd gotten used to it. Once you know where everything is, it's difficult to move it all around. You understand."

"Is there money now?" she quizzed him. "Are they paying you?"

His eyes darted around the room nervously. He coughed. Then he stuttered, "I get a small stipend. I'm just the interim rabbi. Is that why you came here? Are you asking for money for some cause? I do have a little set aside for…"

"No." She shook her head, interrupting him. "I came to see her."

"Her who?" he said, knowing full well who she meant.

She stared at him, knowing that he knew that she knew. Still, she said it anyway. "I came to see Sarah Cohen."

The young rabbi opened his mouth, and then closed it. He had briefly considered denying everything, but after so much time, it was almost a relief to be caught.

"I'll go get her," he said.

Now Chanah shrugged. "No. Don't bother, I'm sure she's

listening. Why don't you go and bring us some tea. I think we should sit here in the parlor."

"You don't want coffee?" he asked.

"Bring us tea," she said.

Chanah hung her coat on a hook and slid into the sitting room. She lowered herself down into the red leather chair that had always been Rabbi Sarnoff's throne. Whenever she'd visited her old friend, he had sat there like a king, while she had perched on one of the rickety velvet cushioned chairs as if she were a supplicant. She'd often wondered what it would be like to sit in his chair, and was delighted to find it was as comfortable and comforting as she had imagined.

Yohon Abrahms watched the caterer and midwife of Chelm settle herself in Rabbi Sarnoff's chair, and then headed toward the kitchen. As he moved through the dining room, Sarah came the other way around the wide table.

"Mrs. Chaipul is here," he said.

"I know." She nodded. "I heard. I was expecting her. She saw me at the fishmonger's shop."

"I'll get tea."

"She likes extra sugar," Sarah told him.

He smiled. "Doesn't everybody from Chelm?"

"Do I look all right?" she asked as he pushed on the kitchen door.

He paused, turned, and smiled. "You look beautiful as always."

"You say that even first thing in the morning."

He nodded. "You look beautiful even first thing in the morning. Good luck."

He pushed through the door, wandered to the sink, and began filling the kettle to refill the samovar.

* * *

Sarah Cohen waited another moment. She stared into the shiny silver platter that always rested on top of a side table. The tray was difficult to polish, because it was crisscrossed with an intricate etching of a mountain landscape. But if you squinted, you could see your reflection. She looked all right. Certainly not her best, but not her absolute worst. She arranged and then rearranged the scarves around her shoulder and then gave up. It would have to do.

She walked into the parlor, smiled, and nodded. "Hello Mrs. Chaipul."

"Hello, Sarah." The older woman was watching as Sarah had entered. She didn't take her eyes away for a second. "Please, call me Chanah. We don't need to be so formal. I would get up to give you a hug, but this chair is so deep that I'm a little bit stuck."

"Would you like some help?" Sarah asked, politely.

"No. Not yet. We might as well talk. If I'm still stuck when it's time to go, then I'll ask for help."

Sarah nodded, and then sat primly in one of the red velvet chairs. It wobbled a little. "It's good to see you."

"Is it?" Chanah said. "I wouldn't think so. The way you stiffened in the fish market, I imagine you were somewhat shocked to be recognized."

"Yes," Sarah said. "But it had to happen eventually."

"Did it?" Chanah asked.

Sarah didn't know how to answer that, so she kept quiet.

Chanah listened to the silence for a moment or two, then nodded. "Do you know why I'm here?"

Half a dozen thoughts raced through Sarah's mind. To bring me back? To blame me? To tell me bad news? To tell me how horrible I am? To tell me my family is suffering? To ask me why?

She didn't answer, and shook her head. "No."

"I didn't come to Smyrna to find you. I was buying salmon. Smoked salmon for a celebration. A bar mitzvah."

"Really?" Sarah said. "That's wonderful."

Chanah waited. Until that moment, she had been certain that what she was doing was right and proper. Now she was surprised. How was it possible that Sarah had drifted so far from her children? Could she truly have forgotten?

"It's your son's bar mitzvah," she said at last. "Yakov's."

Sarah's heart froze. On one level she had known. On another she had completely blocked the event from her mind. "Yakov's thirteen already?" she whispered.

"Almost," Chanah said. "He will be soon. It's been almost three years since you left. He's gotten big. He looks like his father, but his eyes are still the same shape as yours. They have a similar sadness to them, too."

The two women heard the door to the kitchen open, and they fell silent as they waited.

Rabbi Abrahms brought the tea in on a platter, which he set on the writing desk that he never used. He preferred to write in the spare bedroom on the skinny table he had brought with him from Chelm. He set one cup and saucer in front of Mrs. Chaipul, and another in front of Sarah. He put a plate of sweet biscuits on the table, and lifted the tray.

"No sugar?" Chanah asked.

"I already added plenty," he said, defensively.

"Why don't you get us the sugar bowl?" Sarah said.

"There's sugar in the tea," he said.

"How much is plenty?" the old woman asked.

"A lot," he said. "If you need more, just shout."

"I never shout," the caterer of Chelm said.

The young rabbi snorted. "Try the tea. If you need more sugar, I'll bring it."

Chanah smiled. So he had changed. That was good. She picked up her cup and sipped. The sweetness hit her like an ice pick in the top-back-right molar. She kept her expression neutral. "This will do," she said, taking another tiny sip before setting the cup gently down on the saucer.

Rabbi Abrams nodded and excused himself.

"How many people in Chelm know that I'm here?" Sarah asked.

"Just me," Chanah said. "And probably Rabbi Kibbitz. He always seems secretive when he returns from a visit here. Did you know we're getting married?"

"You and the Rebbe?" Sarah said. She grinned. "At your age?"

Chanah raised her head high and nodded. "Absolutely. If I hadn't been waiting for him to propose, we would have done it a decade ago."

"That's wonderful," Sarah said. "Mazel Tov. When's the

wedding?"

"After your son's bar mitzvah."

The silence dropped like a guillotine blade, cutting the conversation in two.

Sarah tried to keep her composure. "Am I invited?"

"To the wedding or the bar mitzvah?" Chanah said.

Sarah's cheek twitched. Her heart was pounding.

"What does everyone on your so-called Council of Wise Women say about me? That I'm horrible? That I'm evil? That I'm bad?"

"It's not my Council," Chanah said. "You are a member too. In absentia."

Sarah snorted.

"We don't talk about you that much actually. We have from time to time, of course. It is impossible not to gossip. Most of the women wonder what happened. Some think badly of you. They wonder if you are dead or alive. They imagine what it must be like to separate from their children and husband. Some of them actually think about it fondly, and wish they had your courage."

Sarah put her hand to her mouth as she listened.

"Mostly we talk about the usual things," Chanah continued. "About births and illnesses. About who needs help. About what to do with this brilliant young girl who lives in our community."

"You mean Rachel?" Sarah said. She stared at the floor as she spoke. "From time to time, I've heard news about her in the market. It's amazing that my daughter is so smart that she is talked about in two towns."

Chanah nodded. "She is becoming quite a young woman. She wrote a scientific paper on the nutritional effects of a cabbage diet on a small rural population. She used me as a resource to compare the health of the villagers before and after the winter of the cabbage and then wrote it all down. It turns out that you really can live on nothing but cabbage and actually get healthier. But who would want to?" She shuddered, and then continued. "Rachel submitted the paper to a number of scientific journals under the name R. Cohen, and the German translation has been accepted and will be published in Vienna next year. She even gave me a research credit."

"My daughter is famous!" Sarah said, kvelling with pride.

"You have a son too, Sarah," Chanah said. "And they both need you. So does your husband."

Sarah bristled. "They seem to have been doing quite well without me. Benjamin could have found me if he had really looked."

Chanah shook her head. "He has two children to raise and a business to run. The world is a big place. He wouldn't think of looking here in Smyrna in the home of his old friend Rabbi Abrahms."

The accusation floated like a thundercloud.

"He's run ads in every Yiddish paper for five hundred miles. Don't you read?"

"I read." Sarah nodded. "It makes me sad, but I read the advertisement every week."

"You know those ads cost him money?" Chanah snapped. "You ever think about answering it?"

Sarah's eyes flashed fire. She bit her tongue, then nodded. "I've thought about it, but what could I say?"

Chanah shrugged, picked up her teacup, sipped the sugary sludge, and winced. "I don't know what you can say to him. I don't know what you can say to your children. I just wanted you to know that Yakov's bar mitzvah is coming up soon, and your family has a hole in it."

Sarah picked up her teacup and sipped. One teaspoon of sugar and a little bit of cream, just the way she liked it. She wondered if her husband, Benjamin, had ever known how she preferred her tea. Probably not, because as far as she could remember, he had never once made it for her.

"Do you think I should go back?" she asked at last.

"Do I?" Chanah wrinkled her brow, then shrugged. "Yes, but that doesn't matter. What matters is what you think. Did you know the fact that you are living here is common gossip in Smyrna, and the rumor is that Rabbi Abrahms will never be hired for the position because of the strange woman that lives in his house?"

Chanah watched Sarah's face carefully and saw that the news

landed hard.

"I didn't know that," Sarah said at last. "No one told me."

"They wouldn't, would they? I doubt you even talk to them. You're hardly treated like the rebbetzin."[57]

"That's not fair!" Sarah said, setting her cup down with a loud clink. "You can't blame me for what they think. You can't blame me for how they treat him."

Chanah shook her head slowly. "Sarah, I am not blaming you. I am telling you what I, a stranger, heard in five minutes in the fishmonger's. I am telling you what I, as the caterer of your son's bar mitzvah, know. I am doing my best not to judge you. I think you are judging yourself."

Sarah put her thumb to her lip, and began biting her nail. "I'm the judge, I'm the jury, I'm the criminal, and I am the executioner."

"Feh," Chanah said, sliding forward in the chair as she prepared to stand up. "Don't be so dramatic. For three years you have done what you've done, and they have done what they've done. Nobody's dead. Nothing has to change, although truth be told everything always changes, whether we like it or not.

"I will tell you one last thing," Chanah said, grunting as she rose as slowly as an underfed sourdough. "What has happened matters. But no matter what you say to yourself, or what anyone else says, you are invited and welcome to come to your son's bar mitzvah. Do you hear me?"

"Yes." Sarah nodded. "Thank you."

"You are also invited to my wedding," Chanah said, finally balanced on her feet. That chair was designed for a man who was comfortable with his life and never had to get up in a hurry. "I would like you, as my friend, to come. We haven't set the date yet. I'll let you know."

She picked her coat up off the hook and grunted her way into it. "I'd better get back to my restaurant. I have to cook some fish

---

[57] The rebbitzen is the wife of the rabbi. She's sort of like a queen who married into a royal family, but not treated with that much respect. It's often spelled "rebbetzin", but in Chelm because the rabbi's name is Kibbitz and Zen is something that gives you patience...

tonight. I'll see myself out."

Chanah looked at Sarah Cohen, who seemed so lost and small even on the narrow velvet-cushioned chair. She leaned down and kissed the lost woman on the forehead. Then she slipped outside and pulled the door shut behind her, trying not to hear the sobs through the thick wood.

Chanah sighed. It was a long walk back to Chelm. If she was lucky, it wouldn't start raining.

Part Nine

The Husband

Chapter Forty-One

Homecoming

Breathless, Rachel Cohen ran into her father's tailor shop and looked around. Yakov was behind the counter. He smiled at her. She darted past him, into the back room, and returned a moment later. She stood in front of her puzzled brother, gasping for breath.

"Where's Papa?" she asked, panting.

"He's not here. Why?"

"Mama's home," she said at last.

"Mama?" Yakov's eyes widened. He smiled. "She is? Wonderful! How does she look? Has she changed? What does she look like? Have you talked with her? Why isn't she here now?"

Even as he unleashed this torrent of words, he was already coming from behind the counter, untying the apron he wore to keep bits of cloth and thread off his fine clothing.

"Yakov," Rachel said, stepping in his way. "Wait. Don't go yet."

"Why?" Yakov asked. He stared at his sister and grinned. "Mama's home. I want to see her."

"Listen first," his sister said. "All right?"

"All right," he shrugged. "Does she know you're here? Did you even see her? Are you lying to me?"

"No," Rachel said. "When have I ever lied to you?"

Yakov sighed. "Never that I've known. Papa says that all women lie."

"Papa is sometimes an idiot," Rachel answered harshly.

Yakov stared at his sister. "How can you say that?"

Rachel flapped her hands at her brother as if chasing a chicken. "Everyone lies sometimes. When you say, 'All women lie,' you are making a statement that is just absurd in its breadth and poor judgment."

"What do you mean?" Yakov said.

"Let's change this around," Rachel said. "All women tell the truth. Wouldn't you agree?"

"Of course," Yakov nodded. "Sometimes they must."

"Exactly!" Rachel pounced. "So what is the point of saying something hateful like all women lie?"

Yakov shrugged. "You know that I have a hard time understanding these sorts of arguments. That's why you do so well at yeshiva, while I would rather be here darning a sock. Now can we go see Mama please?"

"Wait." Rachel said. "I'm sorry for snapping at you like that. Let me tell you what happened."

"Go on already!"

"I am. It's just hard for me," Rachel said. "I was going home to give The Soup a stir when I heard a noise in the kitchen. At first I thought it was a raccoon that maybe got in through that hole in the roof."

"I'm sorry," Yakov said, bashfully. "I know I was supposed to fix that last week, but…"

"This isn't about that. Because the noise was too regular, it sounded like someone pouring tea and setting the kettle back on the stove. So then I thought it was a robber."

"Rachel," Yakov said, rolling his eyes, "what do we have to steal?"

"Exactly my thought as well," his sister agreed. "Yet you never know what stupid people will do when they are hungry or frightened. That is why I peeked in through the window. That is when I saw her."

"What was she doing?" Yakov said, eagerly.

"Making herself some tea."

"And?"

"And sitting at the table."

"And then?"

"And then she began to drink her tea."

"And then?"

"And then I ran here to tell you!" Rachel concluded in a rush. "I didn't know what to say to her. I was frightened. I haven't seen her in three years! I was hoping that… Well, I was half hoping father wouldn't be here and half hoping that he would."

The front door had opened while the young girl was finishing, and a deep and familiar voice asked, "Half hoping I wouldn't be here? Why?"

Rachel looked up, saw her father, and threw her arms around his neck.

Benjamin Cohen, the tailor, laughed and staggered back. "Are you trying to kill me? You want to wrestle me to the ground, like an American cowboy roping a steer?"

"Mama's home," Yakov said, getting straight to the point, because he knew his sister would take all day.

Benjamin Cohen stopped still. His smile froze on his face. His heart began to thud in his chest. Sarah was back?

"Your mother is…" he said. "Where?"

"At the house, Papa," Rachel said, unwinding herself from her father's embrace.

"What is she doing there?"

"Having tea," Rachel answered.

"It is her house," Yakov said.

"Is it?" Benjamin said, under his breath, and then cursed himself quietly, hoping that his children hadn't heard. "Have you talked with her? Is she well?"

"Rachel saw her through the window. Isn't that so?"

The girl nodded.

"Then you should go home," Benjamin said. "Hurry! Your mother is waiting in the house to see you. Don't keep her waiting."

"Thank you, Papa!" Yakov didn't hesitate and bolted out the door.

Rachel paused. "Are you coming?"

"Soon enough," Benjamin told his daughter. "Reb Cantor is due in for a fitting."

"Surely he would understand if you left a note."

"Racheleh, my sweetest," Benjamin said. "Two years ago if you had told me that your mother was home, I would have trampled you both on my way out the door. But now I have learned that I must live in my own time and that the hopes and the dreams I have must be my own.

"It would be better for you and Yakov to spend some time with your mother before I come. You will have much to say to each other, and I would not want to interrupt that."

Rachel nodded, understanding but still curious. "She is your wife, Papa."

Benjamin nodded and smiled at his daughter, his face a mask. "Why are you still here?" he said. "Go home and hug your mother."

Rachel grinned and ran after her brother.

As soon as his daughter sped away, Benjamin staggered backward until his shoulder came to rest on a wall. He closed his eyes and felt as if a wave of racking sobs were about to burst forth like a flood from a broken dam.

* * *

The door opened and shut, but he didn't hear it until Reb Cantor spoke.

"Benjamin? Are you all right? Are you having a heart attack?"

At that moment, Benjamin Cohen, the tailor of Chelm, nearly screamed. A heart attack? He didn't know if he had a heart left to attack.

"Sarah's back," he whispered. There was no point in keeping it secret. Everyone in Chelm would know within the hour.

At first, Isaac Cantor's face broadened into a laugh. "That's wonderful!" he began, but he cut the words off quickly when he realized the state that his friend was in. "Oh. Oy."

"Yes," Benjamin said, laughing a little to try and keep back the tears. "Oy."

"Do you want some tea?" the merchant said. "We can go to Mrs. Chaipul's restaurant…"

"No, no," Benjamin waved his hand. "I'm all right. I don't want to see anyone else right now. Let's do this fitting, and then I'll go to my house and see my wife. After three years of me waiting for her, she can wait for an hour."

"An hour?" Isaac said. "It's going to take me that long? I thought the trousers were all ready."

But the tailor had already gone into the back room of his shop, and the merchant had no choice but to wait. And wait. And wait.

He sat uncomfortably in a chair provided for customers. He looked around for something to do, something to read. "Are you all right?" he called at last.

From the back room, there came the loud honk of a nose being blown in a handkerchief.

Then Benjamin Cohen, the tailor of Chelm, returned to the front of his shop.

"Come, come," he said, waving the merchant into the changing room. "Try these on. They should fit fine. In fact, maybe you don't need to. Perhaps you should just take them home. What, you're still here? All right, all right. Put them on then. I don't have all day you know."

"But… But," said the merchant. Then he sighed, and forgave his friend. "The trousers will be fine. Go see her."

"I don't want to," Benjamin said. He felt like a stubborn child.

"I know," Isaac said. "Actually, I don't know, but I can imagine. Actually, I can't even imagine, but I can try to imagine, and in my imagination, I wouldn't want to go either. Me, I'd probably run away on a caravan to Napoli in Italy. They make the most amazing desserts there."

"Is there a train leaving now?" Benjamin said.

"No," Isaac answered. "You actually can't get there from here."

For a moment, the silence hung in the small shop like a piece of dust floating in the sunlight.

"She is still your wife," Isaac said, putting a gentle hand on Benjamin's shoulder.

"So everyone says," Benjamin answered. "But is she? In law I suppose. But in deed? In body? In mind? In soul and heart? And to be honest, after three years am I still her husband?"

"Don't talk like that," Reb Cantor said, unsure how to react or what to say. "You are still married. And you may stay married, if that is your wish. What do you want?"

"I want it all not to have happened," Benjamin said.

"Ahh." The merchant sighed. He was out of his element. Rabbi Kibbitz or Mrs. Chaipul would know what to say. Isaac Cantor was nothing more than a buyer and seller of things. He didn't know how to ease or answer questions. He was just about to suggest a visit to the rabbi's study when the tailor spoke.

"I missed her so much," Benjamin said. "For days and weeks and months and years, I would have given anything to have her back. No questions asked. Everything back the way it was. Better because I realized how much I loved and missed and needed her. I was angry. I was jealous. I was sad. I was heartbroken. I was burdened. I was lonely. I was embarrassed. I was hurt. I was puzzled and confused. I was guilty. I was incensed. I was outraged. I was empty.

"And then one day all that was gone. And I stopped missing her. And I stopped thinking about her so often. I almost stopped blaming her. And since then, I've done okay. I've been fine, in fact. I've almost felt happy.

"So, now she's back. And I don't know if I want her any more."

The fat merchant listened to his friend and nodded. "You never will if you stay in this shop and hide."

"I know," Benjamin Cohen said. "That's why I'm trying to get you to try on these pants already."

Now the merchant laughed, and the tailor joined him.

The pants, of course, fit perfectly. After the merchant paid and left the shop, the tailor put the money into his cash box.

He sighed, nodded to himself. He hung a sign on the door, "Closed for the day."

And went home to see the woman who had been, was, and might still be his wife.

Chapter Forty-Two

Reunion

As Rachel Cohen walked the short distance from her father's shop to their house, her mind couldn't stop racing and buzzing in all directions at once. Yakov had run ahead, but Rachel was taking her time.

Her mother was home, but what did that mean? Was Mama back for good? Was she only staying for a moment before vanishing again? Would she be the same? Would she be different? Would she recognize her daughter? Would she care?

The speed of her thoughts, the quickness of her pace, and briefness of the walk didn't give her a chance to answer any of the questions.

She paused and, before going in the front door, peeked in the window.

There, as if she hadn't moved, sitting in the same chair she'd been in, was her mother. But sitting on her mother's lap was her brother. They didn't seem to be saying anything. His long arms were around her in an encompassing hug. Her mother was patting her brother's head, stroking his curls like he was her baby.

It was such a beautiful scene that Rachel hesitated to interrupt.

But just then her mother looked up and saw Rachel. She didn't say anything, or stop caressing Yakov, but she smiled and her eyes lit with delight.

Rachel lost all her inhibitions. She ran to the door, yanked it open, ran inside, and shouted, "Move over, Yakov!"

Then she wrapped her mother in a hug of her own that was meant to convey three years of love in an instant.

* * *

By the time Benjamin Cohen walked in the door to his house,

his family was seated at the table, eating bowls of chicken soup with matzah balls.

"Your soup is delicious," Sarah was saying. "I can't believe that you made this by yourself."

"Well," Rachel blushed, "it is Oma Levitsky's recipe and her soup pot."

"Papa," Yakov said, grinning. "Mama's home."

Sarah Cohen's heart was pounding. "Hello, Benjamin."

"Hello, Sarah." His heart was pounding as well.

"Would you like some soup?" she asked, pushing her chair away from the table.

He held up his palm. "I can get it myself. I'm used to that."

The small kitchen fell silent as Benjamin hung his coat on the hook, took a bowl from the shelf, ladled it full of soup, pulled a spoon from the drawer, and brought everything over to his seat. He bowed his head and mumbled a blessing. Then he cut a matzah ball, lifted the spoon, and slurped loudly.

"Delicious soup," he said, conscious that he was repeating what his long-lost wife had just said.

"Mama made the matzah balls," Rachel said. "She showed me why mine were always so heavy. She doesn't cover the pot when she cooks them."

"Ahh," Benjamin said, chewing a bite thoughtfully. He almost cried as he remembered that this was the way Sarah's matzah balls always tasted. Finally, he managed to mumble, "Good."

Again, the room fell quiet. Nobody really knew what to say. Too many questions to ask. Too many answers to avoid.

"Yakov's bar mitzvah is next week," Rachel said.

"I know," Sarah smiled.

"Is that why you came back?" Benjamin asked, not looking up from his bowl.

"Yes." Sarah nodded. "My son is almost a man. And so big! I am very proud."

"So am I," Benjamin said, defensively. "I just hope he learns his Torah portion in time."

"Papa," Yakov said. "It's not so easy."

"I don't think it's fair, Mama," Rachel said. "I know Yakov's Torah portion by heart. I don't understand why I can't be bar mitzvahed."

"Because," Yakov said, testily, "you will never be a man."

"That's not my point," Rachel said. "I just don't think it's fair that you will be allowed to read from the Torah, and I will not."

"Life's not fair," Yakov retorted.

"That's enough," Benjamin said, quietly. He looked at Sarah. "As you can see, nothing's changed."

"That's good." Sarah smiled. "But it's not entirely true. My children are older, and bigger, and both are a little bit wiser."

"Unlike your husband," Benjamin muttered.

"What?" Sarah said.

Benjamin put down his spoon softly.

"Why did you leave?" he asked. "Why did you leave without saying a word? With barely leaving a note?"

"Benjamin, should we do this in front of the children?"

Benjamin looked at his children. "They are not children any more. Yakov is already a man in my eyes. He is responsible and good hearted. He is careful and a hard worker. His designs are brilliant, and he cooks well too. If he needed to live on his own and provide for himself and a family, he could — whether or not he reads from a holy scroll. Rachel is a woman as well. She has been so for almost a year."

Rachel blushed as her father continued. "She cooks and she cleans and she works a job and she studies. She is so brilliant and astute that people come to her for advice, and they actually listen. And she doesn't seem to think that she's anything special, which is in itself a wonderful miracle, because she is such a bright star.

"They are both," Benjamin hesitated, "our children. But they are also grown up enough to hear such a discussion. I think."

"I'm not sure I agree," Sarah said.

"I think we should leave," Rachel said, putting her hand on her brother's.

"I want to listen to this," Yakov said, shaking his head.

Neither twin rose from the table. Sarah sighed and shrugged.

"All right, but don't blame me."

Benjamin bit back his retort and then asked the question that had been plaguing him. "Three years ago, at the Kvetchfest, you said that I didn't give you affection, that I didn't give you praise. You said that you had stopped smiling. When did this happen? Why did you stop smiling?"

"You don't know?" Sarah said. She had a smile on her face, but it was one of disbelief. "I... I need your permission to say something that you asked me not to ever reveal."

Benjamin's eyebrows rose in a furrow. "What are you talking about?"

"You made me promise never to speak a word of this to anyone, especially the children," Sarah said, "and if I'm going to talk about it now, I need your permission."

He shrugged. "I don't remember anything like that. Is it horrible?"

"I never thought so," she answered.

"All right," he said. "So, go."

Sarah pointed her finger at Benjamin. "It started the moment you told me to tell everyone that Yakov was our first born and that he was more important than Rachel. That was when I stopped smiling at you."

"What?" Benjamin said. "You're kidding? I told you that?"

"Do I look like I'm kidding?" Sarah said.

The children sat quietly, pretending that they weren't there.

"No," Benjamin admitted. "I don't understand."

"You said that he was more important than her," Sarah said, aiming her finger from Yakov to Rachel. "You said that it was important for a boy to be first born. You don't remember this?"

Benjamin raised his hands in disbelief. "I thought he was first born."

"You forgot?!" Sarah shouted and rose to her feet. "You want me to go get Mrs. Chaipul and ask her? You swore her to secrecy too. Rachel was born first. Yakov was born second. You told us both to switch it around. We both agreed, and I started to hate you."

"I don't understand this," Benjamin said. "I don't remember.

Such a small thing."

"To you it was small," Sarah said. "To me you were asking for one of my children to be more important than the other. You were asking me to start their lives off with a lie. You were telling me that a man was more valuable than a woman. What a thing to put on a mother just as she has given birth!"

Sarah was pacing the small room. "It was like a rock in my shoe. Like the seam on your shirt that rubs against your neck until your skin is raw and the blood begins to flow. It went on and on and on for years. And then at the Kvetchfest, it all burst out, and I left. I couldn't face it any more."

Sarah stood now with her back against a wall. She looked at her children. "I am so sorry for leaving you two. I missed you every day." Tears began to run down her cheeks. "I wanted to come back. Or write you a letter. But I didn't know where to begin. There was nothing I could say to you that could explain what was going on for me. All my words seemed empty and hollow. And I could not come back here. Not then. Even now, I am not sure I would have come back if it was not for your bar mitzvah. I am so sorry."

Yakov rose, and he hugged his mother. He wiped the tears from her cheek. "I missed you too," he whispered.

Rachel sat in her chair, stunned and torn. She wanted to comfort her mother. She also wanted to comfort her father. She could not do both at once, and she didn't want to choose.

"Mama," she said at last, "I knew that I was first born."

"You did?" Sarah and Benjamin said simultaneously.

Rachel nodded. "A long time ago, Oma Levitsky told me stories. She told me that she could make herself invisible and that she heard certain secrets. She told me that she had once heard Mama and Mrs. Chaipul arguing about who was older, me or Yakov. I didn't really believe her at the time, because nobody can be invisible, but when I thought about it, it made sense and at the same time, it didn't really matter to me."

"It certainly doesn't matter to me either," Yakov said. "What difference does it make if I was born first or second? Rachel is still better at everything she does — except for the things that I like to do. Even though she cooks most of the meals, I'm still a better chef. And I'm better at my needlework than she is. I love the feel of fine linen. I love making a pile of cloth into something beautiful that makes its owner feel good. First born, shmirst born. Who cares?"

Benjamin shrugged. He had been trying to think about how to apologize, and now he realized that he didn't really have to. Or maybe he did.

"Sarah, I was wrong," he said at last. He opened and closed his mouth several times. At last he found what he needed to say. "You know, if you get a rock in your shoe, you don't keep walking until your toe becomes blistered. If the seam in your shirt rubs you the wrong way, you take it to your tailor, and he fixes it.

"I realize that I might have been an idiot... no, that I was an idiot about who was born first and what all that meant to my children in their lives. But how was I to know what my words and my actions did to you if you didn't say it to me? If you didn't tell me."

Sarah sighed, and nodded. "Children, your father and I need to talk."

"I want to listen," Yakov said.

"Not to this," Rachel said, taking her brother by his hand, and leading him away from his mother. "Come, let's go for a walk."

"I don't want to go for a walk," Yakov insisted. "Papa?"

Benjamin nodded. "Go. Get some fresh air. Your mother and I need to talk."

"All right," Yakov said, nodding his head.

He gave his mother a kiss on the cheek and followed his sister out of the house.

"Well?" Yakov asked.

"I don't know," Rachel answered.

"You're the elder," Yakov teased. "I thought you knew everything."

"No." She smiled. "Not even close."

Chapter Forty-Three

Tea

After the children left, Sarah and Benjamin Cohen stared at each other across the kitchen table for a long moment. Three years had passed since they'd been alone together, but neither looked so different. His hair was a little more gray and distinguished. Her hair was a little longer, a little straighter. Both faces were lined with cares, but perhaps they had been there before, unnoticed in familiarity.

Neither knew what to say. Neither knew where to start.

After a time, he got up, went to the stove, and prepared two cups of tea. One he set down in front of her. The other he set across the table. He sat in the chair.

The staring contest resumed. Neither looked away. Neither smiled. Neither moved. Neither blinked. In a way it was like a child's staring contest.

He lifted his teacup, blew, and sipped the warm brew without averting his gaze.

She did the same. Then her eyes flickered down into the cup.

A fleeting glimpse of a smile crossed his lips as he thought, "I won!" but it quickly retreated as the next thoughts came, "What did I win? What have I lost?"

Sarah took another sip of the tea, and then she spoke. "This tea is the way I like it. You knew?"

"Of course I knew." Benjamin nodded. "Two sugars. No milk. I'm glad some things haven't changed."

Sarah looked away. Her eyes drifted to the high shelf where her grandmother's Seder plate was kept. She had missed those family gatherings. Her left elbow dropped onto the table. Her forehead rested on her palm as she tried to rub all the pain out of her head.

"Are you all right?" he asked.

"I didn't know that you knew. About the tea."

He shrugged. "It's tea. Of course I knew. You're my wife. Or you were. Or you still are. Are you? I don't know. What are we going to do?"

She didn't answer.

"For the first year I worried all the time," he said. "I thought perhaps you went insane. You were a little crazy after the twins were born, and Mrs. Chaipul gave me some medicine, but that was long gone, and I had no way to give you any. I was worried that you'd lost your mind and forgotten who you were. I was worried that you were kidnapped or dead. I put ads in the newspaper and waited to hear. I didn't go looking. Perhaps I should have. But the children needed me. And honestly, I was afraid of what I might find.

"For the next year I mourned. I tore a piece of black cloth and kept it pinned under my jacket so that no one would see. I didn't know if you were dead or not, but I thought you might be. It seemed like the right thing to do. I went to minyan every day and said Kaddish for you.[58]

"This past year, it's gotten easier. I had said goodbye. I had done my duty. When Rachel smiles a certain way, she looks exactly like you, and I would feel sad for a time, but then I learned to take that as a way of honoring your memory. When Yakov's nose grew out, I recognized you in him, and saw how lucky we were to have our two children who blend together into better versions of ourselves.

"But recently, I've been so busy that I haven't given you much thought at all. Even with the bar mitzvah coming up, you haven't really been in my mind. Of course when I did remember, I would say a blessing and wish you well.

"Sometimes I felt angry with myself for cutting you out of my life so well, but to have someone go missing like that... It was better to think you were dead. Do you understand?"

Sarah nodded. She did not answer. She knew that for her it had been easier in a way. From time to time, she had heard rumors of her family. When she had asked him, Yohon had brought news of

---

[58] Kaddish is the prayer for the dead. Even in Chelm they don't joke about this.

them from Chelm. She knew how everyone was, and when they
were sick. She had wondered if word had drifted back to Chelm,
but neither Rabbi Kibbitz nor Mrs. Chaipul had betrayed her. It
was the children who mattered the most. Over time, she too had
drifted her thoughts away from Benjamin, coming close to the
point of forgetting that he even existed. Except, of course, that he
did. Except, of course, Yohon had never let her forget that they were
both married and not to each other.

"Did you say something?" she asked.

"Yes, I did," he nodded. "I didn't think that you had heard me."

"I heard everything except for that last question."

He found himself chuckling sadly. "Of course. The easy part you
hear, and the difficult part…"

"I'm sorry," she said, quickly. "Just tell me what you asked."

He nodded. No point in being impatient. Three years of lost
time, a few more minutes wouldn't hurt. "I said, you've been gone
for a long time. I don't know where. I don't know how you've stayed
alive. I don't know where you've been or what you've done. I asked,
'Is there anything you want to tell me?'"

"What?" she said. She couldn't believe him. Didn't he care?
Didn't he have a long list of detailed questions? She would. She
started to get angry.

"Is there anything you want to tell me?" he repeated. "I didn't
think it was such a difficult question."

"Well, it is," she said. "Because it puts all the responsibility on
me."

"Is there someone else who should be responsible for answering
that question?" he asked, testily.

"What do you mean by that?" she shot back.

He looked around the room. "There's nobody else here. Who
else can answer this? What do you want to tell me? Or perhaps the
question is better put, what don't you want to tell me?"

Sarah's face remained expressionless, but she nearly screamed.

She thought, but she didn't say: Do you really want to know?
That I spent three years living in another man's house? Why don't
you ask me directly? He was your friend. He still is your friend. Do

you want to know that? You have lunch with him in the restaurant when he visited Chelm. I lived with him. I made him dinner and breakfast. I cleaned his house. I talked with him late into the night. Why don't you want to ask me these questions? Did we touch? Did we kiss? Did I break my vows? You won't ask? No? Then why should I tell you? Is there anything I want you to know? No, there really isn't anything I want you to know. I don't want to tell you anything.

She waited. She didn't say it. She stared at him for another moment, and then rubbed her forehead with both hands.

"No," she said at last. "There is nothing I want to tell you."

Benjamin closed his eyes. He didn't want to look at her any more. He felt as if his heart was tearing in two.

"I want a divorce," he said, quietly. He didn't open his eyes.

She stared up at him. He seemed so calm about it.

"I wasn't going to ask you for one," she said.

"If you want, then we won't," he said. "I mean if you don't want. I mean… I don't know what I want. Not this. What do you want?"

Now it was her turn to chuckle sadly. "You started by saying that you wanted a divorce. I'm not going to stop you. I couldn't if I wanted to. I told you that I hadn't planned to ask for one."

"No," he said. He opened his eyes and stared into the tea. "That's my job."

"I'll stay at Mrs. Chaipul's through the bar mitzvah," she said. "Can we wait until after that to tell the children?"

"No," he said. "I think perhaps not. We have to tell them. There has been enough hiding and mystery. I think that our children would guess or know. They are fairly bright."

"Yes," she smiled. "We have wonderful children."

They sat there at the table, quietly saying nothing.

"Benjamin," she said at last. "I'm sorry."

He nodded. "So am I. So am I."

Chapter Forty-Four

Family Supper

When she and her brother returned home from their long walk in the woods, Rachel's heart leapt with joy.

Everything was back to normal!

Her father was sitting at the table, reading the Yiddish newspaper. Her mother was at the stove, chopping vegetables for dinner. Yakov quietly went to his room and returned with his bar mitzvah studies and joined their father at the table. It was like they were a family again.

Rachel put on her apron and helped her mother with the dinner. With vegetables and some broth from The Soup, the brisket from earlier in the week became a delicious paprika stew. Rachel showed her mother how Mrs. Chaipul had taught her to make spaetzle dumplings, and felt proud when her mother kissed her gently on the forehead.

Then Yakov started complaining.

"I'm never going to learn my Torah portion! I'm nearly thirteen. I'm supposed to know it by now!" he cried, burying his head in his hands.

Benjamin Cohen looked up from his reading, and shook his head sadly. He'd heard this litany a dozen times already this week, a million times this month. Yakov spent more time complaining than he did studying. He said nothing, determined not to let his son drag him into another distracting argument.

"At least you get to be a Bar Mitzvah," said Rachel. "I don't think it's fair. I know your Torah portion perfectly by heart, backwards and forwards and inside out! I think I should be bar mitzvahed, and you should help Mama by setting the table."

"Now, Rachel," Sarah put her hand on her daughter's shoulder, "you know that girls can't be bar mitzvahed. It makes the men uneasy."

Benjamin frowned and tried to focus on the headlines. They had decided to tell the children after dinner. The last thing he wanted was a fight.

"Exactly!" Rachel said, setting a plate down noisily. "Yakov will be bar mitzvahed, and be respected as a man, while all I'll be doing is learning how to cook, so I can get married and be dismissed as a woman."

Sarah allowed herself a small smile at the words coming from her daughter's lips.

"Rachel my sweet," her father soothed, "we've been over this a thousand times. You had your coming of age party last year. This year it's Yakov's turn."

"She had a coming of age party?" Sarah said, glaring at her husband.

He shrugged and nodded and turned a page, thankful for the escape provided by reading about wars in far away countries. He made a mental note to write to the newspaper and cancel his advertisement.

Yakov interrupted by picking up his head and smirking at his twin sister. "I'm a man, and you're a woman. I am allowed to participate in the shul, and you get to help make the Sabbath dinner. That's the way it is. That's the way it always has been."

Sarah's eyes glowed with anger. "Are you going to let him say things like that?" she asked her husband.

Benjamin's shoulders slumped, and he lowered his newspaper.

"Yakov," he sighed. "If you're such a man, let me hear your Torah portion."

"Well, as I said, I've been having difficulty."

"Really? Let's hear what you have."

Poor Yakov was a very good boy. He had a beautiful singing voice, but was not a great student. He could not even finish the bruchah without trouble. He stumbled and stuttered, and finally put his hands on his face and began crying in earnest.

"You see!" Rachel said. "I know all the blessings and his whole

Torah portion better than he does."

"Yes, you do," said their father. "But the table hasn't been set for dinner. Neither one of you are doing your jobs!

"It's been like this all month," he told Sarah. "One studies and sobs, the other gloats and complains. I'm nearly at my wit's end."

"Well," said Sarah Cohen, "there's only one more week until the bar mitzvah. I think we'll survive."

At the word, "survive," Benjamin's head shot up from his reading. His vision of dying before Yakov's bar mitzvah had drifted from his thoughts with all the chaos and business from Sarah's departure. The feeling of foreboding clutched at his heart, and he felt it beating rapidly. Was this it? The moment?

Sarah looked at him curiously. "Are you all right?"

He nodded. It wasn't all bad. If he keeled over dead, at least the children would have their mother back. Then his heart slowed. Maybe it wasn't the end. Maybe this is what heartbreak felt like. "I'm fine."

"Benjamin, we need to talk about the other subject."

"After dinner," Benjamin said.

Rachel felt her heart skip a beat. "What other subject?"

"We can't eat first?" Yakov said.

"Yakov, go get napkins," Sarah said. She brought the stew pot over to the table while Rachel began assembling bowls and spoons. Yakov got four napkins from a drawer, instead of three, and smiled.

The meal was quick and quiet. No one tasted anything. No one knew what to say, so they didn't speak. When the last of the stew was sopped up by crusts of old bread, they pushed their bowls away.

"So, Papa?" Rachel asked. "What other subject?"

"There's no good way to say this," Benjamin said. "Your mother and I aren't staying together."

"You mean you're getting a divorce?" Yakov said.

Rachel's heart sank at the words. She felt the smile melting off her face.

Benjamin nodded. "Yes." Tears welled in his eyes, but he held them back. "Your mother and I have talked, and we can't work it out."

Benjamin suddenly wasn't sure if he was speaking the truth. In his mind he realized that he had lost his wife years ago. At the same time, he wondered what it would have been like if she had talked to him first, instead of running away. Wouldn't that have worked? Couldn't they both have tried harder? Perhaps they could try again?

"We both love you both very much," Sarah was saying to their children. "That will never change."

"I know, Mama," Yakov said. "But you're just saying that. Are you going to live with us?"

Sarah shook her head. "No."

"Are you going to move away from Chelm again?" Rachel demanded.

"I don't know. At least through the bar mitzvah, I will stay with Mrs. Chaipul. You two will live here with your father, as you have. Nothing really will change."

"But you two won't be married," Rachel said.

"No," Benjamin said, quietly. Certain. "We won't."

Rachel looked at her mother. "If you get divorced what will happen when my husband and I have problems? Why should we stay together?"

"You're married?" Sarah said, surprised. "First you have a coming of age party without telling me, then you get married without telling me?"

"I'm not married, Mama. I'm talking about in the future. If you and Papa don't stay together, why should my husband and I? What lesson are you teaching me?"

"I don't have all the answers," Sarah said. "You will live your life differently from me. You are smarter than I am. You will make different choices."

Benjamin listened to this answer, and wanted to object. He wanted to talk about promises and morality, but he kept his tongue. They had agreed that it would be better to talk with the children together. They had also agreed that taking care of the children would be the highest priority, not arguing or debating or fighting with each other.

"What will happen after the bar mitzvah?" Yakov asked.

"You'll be a man," Benjamin told his son, proudly. "And you will be able to make your own choices. You are welcome to live with me, or if your mother stays in Chelm you may live with her."

"That's true for you as well, Rachel," Benjamin told his daughter. "You are old enough to make such decisions."

"I don't want to," Rachel said. "I want us all together." She began to cry.

Sarah moved to her daughter and put her arm around her. "I don't know what I am going to do yet. I don't know where I am going to stay or live. But no matter where I am there will always be room in my life and in my love for you."

Sarah began running her fingers through Rachel's hair. The hair was so soft and smooth. She had missed so much. It was horrible, but she didn't know what else to do.

"You ran away before!" Rachel said, shrugging her mother off. "You just left. I thought you were dead."

Sarah shifted and knelt down beside Rachel. "I will never do that again. I'm sorry. I didn't know what to do. And when I was gone, I didn't know how to come back. I thought of you every day. I didn't know how to come back. I hope you will forgive me. I love you. I love you too, Yakov."

"I love you too, Mama," Yakov said. "I forgive you."

"Me too," mumbled Rachel.

With that, both Yakov and Rachel began crying loudly.

For more than an hour the family talked and hugged and cried. Even Benjamin, who did his best to hide his tears by pretending to blow his nose into his handkerchief.

The children asked questions, and the parents answered them as best they could.

By the time they were finished it was late in the night and the candles Sarah had lit for dinner were burned nearly to stubs.

Benjamin allowed Sarah to tuck the children into their beds.

Sarah smiled as she helped her twins get cozy. She gave them each a goodnight kiss on the forehead.

"Mama," Rachel asked. "Where are you going tonight?"

"To Mrs. Chaipul's," Sarah said, hoping that it would be all right with the caterer. "I will be back in the morning."

"Do you promise?"

"More than anything," Sarah whispered. "I missed you so much."

"I missed you too," Rachel said. "I love you, Mama."

"I love you," Sarah said. She tried to keep her voice even. The tears falling down her cheeks made no sounds.

She shut the door behind her, and found Benjamin, once again ensconced at the table behind his newspaper. It all felt so familiar and comfortable, and inviting. At the same time, she realized, it was a trap. The anger that she'd felt when she'd left three years ago was still so close to the surface that if she stayed it would burst out like a thunderstorm.

"I'm going to go now," she said.

Benjamin nodded. "I'll talk with Rabbi Kibbitz about getting the Get."[59]

"After the bar mitzvah," Sarah said, suddenly concerned. "I thought we agreed."

"No," Benjamin said, looking up. "I'll talk with him before. But yes, we will formalize it after. Good night."

"Good night," Sarah said. She picked her bag up and walked out the door.

When he heard the door shut, Benjamin put his newspaper down, and sobbed silently into his hands.

---

[59] A Get is a divorce decree. There is some debate about whether you get a Get or give a Get.

Chapter Forty-Five

A Double Mitzvah

The days to Yakov's bar mitzvah flew by.

Sarah was relieved that Mrs. Chaipul welcomed her with a spare bedroom and accepted her help with the preparations in exchange for room and board. It was a little strained to be working for the woman who Benjamin had hired to cater her son's bar mitzvah, but they made the best of it.

The feast that Benjamin had ordered and paid for was truly amazing. Bagels and lox and whitefish salad! Fresh tomatoes imported from who knew where. It would be a magnificent banquet.

That Sabbath morning, the entire village of Chelm gathered in the small shul. Downstairs, the men milled about and shook hands, while upstairs in the balcony the women greeted each other with kisses and hugs.

Many whispered about the sudden and mysterious reappearance of Sarah Cohen, but no one dared say anything to her face aside from congratulatory greetings. No one asked her where she had been or what she was doing. No one told her they hoped that Yakov would survive his recitation without mangling the Torah too badly. Everyone was kind and polite. They held their whispers until they returned to their benches.

In the morning, Benjamin had walked Yakov to the synagogue in silence. Every step seemed like it might be his last. His marriage was ending. His son was becoming a man. Perhaps it would be for the best if he did die. What else was there to do with his life? Work and then come home to an empty house?

While they waited for Rabbi Kibbitz, who was always late on

Shabbos mornings, Benjamin gave Yakov the tallis he had made and watched his son's eyes widen with delight.

White and blue cotton with swirls of purple and long fringes at each corner, it was the most audacious tallis that Yakov had ever seen. The boy read aloud the blessing that his father had stitched in silver, and swirled it onto his shoulders with a flourish, grinning the whole time.

Benjamin put his hand on his heart. Still beating. Not dead! Maybe there is still something else for me to see and do in this world. Relieved and so proud of his son, he smiled and held back tears.

Then it was time.

Rabbi Kibbitz led them into the sanctuary.

Yakov saw that everyone in Chelm was already assembled. They were all watching him.

He smiled and strode up the steps.

Then Yakov's shoe stepped on the fringes of his tallis, and he tripped, fell, and barely caught himself before his nose could smash into the floor.

His face turned red. He heard the laughter, and Adam Schlemiel's shout of "Nice one!" Followed by giggles and loud whispers of "sha!"

Bravely, Yakov stood up and waved at everyone, hiding the fact that his joy at the beautiful tallis had just turned to embarrassment and fear.

He took his seat in the middle of the Bimah. Yakov felt very nervous. He kept his eyes focused on his prayer book, and tried to be as still as possible during the service. To his left was his father. On the other side of the Bimah was wise Rabbi Kibbitz.

Then came the dreaded moment, as Yakov was called to give the blessings and read from the Torah.

His knees buckled, and he could barely stand. If his father hadn't taken him by the elbow, Yakov would probably have run screaming from the synagogue in terror. He moved slowly, careful not to step on the tallis and trip again.

Finally, he stood in front of the Torah. He somehow managed

to get through the bruchah. He took the yad, and pointed its short stubby finger at the Hebrew letters inscribed on the sacred scroll.

Then Yakov's mind went completely blank! He'd forgotten it all. Every word. Suddenly the holy letters on the parchment looked like random patterns stitched with thick black thread into yellowed cloth.

Everyone was watching, witnessing his humiliation.

In utter despair, Yakov stared up at the ceiling, hoping that The Almighty would strike him dead, or at the very least would help him remember how to read Hebrew.

Instead, all Yakov saw was his twin sister, Rachel, sitting up front in the women's balcony. Her lips were moving. She was mouthing something. Words. She was trying to tell him… He squinted.

His Torah portion! She was mouthing his Torah portion!

He smiled, nodded at her, and she began again.

Yakov stared up into Rachel's eyes, and carefully following his sister's lead, while her lips moved silently, Yakov began to sing aloud…

After the service, all of Chelm was buzzing with the news of the miracle. Young Yakov Cohen had actually memorized his Torah portion, and chanted it directly to the heavens!

Only Rabbi Kibbitz suspected that something was amiss. In the social hall, he took the boy aside, and Yakov confessed everything.

His sister had given him the words. He felt ashamed, as if he had lied to the entire community. Tears began rolling down his cheeks.

"I feel like a glomp," he told the rabbi. "I don't deserve this tallis." He started to take it off.

Rachel, who had come over to congratulate her brother, rushed to his defense. "You couldn't possibly have read my lips," she said. "Your eyesight isn't that good."

"Rachel, did you help your brother?" the Rabbi asked. "Do you really know his Torah portion by heart?"

"Of course I do." Then Rachel cast her eyes at the floor. "Yes. I'm sorry."

"Don't be sorry," the Rabbi said. "You have performed a mitzvah today. A bat mitzvah."

"Really?" Rachel's eyes glinted with joy. "A bat mitzvah? I have?"

"Yes," said Rabbi Kibbitz. "You, Rachel Cohen, are a Bat Mitzvah."

"What's that mean?" she asked.

"I don't know." He shrugged. "I just invented it. You're the first."

Without thinking Rachel jumped up and gave the old Rabbi a kiss on the cheek. Then she ran off shouting, "Mama, mama! I'm a Bat Mitzvah!"

What have I done? The old rabbi thought to himself. You have to be careful when you open a door. But whenever she finds a closed door, Rachel Cohen keeps knocking. What can you do? First she comes into the yeshiva. Then all the girls want to come to the yeshiva. Now she's a Bat Mitzvah? Oy. Are all the girls going to want one now?

He glanced up to the women's balcony and saw Mrs. Chaipul beaming down at him. Grinning and winking, she held both thumbs up.

He shrugged and turned to Yakov. "And you," he said, "don't be ashamed. I have never heard the Torah sung so beautifully. Even if you didn't read all the words, you certainly learned the Torah's meaning. That tallis is yours. May you wear it in health and joy for many years to come."

Also without thinking, Yakov jumped up and kissed the embarrassed rabbi on the cheek.

He too ran off to greet his father and grandfather, and to get some of the lox before it was devoured by the hungry hordes.

And with salmon and cream cheese (plain and chives), with noodle kugel and six varieties of Reb Stein's bagels, the brother and sister, their parents, and the entire village celebrated.

Chapter Forty-Five

Grave News

Rabbi Yohon Abrahms glazed over the thin sheets of paper. He stared across Rabbi Sarnoff's kitchen, through the empty space across the table from him.

Yesterday, when he collected the mail from the post office, he had noticed the return address on the envelope. It was from Izzy, one of the last of his Moscow friends. After rabbinical school, Isaac Joelson had secured a position as the third rabbi from the left at one of the major synagogues in the Russian capital. He often penned long and rambling letters full of news and gossip. Years ago, when Yohon first settled in Chelm, he sent Izzy a note describing how he'd helped a goat give birth. Izzy had immediately written back begging his friend to "return to civilization from your exile in the wilderness." Dispatches from Izzy were not the sort of epistles that you opened in public in the post office. He'd shoved the envelope into his pocket to be read later and with a clearer head.

Then news came that Mrs. Lentz, the butcher's cousin's widow, was coughing blood, and Izzy's letter had been forgotten. As was his duty, Rabbi Abrahms had immediately rushed to the poor woman's side to offer comfort, but found that the Widow Lentz only had a slightly bloody nose, was happily brewing tea, and had a platter of sweet cakes ready for his arrival. After checking to make certain that the nosebleed was really an accident, he had managed to extract himself from her clutches, but not before eating three of the rather good cakes, drinking too much tea, and listening to her prattle on and on about her children who had grown up and left the nest, thank goodness, leaving her all alone without a man in the house. It was a relief to return to the peace and quiet of Rabbi Sarnoff's house, empty as it was.

He finally remembered the envelope the next morning, while his tea was steeping, retrieved it from his coat, brought it into the kitchen, sliced it open with a knife, and read.

Izzy took almost two pages to get to the point, describing in detail two art openings, three new books he'd read, and a ballerina, with whom he was flirting, before finally getting to the real news.

After the general pardon of prisoners, Izzy had kept his eyes open for news or signs of Malka. When two weeks had gone by, he visited the prison himself and pretended to be interceding for grieving parents. The bureaucrat in charge took a thick bribe, but promised nothing. Surprisingly, less than a month later, the bureaucrat actually delivered the information that he'd been paid for.

"I'm afraid, my friend," Izzy wrote, "that it is as we suspected and feared. Malka is dead. She has been dead for quite some time. The cause was pneumonia. You remember I wrote to you about the epidemic four years ago? According to the records, she succumbed and was buried in a mass grave with fifty-five other women from the prison. The senior executive clerk told me there was no next of kin listed on her paperwork; otherwise we might have learned all this sooner. Or not. You know how the government here works.

"I am sorry, Yohon. I know that this news is both sudden and perhaps unsurprising. Your devotion to Malka is legendary here in Moscow. I hope that the certainty of the truth will give you some freedom and some relief. I have said a Kaddish for her, and you, of course, are in my prayers. I know that you are a big shot now in the tiny town of Smyrna, but if you ever come to Moscow, you are always welcome in my home.

"Be at peace. Izzy."

So there it was. His wife was dead.

Yohon read the last page over a dozen times. His eyes glazed over as he chewed the knowledge around in his brain. It was hard to grasp.

On the one hand, he had suspected that she was dead. Malka had been gone from his life for so long that the only way he truly remembered what she looked like was to take out the secret sketch that one of her artist friends had drawn of her. He kept it hidden in an atlas on the pages that showed France, where they had always talked of visiting. It was a charcoal nude, quite scandalous at the time. But it had captured her likeness and her shape and her face and the glint in her eye.

As a man of integrity, Yohon Abrams had lived his life as if she was still alive. He had honored her as his wife. He had kept his promises even while Sarah had lived with him in Rabbi Sarnoff's house.

Yes, he had kept his promises and been true to his wedding vows, but he had also longed to break them at every moment. Awake and asleep, Sarah's presence had been a constant source of both delight and temptation. In his dreams and thoughts he had fantasized that Malka was dead and Sarah was in her place.

Of course, as someone who had lived in Chelm for a long time, it all would have gone wrong. If he had married Sarah, (after she was divorced from Benjamin) then a week after the wedding, Malka would have almost certainly arrived at Rabbi Sarnoff's door demanding to see her husband. Then, instead of just sinning in his thoughts, he would have been a bigamist.

Was it integrity or fear that had kept him from consummating a relationship with Sarah? And did it matter now? Malka was gone, but so was Sarah. She had returned to Chelm, and he had received no word from her since. He hadn't dared ask.

He stared at Sarah's empty chair on the other side of the kitchen table. He felt miserable and alone. Sarah was gone.

And Malka was dead. Was it his fault? He had been a poor husband, saving himself and leaving his wife to rot and die in a Russian prison. What had she thought of him? How could he have done that to her? Yes, she had defied the authorities. Yes, she had brought the trouble on herself. Yes, she had told him, as they dragged her off, "Go, Yohon! Save yourself and live a good life." He could have tried to find her, tried to have her released. But he'd taken her words and treated her as if she was dead. But not.

Now that he knew for certain, it wasn't for her he was sad. It was for himself.

The knocking at the door startled him from his reverie. He checked to make sure he was presentably dressed before walking through the dining room and study.

He smiled as he realized that perhaps for the first time in years the knocking at the door hadn't immediately brought the thoughts of the secret police. Now that he knew Malka was at rest, perhaps that fear would rest as well. Perhaps he could forgive himself.

He turned the knob and opened the door to see Reb Zalman, the fishmonger, one of the leaders of the Smyrna synagogue.

"May I come in?" Reb Zalman asked. "I have good news."

Rabbi Abrahms shrugged and stepped aside. He followed the scent of salmon into the study. "Can I offer you some tea? It may be a little cold. I don't have any help."

"No, no," Reb Zalman said, waving his hand. "That is part of the reason why I came to see you… You look pale. Are you all right?"

"No." Rabbi Abrahms dropped into Rabbi Sarnoff's chair and shook his head. "She's dead."

"Who's dead?" Reb Zalman said. "Certainly not Mrs. Lentz. I thought that was just a ploy so she could have your company."

"My wife is dead," Rabbi Abrahms said. He knew he was not making much sense and that perhaps he had no right to share this information with someone who wasn't prepared to hear it, but he had no one else to talk to.

"You were married to her?" Reb Zalman said.

"Of course!" Rabbi Abrahms said. "Who else would I be married to, but my wife? Every husband I've ever heard of is married to his wife, and every wife is married to her husband."

"All right, all right," said Reb Zalman, waving his hands to calm Rabbi Abrahms down. "I'm sorry for your loss. If we'd known you were married to her then we would have done this years ago."

Rabbi Abrahms was puzzled. "Done what years ago?"

"Offered you the job of Chief Rabbi of Smyrna," Reb Zalman said. "We have confirmed you in the position that you have held for so long and have done so admirably with. I realize that this does not replace the loss of your wife, but perhaps it can be some small consolation that you are a valued and respected member of our community."

Rabbi Abrahms felt his right eye begin to twitch.

"Now?" he said. "Why now?"

Reb Zalman shrugged. "Well, we noticed that the woman who was living here wasn't there any more. We assumed that she had left, and that you were living by yourself, which was true. It wouldn't have been appropriate to confirm your position while she was here, but as I said, if we'd known that you were married to her that would have been different. You have to understand that no one in Smyrna knew who this woman was or why she was living here. Why didn't you simply tell us you were married? Why did you wait until she was dead?"

"What?" Rabbi Abrahms said. "She's dead?"

"You just told me she was," Reb Zalman said. "It's a little early in the day, but maybe we should have something stronger than tea."

Yohon Abrahms laughed. If he had been living in Chelm, he would already have been out the door to find out how Sarah had died and that would have been a whole mishugas. Now, his heart was racing as he tried to sort through the morass. Reb Zalman didn't know who Sarah was, and now assumed that they had been married. So, Sarah wasn't dead. Malka was. Enough of this confusion, he thought.

"Listen, Reb Zalman, my wife has been dead for more than four years."

Now it was the fishmonger's turn to look puzzled. "How is that possible? She's been living here for quite some time. She wasn't a ghost, was she?" Reb Zalman hastily made the sign against the evil eye.

"No. Not a ghost. That woman wasn't my wife," Rabbi Abrahms admitted. "She was my friend."

"Ah ha!" Reb Zalman exclaimed. "I knew it. But she's gone now, am I right? Or is she dead too?" Suddenly, Reb Zalman had a frightened image of this young rabbi as a mass murderer of women and he began to fear for his own safety.

"No, no," Rabbi Abrahms shook his head. "I don't think so. I hope not. I doubt it. She left. She returned to her home. It is my wife who is dead."

"All right. So you keep saying. Why didn't you just marry your friend? You would have saved us all a lot of trouble."

"Wait, let me understand this," Rabbi Abrahms said. "You mean to say that you people would not offer me the job of chief rabbi while Sarah was living here?"

"No." Reb Zalman shrugged. "How could we? We need to have a religious leader who is an upright and moral man. Our chief rabbi needs to set an example for the community. You had a woman living with you. How were we to know that she was your wife? But she wasn't your wife. What was she doing here and why didn't you just marry her?"

Rabbi Abrahms stood up from Rabbi Sarnoff's chair. He suddenly felt the need to stand on his own feet. He shrugged off Rabbi Sarnoff's coat and hung it over the chair.

"I am going to explain this once and then the subject will be forever closed," he said. "My wife was in prison in Moscow. She has been dead for four years, but I did not know that until this morning. Sarah, the woman who was living here, was already married to someone else. She was living here because she did not want to be with her husband. She cleaned my house and she made my meals and she was my friend, but there was nothing more between us for the entire time that she lived here. Not once did any of you people from the synagogue have the courage to ask me directly about her. Instead you all whispered and gossiped and waited until she was gone or dead for all you knew. Now you offer me this position, claiming that you need to have a man of unblemished character as your religious leader? This is who I am. Is there anything else you need to know about my personal life?"

Reb Zalman had listened to the young rabbi with astonishment. He had never heard the man speak so clearly before. "Do you have any children?" he asked.

Rabbi Abrahms shook his head. "No."

"Then my offer is still open. I have heard your story. I will tell no one..."

"Tell anyone you please," Rabbi Abrahms interrupted. "I am tired of deception by silence."

Reb Zalman nodded. "I will tell people that you are exactly the kind of a person that we in Smyrna need to have as our Chief Rabbi. The position is yours."

"If I want it," Rabbi Abrahms snapped back.

"What do you mean?" asked the confused Smyrnan.

"Maybe I just want to go back to Chelm and be a school teacher."

"Are you crazy?" Reb Zalman said. "You spend three years auditioning for a job, and now you're going to walk out? I'm offering you lifetime security. I'm offering you a home and a community and respect and back salary."

"And a raise?" Rabbi Abrahms said.

"And a raise!" Reb Zalman agreed before he realized what he'd said. "Ummm... I'll have to consult with the others before I can tell you how much."

Rabbi Abrahms pursed his lips. "I'll have to consult with myself before I can tell you whether it's enough."

Reb Zalman laughed as he rose to his feet. "Come now. No matter how much or how little we offer, it has got to be more than what they can give you in Chelm!"

"Maybe," Rabbi Abrahms said. "There are other things besides security and money and a good job."

Reb Zalman stopped on his way out the door. "Does she, this Sarah, live in Chelm?"

Rabbi Abrahms nodded.

Reb Zalman nodded back. "I'll let you know about the money. You let me know what you decide. Don't take too long."

Rabbi Abrahms raised an eyebrow. It had stopped twitching. "You make me wait for three years and now you want an answer right away?"

"Take your time." Reb Zalman laughed. "You negotiate quite well. Are you sure you lived in Chelm?"

They shook hands. As Rabbi Abrahms shut the door he whispered, "Yes. I'm sure."

Chapter Forty-Six

Getting the Get

Sarah Cohen was biting her cuticle outside the front of the synagogue, when Mrs. Chaipul tapped her on the shoulder. Sarah nearly jumped out of her skin.

"Nervous?" Chanah Chaipul asked.

Sarah nodded. "It's not every day you get divorced."

Chanah nodded back. "My dead husband, Sam, may he rest in peace, always said that a good marriage started new every morning, but a bad marriage was like a fish that began to stink after a while."

They stood for a moment in silence.

"Were you married long?" Sarah asked.

"Oy," Chanah nodded. "Sometimes it seemed like forever. Sometimes it seemed like it was only a minute."

The two women stared across the round village square, watching as men meandered to and from their businesses, as wives trudged up the hill to draw water from the well.

"Do you think I should do this?" the younger woman asked.

"Does it really matter what I think?" the caterer said. "If I say yes and you're miserable will it be my fault? If I say no, and you go ahead anyway, what difference will it make?"

"Does everyone in Chelm hate me?"

"Why would they hate you?"

"I deserted my husband and my children."

Chanah Chaipul let those words float for a few moments on the air. She thought for a moment and then spoke.

"There are some who will never understand. There are some who are jealous. The ones who are jealous probably gossip the most. Either way it is none of their business. It seems to me that you didn't abandon your children, so much as leave them alone in good hands for a while. After all, you have returned. My question to you is, do you hate yourself?"

Sarah nodded. "Sometimes. Not all the time."

Chanah sighed. "That's hard."

They stood for a moment. It was a beautiful day. The sky was clear. The air was warm. The breeze cooled their cheeks.

"I need to go inside," Chanah said. "I'm one of the witnesses."

A look of panic crossed Sarah's face. "You're not going with me?" She reached out and grasped the caterer's strong forearm.

"This you have to do yourself," Chanah said. "But I will be in the room. Remember, whatever he does, you also do. Don't let this intimidate you. You were married. Now you will be divorced. In between were good times and bad. After will be good times and bad. This is just a moment. Just a transition. All right?"

Sarah let go and shrugged. "I suppose."

Chanah kissed her cheek. "Come in when you are ready."

* * *

In the synagogue's small meeting room, Benjamin Cohen shifted from foot to foot. Rabbi Kibbitz, sitting behind the long table, watched the tailor fidget, and then said, "You know you can sit down."

"I'll stand," Benjamin said, waving a hand. "There will be plenty of time for sitting later."

Mrs. Chaipul entered the room and sat next to the rabbi.

Benjamin stopped moving. "What is she doing here?"

"In cases like this," Rabbi Kibbitz explained, "where people's lives are at stake, we confer a rabbinical court. In most communities, this Beit Din requires three adult men, so that someone can break a tie. For criminal offenses and such. You understand?"

Benjamin nodded.

"Here in Chelm, we changed the rules a little," Rabbi Kibbitz continued. "We only have two people, so if it's a tie we have to err on the side of compassion."

Again Benjamin nodded.

"Usually, I would ask another rabbi to help officiate at such an important rabbinical court, but I'm afraid that's impossible at this time. So I have asked Mrs. Chaipul, as a respected community leader, to participate instead. Is that all right with you?"

Benjamin shrugged. He began shifting his feet again.

Sarah poked her head in the door, saw that she was in the right room, and entered.

"Hello," she said.

"Hello," he said.

He felt a lump rising in his throat.

She looked away from him, and smiled at Mrs. Chaipul, who did not return the favor. It was not a time for smiles, she realized. She sighed quietly, and waited.

"Benjamin and Sarah?" Rabbi Kibbitz said at last. "Are you here of your own free will?"

They both nodded.

"Do you both wish to divorce and dissolve your marriage?"

No! Benjamin thought. No, I don't. Not really. Not at all.

Sarah nodded her head, yes. It's been dissolved for a long time, she thought.

Benjamin closed his eyes, holding back his tears. Then he, too, nodded his head.

"Benjamin," the rabbi said. "I need you to sign this." He slid a piece of paper across the desk, and offered a pen. "This is the divorce decree. It assigns no blame to either of you. It offers no consequences or punishments. It declares that the vows that you made to each other have been rescinded, and will no longer be binding. It gives you both permission to remarry."

Remarry? Benjamin thought. He wanted to laugh. I can't even conceive of it.

Remarry? Sarah thought. I don't know.

Benjamin glanced at the papers without really seeing them, and signed his name.

"Sarah," Mrs. Chaipul said, as she brought a piece of paper out from a pocket in her skirt, "will you sign this as well?"

Rabbi Kibbitz's face turned somber. He frowned. "What is this?"

"It's a Get for her," Mrs. Chaipul said. "It's basically the same document as his."

"There is no such thing as a man getting a Get from a woman," the rabbi said. "Only men give a Get. A divorce is final when a man signs a Get, gives it, and the woman takes it. Not the other way around."

Mrs. Chaipul stared at him. "Does the law say that women can not also give a Get? Will a man getting a Get from a woman make the man's giving a Get invalid?"

Rabbi Kibbitz rubbed his forehead. "No," he said, "but what's the point? Give a Get. Get a Get. It's all the same."

"Balance," Mrs. Chaipul said. "Fairness. Equality."

Rabbi Kibbitz took a deep breath. "You know, every time I turn around someone is talking about equality between men and women. We aren't the same, you know."

"Yes, I know," Mrs. Chaipul agreed. "I for one appreciate the differences. But I don't think that men should make all the laws, have all the rights and all the responsibilities. When this ceremony is completed, Sarah will live her own life. She will share her children with her husband, but provide for herself. I don't see why she should not take responsibility from the beginning, rather than allowing it all to fall upon Benjamin."

"Get on with it," Benjamin said quietly. "I'll give a Get and I'll get a Get. It's fine."

"Will it hurt?" asked Sarah.

"No, it won't hurt," the old man said. "This is why I don't like to have women involved in these processes. It changes everything. Fine! Sarah, you sign that one. Benjamin, you sign that one."

They both picked up pens, dipped them in ink, and signed.

"Now, give the documents to each other."

Awkwardly, Benjamin and Sarah traded the papers.

"Now, walk to the door."

They bumped into each other and laughed nervously.

Benjamin allowed Sarah to precede him. They stopped at the door.

"Wait!" the rabbi said. "Come back now, and give the documents to me."

They returned to the table and held out the papers.

Rabbi Kibbitz took the one from Benjamin. Mrs. Chaipul took the one from Sarah. They each signed their name at the bottom of each piece of paper.

The rabbi dripped wax at the bottom of each document and took out the synagogue's seal, which was a symbolic representation of the village itself. It showed a square representing the synagogue, and with the two round shapes of East and West Hills above, and another circle that depicted village square at the bottom. He pressed the seal firmly into the wax on each Get.

When the wax had hardened, he handed Benjamin's to Sarah and Sarah's to Benjamin.

"Benjamin Cohen," he said, "you are no longer married to Sarah."

Benjamin nodded, the piece of paper clutched in his hand.

"Sarah…" the rabbi began. "You know I don't remember… What's your maiden name?"

"No," Sarah said. "I don't want to take back my father's name."

"What?" the rabbi said.

"I went from the house of my father to the house of my husband. Tonight, I will be living in my own house. I want my own name."

"We can't just call you Sarah," the rabbi said.

"Why not? In the Torah there are many women with only one name."

The rabbi's mouth opened and closed in astonishment. Sometimes he wasn't sure what to say, but he usually was able to find something reasonably apt to fill the gap. It was rare for him to be left completely speechless.

At last Mrs. Chaipul spoke softly, "You need a second name, because there are other women named Sarah who live in Chelm and it will be confusing."

Sarah nodded with understanding. "All right. Then call me Sarah Sarah."

"I already explained that I can't just call you Sarah," said the exasperated rabbi.

"No," she said. "Call me Sarah Sarah."

"Sarah Sarah?" the old man said. "Which is your first name and which is your last."

"Sarah will be my last name," she said. "And Sarah will be my first."

Rabbi Kibbitz felt a splitting headache coming on. "All right. Sarah Sarah, you are no longer married to Benjamin."

"May you both have long and healthy lives."

With that, Rabbi Kibbitz and Mrs. Chaipul rose and left the room, leaving the ex-husband and wife alone for a few moments.

Benjamin and Sarah stared at each other.

"Well, it's done," Benjamin said at last.

Sarah nodded. "At least we can still talk."

"Talk?" he snorted bitterly. "Sometimes I think that's all we did. Talk and work. And look what happened."

"What else is there," she asked.

"Did we have a good life together?" he asked.

She shrugged. "Some of it. And we made beautiful children."

"Yes," he smiled. "We did. Good luck." He left the room without looking back.

"You too," she said as the door slowly closed in her face.

* * *

Outside the synagogue the light was bright and it hurt Benjamin Cohen's eyes. He nearly ran into the skinny shape of Rabbi Yohon Abrahms.

"Excuse me," Benjamin said. "I just got divorced and it's a little disorienting."

"Benjamin," Rabbi Abrahms said. "I am sorry. I am so sorry."

The tailor looked at the rabbi and shrugged. "Me too. I hadn't expected this would happen in my life. Marriage was supposed to be until death. Oh, well. I think I'd better go back to work. I have a commission for another suit for Reb Cantor. He keeps wearing through his pants at the thighs. He keeps suggesting that I make him a suit with two pairs of pants, but that's just craziness."

With that, the tailor turned and hurried off.

Yohon Abrahms watched him go. He was about to open the

shul's door when it slammed opened, banging him right in the nose.

"Ow!" he yelped.

"Oh, I'm sorry," Sarah sputtered. "Yohon?"

"Sarah?" He said, rubbing his swollen shnoz.[60] It was the first time he had seen her since she had left his house.

"I got divorced," she said. "I'm Sarah Sarah now."

"Of course you are," he said, smiling.

"Are you bleeding?" she asked.

He checked. "No. Do you wish that I was?"

Now she too smiled. "Only sometimes when you're being stubborn. By the way, I understand that they finally offered you the job in Smyrna. Congratulations!"

"Yes, well I haven't accepted it yet."

"What?" She stared at him with amazement. "Are you crazy?"

"I wanted to talk with you first."

"With me?" she said. "Why?"

He snorted. "Let's go for a walk."

"No." She shook her head. "I was just divorced. I'm a single woman now and you are a married man with a respectable position. You should not be seen alone with me. Even now, I'm sure people are talking already."

"It turns out," Yohon Abrahms laughed sadly, "that I'm not so married anymore."

"What do you mean?"

"I shouldn't laugh because it is sad, but it turns out that my wife, Malka, has been dead for years. She died in prison. I don't know exactly when. I just found out. That is why the town of Smyrna offered me the job."

"You mean that I'm unmarried and you're unmarried?" Sarah pointed at herself and then at him. "Both at the same time?

Yohon nodded. "It makes for a change."

"No. I'm not getting married again right now," Sarah said, suddenly and firmly. "I'm not even single for five minutes!"

---

[60] A shnoz is slang for a nose. Usually a big nose, a long nose, a large nose, perhaps even a huge nose.

"I didn't ask you to," he said, half wishing that he had. "But I do miss your cooking."

"I'm sick of cooking for men," Sarah said. "I have made arrangements for a little house that I'm renting from Reb Cantor. It's tiny really, but that's all I need. I will be cooking for myself and my children. And of course for everybody in Mrs. Chaipul's restaurant, which is where I'm going to keep working. But that is for money and not for…" She almost said 'love' but stopped herself. "…not for obligation."

The young rabbi nodded, keeping his emotions in check. "I understand. As a mashgiach, I'm in charge of making sure everything's kosher. But I get tired of observing ritual slaughter all the time. You have to eat, but there's so much blood."

As soon as he said it, he realized that he had just compared romance and marriage to butchering, and wished he'd kept his mouth shut.

She gaped at him and then laughed. "I don't think that cooking and slaughtering are the same."

He shrugged and smiled, glad she hadn't taken it poorly. "You need the one before you can do the other."

"I suppose," she agreed. "So, what will you do?"

"I think I'll take the job. It would have made my mother happy."

"Will it make you happy?" Sarah asked.

He looked at her and thought to himself, if you were my rebbetzen, everything would be perfect.

Instead, he said, "I don't know. But if I don't take it I will never find out."

"Then congratulations!" she said. "You earned it. Now you will have to excuse me, but I have to go to work."

"Me too. I have to pay an official visit as the newly appointed Chief Rabbi of Smyrna to the Chief Rabbi of Chelm. I heard there was going to be a Beit Din, and thought that I could… I'm late, aren't I?"

"Mrs. Chaipul filled in for you." She nodded. "It probably wouldn't have been appropriate anyway."

"I suppose not," he agreed. "Does Benjamin know about us?"

"Know what?" Sarah said. "Nothing happened. There is nothing to know, is there?"

Yohon didn't quite know how to answer this. "Can I see you?"

"Are you blind?"

"You know what I mean."

"No." Sarah shook her head. "Not for a while. Give me six months or a year. Then we'll see what is what and who is who."

"Goodbye, Sarah," Yohon Abrahms said.

"Call me Sarah Sarah," she said. "It's more formal."

"I'd rather not," he said, softly. He stared into her eyes.

She looked back and whispered, "I know."

"Goodbye Sarah Sarah," he said.

"Goodbye Yohon Abrahms," she said, "Chief Rabbi of Smyrna."

And off she went, across the round square to Mrs. Chaipul's restaurant.

He watched her depart and sighed. A year? Six months? Not long. Too long.

He reached for the door to the synagogue and hesitated. When it didn't slam open in his face, he turned the knob and stepped inside.

Part Ten

The Renewal

Chapter Forty-Six

Meeting the Council

Rachel Cohen was buzzing with excitement. It was just after dawn, and she was quietly walking beside her mother through the gradually brightening streets of Chelm.

Sarah Sarah had woken Rachel while it was still dark, and told her to get dressed. Her mother's new house was small, a single room with a bed, table, three chairs, and a stove. All of Sarah's possessions were either on shelves along the walls or tucked into a chest that was slid underneath the bed. By the time Rachel pulled on her dress and pulled up her socks, her mother had set a cup of tea on the table next to a bowl of warm porridge.

"I don't really like tea," Rachel had said. "I prefer coffee."

Sarah had sighed and shaken her head. She had missed so much by being gone.

"Why does that bother you?" Rachel had asked.

"That's a good question." Sarah had smiled. "Tea is an important part of a woman's life. Making tea is a small activity that is almost completely in your control. When everything else is going badly, making tea is something you can do, and do well, without really thinking. Making tea focuses the mind and steadies the hand. It provides comfort and assurance and stability. As does drinking tea. Tea is solace when you are alone and social when you are with company. Do you understand?"

Rachel had nodded. "I just don't like the taste."

"Truth is, I don't like tea much either." Sarah had shrugged. "So I add milk and sugar."

Rachel had added one, two, three, and finally four teaspoons of sugar and just a splash of milk. By the time she had finished the cup, she had felt her heart racing as she became certain that something special was happening.

The night before her mother had asked Rachel to come and spend the night in her new house without Yakov. That in itself had been odd. Usually when the children stayed with Sarah, all three of them squeezed into her small house in an intricate process that involved borrowing a mattress and shifting the furniture around before bed and then moving back again before breakfast. That evening, mother and daughter had shared a quiet meal before climbing into bed beside each other. They hadn't talked much. There wasn't much new to say. They saw each other every day while they worked in Mrs. Chaipul's restaurant, so by the time dinner was done and the dishes were cleaned, exhaustion replaced conversation and they both slept deeply.

When Sarah had nudged Rachel awake and told her that they had somewhere to be, Rachel thought she knew what was going on but she wouldn't say, because that would spoil the surprise.

They left the house in silence and began to walk south, away from the village.

"Are we going to the mikveh?" Rachel asked.

Sarah smiled. "Near enough."

It was a lovely spring day and the sky was brilliant red and gold as the sun inched up over East Hill.

At the ritual bath house, Sarah opened the door and let her daughter in. They walked through the bath area, past the pool, and through a small door in the far wall. Beyond this was a short narrow passage with a low ceiling. It dead-ended in another even smaller door.

"Close the door behind you," Sarah told Rachel in a soft voice.

Rachel did, and for a moment felt her heart sink as all light was erased from the world.

"Listen," her mother said.

They were both quiet. The darkness and silence seemed absolute. Rachel could hear her heart pounding and the blood flowing through her veins.

"What am I listening for?" Rachel asked.

Sarah sighed. "You're not listening for anything. You're just not talking."

Again they fell silent.

Rachel found thoughts speeding through her head. She remembered the first day she had gone to the yeshiva and how terrifying that was. She remembered riding behind Oma Levitsky on the wheeled chair. She remembered the sharp moment that light and sound had entered her life.

"Oh my," she gasped.

"What?" her mother hissed.

"I think I just remembered the day I was born. Was it winter time?"

"Yes," her mother said. "You know when your birthday is. Now be quiet."

"But I remember going from a warm place to a cold place. From darkness to light. I remember hearing noises."

Sarah felt around and put one hand on her daughter's shoulder and a finger on her daughter's lips. "How long do you want to stay here? The rules say that we have to be completely quiet for five minutes."

Rachel nodded.

The five minutes took forever.

At last, the small door opened. The light from the room on the other side was so warm and bright that Rachel felt as if she'd gone to heaven.

Sarah stepped aside and let her daughter pass through the door first.

Rachel was grinning broadly as she stepped from the stone floor onto the carpeted floor of the chamber.

All around her the women sat in their chairs, or on the sofas. All of them were drinking tea.

"Welcome," Mrs. Chaipul said.

"Good morning," greeted Mrs. Stein and Mrs. Schlemiel.

Sarah smiled, gave Rebecca Schlemiel a hug, and sat beside her.

"That wasn't a new record," said Mrs. Cantor, "but at the same time, it wasn't the longest time ever spent in the hall of silence."

"I didn't realize it would be so difficult," Rachel said, as she admired the woven tapestries on the wall, and found a seat on a couch beside Perel Dov.

"Didn't know what would be so difficult?" Mrs. Chaipul said, suspiciously.

"Nothing," Rachel said, jumping back to her feet. "Nothing. I'm sorry. May I sit here?"

"Of course," Perel said, patting the cushion. "It will be wonderful not to be the youngest member any more. They make you fetch everything."

"Thank you," Rachel said, sitting back down. "So. I didn't expect to be here so soon."

"She told you, didn't she?" Mrs. Chaipul asked, a curious look in her eyes.

Rachel nodded.

"Who told her what?" Mrs. Meier asked.

"Oma Levitsky told Rachel all about the Council," Mrs. Chaipul said. "Didn't she?"

Again, Rachel nodded.

"Oy! That old woman. Even when she's dead she interferes!" Shoshana Cantor waved her hands. "Look, I don't mind that we changed the rules to let Sarah back in. I don't even mind that we changed the rules again to let Rachel in before she's married and has children. This is a young woman who needs to be kept under observation. She's dangerous."

Under this harsh gaze, Rachel was suddenly feeling quite frightened. "I am? Really?"

"No, I don't mean that in a bad way," the large woman said, softening her tone slightly. "The amazing things that you have done in your short life have given me no end of frustration, annoyance, and occasionally pain in the tuchas. Nevertheless, I agreed that we should break our rules, change our rules, modify our rules to admit you into our company, and the least you could do is act surprised!"

"I'm sorry, Mrs. Cantor," Rachel said, quietly.

"Feh," the chubby woman said. "Forget about it. At least you don't know everything. In this room we do not call each other by our husband's names. Please call me Shoshana."

"All right," Rachel said, hesitantly, "Shoshana."

"Here, have something to eat," Shoshana said, passing a china plate to Rachel.

Rachel's eyes widened. "Is this the mandel bread?"

Shoshana chuckled and shook her head. "The old woman told you about the mandel bread, too?"

"Yes," Rachel said, reverently taking a long cookie. "She told me it was special."

"Like a special rock," Perel whispered.

"Enjoy," Shoshana said.

"Perhaps I should start at the beginning," Chanah said. "How did we come to be here? Where did this all begin? What is The Council of Wise Women?"

"Oy, here we go again," muttered Shoshana, rolling her eyes.

But even though they had all heard the story many times before, one by one the women in the cave fell silent as they listened to Chanah tell the story of a family, of women, who came together in the spirit of reconciliation.

Rachel Cohen felt a warm glow in her heart. She lifted the mandel bread to her lips and bit down hard.

"Ow!" she said, quietly.

"It helps if you dip it into the tea," Perel whispered out of the side of her mouth.

"Oma Levitsky didn't have any teeth," winked Shoshana. "She could gum a piece of that mandel bread for hours. She claimed it was exercise."

Chanah glared at them. "May I continue, or are you all going to just keep talking?"

The conspirators tried to keep it together, but a moment later, the room exploded with giggles and laughter, as the Council of Wise Women of the village of Chelm was called to its usual level of disorder.

The End

About the Author

Izzy Abrahmson is a pen name for Mark Binder, a professional storyteller, and the author of more than two dozen books and audio books for families and adults. He has toured the world delighting readers and listeners of all ages with his stories, interspersed with his unique klezmer harmonica sounds.

Under his "real" name, Mark began writing about The Village as the editor of *The Rhode Island Jewish Herald*. These stories were so popular that they have been published in newspapers and magazines around the world. His epic *Loki Ragnarok* was nominated for an Audie Audiobook Award for Best Original Work, and *Transmit Joy* won a Parents' Choice Gold Award for Audio Storytelling. Mark is also a playwright, and the founder of the American Story Theater. In his spare time he bakes bread and makes pizza. He lives in Providence with his wife, who is a brilliant ceramic artist.

For tour dates, news, and bonus material visit:
izzyabe.com and **markbinderbooks.com**

Thank you

We hope you've enjoyed this book.

Please consider telling your friends
and writing a review.

May we send you a bonus story as a gift?
Subscribe to our email newsletter at
izzyabe.com

You'll also find tour dates, podcast and blog posts

You can also tag us on social media
#TheVillageLife
@IzzyAbrahmson

We value your readership.
Have an excellent day.

A Village Glossary

"A word clearly spoken is like a pattern of golden apples on a silver mosaic." –Proverbs 25: 11

Yiddish is a language of sound and subtlety. Hebrew is an ancient tongue. These are the villagers' interpretations of words you may, or may not know.

Chelm: The Village. The place where most of the people in this book live. A traditional source of Jewish humor. The "ch" in Chelm (and most Yiddish and Hebrew transliteration) is pronounced like you've got something stuck in your throat. "Ch-elm."

Chelmener: the people who live in The Village. Often known as the wisefolk of Chelm. Sometimes called Chelmites. Sometimes called, "The Fools of Chelm".

babka: a delicious cake. Usually served with coffee, tea and gossip

bar mitzvah: the Jewish coming-of-age ceremony for boys. Celebrated at 13. Almost always catered.

bimah: the platform at the front of the synagogue where the rabbi stands so that everyone can hear him.

bris: a ritual circumcision ceremony. Usually catered.

cantor: a person who leads a religious service with song. Not to be confused with Reb Cantor the merchant.

challah: a braided egg bread. In English, the plural of challah is challah.

Chanukah: the festival of lights. Celebrated in the winter, it commemorates the victory of the Maccabees over King Antiochus. The miracle of Chanukah was that one day's measure of oil burned in the Temple for eight days. Sometimes spelled Hanukkah. Or Hanukah.

chanukia: the Chanukah menorah. A lamp or candelabra with room for nine candles: one for each night of Chanukah, plus another, called the shammos.

cheder: the school for young people. Not cheesy. See also yeshiva.

cholent: a slow-cooked stew usually prepared on Friday and left to simmer for Saturday's dinner. Delicious… unless it's burnt.

chometz: all sorts of delicious baked goods that aren't matzah. Only obsessed about during Passover.

chuppah: the wedding canopy.

daven: to rock back and forth in prayer.

dreidel: a four-sided top spun in a children's game during Chanukah. The game of dreidel is usually played for high stakes, like raisins or nuts. Although immortalized in song, rarely are dreidels made out of clay, because clay tops are very difficult to spin. The Hebrew letters on the dreidel are Nun, Gimmel, Hay, and Shin. They signify the words, "Nes Gadol Haya Sham" or "A great miracle happened there." In Chelm, where Yiddish is spoken when the game is played, the Shin, means "stell" or put one back. Hay is "halb," so you would take half. But, Gimmel, instead of getting the pot means "gib" or give everything back into the pot. And Nun, instead of nothing means "nimm," or take everything. Confusing, isn't it?

erev: the evening that begins a holiday. Jewish holidays start at sunset and end after sunset.

gelt: money. In the old days, Chanukah gelt was given to teachers. Today gelt means foil-wrapped pieces of chocolate shaped like money.

goyishe: something that is not Jewish.

goob (English): when something is so delicious that you can't pronounce the letter "d" because you're too busy eating, it's "goob."

hamotzi: blessing over the bread – or matzah.

kafratzed: Completely messed up. Incapable of working.

kabalah: Jewish mysticism, often numerological. It's secret: shhh!

kasha varnishkas: buckwheat groats with noodles. Serve it with brisket and gravy. Mmm.

kiggel/kugel/keugel: a baked pudding. Mmmm.

klezmer: Jewish jazz. Very danceable!

knaidel (or, if you're in a spelling bee, kneydl): a matzah ball dumpling, usually found in chicken soup. Often served during Passover. The plural of knaidel is knaidlach. After lead, one of the densest materials known to Chelmener.

knish: dough stuffed with meat or potatoes. Sort of a Jewish calzone.

kreplach: Jewish wontons. Yiddish ravioli. Filled dumplings that are sometimes boiled, sometimes pan fried.

kugel: an incredibly rich pudding. Sometimes savory, sometimes sweet. Often made with noodles. Mmmm.

kvell: to glow with pride.

kvetch: 1. To complain. 2. To really really complain. 3. A complaint. 4. The complainer.

latke: a pancake fried in oil. At Passover, latkes are made with matzah meal. At Chanukah they are made with potatoes.

mandlebread: a twice-baked cookie, Jewish biscotti.

mashgiach: the rabbi in charge of making sure everything's kosher.

matzah/matzoh: unleavened bread made from flour and water with no salt or yeast. Sometimes spelled "matzoh." Eaten during Passover, the holiday celebrating the Israelites' exodus from Egypt. Also known as the bread of affliction, perhaps because it is tasteless, bland and often binding.

matzah brie: fried matzah. Mix damp matzah with eggs and salt and fry it to make matzah brie. Yum!

menorah: a candelabra. Usually with seven branches, but on Chanukah it has eight (plus another one for the shammos) and is called a chanukiah.

mensch: a good man. A nice fellah. Charitable, wise, intelligent, kind-hearted. The sort of man who, if he had a little money as well, you'd want your sister to marry.

mishugas: craziness.

mikveh: the ritual bath.

mitzvah: a commandment, often a good deed. Not to be confused with a Bar Mitzvah, which is the coming of age ceremony for boys.

nachas: joy, pride, and happiness. Especially something you get from good children.

Omama/Opapa: Grandma/Grandpa.

oy: an expression of excitement and often pain. "Oy! My back!" or "Oy, I can't believe you're wearing that to a wedding!"

Passover/Pesach: the celebration of the Exodus from Egypt. Celebrated for eight days in the diaspora or seven day, depending on where you live and what you believe.

plotz: to explode. As in, "I ate so much matzah brie I nearly plotzed."

Purim: another holiday involving survival and food. The original gift-giving holiday. Nowadays, presents of food and treats may be given on Purim.

Rabbi: a scholar, a teacher, a leader in the community.

Reb: a wise man. And, since everyone in Chelm is wise, the men are all called Reb... as in Reb Stein, Reb Cantor, and so on.

Rebbetzin: The rabbi's wife.

Rosh Hashanah: the Jewish New Year.

schlep/shlep 1. To walk, but not a happy joy-filled walk, more like a burden. 2. To carry a burden. 3. Someone who is a burden.

Seder: the Passover feast. A huge meal with lots of prayers, songs and stories. No leavened bread. No challah. Just matzah. Followed by seemingly endless days of matzah. Oy.

Shabbas/Shabbat/Shabbos: the Jewish Sabbath. Starts Friday at sundown and ends Saturday after sunset.

shalom: Sometimes hello, sometimes goodbye, but especially peace.

shammos: the candle used to light other candles on the Chanukah menorah.

shmaltz: chicken fat. Used in cooking and spread on bread. Source of many heart attacks.

shmear: a big hunk of cream cheese usually spread on a bagel, but during Passover you can shmear matzah.

shemini: Hebrew for eighth. Shemini Schlemiel was born on the eighth day of both Chanukah and her mother's labor.

shmootz/shmuts: dust, dirt, those little brown flecks of stuff that you find here and there.

shmooze/shmoozing/shmoozed/shmoozer: to chat at length about nothing or everything. A shmoozer shmoozes, shmoozing until shmoozed out.

Shmura Matzah: a special round matzah made from carefully guarded wheat. Often burned. Don't use it for matzah brie.

Shul: the synagogue.

shvitz: to perspire.

Shul: the synagogue.

simches: joy. See also *nachas*.

Smyrna: the town nearest to Chelm. Lots of nice people and a few practical jokers live there.

tallis: is a fringed prayer shawl. (plural: tallisim or tallit)

Tante: aunt.

Torah: The Five Books of Moses. The first five books of the Hebrew Bible, which is frequently called the Old Testament.

tsedaka: a gift of charity.

tsuris: woe, trouble, aggravation. Especially something you get from rotten children.

tuchas: the posterior. The behind. The bottom. The part of the body you sit with. The southern end of a north-going Chelmener. Clear enough?

yad: a pointer. You're not supposed to touch the Torah Scroll as you read, so instead of pointing with your finger, you use a yad. The word means hand, so it often looks just like a tiny hand with its index finger outstretched.

yarmulke: the skull cap worn during prayers. Often abbreviated as **kippah**, which is not to be confused with the fish.

yenta: a gossip, a busybody.

yeshiva: the religious school. In Chelm, the yeshiva is the only school.

Yom Kippur: The Day of Atonement. No one eats or drinks. No kiggle, knaidel, babke, challah, or shmaltz or even matzah. Always followed by the break-fast, a sumptuous meal served after dark. All the food at the break-fast is eaten in a matter of moments.

zaftig: plump, but in a good way. Rubenesque.

Acknowledgements

Like many stories about Life in Chelm, this tale takes place over many years. Chronologically it begins during the early part of The Brothers Schlemiel and well before the end of The Misadventures of Rabbi Kibbitz and Mrs. Chaipul.

Listeners: Jeanne Donato, Angel Hutnak, Vida Hellman, Susan Letendre, Anke Steinweh, Judith Black, Tom Brillat, Rose Pavlov, Heather Binder.

Gracious and deep thanks to Andrea Kamens for her careful editing and brilliant guidance. More thanks to Nina Rooks Cast for her proofing. Even more thanks to Jessica Everette for her amazing proofreading and suggestions.

Thanks to the folk at Light Publications: Beth Hellman, Stephen Brendan and Lou Pop. Without you, everybody would blame me for everything.

Thanks always to Heather, for her love and keeping me sane.

If I missed thanking anyone, I apologize. Let me know and we'll add it to the next edition...

The Village Life Series

"The Village is snuggled in an indeterminate past that never was but certainly should have been, a past filled with love, humor, adventures and more than occasional misadventures. And when you go, be sure to bring the kids." – *The Times of Israel*

The Village Twins - a novel

When the seventh daughter of a seventh daughter has twins, you know there will be trouble. Abraham and Adam Schlemiel star in this warm comedy that blends ordinary life with adventure and epic confusion.

"In the spirit of Sholem Aleichem… identical twins, confused from birth, will charm with their simplicity and sincerity." – *AudioFile*

A Village Romance - a short novel

He's the wisest man in the village. She runs the only restaurant. They are both widowed…. What could possibly go wrong?

"engaging tales… Village stories that deftly lift a curtain on a world of friendly humor and touching details of Jewish life." – *Kirkus Reviews*

Winter Blessings - eleven Chanukah stories and a novella

National Jewish Book Award for Family Literature Finalist!

"Parents and grandparents will enjoy reading selections aloud and retelling the stories." – *AJL Newsletter*

The Village Feasts - ten tasty Passover tales

Cabbage Matzah? Who stole the afikomen? Delightful and amusing.

"Readers young and old will be delighted…" – *Publishers Weekly*

The Cracked Potter – a short novel

Nava Ortlieb says she's a potter and an artist. Shoshana Cantor isn't so sure. The two women find common ground, and seize an opportunity.

The Council of Wise Women - a novel

More twins? Oy! The birth of Rachel and Yakov Cohen bring new blessings and new challenges to the village.

Buy books, ebooks, and audiobooks from your favorite retailer
For more books and news – plus tour dates – visit
IzzyAbe.com

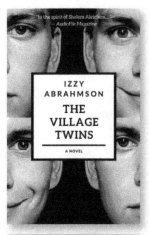

"In the spirit of Sholem Aleichem..."
— *AudioFile Magazine*

IZZY
ABRAHMSON

THE
VILLAGE
TWINS

A NOVEL

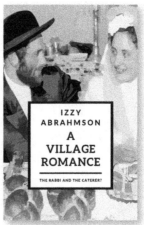

IZZY
ABRAHMSON

A
VILLAGE
ROMANCE

THE RABBI AND THE CATERER?

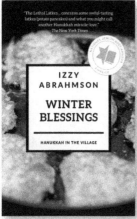

"The Lethal Latkes...concerns some awful-tasting
latkes (potato pancakes) and what you might call
another Hanukkah miracle love."
— *The New York Times*

IZZY
ABRAHMSON

WINTER
BLESSINGS

HANUKKAH IN THE VILLAGE

IZZY
ABRAHMSON

THE
VILLAGE
FEASTS

PASSOVER IN THE VILLAGE

The Cracked Potter

by Izzy Abrahmson

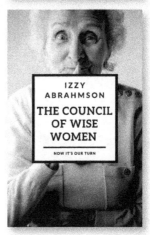

IZZY
ABRAHMSON

THE COUNCIL
OF WISE
WOMEN

NOW IT'S OUR TURN

Printed in the USA
CPSIA information can be obtained
at www.ICGtesting.com
CBHW030810110324
5199CB00001B/1

9 781940 060637